A READER

Self-governing Socialism

VOLUME TWO

Sociology and Politics
Economics

Edited by
BRANKO HORVAT
MIHAILO MARKOVIĆ
RUDI SUPEK

Helen Kramer, *Assistant Editor*

iasp INTERNATIONAL ARTS AND SCIENCES PRESS, INC.
WHITE PLAINS, NEW YORK

901 North Broadway, White Plains, New York 10603

Library of Congress Catalog Card Number: 73-92805

International Standard Book Number: 0-87332-061-1

Printed in the United States of America

Self-governing Socialism

VOLUME TWO

VOLUME ONE

Historical Development

Social and Political Philosophy

VOLUME TWO

Sociology and Politics

Economics

Contents | Volume Two

Part III Sociology and Politics

1. RUDI SUPEK The Sociology of Workers' Self-management 3

General

2. HENRI LEFEBVRE Elements for a Sociology of Self-management 14

3. GEORGES GURVITCH Three Paths to Self-management 20

4. ROGER GARAUDY The Possibility of Other Models of Socialism 29

Self-management and the Political System

5. NAJDAN PAŠIĆ The Idea of Direct Self-managing Democracy and Socialization of Policy-making 34

6. YVON BOURDET The Two Fundamental Principles of Self-government 41

7. Bogdan Denitch Forms and Intensity of Participation in Yugoslav Self-management 45

8. Rudi Supek Organization as an Intermediary Between the Individual and Society: The Democratic and Humanitarian Form of Organization 49

Self-management and Organization of Enterprises

9. J. Y. Tabb and A. Goldfarb The Typology of Systems of "Participation" 61

10. Gerry Hunnius Workers' Self-management in Yugoslavia 64

11. Josip Županov Participation and Influence 76

12. Janez Jerovšek The Self-management System in Yugoslav Enterprises 88

13. Veljko Rus Problems of Participatory Democracy 101

Workers' Movement, Workers' Control, and Self-management

14. André Gorz Strategy for Labor 112

15. Serge Mallet Workers' Power 122

16. Ken Coates and Tony Topham The Trade Union as Opposition 127

Part IV Economics

General

1. Jaroslav Vanek Identifying the Participatory Economy 135

2. Mario Zañartu Self-management, Oligarchy, and Proprietary Socialism 141

3. ALEKSANDER BAJT Social Ownership—Collective and Individual 151

The Firm

Organization and Efficiency

4. BRANKO HORVAT The Labor-managed Enterprise 164

5. ICHAK ADIZES Balancing Environmental Requirements and Personal Needs Through an Organizational Structure 177

6. GUDRUN LEMÂN Economic Units in Yugoslav Enterprises 190

7. SEYMOUR MELMAN Industrial Efficiency under Managerial versus Cooperative Decision-making 203

8. MITJA KAMUŠIĆ Economic Efficiency and Workers' Self-management 221

9. JAN TINBERGEN Does Self-management Approach the Optimum Order? 225

Analytical Aspects

10. BRANKO HORVAT On the Theory of the Labor-managed Firm 229

11. BENJAMIN WARD The Illyrian Firm 241

12. SVETOZAR PEJOVICH The Firm, Monetary Policy, and Property Rights in a Planned Economy 261

National Economy

13. DEBORAH MILENKOVITCH Plan and Market in Yugoslavia 272

14. OSKAR LANGE and FRED M. TAYLOR The Trial and Error Procedure in a Socialist Economy 282

15. BRANKO HORVAT The Pricing of Factors of Production 294

16. BRANKO HORVAT An Institutional Model of a Self-managed Socialist Economy 307

Notes on the Editors 329

PART III

Sociology and Politics

Introduction

1. The Sociology of Workers' Self-management

RUDI SUPEK

Sociology means the study of society from the viewpoint of its totality. The sociology of self-management shows us that all those attempts at and conceptions of self-managed production organizations that did not take into consideration workers' self-management as an integrated social, economic, and political system—from Robert Owen to guild socialism to the Soviet and German workers' councils—were condemned to failure. Workers' self-management, therefore, represents an entire social organization, on the one hand, and the corresponding social forces capable of realizing it, on the other. Yugoslavia today is the only country in the world that is attempting to create and apply an integrated system of workers' self-management. It remains an open question for scholarly discussion, however, whether the implementation and very conception of workers' self-management does not require a certain level of development of economic and social forces; that is, whether, according to Marx's conception, it represents a "new form of social relations" that presupposes "a certain level of development of the productive forces." From that viewpoint one can examine whether Yugoslavia possesses the best "objective conditions" for the construction of a self-governing society. Such a dilemma is not new;

Translated by Helen Kramer.

Lenin faced a similar question in connection with socialism. But once history is in action as a revolutionary force, it usually subordinates "objectivity" to the "human project," within certain limits, by particular anticipations or "leaps" (Lenin). The virtues of the Yugoslav experiment lie in its revolutionary anticipations; its weaknesses, in the "objective necessities" of historical development. This, of course, by no means frees the creators of the new society of their subjective responsibility for attempts as well as for mistakes.

Although the idea of workers' self-management historically developed from the parts toward the whole, from individual attempts of various visionaries and social reformers to an overall inclusion in the social system of a revolutionary class, the practical realization of workers' self-management, applied within the framework of a concrete society, seems to flow in the opposite direction, from the whole toward the parts, from state power toward the transformation of production organizations. This is especially true in those countries that underwent a socialist revolution which at first took an etatist form and gradually oriented itself to workers' self-management; we have seen such attempts in Poland, Hungary, and Czechoslovakia, and this is probably that trend toward the democratization of society that Gurvitch calls "reformist." It is valid to assume, as does Gurvitch, that the establishment of workers' self-management will take place both "from the bottom up," by the takeover of factories by workers' councils in revolutionary circumstances, and "from the top down" in those countries, usually socioeconomically backward, where industrialization and the lack of suitable personnel will impose a more statist form of organization. Hence workers' self-management appears simultaneously as an element of labor strategy in winning power and as the basis of a new socialist order (H. Lefebvre).

There is a widespread opinion that workers' self-management is a theory elaborated especially by Proudhon and the anarchosyndicalists and that it cannot be connected with the Marxian conception of socialism. This conception is advocated in particular by the proponents of so-called statist socialism, which today is the dominant system in the East European countries. However, those acquainted with the works of Marx and Engels know that workers' self-management is the logical consequence of Marx's critique of bourgeois democracy, at the center of which is the organization of rule in the form of the state, as well as of Marx's theory of the alienation of labor. In fact, we find three dominant ideas in Marx that lead us to workers' self-management:

a) the idea of the withering away of the state and its replacement by the "free association of the producers";

b) the idea of the "expropriation of the expropriators," the owners of the means of production, by the workers, and direct control of workers over the produced surplus value or surplus labor;

c) the idea of the abolition of the technological division of labor or "split-up labor" and of the crippling of the worker's personality, through institution of a system in which workers will successively perform different functions, from manual to managing, in the productive process itself; this is possible only by the creation of a "work community," a self-managing productive organization in which the worker directly participates in all essential productive functions.[1]

For Marx, the political alienation of man—which means the alienation of social forces in the form of political power and the state—has the same root as alienation in work—that is, in the class relations between the capitalists and workers—for the state is an instrument of the class rule of the capitalists. Hence the abolition of the state and of representative democracy is just as much the precondition of the emancipation of the working class and of people in general (for the working class is the emancipator of the whole society) as is the socialization of the means of production. Nationalization of the means of production by the state, regardless of whether the state is bourgeois or proletarian, means, as Engels once expressed it, only the transformation of the state into a "general capitalist." Hence the essential precondition for the "withering away of the state" is not the nationalization but the *socialization* of the means of production, where work collectives or the associated producers themselves independently manage production as "good entrepreneurs." The means of production are not the property of the state, but neither are they group property. They are social property, which means that self-managing organizations do not have the right to misuse these means (*jus abutendi*): they dispose of the fruits of their labor, but they do not have the right to destroy the means of production. The political system that corresponds to a self-governing society is that whose anticipation Marx saw in the Paris Commune of 1871, that is, direct democracy, which eliminates every form of state bureaucracy and is based on the direct representation of workers' or people's delegates, who remain under the closest control of their electors for the duration of their mandate.

The Marxist-Leninist strategy of socialist revolution assumes a transitional period between capitalism and socialism which is generally called the "dictatorship of the proletariat," and about which there are various theories; one of the essential factors in that period is the takeover of the state by the proletariat and the adoption of measures to insure that the "state begins immediately to wither away" (Lenin). The first of these measures is quite understandably the establishment of the power of workers' councils (soviets). However, the etatist course already being followed in Lenin's time, and especially the later rejection of the withering away of the state in the name of "strengthening the workers' state" (Stalin)—even in both socialism and communism!—curbed the control organs in the factories and made them purely consultative, while in the townships and the state they were transformed into classical bourgeois representative bodies. The rehabilitation of the idea of workers' self-management in the transitional period means the establishment of the power of workers' councils in production and other organizations as the counterweight to the power of the state, which is inherited from bourgeois society.

The essence of self-governing democracy lies in the disappearance of politically organized power above society; this means power not only of the state but also of political parties and, in general, of all forms of mass organization insofar as they are the carriers of the bureaucratization of social life. Thus, one of the first moves in Yugoslavia was the demand for the separation of the Party from the state, for the duplication of functions is typical of statist socialism, where the Party controls all the important administrative activities of the government. The shift of the Party's control from the executive sphere toward the legislative—that is, toward the area of civic life and public opinion—is characteristic of the process carried out in the transition from statist to self-governing socialism, although the Party, as the dominant political force, does not change its "democratic-centralist organization." It does, however, necessarily change its social role, receding more and more before the autonomus activity of self-managed production organizations and communes, as well as of the basic political-territorial organizations, which also enjoy full autonomy in a direct democracy.

Here attention should be called to a problem concerning the relation of a political party to workers' self-management. In his testament, Togliatti already had raised the question of whether the "dictatorship of the proletariat" will be the expression of the power of one party (the Communist), or whether a coalition of leftist parties, ready to carry out socialism, might be possible. The answer can be given roughly as follows: in "socialist" systems with a markedly statist structure of power (state power, centralization of functions, subordination of the planned economy to the state, etc.), it is quite probable that the very phenomenon of combining political party and state administrative power (the predominance of the executive functions over the legislative) will favor the establishment of a one-party system, while socialist systems with workers' self-management (power at the base, decentralization, freeing of the economy from state administration, etc.) will favor the preservation of a coalition or multiparty combination of power, since the essential *integration* of society is carried out not by political means from the top down but by sociocommunitarian means from the bottom up.

As a way of abolishing representative democracy, socialist self-management aims at abolishing professional political representation, which is remote from the electoral masses, by introducing a delegational system. The idea of the delegational system is to enable associated producers and citizens to exert direct influence on decision-making on social matters in the representative bodies, the parliaments (Šuković, Bourdet). It expresses the right of every individual to participate in making social decisions and to control them directly. Thus the natural right to man's self-determination as a producer in production organizations is carried over to the society as a whole.

One of the problems that has been resurrected in the organization of self-governing socialism is the problem of the *legal equality* of individual production organizations and other economic organizations that, in a market economy, necessarily gives rise to *economic inequality*. The market economy, for many reasons (bearing on an economic organization's initial stock of capital, rate of accumulation, monopolistic position on the market, better organization, etc.), acts to create inequalities among economic organizations. Thus, in Yugoslavia, the concentration of financial and trade capital quickly led to their domination over industrial capital, which found itself in economic difficulties and was exposed to economic exploitation by financial and trade capital. Hence, for example, workers and employees in the former area earned lower incomes than those in the latter. This fact poses the fundamental question of the control of income at various levels of social organization, and hence the question of control of the basic production organizations over intermediaries (banks, trade, insurance, etc.). Control over intermediary organizations means the necessary limitation of their self-management autonomy by society. Here social self-government is limited in the name of *social management* by the introduction of representatives of other social organizations into managerial organs or by legal measures (R. Supek). What is essential in this problem is to honor the principle that man as producer should control the produced income on all levels of social organization or in all forms of its economic transformation. The honoring of this principle leads to a *functional organization* of self-governing society, to the linking of the principle of functionality to the principle of democracy. It is not a question of functionality as conceived by the guild socialists, *nota bene*. Rather, it is a question of functionality defined on the basis of humanist axioms, and not economic or technological ones, which remain subordinated to the humanist.

The relations of economic efficiency, technological functionality, and humanist organization are sharpened especially at the level of the production organizations, and here the theoreticians of workers' self-management encounter a series of theoretical and practical problems.

Today all forms of participation, workers' control, and workers' self-management are included under the concept of "industrial democracy." In fact, "industrial democracy" as introduced into sociology by Proudhon, and as follows naturally from its definition, is identical with workers' self-management. We see this not only from the typology of various forms of participation (J. Tabb and A. Goldfarb), but also in the actual workers' movement, which aims at achieving "full participation," as it is conceived by libertarian socialism in Latin America, or full "workers' control," that is, the authority of workers' councils (A. Gramsci, K. Korsch). We must immediately mention here that it is a mistake to equate workers' self-management, as the highest form of the "participation" of workers and employees in managing the enterprise, with self-governing socialism, which is a longer process of social transformation in the direction of achieving direct democracy as well as the full control of the producers over national income or labor and, at the same time, full control of consumers over the production of those consumer goods that truly correspond to real "human needs."

Experience has shown that the realization of a self-managed production organization depends on a number of internal (intraorganizational) and external (interorganizational) factors. The basic precondition for the autonomy of a self-managed organization is its "material base," that is, independent disposal of the income produced. Yugoslav experience shows that this material base was very narrow in the beginning, and that it widened increasingly from 1955 to 1965, as state intervention in the economy declined and market mechanisms were gradually freed. It goes without saying that the widening of the material base went hand in hand with the process of decentralization of management in the economy (V. Rus). This process is connected with various conflicts between tax payments (to the federation, republic, and communes—in all, about 40 percent of net income) and the possibility for independent investment, as well as between economic initiatives from the bottom up and state planning interventions from the top down. These conflicts remain inherent in the system itself and represent a kind of internal dynamics.

In its external relations, the self-managed production organization is exposed to various influences to which it must actively adjust: state planning interventions (price controls); the market mechanisms of supply and demand; and different, more or less connected relations with other production organizations (problems of integration and independence) which are equally under the influence of market, economic factors and technological, developmental factors. Thus we can speak of a pluralist model of self-managed organizations with respect to their socioeconomic relations.

One of the most important problems concerning the internal situation is the transformation of *formal rights* of participation into *actual or effective* participation, which is most closely connected with the power relations within the organization itself. It is obvious that the lack of development of class consciousness or of motivation for participation in decision-making enables smaller groups or cliques to monopolize decision-making in a self-managed organization. This has been the subject of a large number of research studies in Yugoslavia (V. Rus, J. Županov, J. Obradović, R. Supek). It is clear that a certain passivity on the part of workers and employees—and also the lack of adequate education—permit the maintenance of an authoritarian type of management, so that the role and influence of the director or management board remain dominant. This is promoted, of course, by the prevailing economic insecurity and the political connections of the director and managerial personnel in the enterprise with powerful political and economic elements (banks) in society, as well as by a certain passivity on the part of the trade unions, which have retained in Yugoslavia the same role they had in statist socialism—that is, they transmit Party decisions and perform the role of educating and disciplining the working class, but they do not represent the latter's class interests independently. (Bureaucrats usually hold that workers cannot have any "special interests" opposed to the administration, which leads "in the name of the working class"; but in actuality workers do not share this opinion, as can be seen by the very large number of wildcat strikes.)

Among the main reasons that relations within self-managed organizations are authoritarian, in addition to the lack of development of the working class itself (often 80 percent are "worker-peasants"!), one of the factors often cited is the contradiction between the horizontal structure of relations, adapted to self-management autonomy, and the vertical structure of relations between the base and higher jurisdictions, from the commune to the federation, where state and Party control still dominate (the Party itself retains the principle of "democratic centralism" in spite of the pressures of self-government relations in the opposite direction). In addition to this contradiction between the horizontal and vertical organization of self-management (J. Županov), the conflict between producing organizations and intermediary organizations (banks, trade organizations, village cooperatives that have transformed themselves into trading or middleman organizations) can be stressed. One can ask if the authoritarian structure is favorable to economic efficiency. Research in Yugoslavia as well as in some other countries (Likert, Tannenbaum) confirms that organizations with developed participation are much more efficient than organizations with an autocratic type of management (J. Jerovšek).

When the concept of "industrial democracy" is used, it is essential to distinguish among various forms of participation or "participatory democracy" and workers' self-management. Participation includes collaboration or "antagonistic participation" with employers (private or state), while workers' self-management presupposes independence and social ownership. Likewise, "workers' control" must be distinguished from workers' self-management, for workers' control involves class antagonism toward employers and the existence of antagonistic class power relations, while workers' self-management represents the surmounting and disappearance of class antagonistic relations and the creation of a new work community of producers, and this means that, in addition to the workers, all other "working people" (employees, technical staff, directors, etc.) also manage the enterprise. In modern capitalism, participation represents an attempt to integrate the working class into the existing system, although at the same time it indicates a certain broadening of workers' control with respect to power relations, while workers' self-management means the elimination of every form of integration of the working class into a private or state capitalist system of managing economic organizations. As regards the "new unionism" or "enterprise unionism" (S. Mallet, A. Gorz, K. Coates and T. Topham, et al.), it is a matter of widening the base of the class struggle (to include both workers and technicians, that is, both the manual and intellectual workers in the enterprise), with the aim of their joint control in enterprise management. The traditional function of enterprise management by owners is slowly dying out, as Marx predicted. In contrast to the transfer of power to the managers (the "managerial revolution"), here it is significant that what is involved is the takeover of management by the entire work collective, and hence the abolition of the traditional hierarchical relations in the enterprise—in effect, the debureaucratization of the enterprise.

Enterprise unionism therefore faces the task of struggling not only against bureaucracy in the enterprise, but also against bureaucracy in the trade unions, whose leadership is accustomed to the traditional, ritualistic resolution of conflicts together with the employers' representatives. Hence, the new unionism emphasizes a more independent role for work collectives in the struggle not only for material improvement but also for qualitative changes (greater influence in decision-making, work security, social security and health protection, control of influences, etc.), and at the same time initiates action from the bottom up (the phenomenon of wildcat strikes) and introduces an element of spontaneity, initiative, and group solidarity in the spirit of industrial democracy. As opposed to state and union bureaucracies, it emphasizes the autonomy of work collectives.

All these contemporary trends of the workers' movement show that it is heading toward workers' self-management as the strategic goal, especially in the developed countries. The broadening of workers' control in the sense of workers' self-management here means the mobilization not only of the traditional proletariat (blue collar workers) but also of all those people who stand in a *wage labor relation* in various economic and noneconomic organizations and in education, health, and mass media, who strive to eliminate the monopoly of power by bureaucratic and managerial groups. The very strategy of the workers' struggle in the developed countries—the struggle against state centralism, bureaucracy, and technocracy, against all ideologists of a "third way" or "convergence" of the capitalist and socialist systems into some sort of "postindustrial technocratic society," in which the need for democracy dies out (H. Schelsky)—leads today toward an ideal of industrial democracy as the foundation of direct and self-governing democracy. It is also for this reason that the model of so-called statist socialism, with power held by a revolutionary elite or "workers' avant garde," is less and less attractive and acceptable for the developed countries.

The revival of the idea of participatory democracy, when conceived in its elaborated form, is not at all the revival of a utopian vision of the human community, but becomes a certain social necessity in a society in which the functional complexity of production favors the growth of an alienated, centralized, and bureaucratic form of power over people, the reduction of the decision-making role of people as producers and consumers in social organizations, and the crippling of the role of citizens and civic responsibility in society in general. Today, against the very powerful and forceful tendencies striving to establish final authority over man and society, similarly powerful tendencies are arising in the direction of a true democracy; nevertheless, neither the workers' movement nor progressive circles have yet clarified many conceptions about how best to eliminate the danger that threatens human freedom and the dignity of the human personality.

NOTE

1. For Marx's critique of the state and bourgeois democracy, the following of his works are particularly important: *Critique of Hegel's Philosophy of Right* (1844), "On the Jewish Question" (1844), *Critique of the Gotha Program* (1866), *The Civil War in France*

(1871); also, Engels's *Anti-Dühring* (1878). For the theory of alienation, see especially Marx's *Economic and Philosophic Manuscripts of 1844* and *Capital* (1868), in which there is a sharp criticism of the consequences of the division of labor for the worker's personality. For Marx's conception of workers' self-management, the reader may consult the well-documented study by Y. Bourdet, "Karl Marx et l'autogestion," *Autogestion,* No. 15 (1971); and for the theory of alienation, the book by J. Israel, *Der Begriff der Entfremdung* (Rowohlt, 1972).

General

2. Elements for a Sociology of Self-management

HENRI LEFEBVRE

The "managerial" theory of Proudhon and Proudhonism are currently being revived. In effect, according to Proudhon, an economic society that can and must become the entire society establishes itself spontaneously.

Opposed by its very nature to the political society, to the state, this economic society has its separate "reality, individuality, essence, life, its own rationale" *(Idée générale de la Révolution)*. The producer and the workshop negate the ruler. The state is only the abstract representation of consumers, while the real society is a concrete whole of work and production. Below the state apparatus, in the shade of political institutions, society slowly and silently produces its own organism—the economic or, rather, socioeconomic formation. There then exist two formations, incompatible by nature. The socioeconomic formation tends to subordinate and to absorb the political system. . . .

No doubt Proudhon conceived of the managerial associations as installed at the privileged and hence the strong points of the existing society, in the economic and social sectors well placed from the standpoint of the market and competition—the banks,

Reprinted from "Problèmes theoriques de l'autogestion," *Autogestion,* No. 1 (December 1966), 62–64, 66–70, by permission of the publisher. Translated by Helen Kramer.

for example. Experience, or social practice, has not confirmed Proudhon's views on this matter. The managerial associations formed by workers, which tried to install themselves at the "strong points" of the bourgeois society, turned out badly. Either they failed or else with rare exceptions . . . they were absorbed by capitalism; they functioned like capitalist enterprises under a "communitarian" or "cooperative" label.

Very recently Serge Mallet has proposed a theory which . . . is connected to the same hypothesis.

Serge Mallet has studied with much insight "the new working class" found in the industries technically in the avant-garde. He believes that some political conclusions can be drawn from this socioeconomic study. For him, the new working class is turning away from "obsolete ideologies" incapable of expressing the workers' felt needs. He finds indications of a "politicization of a new type, of a superior character, resting on a positive claim of the responsibilities of the working class," and emanating from the trade union movement. "We emerge here at the problem of participation, of responsibility in management itself, whatever the forms of this management may be." The questions discussed between the management and the trade unions tend on the workers' side to be posed "on the plane of control of management, control of the organization of production."

It is still too early to condemn this hypothesis resolutely. One can, however, consider confirmation of these views to be lacking. Hasn't Serge Mallet yielded to the temptation to extrapolate on the basis of his brilliant analyses, to jump from the socioeconomic to the ideological and the political?

Our hypothesis here will be entirely different. Experience (social practice) shows, in our opinion, that the managerial associations, in their purest and most interesting form—that is to say, self-management—appear at the *weak points* of the existing society. In every society one can perceive strong points which as a whole constitute its armor or, if one prefers, its structure. The social whole has a certain cohesion, a coherence. The existing state rests on these strong points. The statesmen occupy themselves with filling in the cracks by all the means at their disposal. Nothing passes around the reinforced places once they are consolidated. But between them there are weak zones or even gaps. It is there that something can penetrate. Some initiatives, some social forces act, intervene in these gaps, occupy them, and transform them into strong points, or, on the contrary, into something other than what exists in a consolidated way. The weak sections, the empty spaces, are revealed only in practice, by the actions of individuals capable of taking an initiative, or by the groping investigations of groups capable of intervening. While the weak points can thus be changed into strong points of the whole social structure, they can also lead, conversely to a bending or collapse of the whole (destructuration) . . . .

How do attempts at self-management arise? . . .

We know that self-management is born spontaneously, but that it is not born no matter where, no matter how. On the contrary. We have perhaps succeeded in localizing this birth, in defining certain necessary conditions. A conjunction is needed, a privileged place.

For a royal road, a route traced in advance, does not spring up before it simply because it appears. In whatever place and at whatever moment self-management manifests itself spontaneously, it carries in itself its *possible* generalization and radicalization; but, simultaneously, it reveals and crystallizes before itself the contradictions of the society. As soon as the optimal and maximal prospect is opened, it means the overthrow of the entire society, the metamorphosis of life. But in order for self-management to affirm and extend itself, it must occupy the strong points of the social structure, which immediately resist it. From a privileged sector it must become a whole, a totality, a "system." This is a difficult advance along which self-management may even enter into conflict with itself. To manage an estate or an enterprise, and even more so a branch of industry, are not skills, experts, accountants, technicians needed? Thus, a bureaucracy tends to establish itself within self-management, a bureaucracy which negates the essence of self-management and which must be reabsorbed lest self-management contradict itself.

The principal contradiction that self-management introduces and provokes is its own contradiction with the state. In essence, it puts the state in question as a constraining power erected above the entire society, capturing and monopolizing the rationality inherent in social relations (in social practice). From a point at ground level, in a fissure—the humble plant—the enormous statist edifice is menaced. The statesmen know that, as it develops, self-management tends to overrun the state, that is, to lead toward its withering away. It sharpens all the contradictions at the heart of the state, notably the supreme contradiction, expressible only in general, philosophic terms, between reasons of state and the human claim, that is, liberty.

To generalize itself, to change itself into a "system" on the scale of the entire society—production units, territorial units, including so-called higher jurisdictions and levels—self-management cannot avoid conflict with the statist-political system. . . . Self-management cannot escape the hard obligation to constitute itself as a power that is not statist.

Self-management will have to confront a state which, even weakened, even shaken, even withering away in the sense foretold by Marx, will always be able to attempt to reaffirm itself, to consolidate its own apparatus, to change self-management into an ideology of the state in order to suppress it in practice. The state, whether bourgeois or not, by its very nature opposes a centralist principle to the principle of self-management, which is decentralist, acting from the base to the summit, from the element to the totality. By its nature, the statist principle tends to limit the principle of self-management, to reduce its applications. . . .

Self-management must also confront and resolve the problems of the organization of the market. In neither its principle nor its practice does it negate the law of value. One does not pretend in its name to "transcend" the market, the profitability of enterprises, the laws of exchange value. Only centralizing statism has had this inordinate ambition.

Only in a narrow and condemned conception does self-management tend to dissolve society into distinct units, the communes, the enterprises, the services. In a broader conception, it is proper to propose and to impose forms of self-management at all the levels of social practice, including the coordinating bodies. The principle of self-management revives the contradiction between use value and exchange value. It tends to give primacy to use value. It "is" use value of human beings in their practical relations. It validates them against the world of commodities. It calls into question the world of commodities, but it does not deny the laws of this world, which must be mastered, not ignored. To limit the world of commodities does not mean to claim to liberate oneself of it by magic. Self-management makes it possible to give content to ideas of democratic planning, putting in the forefront social needs formulated, controlled, and guided by those concerned.

The organization of the market and democratic planning are not without risk. The principle of self-management implies the refusal of "co-management" with an economic apparatus, with a planning bureaucracy. It excludes toleration of a relapse toward capitalism while it contents itself with a share granted to the "workers," which would quickly be denied them.

The concept of self-management consequently has, in itself and by itself, a *critical import.* This critical import is major and decisive. As soon as one conceives self-management, as soon as one thinks of its generalization, one radically contests that which exists, from the world of commodities and the power of money to the power of the state.

Before this reflection, the true character of institutions and of the commodity world is revealed. On the other hand, as soon as one challenges the statist and bureaucratic institutions or the generalized world of commodities, how can one fail to evoke that which could replace them? As soon as self-management appears spontaneously, as soon as thought conceives it, its principle shakes the entire system or systems of the establishment. But this principle itself is immediately called into question, and all seek to crush it. If we now try to give shape to these reflections, we can propose the following formulations:

a. Self-management is born and reborn in the heart of a contradictory society that tends, under various influences (those of the state, those of technologies, bureaucracies, and technocracies) toward an overall integration and strongly structured cohesion. Self-management introduces and reintroduces the only form of movement, of effective challenge, in such a society. Without it, there is only growth without development (quantitative growth of production, qualitative stagnation of practice and social relations). In this sense, the idea of self-management coincides with the idea of liberty. It is the theoretical essence of liberty, today concentrated in and identified with a practical and political notion.

b. Self-management is born of these contradictions, as a tendency to resolve and surmount them. It is born as an actual and universal form (though not exclusive of other forms) of the class struggle. It adds a new contradiction to those of the society in which it arises—an essential, principal, superior contradiction with the existing state apparatus, which always claims to be the sole organizer, sole rationality, sole unifier of the society.

c. Self-management then tends to resolve the totality of various contradictions while it surmounts them in a new totality; but this occurs in the course of a theoretical and practical paroxysm, while the whole of these contradictions is pushed to the extremity, to its dialectical limit. This presupposes a historic moment and favorable circumstances.

d. Self-management must be studied from two different aspects: as a means of struggle, breaking the path; and as a means of reorganization of society, transforming it from bottom to top, from daily life to the state.

Its principle implies its extension to all levels of society. In this process, the difficulties and obstacles encountered will be all the greater as self-management calls into question the higher levels of society, the authorities.

It should never be forgotten that society does not consist of a sum of elemental units, but constitutes a whole. Any self-management, even a radicalized one, which installed itself only in individual, partial units without encompassing the whole would be doomed to failure. For the whole contains the level of strategic decisions, of politics, of parties. . . .

Since the state is unable to coexist peacefully with radicalized and generalized self-management, the latter must submit to democratic control "from the base." The state of self-management—that is, the state within which self-management raises itself to power—can only be a state that is withering away. Consequently, the party of self-management can be only the party that conducts politics toward the limit and end of politics, beyond political democracy. . . .

Would this be a utopia? No, insofar as this conception does not evoke the image of a spontaneous explosion, of an effervescence infecting the entire society, but rather of a long sequel, of a lenthy process. Self-management can be only an element of a political strategy, but it will be the essential element without which the rest is worthless, and which validates the rest. The concept of self-management today is the *opening* toward the *possible.* It is the way and the end, the force that can raise the colossal weights that oppress and crush society. It shows the practical way to *change life,* which remains the password and the goal and the meaning of a revolution.

Only by self-management can the members of a free association take their own life into their hands, so that it becomes their work —an action which is also known as appropriation or dealienation.

3. Three Paths to Self-management

GEORGES GURVITCH

The history of workers' councils in the capitalist countries from the Whitley Councils of 1916 in England, the works councils anticipated and established by the Weimar Constitution, and those created in several European countries (Austria, Norway, and Sweden in the twenties; France and Great Britain after the Liberation in 1945) has shown that they cannot succeed without nationalizations and total planning. The failure of the experiences realized up to the present in the noncollectivist countries represents only the defeat of *reformism*, which, relying on works councils, hoped to transform capitalism peacefully into socialism. The first attempts of industrial democracy under a capitalist regimen achieved no palpable result. . . . Industrial democracy will be either revolutionary or postrevolutionary, or else it will not be. This statement deserves more detailed explanation.

1. Workers' councils are incompatible with the existence of the management, which is always stronger. The state claims to play the role of arbiter, but it always retreats before the higher claims of capitalist profits and productivity. In fact, the collusion between the state and organized management engenders a force that literally crushes all pretense of worker representation; in practice,

Reprinted from "Les conseils ouvriers," *Autogestion,* No. 1 (December 1966), 50–57, by permission of the publisher. Translated by Helen Kramer.

the role of the latter is restricted to limiting some vexations and camouflaging the authoritarian economic power and privileges of the management.

2. Private property in the means of production leads, in fact, to reduction of all the power of the workers' councils to, in the best of cases, the right of control over the elaboration of workshop rules; participation of these councils in enterprise management is excluded. These are *control councils,* not *management councils.* All the more reason that the workers' councils do not have the authority to participate in the elaboration of enterprise and investment plans.

3. The weakness of the works councils and the limitation of their jurisdictions under a capitalist regimen prevent them, in the third place, from entering into a chain, into a more comprehensive economic organization that rises by tiers from the basic cells to industrial councils, to regional economic councils, and from there to a national economic council. It is not without reason that even when such a chain of organization is foreseen—as in the Weimar Constitution or in the preliminary drafts of the partial nationalizations in France and England—it is not actually realized.

4. Since the enterprise councils remain isolated fragments with limited jurisdiction and without any real power, they provoke at the same time the suspicion of the trade union organizations, which fear the influence of the management and the egoism of the particular enterprise.

5. Even when it is works councils in nationalized sectors of industry that are involved, and their representatives are called upon to sit in the managerial and executive councils (as in the case of certain French, British, and Canadian experiments), they are always in a minority, overwhelmed by the representatives of the bourgeois state and of the higher technical personnel.

6. Even when the workers' councils under a capitalist regimen succeed particularly well, as was the case in republican Germany between 1920 and 1930, their success, which threatens to become the preamble of a social revolution, comes into conflict with strong forces of resistance capable of reaching disquieting proportions. It is well known that at the beginning the Nazi movement was financed and armed by American and British capital and that the death of the Republic was preferred to the imminence of a social revolution.

One cannot, therefore, separate the workers' councils from na-

tionalization of all the important sectors of the economy and from the abolition of the absolutism of private profit—that is to say, from a social revolution. . . .

7. To conclude these negative remarks on the possibility and efficacy of workers' councils in the capitalist countries, let us note that in our superindustrialized and superorganized epoch, nationalization of the means of production implies comprehensive planning. This planning can bring about an enormous good by giving to the society, to the group, and to man the possibility of controlling their own fates, thus assuring the triumph of human liberty, collective as well as individual. . . . But this planning can also produce a no less enormous evil by literally crushing man, by subordinating him to things, by sacrificing him as much to the private interest as to the arbitrariness of uncontrolled planners. While workers' councils remain shadows without reality in all systems where the collective nationalization of the means of production is not achieved, this *nationalization linked to planning is socialist only when the planning gives every guarantee against arbitrary power*. To be democratic and humanist, planning must be decentralized and based on the self-management of the workers.

Collectivist, that is to say, democratic, planning and the workers' councils are only the two ends of one and the same chain; that is why the former calls for the latter.

The workers' councils must be not only the executive organs of planning but also active cells in the *elaboration of local and central plans*. Therefore, the extent of their jurisdictions must be wide and must permit them to establish at the same time: (a) control organs; (b) management organs; (c) organs for raising productivity; (d) income distribution organs; (e) organs for participation in general planning.

It seems to me that the development of workers' councils in Yugoslavia has not yet ended, since it has provoked a reorganization and strengthening of the Chambers of Producers.[1] The reason is that the Chambers of Producers do not rest on the factory councils from which they should emanate. For it is in this way that the workers' councils should become the machinery for planning the entire collectivist economy. The direction and planning of the economy should be confided to an Annual Congress of Workers' Councils which would replace the Chamber of Producers in the Parliament. Consumers and users would also have to be

1. Reference is to developments as of 1957, when this text was written—*Trans.*

represented in this new Chamber. Workers' councils mus permitted to become a source of denationalization and deplanning. They would be the first to suffer from such a situation.

We are thus led to envisage the prospects for the development of self-management by means of workers' councils that are opening up in the other socialist countries and in the USSR itself.

It is certain—and I think that the whole world is now in agreement on this fact—that there are *many ways* to reach collectivism, setting out from *worker self-management in a nationalized and planned economy*. Let us specify certain of these ways:

1. In the first place, workers' councils can be born spontaneously, in the fire of the social revolution itself, and remain afterwards as the determining factor of the nationalized and planned economy. Since workers' councils would then be simultaneously executors and beneficiaries of the social revolution, all risk of autocratic technocracy in planning and management would be excluded and an immediate blossoming of worker self-management would follow.

2. In the second place, workers' councils can be installed by a political government which has sprung out of the social revolution and which, after having first succeeded in stabilizing itself and eliminating the adverse forces, is all the more convinced that the best means to implement planning that is both democratic and capable of yielding the maximum returns is to disposses itself in favor of the direct representation of the workers. This is the Yugoslav way.

3. In the third place, the workers' councils can develop by stages, modifying over a rather long period the autocratic and bureaucratic organization of the economy imposed on a large scale by the political government that has sprung from a social revolution. This process can be very slow or more accelerated, depending upon the concrete structure of political power and on internal and external circumstances. Thus, it is still almost embryonic in the USSR, Czechoslovakia, Bulgaria, and Romania, but more pronounced in Hungary and especially in Poland. I do not have sufficient information to judge the situation in China. But what appears to me essential is to throw into relief the imperious reasons that lead me to believe in an imminent postrevolutionary evolution toward self-management by workers' councils and toward decentralized planning of all the nationalized and planned economies. The emancipation from the absolutism of private profit—gained by nationalization and planning realized and in-

terposed in the aftermath of a social revolution—cannot be stopped midway. While the collectivist regime assures the working class that it is in power, it contradicts itself if it allows the working class, in the daily life of the factories, enterprises, and the implementation of plans, to remain subject to the uncontrolled orders of bureaucrats; it risks in the long run provoking both confusion and discontent among the working masses. At the same time, the voluntary cooperation and initiative of all the participants are indispensable for the realization of plans, and these can only be obtained if all the interested parties—the workers first of all (their factory councils and regional councils), then the consumers and users—are represented in the elaboration of plans.

Each of the three paths to self-management of workers' councils has its faults and its advantages, and it would be contrary to sociology to choose among them in an abstract manner. These paths are imposed according to the circumstances, sometimes combining with or substituting for each other. The faults and the advantages of each are accentuated differently depending on the obstacles that self-management of the economy by workers' councils finds in its path in each concrete situation. Setting out from these various points of view, we shall examine each of these three paths and present some concrete examples.

I. As regards the first path, it is the Russian Revolution, the first, which actually experienced—for too short a period, alas!—the spontaneous rise of workers' councils in the very fire of the social revolution. Let us recall the facts: the workers' councils were born spontaneously in Russia in the memorable days of February 1917; it was they which in large part made the revolutions of *February* and *October*. Not contenting themselves with control and management of the factories and enterprises, the workers' councils elected delegates to the *local, regional, and central soviets,* these peoples' committees which became first the competitors of the provisional government and then, in October 1917, the sole legally recognized power. Was it not with the slogan "All power to the soviets" that Lenin and the Communist Party overthrew the provisional government and carried the majority in the soviets? But, after having been the architects of the new political power, the workers' councils in the factories submitted to a paradoxical, even tragic fate. *Their too great success, in turning them away from their first inclination of workers' self-management of industry, dealt them a harsh blow.* By a decree of April 1917, the provisional government of Lvov-Kerensky tried to reduce their functions to the control of the disciplinary power of the employers. This decree was attacked very violently by Lenin and by all of the extreme Left, which rightly demanded management and direction of the factories by the councils and the elimination of the employers. After the October Revolution, they went further, even too far, in affirming that the factory councils could replace the technicians and engineers. But this experience lasted only several months in all. Stalin need not be accused of things of which he is not guilty; his errors are surely numerous enough without that. It is Lenin himself who, conscious of the need for great efficiency of production at a moment when the civil war made the rapid production of arms indispensable, replaced the workers' councils in the factories of the USSR by work inspectors appointed from above. They were very badly received by the workers, who regarded them as policemen. Thus, the workers' councils in the USSR, after having been the organs of the social revolution, were engulfed by the revolution's very tide. It would be entirely erroneous, however, to believe that the workers of the USSR have forgotten about workers' councils. Quite to the contrary, these continue to hold a place in their consciousness and in their memory. To convince oneself of this, one need only read the declarations of the Soviet leaders, who, during the most bureaucratic and most authoritarian period of the Stalinist regime, never openly denied the principle of workers' self-management. They have sought only to justify the nonrealization of this self-management by invoking the necessity for an accelerated pace of industrialization, the circumstance of civil war, the menace of Western imperialism, the needs of postwar reconstruction, and so on. These justifications of very unequal validity appeared to be necessary, for the idea of the control and management of the factories by the soviets has remained very popular among the Russian workers. They rightly consider that self-management represents the principal form of "democracy at the base," a concept still officially approved by the leaders of the USSR.

It is not my task here to review the history of the Russian Revolution, or to judge it. However, I must affirm my continuing opinion that Lenin, distracted by the grave threats that weighed on the very existence of the soviet regime of the USSR—the sole soviet regime in the world at that moment—committed a serious error in temporarily putting the workers' councils to sleep; it would have sufficed to have organized them better while defining their jurisdiction. As Goethe said, it is only the temporary that endures. And this provisional state opened wide the way to the bureaucratization of the planned economy of the USSR; from such a point, after having begun with the birth of all-powerful workers' councils, the USSR must now follow the third path that we indicated, that of a slow evolution by stages toward these same councils.

Let us note in addition that the failure of the first path to worker management in the USSR does not at all signify that this path of spontaneous appearance of workers' councils cannot succeed at the time of social revolutions in countries with old democratic traditions, such as Great Britain, France, and the Scandinavian countries, which also enjoy powerful trade union organizations independent of the state. But here everything depends, on the one hand, on the resistance that the employers will be prepared to offer, and, on the other, on the ease with which the political advancement of the working masses, who arrive at economic power through the workers' councils, can be carried out. For it is not solely the narrow collaboration of economic and political power that can enable the workers' councils to become the determining factor of the nationalized and planned economy. We are here before an equation with several unknowns, and we can only wish for the old Western democracies that they choose at the decisive hour the most direct way toward a spontaneously arising worker self-management of the economy.

II. The second path, that of the granting of workers' councils by a stabilized political government sprung from the revolution —the Yugoslav way—presupposes a favorable conjunction of events and circumstances. In Yugoslavia, this consisted in the struggle for national independence after the country's liberation, in which the peoples' committees and the Popular Front played a very important role. The very difficulties encountered with the Cominform impelled a search for ways of socialization and planning different from those current in the USSR during the Stalinist era. Worker self-management was, so to speak, in the air before it was officially introduced by the government. The local peoples' committees had paved the way for it. However, some difficulties remain to be surmounted: (1) the integration of factory councils in the planning bodies is not sufficiently realized; (2) the profits of the enterprises governed by worker self-management and the profits of the nation as a whole ought to be better distributed; (3) the relations between the workers' councils and the trade unions should be specified and improved.

Moreover, in other countries and in other circumstances, this path to workers' councils could encounter the resistance of a too deeply entrenched administrative and bureaucratic apparatus whose confidence would go more voluntarily to its officials, technicians, planners, and experts than to the workers' representatives. In addition, the latter's demands could appear to a state sprung out of the social revolution not only annoying but even counterrevolutionary. Truly favorable circumstances, such as the pressure of a powerful, well-organized workers' movement or the imperious requirements of productivity, are therefore necessary to lead a political government sprung from the social revolution to take the initiative of transferring a large part of its power to the workers' councils.

III. It remains for us to examine the third path to self-management of workers' councils—the slow path of proceeding by stages. . . .

a. Bureaucratic management of the economy was not always total in Russia, despite all the power attributed to the director, who was appointed from above. While the workers did not have the right to force the recall of their superiors, they maintained the right of criticism, exercised within the framework of the trade union, the Communist Party cell, and the local soviet. These criticisms are transmitted to the local or central authorities voluntarily or involuntarily by the directors, managers, and technicians, thereby becoming possible victims of sanctions, sometimes exaggeratedly severe, for sabotage, abuse, and so on. It will perhaps be said that this way of exercising control is rather primitive and at the same time limited, for this right is impotent against those responsible for planning, the heads of the Party. I would be the last to deny it. But it should not be forgotten that we are speaking of potentialities, and that, in addition, the political power of the USSR holds its technobureaucrats well in hand until the new order is established.

b. The development of "wall newspapers" in the Russian factories over a rather long period is another manifestation of the same potentialities. The complaints formulated there are often effective, and the administration is forced to take account of them.

c. Some "workers' committees" have been introduced in the

large factories. While up to the present they have not had any right to make demands, and have had a tendency to be cast into organs of the executive, whose sole function is to explain to workers the latter's decisions, the "workers' committees" can, when discontents or serious conflicts arise, change in substance and become embryos of real workers' councils.

d. The recent measures of deconcentration and local decentralization of heavy industry and its planning bodies could in the long run work in favor of the resurrection of workers' councils. In effect, when the great planners and directors are on the spot, it is easier to touch them, to observe them, to criticize them, and these criticisms become more effective. Deconcentration and local decentralization have a chance of becoming a stage toward worker self-management of the planned economy.

e. Is it not significant that several months after this local decentralization, the Soviet government decreed the right of every worker to lay a complaint before any court against the abuse of power by directors of factories and enterprises?

In realizing this right, will not the Soviet workers choose to exercise it as a group, electing their representatives? Here once again the workers' councils spring up in germ.

f. This development . . . toward workers' councils, under a new form, can only be encouraged by the fact that in the countryside, the organization of agricultural production is giving place to a rather intense manifestation of self-management of kolkhoz members. The kolkhozes are bound to the direct participation of all members in management.

4. The Possibility of Other Models of Socialism

ROGER GARAUDY

In our time, the major problem in the elaboration of a model of socialism is that posed by the new scientific and technological revolution: how to surmount the possible contradiction between the scientific organization of production and the workers' autonomy.

This contradiction, as we have seen from the experience in the United States, cannot be surmounted in a capitalist system; its solution requires a radical change in the relations of production. As long as technocracy, in terms of the essential, is controlled and oriented by the private owners of the means of production, by the big monopolies, there will be osmosis between the imperatives of profits and the imperatives of growth for the sake of growth; the alienation of the workers and of the entire society will continue to increase.

To begin to force this alienation to recede, the first condition is to put an end to the private ownership of the means of production, which is the point of departure of the construction of socialism.

This is a necessary but not a sufficient condition. The analysis of the Soviet model has shown this.

Translated from *Le Grand tournant du socialisme* (Paris: Gallimard, Idées, 1969), pp. 172–79, with permission of William Collins Sons & Co., and Grove Press, publishers of the English-language version, *Crisis of Communism* (London, 1970; New York, 1972). Translated by Helen Kramer.

What characterizes the Soviet model of socialism is the identification of collective ownership of the means of production with state ownership.

Now, it does not at all follow from the revolutionary role of the proletarian state that it should transform itself into management.

The socialist revolution necessarily implies the seizure of political power by the working class and its allies precisely in order to change radically the relations of production and their legal expression, the right of property.

The revolutionary function of the new class state, as far as the problem of property is concerned, consists not only in abolishing private ownership of the means of production and in instituting a social ownership, indivisible and inalienable, but in establishing "rules of the game" that will prevent their reversion to private ownership, whether in individual form or as the property of groups that can hire and exploit wage earners or transform themselves into private shareholders.

If, in its economic function, the state goes beyond this transformation of the relations of production and the establishment of the rules of the game, its revolutionary role becomes a managerial role.

In the first stages of the revolution it can be led to fill this role for historical reasons: scarcity of products and personnel, counterrevolutionary attempts requiring a war economy and an extreme centralization of resources and of power.

But if the managerial role, legitimate and necessary in a period of "war communism," is perpetuated beyond that period, this state ownership, which during the period of attack of the revolution could be the first form of social ownership of the means of production, will distinguish itself from the latter more and more.

The state is not society. It is a class's instrument of domination and repression. Even when it is the working class's instrument of domination and repression, it remains distinct from society as a whole, and even from the working class as a whole. We can recall Lenin's judgment of 1919 and 1920 on this phenomenon: "Our state is a workers' state presenting a bureaucratic deformation . . . the soviets, which according to their program, are the organs of government *by* the workers, exercised by the advanced stratum of the proletariat and not by the working masses. . . . we must use the workers' organizations to defend the workers against their state."

The state, in effect, is not an abstraction but is incarnated in a group of people: "The bureaucracy," wrote Marx, "possesses the substance of the state . . . it becomes its property."[1]

In a model of socialism in which social ownership is identified in a permanent way with state ownership, the monopoly of management becomes the specialty, the profession of a particular social group. Its essential social prerogatives are:

1) the monopoly of management of state property;

2) the monopoly of political decision, which flows from the preceding prerogative by the determination of objectives and programs;

3) the monopoly of use of the newly created values, of surplus value.

This bureaucracy does not constitute a social class for two fundamental reasons: it does not own the means of production, but only manages them; and this management function is not transmitted through inheritance as is property.

Nonetheless, this conversion of social property into state property, in a centralized and bureaucratic state, in particular, does not permit the satisfactory resolution of:

—either adaptation to the new scientific and technical revolution, which requires the widest participation, creative initiatives, and the responsibility of all;

—or disalienation, which is the major objective of socialism, for in such a system the worker is transformed once more into a wage earner, no longer of a private employer but of the state.

The elaboration of a different model requires, first of all, a clear consciousness of the fact that state property is only one form of social property among others. For this, it is necessary to recall the multiple components of property and of the concept of the state.

Marx distinguished between property as the appropriation of nature by man's labor, which transforms it, and property (alienated in all class societies) in which the determination of the ends and the methods of work and the disposal of the fruits of labor are the privilege and monopoly of the owner of the means of production.

This analysis of Marx enables one to give a precise content to the classical legal distinctions concerning the right of ownership of the means of production: *usus, fructus,* and *abusus.*

Usus is first of all the power to determine the ends of produc-

---

1. Karl Marx, *Critique of Hegel's Philosophy of Right.*

tion—for profit, or for individual or social needs, or for any other end.

Next it is the power to determine the methods, organization, and pace of work, and to secure the technical management of the enterprise.

Fructus is the disposal of the fruits of labor, that is, the appropriation of the surplus value, and the determination of its use and distribution: immediate consumption, investment, and so on.

Abusus is the right to "dispose like a master" of the possessed object, to use it and abuse it, that is, as regards a means of production, to destroy it or sell it in order to transform it entirely into consumer goods.

The holder of this property can be an isolated individual, a group, the state (under the form of state capitalism or state socialism), or the whole of a society's workers. There can also be mixed forms, such as, for example, the "workers' control" instituted by Lenin, which, while leaving to the employers the ownership of certain means of production, first of all excluded *abusus,* that is, the destruction of the means of production by dilapidation or sabotage, and controlled *usus* and *fructus—usus,* by verifying the quantities of merchandise produced while orienting production toward the most urgent needs, and by controlling technical management so that it insured the necessary supplies and respected working conditions; and *fructus,* by intervening in pricing or by taxing to limit profits.

The state exhausts its revolutionary function in the act of abolishing private property and instituting the rules of the game to prevent any return to private ownership, individual or collective; this does not mean, however, that production and economic life as a whole are abandoned to spontaneity. If the revolutionary state renounces its own transformation into the universal management and entrusts to the workers themselves the right of ownership and disposal of the surplus value, it can leave to other factors of social integration, which are neither administrative nor authoritarian, the task of orienting production in terms of needs and of creating forms of management that will assure maximum productivity through the maximum participation of workers in this management.

What are the characteristics of this "model" following from the four criteria of ownership defined above?

In contrast to the situation under capitalism, production is oriented not in terms of profits but in terms of the needs of society.

It is such an orientation which defines all forms of socialism. But in contrast to the etatist and centralist (Soviet) model, in this model these needs will not be defined "from above" by central directives of the Party and the state, but by the play of the *market* and of the demands that emerge from it. If one remembers that it is socialist enterprises, and not private owners, that are confronting each other on this market, then one cannot consider this market economy a capitalist economy. On the other hand, it is true that the individual needs which exert their pressure there are influenced, if not determined, by the level of productive forces, previous privatizations, external models, and so on. But one cannot escape that without falling into subjectivism and idealism, without believing in the magic power of determinations "from above" which emanate from omniscient rulers who substitute themselves for the workers and make infallible interpretations of the latter's needs; without believing in the magical powers of an "ethics" detached from its material conditioning. Marx's comment on the law is equally true for all social rules: "Law can never be more elevated than the economic state of the society and the degree of civilization that corresponds to it."[2]

With respect to property, the Yugoslav Constitution of 1963 proclaims (Part I, Title II) that the inviolable base of the system is social ownership of the means of production, the aim of which is to abolish "alienation of man from the means of production and from other conditions of work."

The characteristic of self-management, specifies Title III, is that "no one can have a right of ownership of the social means of production—neither the sociopolitical community, nor the work organization, nor the worker, taken individually; no one can appropriate, in virtue of any legal deed of ownership whatever, the product of social labor. . . . Man's work is the sole basis of the appropriation of the product of social labor as well as the basis of the management of social means."

Thus, in order to exclude all alienation of the conditions and the product of labor, the Constitution does not confer to any titulary the monopoly of social ownership. The factories, for example, are no more the property of the work collectives than they are of the state; the collectives manage them in the name and in the interest of the whole society.

---

2. Karl Marx, *Critique of the Gotha Program.*

5. The Idea of Direct Self-managing Democracy and Socialization of Policy-making

NAJDAN PAŠIĆ

The social emancipation of labor in the sphere of material production and income distribution is the point of departure for the historic process of socializing policy-making. In the organization of production and distribution on the lines of self-management, all the basic social forces and powers—forces whose actual source lies in associated, combined human labor—themselves come under the control of the associated workers rather than bossing them. According to Marxist theory, the forced alienation of the product of social labor from the producers, under a system of exploitation, lies at the root of pitting the common and general social interests against the concrete and personal interests of individual citizens (man as a private person in the specific system of production and social relations and man as an abstract citizen, a member of the "body politic"), consequently at the very root of the alienation of public power (the state) from society.

Placing the associated producer in the position of directly and jointly controlling the social conditions of his labor and his material existence, self-management *ipso facto* removes the principal social causes and roots not only of authoritarian forms of political organization but also all forms of rule and "bossing" by aloof po-

Reprinted from "Self-management as an Integral Political System," in M. J. Broekmeyer, ed., *Yugoslav Workers' Self-management* (Dordrecht, Holland: D. Reidel, 1970), pp. 3–9, by permission of the publisher.

litical forces above the working man and the social conditions of his existence. In consequence, the self-managing transformation of production relationships opens up for society the prospect of such consistent democratization of managing society's affairs, of the merger of self-managed organization of labor with the global organization of society, as will logically lead to the withering away of the state, that is, to the complete socialization of policy-making.

Such and similar Marxist conceptions on the revolutionary change to which the social emancipation of labor regularly leads throughout the entire fabric of society, and particularly in the forms of its constituting itself politically, are the theoretical basis taken as the starting-point by all conscious socialist forces in Yugoslavia in the development of the political system on the basis of self-management. The central focal point of the new political system becomes man in associated labor, to an increasing degree. Through the system of self-managing relationships in the working organization itself and through association between working organizations amongst themselves and also with the community at large, labor and the management of labor, production and appropriation and the disposal of the products of labor are linked together. Thereby the democratization of the political system, the democratization of the management of joint social affairs, regularly and inevitably transcends institutional forms and the limits of political-representative democracy which has been and remains the only possible form of democracy under conditions of the division and opposition of public power and society, of those who rule and those who are ruled.

As the development of self-management and the resulting liquidation of the causes of division between public power and society become the fundamental objective determinant of the transformation of political relationships, so does the transformation of political-representative democracy into direct social democracy become the basic law governing that transformation. Understanding this law is an essential condition for comprehending the meaning and perceiving the prospect of constituting the political system on the basis of self-management and for arriving at historically relevant criteria, rather than inadequate analogies looking to the past, for appraising concrete manifestations and the forms through which the process of socializing policy-making in a self-managing society are realized.

In the concrete historical example of Yugoslav society, the process of transforming political-representative relationships and institutions into an integral system of direct self-managed democracy has several basic aspects.

First of all, there is an expansion of the sphere of free, self-managed association by people to satisfy common requirements under their joint management and control. This refers above all to the local territorial communities (e.g., local communities in which the citizens, voluntarily and at their own initiative, pool their resources and efforts to solve problems relating to their common life in the small area in which they reside) and to social and public services in the field of education and culture, employment and social welfare, health protection, etc. Growing freedom in disposing of the income they earn in associated labor (gradual replacement of taxes and other fiscal levies by voluntary or compulsory contributions of an agreed amount and for agreed purposes) makes it possible for the working man, acting through forms of direct democracy (assemblies of beneficiaries, delegates in the assemblies and other organs of the community of interest, etc.) to participate in guiding the activities that serve to satisfy his vital needs.

Secondly, a place of importance in the organization of the political system is held by institutions of directly democratic decision-making and participation in policy-making, such as assemblies of voters in parts of the territory of the local communities, assemblies of working people in the enterprises and institutions, assemblies of those who utilize the services of communal and other enterprises, referendums in the working organizations and in the socio-political communities, etc. These and like institutions of direct democracy are not unknown to history, and in certain revolutionary periods and in various countries they have managed to assert themselves in their democratic function. However, the tremendous burgeoning of centralized state machinery and the growth of its monopoly over the bureaucratic management of society's affairs (which is characteristic of the present epoch) has resulted in the disappearance of these institutions or in their complete degradation. The development of self-management paves the way for a new and historic turning-point in this respect as well. The fuller affirmation of the aforementioned forms of direct democracy is made possible first of all by the altered position of the working man who, as part of self-managed production relationships and disposing of the surplus of social labor, becomes increasingly interested, capable and competent in terms of orienting himself and of making decisions on all political problems concerning his own special and the broader community. Secondly, the work of these institutions has a firm and broad normative basis, the support of laws and the backing of organized political forces. Legal and self-managing norms regulate the role and manner in which the assemblies function and the holding of referendums, and provision has been made for certain other important activities (nominations for representative bodies, establishment of development plans, the submitting of accounts by self-managing organs in the enterprises and in the local community, etc.), in which application of these forms of direct democracy in political decision-making is compulsory.

Thirdly, an important component in the process of developing direct democracy and socializing policy-making is decentralizing the management of social affairs in a manner that brings decision-making as close as possible to the working man himself and eliminates, wherever possible and to the greatest extent possible, decision-making and political mediation in his name. The most meaningful and the fullest expression of that self-managing decentralization is the conception of the commune as the basic socio-political community, the fundamental form of territorial integration of self-management and its merger with the mechanism of political power of the working people.

The commune is the basic socio-political community, above all in the sense that in it the working people exercise self-management, regulate their mutual relations and independently solve all problems connected with their work and their social existence with the exception of those which, because of their nature, must be entrusted to the broader socio-political communities—the provinces, republics and federation. This "preference of competence" favoring the commune derives from the inalienable right of the working people to make decisions, on the basis of self-management, not only about their work but about all other matters concerning their social position and the satisfaction of their personal and social requirements. Accordingly, the new position of the commune in the Yugoslav political system is the direct expression of self-management and not of administrative delegation of competence by higher, superior instances.

If the volume and significance of the function discharged by the commune as a local organ of power and self-management has grown tremendously over the past 13 or 14 years, and if the Yugoslav system stands out in this respect, in terms of the tendencies prevailing in the present-day world, then this fact can be explained only by the development of self-management at the base of society.

Naturally, we should not lose from sight the existing and palpable difference between the normative and the actual, between the theoretical and the constitutional-legal conceptions of the commune and its nature and position in political life. Nonetheless, certain important facts testify that development is going in a certain direction which, in perspective, should lead to elimination of the present disparity between the normative and the actual. In the final distribution of "public resources," which serve to cover the general requirements of the community (budget, social and public services), the commune has at its disposal greater resources than the federation or republic, attesting the extremely significant expansion of the material basis for self-management in the commune. In applying this yardstick, we may conclude that the local organs of government and self-management in Yugoslavia enjoy stronger positions than those enjoyed by the corresponding organs in either capitalist or socialist countries.

The commune is the basic socio-political community also in the sense that it provides the framework for the first step in horizontal integration and coordination of self-managed social activities, as a result of which the commune acquires the character of a community in which the working man maintains direct control over various aspects of his social existence. And it is precisely in this sense, as the basic cell in the territorial integration of self-management, that the commune provides the foundation from which the broader socio-political communities derive directly—the provinces, republics and the federation. Unless integration of self-management is realized in the commune, it would be impossible to forge unity in the broader community on the principle of self-management.

Fourthly, the replacement of a political-representatives system by the system of direct democracy is also reflected in changes in the character of the mandate of deputies and councilmen. For the representative bodies to shed their parliamentary nature and acquire the character of working bodies, they must be composed not only of independent political representatives but also of delegates who retain firm links with the self-managing structures (the working people organized along the lines of self-management), who delegate power to them. Normatively, this change is expressed in the Yugoslav Constitution, which defines the assemblies of socio-political communities as "elected delegations of all citizens, and particularly of the working people in their working communities, constituted in and replaceable by the communes." The deputies are responsible to their voters and may be recalled in accordance with procedure established by law. Constitutional and other legal provisions dealing with the rights and duties of deputies establish the conditions and premises for deputies to act as a direct permanent link between the assemblies to which they have been elected and the assemblies of the communes or republics where they have been elected. The professional discharge of the deputy's functions is strictly limited, also as a result of the principle of delegating representatives. As a rule, the deputies of large working communities remain at their jobs in their working organizations. All these are elements reflecting essential changes in the nature of the deputy's mandate which have been designed to assure that the assemblies have a self-managed, directly democratic and working character rather than being political-representative and parliamentary bodies.

Fifthly, the key element in transforming representative-political into direct democracy is the change in the character and role of the political organizations, particularly the political parties. All advanced systems of representative democracy are systems of party rule (partocracy): a number of parties, struggling amongst themselves for power, or one party holding an actual monopoly on political decision-making. Direct democracy, based on self-management, if it is genuine, signifies the negation of monopoly and is consequently, in essence, irreconcilably at odds with the system of party rule. This is empirically confirmed in all cases where social affairs are run in a self-managing form (as is the case with nationalized industry in France, with local self-management in India, etc.).

In Yugoslavia, too, the outlines of this problem began to appear during the very first years of development of self-management and the formation of workers' councils in the enterprises. The Communist Party itself soon became aware of the problem. At the Sixth Congress of the Communist Party of Yugoslavia held in 1952, only 2 years after the promulgation of the law turning state enterprises over to the working collectives to manage, decisions were adopted mapping out the transformation of the Party from the center and backbone of the system of all-embracing and direct state management of the entire process of social development (which began to forge ahead rapidly right after the war) into an ideological and political force acting as an integral part of the system of self-management, in keeping with the democratic principles on the basis of which that system had been constituted. Thus began the process of transforming the Communist Party into the League of Communists.

6. The Two Fundamental Principles of Self-government

YVON BOURDET

The first of the fundamental principles of self-government was formulated by Marx himself in *The Civil War in France*. It is the right to recall deputies, delegates, or any type of leaders at any moment. This rule, as simple as it is radical, aims at preventing the division of society into two categories of people, those who command and those who obey. This division, which in the beginning can pass as a simple technical convenience "for the good of all," has shown itself in history to be one of the causes of the division of society into antagonistic classes. Contrary to Hegel's postulate, the dialectic of the master and the slave does not always have its origin in a life and death struggle that gives power to courage and servitude to cowardice. Whatever there may be, after all, to this supposed "origin," the fact remains that the foundation of the power of the dominant class is only rarely an act of courage and, even if it is, it assures power only because it forces compliance with a class structure to which one can also gain access by birth, cunning, election, or cooptation. Rousseau knew well how to demonstrate that a cohesive society of equals can be achieved only by suppressing all heterogeneous power

Reprinted from "Les conditions de possibilité de l'autogestion," *Autogestion,* No. 9–10 (1969), 64–67, by permission of the publisher. Translated by Helen Kramer.

(whether it is of divine origin, born of violence, or perpetuated and reinforced by habit and tradition). But while he shows that the only "sovereign" compatible with our dignity must be a creation of our liberty, he does not sufficiently emphasize the risks of deputation or does not believe it possible to avert them (in which he was perhaps right, in his own epoch). Since then, experience has abundantly shown that the delegation of power, even for a fixed time, causes a break. The elected is exalted to a different status, he is *ipso facto* invested with a power that comes to him from the laws, the constitution, and, in spite of appearances, in an obscure way from the kings and gods of the past as well.[1] To be sure, toward the end of his mandate, to the extent that he wishes it to be renewed, he sometimes condescends to some sort of demagogy in order to keep the key to a kingdom to which election sometimes gives access but which it does not constitute. In fact, the elector can only recall Charles by naming George or another in his place, and the only difference is one of personality. The structure of domination remains unchanged. *Recall at any moment,* on the contrary, for the first time breaks the dual structure. There is no more *delegation* into a distance that is more than just temporal; the delegate "goes far," even when he returns to "our milieu"; he is invested for the duration of his mandate with an imaginary aura which assumes the quality of "strangeness." But if the delegation can be withdrawn at any moment, there is no more break; the "sovereign" no longer acquires independent existence; he remains supported at every instant by the arms of his mandate, which can let him fall at any moment. Thus, due to this continual control, power can never become a *separated jurisdiction;* it is embodied in a simple, mobile structure of the group that assumes one form or another according to the needs of the case. This effective organization, adapted to the objective of the moment, is no longer a *delegation* but an *expression* of the will of all.

We have previously insisted on the practical difficulties of implementing this rule,[2] but these problems are of a conjunctural

1. In this connection, it is enough to recall the "charismatic power," in Max Weber's sense, not only of a Hitler but also of a de Gaulle, who, while submitting to the popular verdict, never hid the fact that "his legitimacy" came from elsewhere and from further away.

2. See Max Adler, *Démocratie et conseils ouvriers* (Paris, 1967), pp. 39–44.

nature and do not at all call the principle into question. It must be seen especially that the *two* fundamental principles are *jointly* the condition for the possibility of self-government and that, because of this fact, they cannot be judged separately.

The second principle is the following: there is no democracy —or, with even more reason, self-government—if people are not in a position to *decide with full knowledge of the matter*. To be sure, it is a question here of an "evidence" that has always been perceived and the theory of which Plato formulated. But many consequences have been deduced from this "evidence," the principle one being that, given the ignorance of the people, democracy (in the proper sense of the term as self-government of the people) is not possible, that it is the best theoretical system but that it could only function with a "people of gods." In their actual state of incompetence, backwardness, indeed, of degradation, the people will always be made fools of by the able, will remain humble before the powerful and erudite, unconscious of their own good. Consequently, democracy will be perverted into demagogy so that the education of all the citizens will not be realized. . . .

Even if the general education of the people is assumed to be accomplished and private capitalism suppressed, the question of the circulation of information is again raised. We must return to the detailed criticism we made of the pretenses of the abusive system called "democratic centralism."[3] In this system, the ruling apparatus in fact enjoys a monopoly of decision-making power. Certainly, there is no absolute break between the population and the central political bureaucracy . . . but although the circulation moves in the two directions, it does not have the same nature for both; the adherents of the base can, by following certain rules, transmit *information* to the summit, which responds (if it responds) not with different information but with a *decision,* possibly motivated by argumentation whose supposed evidence permits the leaders to think that they are not commanding but elucidating, and the led to think that they are deciding according to what appears to them true and opportune after the superior authorities have explained the "correct line." This appearance cannot always be maintained, whether because a mili-

3. *Cahiers de l'autogestion,* No. 5–6.

tant at the base persists in his point of view (and, in this case, it would sometimes be necessary to "advise" his cell to exclude him and, if it refuses, to "dissolve" the cell), or because the decision communicated to the base is founded on information it is judged better not to divulge. Thus, the ruling apparatus disposes not only of the power of decision but also of the *monopoly of conditions of decision-making* in arrogating to itself the right, like any state, to have its "secrets." The militants at the base are then in no position to determine or to judge the leaders' acts with full knowledge.

7. Forms and Intensity of Participation in Yugoslav Self-management

BOGDAN DENITCH

Before discussing the relevance of Yugoslav self-management to other polities, it is useful to examine the extent of popular participation which it involves at this time. There are three areas of self-management: enterprise, including co-operatives, communal councils, and bodies; social services; and institutions. In the economy where self-management is most widely developed, the number of persons involved on various levels is huge. Four specific groups of participants in self-managing bodies can be distinguished in the economy:

1. Workers' councils elected in enterprises large enough to have councils and managing boards; there are 145,488 members of councils in this category.

2. The second group includes managing boards of enterprises which are too small to have both a council and a board; there are 10,016 members of such boards.

3. The third and largest group consists of members of self-managing bodies in *parts* of enterprises. This is a group which can be expected to grow for a number of reasons, one of which is the growth of large complex enterprises in Yugoslavia. There are a

Reprinted from "Notes on the Relevance of Yugoslav Self-management," paper presented at the First World Conference on Participation and Self-management, Dubrovnik, December 13–17, 1972, pp. 8–12, by permission of the author.

total of 303,328 persons participating in self-managing bodies on this level.

4. The fourth group consists of self-managing bodies in agricultural co-ops; there are 35,469 persons in these councils.

The grand total for the economy therefore comes close to half a million persons in this area alone, participating in various self-managing bodies.

In the field of communal self-government, the communal assemblies (there are 500 communes in Yugoslavia) include 40,791 persons, roughly one-half of whom are elected at large, the other half being elected by the working communities. In addition, there are local community bodies on a lower level which include 92,725 persons, a total of 133,516 persons.

The third area officially defined as "Social Self-Government in Institutions of Social Services" includes: primary and secondary schools; higher schools and universities, scientific institutions; cultural, educational, art, and entertainment institutions; health institutions and social welfare institutions. The self-managing councils include 210,384 people, of whom roughly one-half come from the primary and secondary schools.[1]

The point of all these figures is to show the enormous numbers of people involved in one way or another in the institutions of self-management participating with various degrees of intensity and effectiveness in *managing some aspect of their social existence.* (To put it in another perspective, out of an employed population of approximately 4 million, 838,201 persons participate in some type of self-management!) It is important to note that while the largest number are in the enterprises, massive numbers are found in the other two fields. This wide involvement of nonprofessionals in managing major institutions in their society, no matter how limited, obviously affects the entire political culture of the polity over time. *Self-management thus becomes not an instrument of the society but the very fabric of the society.* This is not to say that abuses do not exist, that participation is not sometimes only nominal and that the general political climate of the society at a given moment does not also have an effect on the workings of these bodies. *All that I am asserting is that the norm of participation is now firmly rooted and, given the system of rotation which is used in electing representatives to*

---

1. *Statistički godišnjak Jugoslavije 1970,* pp. 66, 67, 68, 69. The figures are somewhat dated (1969–70) but adequate.

self-managing bodies, this means that a major part of the working population at one point or another participates in running its own institutions. This however also underlies my earlier point that self-management is not a *partially* transferrable system.

Accompanying self-management itself has been a process of decentralization from the federal to the republic and provincial governments down to the communes. This process began relatively early in Yugoslavia and can be seen in the shift of the personnel in the federal administration from 47,300 persons in 1948 to 10,326 persons by 1956, with the process continuing even today.[2] There are two underlying theoretical approaches to this process of decentralization. The first emphasizes the sovereignty of the republics and regards the decentralization as primarily a reflection of the multinational character of Yugoslavia. The second stresses *structural* decentralization and thus emphasizes decentralization to the level of the self-managing bodies in the communes and the enterprises. While the two processes are simultaneous, they are in my opinion ultimately contradictory, and it is the second process which seems most naturally to flow from the basic needs of a self-managed society. (The emphasis on republics is rooted in the *specific* historical needs of *multinational Yugoslavia,* not in self-management as a system.) It can be argued however that the first stage of decentralization necessarily required an emphasis on the republics in order to dismantle the central federal structure. I believe that the future will show a greater emphasis on the second process accompanied in all likelihood by attempts to solidify nationwide institutions such as the League of Communists, the unions, and the unified market.

The two decades of development of self-management have had a profound and long-range effect on the political culture of Yugoslavia. Findings from surveys of workers and the public at large confirm the fact that, although there are criticisms of specific practices and abuses in self-management, it is taken at least as the desirable norm and the most characteristic feature of Yugoslav socialism. This was also confirmed in 1968–69 in the study of *Yugoslav Opinion-Makers,*[3] where the leading opinion-makers of the

---

2. Dušan Bilandžić, *Borba za samoupravu socijalizam u Jugoslaviji 1945–1969* (Zagreb, 1969), p. 73.

3. Reports on the study are found in: Firdus Dzinic, ed., *Stvaraoci javnog mnenja u Jugoslaviji,* Vols. 1–4 (Institut Društvenih Nauka, 1969). English versions of the major papers can be found in: Allen H. Barton, Bogdan Denitch, and Charles Kadushin, eds., *Opinion-making Elites in Yugoslavia* (New York: Praeger, 1973).

major institutional areas of Yugoslav life were asked, among many other things, what they thought were the major achievements of Yugoslav socialism. The question was broken down into three parts: what were the major achievements of Yugoslav socialism for Yugoslavia proper, as an example to developing countries, and as a contribution to socialist theory. In all three cases, self-management, either in the economy or in the polity, came out convincingly in first place. For Yugoslavia proper, self-management as the first choice ranged from 72.3 percent for the legislative leaders, to 53.8 percent for intellectuals, with the second and third choices being not unrelated, i.e., freedom and socialist democracy, and the solution of the national question.

In contrast, self-management *in industry* was not viewed as an exportable item for underdeveloped countries. There the answers ranged from 27.3 percent for economic leaders to 16.8 percent for journalists and personnel in mass communications. For underdeveloped countries, it was *political* self-management and economic development which were considered to be the Yugoslav contribution for emulation.

In the field of theory, again self-management was regarded as the major Yugoslav contribution, with 58.2 percent emphasizing industrial self-management and 27.1 percent communal self-management. Interestingly enough, again intellectuals were the least enthusiastic, although a substantial majority did pick self-management.

This is a finding which should be taken in its proper context. There is, after all, in most societies a gap between normative descriptions of the system and its performance. However, what is clear is that the leaders of Yugoslav society agreed that the major innovation of Yugoslav socialism was self-management. All major economic, political, and social reforms since that period have basically concentrated on working out the kinds and details of a system to which they are generally committed.

8. Organization as an Intermediary Between the Individual and Society: The Democratic and Humanitarian Form of Organization

RUDI SUPEK

III. . . . The *democratic conception* of a production organization is, in fact, based on worker self-management, since this presupposes the full participation of the producers (workers and employees) in managing the enterprise, and not only limited forms of participation. What are the essential characteristics of this democratic model of organization?

1. First, it means the very simple and logical application of a "democratic society," as it was already thought out at the time of the bourgeois revolution, to the production organization. And this means that the administrative (or legislative) authority is under the control of "all citizens," that is, producers, just as this is assumed for the *overall* society. The structure that bourgeois democratic society postulated for the overall society is here applied to the production organization as well, and in that way the traditional gap between the "democratic order in bourgeois society and the despotic order in economic organizations" (Marx) is overcome. It is obvious that the executive authority, regardless of the degree of its authoritativeness or hierarchy, is limited by

Reprinted from *Teorija i praksa samoupravljanja u Jugoslaviji* (Belgrade: Radnička štampa, 1972), pp. 923–31. Translated by Helen Kramer.

some technical and working requirements and becomes subordinated to the managerial power of the work collective, which exercises its power directly in the form of referendums (conferences) or through its elected bodies (workers' councils). From the viewpoint of the sociology of knowledge, it is interesting to establish that this very simple and plausible hypothesis about the transfer of the global model of the democratic structure to the production organization or to social organizations in general was never taken into consideration in the numerous works of contemporary industrial sociology, which is concerned with problems of organization both within and outside of production, although much energy was expended in describing and criticizing bureaucratic organization. Not even the most progressive spirits did this. Is this not one proof of the strength of social prejudices, which in this case are rooted in respect for "private or state ownership"?

2. We can find the theoretical base of the democratic model in two dominant theoretical currents in contemporary sociology: in the *theory of participation* (which was especially elaborated by the Michigan school) and in the *theory of alienation,* whose representatives, from Marx until the present, are found in various countries, and not exclusively in the channel of Marxist thought. Both theories assume that the inhuman and negative consequences of the exaggerated division of labor or of hierarchical (and class) relations can best be resolved, under modern conditions of technological development, by once again giving the producer all those functions that he performed as a creative being (planning, executing, control and disposal of the product), and hence, in addition to the function of production, the function of management as well. The latter means entering into the problems and goals of production, and thus also into the *basic values* that production must serve.

Within the framework of this theory, various approaches to the broadening of human labor or work that liberates man from rigid binding to the job assignment (job enlargement, job enrichment) were worked out. The theory then examined various consequences of and possibilities for participation of workers in decision-making in the life of the production organization, although that participation was necessarily limited by the ownership and class character of a particular organization. It came to be understood very early that radical solutions depend on the *entire* social organization, and that they cannot be achieved in the framework of the existing (capitalist) society.

3. The democratic model (or self-management form) of organization radically breaks with all *reformist* speculations that the forms of workers' participation should be introduced in limited amounts that would allow the preservation of the capitalist or state capitalist form of production and simultaneously integrate the working class into the production organization—and with the false consciousness that it is the subject of such an organization or that it has succeeded in realizing in it a type of "social community." Between various forms of participation, on the one hand, and self-management, on the other, there is a radical leap, a qualitative break with the subordinated role of the producer, a true revolutionary transformation which does not usually occur without general social changes. This does not mean, however, that the development of various forms of participation will not, by creating an awareness of the "naturalness" or "necessity" of such a qualitative change, ease the transition to self-management.

4. Insofar as the democratic model of organization on the basis of self-management is conceived as the transfer or application of the classical form of democracy to the production organization—and such conceptions are widespread, especially as regards the economic aspect—then similar relations are created between individual self-managing organizations as exist between individual global democratic societies in the field of production: relations of free exchange of products, contractual relations, and competitive relations (with the corresponding conflicts and compromises). Just as it is typical in authoritarian forms of organization for there to exist some *law* or *order* outside of and above the organization that supports its authoritarian structure, it is typical in free and independent democratic organizations for the organizations themselves freely to determine their norms of business operation on the basis of contract and to manage the sphere of social exchange on which they base their independence with initiative and freedom in disposing of the results of work. This independence of the production organization and its contrast to relations of exchange regulated by the superimposed state and its legislative bodies gives the production organization a sovereignty which leads some to brand it as a "state within the state"; but it is forgotten that the capitalist corporations were always "states within the state," not on the basis of free association, but as markedly

forced creations, which also correspond to the nature of the state.

Here we encounter a characteristic of the self-managed democratic organization that is the subject of rather lively discussions, so we will elaborate on it somewhat. The definition of a "free association of producers" that is taken as the essential definition of a democratic production organization can move between the form of "utopian communist association," which is a society in the microcosm, and, as such, closed toward the outside society with respect to its internal organization, and whose goal is to develop harmoniously all the essential social functions for all its members (a "polyvalent form of organization") ; and the form of a "social subsystem," that is, an organization which, as an integral element of the wider social organization, is in various ways subject to the social division of labor and social principles of general organization. For the former, the essential law of its organization and its life lies in it alone, and hence it is essentially an *autonomous* social community; for the latter, the law lies outside it, and hence it is essentially a *heteronomous* social community. Between these two extreme forms, the "free association" attempts to find a compromise that represents the most favorable solution in view of the concrete conditions of the given social system. The utopian socialists already faced the problem of these dilemmas and compromises; among them, probably the most interesting with regard to the theoretical consideration of a classical democratic association is Pierre Joseph Proudhon, with his theory of *mutualism* and *federalism*.

Although Proudhon's ideas are founded on the liberal economic conception that individual and collective interests can be reconciled by the spontaneous play of market economic laws, and that this spontaneity is the precondition of civic freedom, he does not arrive at the functionalist position that these laws insure a certain harmony of social development. Society remains basically contradictory, for political and economic, or private ownership and political-civic, contradictions, which Marx analyzed so well, remain present and unresolvable. This gives Proudhon's conception a certain "dialectical character." "Since two principles, Authority and Freedom, are at the foundation of every organized society, and on the one hand are contrary to one another and in a constant state of conflict, and on the other hand cannot exclude or annul one another, some sort of compromise is necessary between them. Regardless of how the system is conceived, whether it is monarchical, democratic, communist or anarchist, its life duration will depend on how much the opposite principle is taken into account."[1]

The longevity of the regime depends, accordingly, on the extent to which it takes care to honor simultaneously the freedom of economic activity and initiative on the basis of contract and exchange, and the striving for equality in people's social and political relations. These two principles will find themselves in constant conflict and will therefore call for a permanent arbiter. Who is this arbiter? Is it that political organization which represents the "long-run interests of society"? Proudhon says nothing about this.

With the democratic model of production organization, we entered into dilemmas that are currently faced by worker self-management, insofar as it is placed in the framework of a higher "liberal economic conception" with the focus on the free operation of market laws, or of a higher "political-organizational conception" with legal regulation of general relations that guarantee the equality of production organizations and the equality of the living conditions of individual producers. We know how urgent this dilemma is for contemporary Yugoslav society, whether it is viewed from the standpoint of the role of the trade unions, which serve as the advocate of "general class interests"; from the standpoint of the economy, which finds itself caught between the needs of integration and decentralization; or from the standpoint of political legal theory, which is attempting to replace governmental legal regulations with contractual agreement on a social and local basis. We need not enter into this dilemma here. It is sufficient to know that this conception of democratic organization necessarily generates such a dilemma.

IV. Finally, we come to the *humanist conception* of the production organization. Let us say immediately that the democratic model, with the focus on the production and exchange of products, is a necessary result of industrial society, especially of societies in the process of rapid industrialization. The humanist model involves a certain overcoming of this "industrial situation," for it is not the principle of exchange and contract, but rather the principle of human needs and the all-around development of the personality, that lies at the center of interest here. Man appears just as much as a consumer as a producer.

The humanist organization, after all, depends like all others on

1. *Selected Writings* (New York: Doubleday, 1969), pp. 103–104.

the objective conditions of social development as well as on the *goals* that people want to attain by means of it. The very objective and material character of social organization prevents the conception of organization as an entirely subordinate and adaptable means for the attainment of certain goals. In its technological characteristics (various forms of the division of labor, carrying out of work tasks, coordination and communication in work, etc.), it is in direct contradiction to the posited goals. But these goals are no less limited by the purely social requirements or traits of every organization (certain interpersonal relations based on cooperation or hierarchy, relations of management, negotiation, control, etc.). The humanist organization tries to overcome, insofar as is possible, the restraints and resistances that operate inhumanely within the organization as such in relation to its inherent requirements (so-called technological-functionalistic requirements), as well as the inhumane contents that operate on the level of the very goals of the organization (the production of material or spiritual objects). Developed production in a modern industrial society has changed the conditions of production in the following ways:

1. In the transformation of nature, the worker is no longer essential as a mediating factor (as a source of physical energy, as a manual worker), for the role of that mediation has been taken over by the "technological-industrial process" (Marx) itself, while the role of man has increasingly been carried over to the role of planning, control, and maintenance of the production process.

2. The focus of the "productive forces" has been transferred to the development of the natural (and social) sciences, the application of science in technology, and automation and organization of the production process. Thus, intellectual work has attained greater significance than manual labor, or manual labor has increasingly taken on the characteristics of intellectual work (operators in automated production). In terms of the structure of the labor force, this has led to a continual decline of manual and unskilled labor in favor of intellectual and skilled labor, which was reflected both in the attitude toward the profession as a vocation or calling, and in relations among individual professions (engineers, technicians, operators) or "social classes." Within the framework of the production organization, the class difference between highly skilled and unskilled labor which was typical of production in the nineteenth century was eradicated. (Although

Marx dealt with relations in production, he nevertheless overlooked this development.)[2]

3. The development of production led to the pronounced *socialization* of human labor, both in the performance of the work operations themselves (in automated production, piecework or individual efficiency disappears) and in the planning and organization of production, for the role of modern science, technology, and the scientific organization of work cannot be reduced to "individual work," nor can payment be made according to the criterion of the "production of surplus labor." This type of work is still the "natural gift of man" (Marx) to a greater degree than is manual labor, and in principle it remains "unpaid," as is best demonstrated by the constant drop in the pay of intellectual and scientific workers over the last hundred years, in spite of the fact that this work is becoming increasingly important for the development of the productive forces of the whole society.

4. A special form of the socialization of work efficiency or surplus labor is that part of human labor that is increasingly devoted to the social education of producers (vocational and general education), health protection, social security, construction of housing and communications, and various other "social funds" which were as unknown to the peasant of a hundred years ago as to the social administration itself, which also swallows an ever greater part of the "production surpluses," most often outside the control of the producers themselves.

5. The socialization of human labor is also reflected in the very well known concentration of capital or of means of production, as well as in the ever greater interdependence of individual production organizations, whether in the course of production or on the market. This mutual dependence is best seen in the efforts to rationalize production by means of planning within the framework of the given organization, branch of production, or society as a whole, and to establish some reasonable equilibrium between planned and spontaneous processes in social production. The need for planning imposes itself as much upon "organized capitalism" as upon "state socialism" or "self-governing socialism," although the goals and methods of planning differ to some extent in individual "industrial societies."

6. The development of modern industry led both to mass

2. See R. Supek, "Marx i automatizacija," in *Sociologija i socijalizam* (Zagreb: Znanje, 1966).

production (large production series and industrial concentration) and to mass consumption (the noticeable increase of consumer purchasing power and the psychosis of buying with the aid of massive publicity and advertising). Thus, Marx's proposition that for the capitalist his own worker is above all "labor power," while at the same time that same worker is for another capitalist a "consumer," is being increasingly realized. Now, while the area of production was exposed to increasing rationalization, as well as to a certain "humanization" (growing out of the perception of the significance of "interpersonal relations" in production itself), the area of consumption was, for the most part, left to the operation of the "law of supply and demand," to that "invisible hand" of Adam Smith, which is present in modern society as a huge and irrational, although superbly "scientifically organized," force which operates by means of suggestion and propaganda in the form of modern publicity. This form of the manipulation of human consciousness did not limit itself to material goods but deeply penetrated the marketing of "spiritual goods" in the field of culture and education as well.

One of the essential characteristics of the humanist model of organization is that it does not separate man as producer from man as consumer, does not divide human existence into "working time" and "leisure time," does not consider man to be one being with regard to his work capabilities and another with regard to his needs for enjoyment. What is more, the humanist conception of organization *focuses its interest on "man with needs,"* human needs, and above all human social needs, which were already recognized in the sphere of production for purely "productive" or "capitalistic" reasons (from Taylor to Ford), and which now necessarily transcend the limits of the production organization just as consumption passes the limits of the production of a certain good. By placing human needs at the basis of the production organization, the cycle that flowed from the production of use value to the circulation of exchange value to purchase or transformation of exchange into use value to consumption or the transformation of use value into labor power, is closed. The goal is no longer exclusively the sale or purchase of some use value (hence, the realization of profit), but the "renewal of labor power," in other words, the relation of man toward use value as such. Since within the framework of the production organization man the producer is no longer renewed—that is, no longer lives—only as crude "labor power" (as a part of natural or physical force) but is renewed as a natural and social being, as an integral personality, this is a man who is highly educated; whose knowledge surpasses the limits of the direct work process; whose responsibilities, as a result of the socialization of the work process, become equal with those of the entire work community; who appears, therefore, as a "collective worker" but, because of this, appears at the same time as a "collective consumer"; who can no longer exist as an "individual" or "private consumer" under the control of market forces because of his participation in the management of production, directly or as a citizen in the commune, republic, or state, but, precisely for the protection of his individuality, must appear both as a "collective worker" and as a "collective consumer." In addition, it should immediately be added that his situation as a responsible person in the form of the "collective worker" is incomparably easier than his situation as "collective consumer," for the simple reason that contemporary organizational science has worked out man's problems as a producer from all sides, while the questions of human consumption and its corresponding organization are still open. However, our assumption is that one of man's basic needs is to be *free*, and to be free on the level of social organization means to have the full opportunity of participating in all decisions that concern one personally. Our entire model of humanist organization is based on this "minimal conception" of human needs—on taking account of only some needs, namely, the need to be free and the need to be social, needs which are often combined in the concept of "human dignity."

What are the basic differences between the democratic and humanist models of the production organization?

In the first place, the humanist conception is not limited to the integration of laboring and managing functions as is the democratic conception, but also takes into account another form of integration, that between the work community and the living community, or between man the producer and man the citizen, a concept in which we included man with civil rights, whose basic need is freedom, and man the consumer, man with all those needs we usually place in "man's private life." This integration of the work community and the living community means still far greater broadening of the "productive functions" of man the producer than occurred within the framework of the managerial or self-managerial functions in the enterprise, for he now can engage himself much more directly in the "renewal of his work capabilities," that is, in the questions of education, housing, rest or entertainment, biological renewal in the family, and so forth, in all of which the living community is engaged. While in the work community the question of man's needs entered only as an element of the "social policy" of the enterprise itself, as something foreign that interfered with the problems of production and about which the traditional liberal capitalists did not even wish to hear, to the living community human needs are the essential content of activity, for this community considers man in his total biological, social, and cultural production and reproduction. It is natural that the basic principles of a certain "social policy" should be determined *first of all* in the framework of the living community and that, after this, the attempt should be made to carry out these principles along with the participation and help of the work community.

Such widening of social functions enables one, on the basis of the theory of dealienation, to pose the problem of "dealienation in work" much more broadly by introducing into the sphere of production a number of new criteria and activities which the classical work organization did not take into very great account. Does not such an integration mean that old solution of achieving human association on the basis of two heterogeneous organizations—production organization and living organization—when it has become obvious that the full polyvalence of human functions and the integrity of social development cannot be achieved within the framework of the production organization alone, as dreamed of and still dreamed of by the utopian socialists (kibbutzim and other utopian organizations)? We need not enter here into a description of the very complex and diverse individual and group activities that are connected with the problems of dealienation of labor, compensation effects of partial dehumanization, changes in the structure of power in the sense of real democracy of interpersonal relations, and so on. It is important to keep in mind that we are in a situation in which the relations of the individual and the social organization or social group are resolved so that man is considered a much more integrated personality, and organization is considered a much more democratic and more complex institution.

Furthermore, the very broadening of social functions due to the integration of the work community and living community carries special importance in those types of production that fall into the area of "cultural goods" and mass communications. This area enters more into the global society itself and into general social consciousness, and cannot be narrowed to the political-territorial relationship of the commune and the factory. Cultural goods relate to all people in the national and international framework, and the role of the political-territorial community, or of the close cooperation of the production community and living community, is to insure the *conditions* of such production, not to determine its content or "productive goals." This production is the affair of every individual and the entire society.

In this area, however, the tendency often appears to reject responsibility to the society as a whole in the name of the "self-managing" nature of such an organization, and to limit responsibility to the "self-managed organization" itself. Such tendencies can be seen in our country in the press, publishing houses, radio and television, and similar institutions. In the area of culture, the basic problem is to remove those "social intermediaries" who try to subordinate cultural creators and the public (cultural receivers) to themselves in the production of cultural goods, and to put these intermediaries under the social control of the creators and consumers. In this area, the basic task is for the producer or creator and the consumer or enjoyer, who as a rule represent one and the same person, to reach agreement, to unite, and to organize so that they can dispose of their creativity and their enjoyment of spiritual values with complete freedom. Just as the very act of cultural creation presupposes a certain unity of conception, materialization, and enjoyment, so the basic organizational principle in that area can be only the integration of the creator and the consumer in the name of their own needs, and not in the name of needs (imposed and artificial) dictated to them by an intermediary. While in the field of culture the primacy of human needs was always emphasized, as opposed to the conditions of production themselves, at the same time the question of the social organization that must correspond to that principle remained theoretically untouched for the simple reason that the role of social intermediaries in the material reproduction and market placement of cultural goods was never so great as today, when we speak of the "commercialization of culture," "manipulation of the human consciousness," "inauthenticity of cultural values in conditions of mass production," "instrumentalization of education," "technocratic indifference to humanistic values," and so on.

Thus, we enter into a new theme, possibly most important when it concerns the principles of a production organization, for these principles depend directly on the goals adopted by such an organization, and goals can be defined only on the basis of the fundamental values that a society and culture wish to attain. Since the democratic conception of organization appeared under conditions of the rapid industrialization and social backwardness of the country carrying out such industrialization, it is no surprise that it began to be viewed more from the economic and vulgarly materialistic standpoint, which today coincides with the so-called philosophy of the welfare state, than from the humanist standpoint, with the ideals of human equality and freedom held as the fundamental values of human organization. The rationalism of the industrial era imposed functionalistic and shallowly utilitarian viewpoints on social organization and necessarily led to the subordination of the individual and human group to the organization, and not the reverse! The humanist approach will correct this unnatural situation and return us to the humanist ideal of freedom, the ideal of man who has mastered the conditions of his existence and achieved his freedom according to his own standard, and not the standard of external factors—of a physical or biologic nature, god, the state, functional organization, abstract organizational rationalism, the transformation of man's totality into the cog of an all-powerful machine with its axis driven into the cosmos or into the state-god.

Self-management and Organization of Enterprises

9. The Typology of Systems of "Participation"

J. Y. TABB AND A. GOLDFARB

The world of "participation" is divided into various types and subtypes of "participation." There are four major types: workers' participation in the firm's profits, workers' or their representatives' participation in consultation, workers' or their representatives' participation in managerial decisions, and workers' involvement in making all decisions within a defined area of authority. In each case the socio-economic structure, culture, traditions, and other factors that are an integral part of the nation and determine its unique characteristics, influence the structure and mold the type of participation that is developed.

As a basis for classifying and analysing this typology, four criteria may be useful: (a) the normative basis, (b) the extent of participation, (c) the degree of participation, and (d) the material rewards offered.

The first criterion refers to the formal procedural basis upon which the structure depends: it identifies the source that enables the workers to participate; i.e., it establishes from where and from what the participation derives its authoritative power and the rules that determine its role and function. Many such "bases" or sources can exist but for the sake of convenience they

Reprinted from *Workers' Participation in Management* (New York: Pergamon Press, 1970), pp. 17–20, by permission of the authors.

can be limited to four main ones: (1) local collective agreement, (2) national collective agreement, (3) law, and (4) constitutional statute.

The first indicates a structure whose origin is to be found in an agreement between an employer and his employees, and its validity holds only for the members of the enterprise concerned. The term "national agreement" refers to agreements signed by a national employers' association with a national trade union or unions covering all or most of the country's workers (as, for example, in the Scandinavian countries). The remaining two possibilities imply structures whose origin is in national legislation at two respective levels.

The second criterion—"extent of participation"—identifies the relative size of the work-group that is directly involved in management or decision-making of the enterprise. Different structures are based on different numbers of participants. There are those ("minimum") that are built on a very limited number of elected representatives like the enterprise committee representing the mass of workers; others ("medium") may be based on a number of departmental or functional groups, and involve a large number of workers—up to and including the involvement of the entire mass of employees in managerial decisions, through general meetings, referendum, and the like ("maximum").

The third criterion—"degree of participation"—classifies the various structures according to how far the workers are permitted, in the given structure, to participate in decisions, what the nature of the decision is, and to what degree the enterprise and its management are obligated to execute these decisions. This criterion can be subdivided into five classes: (1) no authority, (2) consultation and advice only, (3) control, (4) joint management, and (5) self-management.

The last criterion brings in the question of "material rewards" as a basis for participation, i.e., it asks whether the workers are partners in the fruits of participation (be it in form of cash, shares or otherwise) and whether these fruits are distributed among them, beyond and above their regular salaries, as a reward for their active participation and creative effort. This criterion offers only two possible answers: (1) yes, (2) no.

If we assume that the classes of criteria not only indicate existing and possible alternatives, but also constitute a ranking order, then it is possible to introduce a value-scale into this classification, and to see different systems of participation as different de-

The Typology of Systems of "Participation"

(a) Basis	(b) Extent	(c) Degree	(d) Rewards
1. Local agreement	1. Minimum	1. None	1. Yes
2. National agreement	2. Medium	2. Consultation	2. No
3. Law	3. Maximum	3. Control	
4. Constitutional statute		4. Joint management	
		5. Self-management	

grees of advancement on the road to effective application of the idea of workers' participation in management. Following this line of thought the system limited only to profit-sharing (i.e., a_1, b_1, c_1, d_1) would constitute the "beginning of the road," while the system of self-management (i.e., a_4, b_3, c_5, d_1) would probably constitute the "end of the road."

This approach makes it possible to assume a ranking continuum of structures and systems of workers' participation that provides us with a uniform method of analysis of the system's advantages and disadvantages at each point in the continuum.

This is not, however, enough. In order to analyse and evaluate a given system, it is essential to examine the forces—objective and subjective—which give rise to the system and influence its action, the values that give meaning to this action, and the goals and the means of achieving them. In other words, many factors leave their impact on the pattern and developmental paths of a system of social action. Thus, an understanding of a specific system is dependent on the discovery and analysis of those conditions and causal factors—external and internal—that give rise to it and determine the unique character of its development or lack of development.

10. Workers' Self-management in Yugoslavia

GERRY HUNNIUS

Structure and function of workers' self-management

Yugoslav legislation defines an economic organization as a work organization

—that is founded according to the law;
—that performs a given type of economic activity (in commodity production, trade, services, or finance);
—that performs its activity autonomously in conformity with its statute and other provisions;
—that manages a share of social property directly or through its elected organs of self-management.[1]

Yugoslav economic legislation and practice are based on the concept of the self-managing enterprise as a "Socialist commodity producer."

The workers employed in an enterprise organize work and management according to the following objectives:

1. Optimum utilization of the socially owned means of produc-

tion and constant increase of productivity.

2. Promotion of the direct interest of the workers in their work and their most effective participation in the management of all productive and other activities.

The internal organization of the enterprise is regulated by its statute. Since the passing of Amendment XV, the only structural requirement is the establishment of a workers' council. Other and additional self-management bodies are to be regulated by the statutes of each enterprise.

In contrast to the vertically (hierarchically) structured industrial organizations where status, prestige, rewards, and power increase as we ascend the pyramid, and administrative and legislative power is united in management, the Yugoslav model is horizontally (democratically) structured with the following features:

1. Decision-making power is divided by distinguishing between administrative and legislative power.

2. The veto power is in the hands of the general membership or its elected representative bodies instead of being in the hands of the director or general manager.

3. Tenure, admission, and dismissal of all personnel are decided by the general membership or its representatives. Administrators are elected and recalled, depending on how successful they are in the view of the general membership and its elected organs.

The division between administrative and legislative power implies two hierarchies. One, concerned with self-management, includes the working units, the workers' council, the managing board, and the director. The second hierarchy approximates the conventional chain of command with workers on one end, followed by supervisors and heads of working units, and managers at the other end.[2]

Another way of looking at the functioning of the self-management system within an enterprise is to see it in terms of two levels of authority—the professional, dominated by skilled, highly skilled, and lower managerial personnel, and a second level which bases its judgments on the social and political values of the wider community. The protagonists of this second level are the sociopolitical organizations represented within the enterprise. This is again a typically Yugoslav solution insofar as a function of the central government has been replaced by non-governmental organizations which base their influence largely on persuasion.

The organizational framework in enterprises

Yugoslav enterprises operate within a framework of workers' self-management. The supreme authority within each enterprise is the workers' collective which consists of all members of the enterprise. In all but the smallest enterprises, the workers elect a workers' council which meets approximately once a month and is charged with making decisions on all major functions of the enterprise (prices on its products whenever these are not controlled, production and financial plans, governing of the enterprise, allocation of net income, budget, etc.). The workers' council elects a management board, in practice largely from its own ranks, which acts as executive agent. At least three-quarters of the members of the management board must be production workers.[3] The board meets more frequently than the workers' council and works in close cooperation with the director, who is an *ex officio* member. The workers' council is elected for a period of two years, half of its members elected every year. Its composition is supposed to approximate the ratio between production workers and employees. Meetings of the workers' council are usually open and every member of the working collective is entitled to attend. Decisions are made by majority vote and the members of the council, individually or as a group, can be recalled by the electors. No one can be elected twice in succession to the workers' council, and more than twice in succession to the management board.[4] The management board is elected for a period of one year and is answerable for its work to the workers' council, which may recall individual members or the whole board at any time. Service on management boards and workers' councils is honorary and members do not receive payment. The director is the actual administrative manager of the enterprise. He is responsible for the day-to-day operations and he represents the enterprise in any external negotiations. In theory, but only infrequently in practice, he can be removed by the workers' council, which also determines his term of office.

The most recent innovation in the organizational structure of the enterprise is the emergence of the working (or economic) unit.[5] The working unit may represent a department or, in large enterprises, an entire plant. The establishment of the working units introduces significant additional elements of direct industrial democracy into the system of self-management. The current controversy about their role centers largely on their degree of authority in relation to the distribution of the income of the enterprise as well as the distribution of personal income to the members of the working units. Increasingly, entire enterprises are being divided into working units, including the managerial staff, the accounting service, and the production departments.[6] Relations between these units are conducted on the basis of contracts and payments for services rendered. Disputes arising between working units are dealt with by an arbitration commission appointed by the central workers' council.[7]

Small working units are managed directly by the entire membership. Decisions are made at meetings, usually called "the conference of the working unit." The introduction of direct decision making is the main feature distinguishing the smaller working units from the enterprise as a whole. In the latter, direct decision making is largely limited to occasional referenda and voters' meetings prior to election.[8] In large working units the conference elects a council which it can recall at any time. The conference also appoints a manager (foreman) after announcing an open competition for this post.[9]

One of the democratic features operative in the Yugoslav system is the recall. Figures on the frequency of recalls are not easy to come by, but information available for 1956 shows the following: 999 members of workers' councils (0.8 percent) and 476 members of boards of management (1.2 percent) were recalled in enterprises with thirty or more workers. Of this total 1,474 recalls, 254 were initiated by a government department or agency, 181 by the director of the enterprise, 542 by an organ of self-management, 372 by the entire collective of the enterprise, and 124 by sociopolitical organizations. No data are available on the frequency of recalls of elected communal deputies, but it appears to happen only infrequently. Responsibility on the part of elected deputies to the voters has not yet reached the level hoped for and voters, as a rule, do not yet constitute an organized political force permitting the effectual use of the recall. We should note that in 1956, the system of self-management in industry was only just beginning to be put into practice.[10]

The authority of the foreman is usually limited to the implementation of decisions made by the self-management bodies. He alone cannot discipline a worker, or register complaints. The final verdict in a disciplinary case will be given by the disciplinary committee of the working unit.[11] The foreman's basic responsibility, in addition to the implementation of decisions already made, lies in the area of training and coordination (with other economic units as well as with the central workers' council).

To describe the legislative and administrative functions within an enterprise would go beyond the scope of this article. Very briefly, they may be summarized as follows:

1. Legislative functions and organs

Referenda. As indicated before, mergers, relocation of plants, disagreements between working units and the central workers' council are among the decisions made by referendum. The referendum is one of the key elements of direct democracy within enterprises. Preparations for referenda are extensive and the sociopolitical organizations operating within the plant are involved in organizing discussions on the purpose of the referendum.

Zbors (conventions). Zbors elect and recall the governing bodies and pass amendments on the enterprise statutes. They are consulted on all key decisions such as manpower policies, modernization, and wages.[12]

Working (economic) units. Working units and their councils, the central workers' council, and the managing board have been discussed above.

2. Administrative functions and organs

The administrative branch of an enterprise is made up of the director of the enterprise, director of plants and departments, and the foremen of the working units.

The director. The role of the director is of particular importance and continues to be surrounded by controversy. Prior to the passing of Amendment XV, his term of office was four years. Today, his term is decided upon by the workers' council, which also appoints him and dismisses him.

During the administrative period, prior to 1950, the director functioned as an agent of the state. While he had almost complete power within the enterprise, his responsibilities were limited since all decisions on the operation of his enterprise came from Belgrade. The typical director during this period was a person whose main qualification was his political reliability. With the introduction of workers' self-management and the increased autonomy of the enterprise, the role of the director has become somewhat more ambiguous. As the chief executive officer of the enterprise he is directly responsible to the central workers' council; at the same time he is supposed to act on behalf of the wider community. He retains a veto power over decisions of the workers' council which in his view violate the law; the commune, however, as representative of the wider community, retains some influence in his appointment and dismissal. His skill and educational background are now of far greater importance than his political loyalty. Increasingly, relations between the director and the workers' self-management bodies have come to play an important part in the development of the enterprise.

Pressures put on the director to maintain economic efficiency and at the same time adhere to national guidelines, combined with his responsibility to the self-management bodies have made it increasingly more difficult to attract qualified people to the position.

The legal duties of the director are mainly administrative ones. In theory, he has virtually no right to make decisions, since these are reserved exclusively to the general membership and their elected representatives. In practice, however, . . . the director has extensive influence[13] and the ambiguity of his position is very real. The director has great influence but little legal authority, and hence, little clear-cut responsibility, while the workers' council has legal authority but lacks influence.

Another reason for the confusion surrounding the role of the director is the fact that, until recently, his role was circumscribed by a vast profusion of legal statutes, beyond those found in the statute of the enterprise. Changes in federal law have been so frequent that it has been virtually impossible for anyone to be fully aware of them.

As of 1969 (after passage of Amendment XV) enterprises were given the right to define for themselves the role of individual as well as collective executive bodies. In many enterprises this has meant a strengthening of the managerial bodies including that of the director. New executive bodies, such as directors' boards and business boards, have been created, thus legitimizing to some extent the actual influence of the director and the managerial groups. Opposition to this trend, and particularly to the effects of Amendment XV, has come from sections of the League and from the trade unions.[14]

The Collegium and the Extended Collegium. The Collegium is composed of the top administrators, including the heads of departments, and is presided over by the director. Its purpose is to aid the director in carrying out the policies of the enterprise entrusted to him. The Collegium has no decision-making power and performs, in essence, the function of a staff meeting.

The Extended Collegium includes foremen and experts in addition to the top administration. It discusses matters submitted to it by the Collegium.

The Politikal Aktive. The Politikal Aktive, another nonelective body which, like the preceding two, exists in almost every enterprise, comprises all sections of the self-managed enterprise. In addition to top management, the heads of *all* governing bodies are represented as are the secretaries of the plant committee of the League, the trade union, and the Youth Brigade. The existence of these three groups is not stipulated by law or in enterprise statutes. According to Adizes, "their existence and functioning seems to be dictated by organizational necessities; a central, unifying group is needed as a centripetal force when the organization's authority and power are highly segmented. . . ."[15]

Informal groups. Informal groups within enterprises include the many clubs established by the local trade union branch and the Youth Brigade, and the Majstors (masters) composed of skilled workers who repair the machines.[16] . . .

Influence structure in Yugoslav enterprises

A great deal of research has been done on the perception of influence among workers. Tannenbaum and Županov, in their study of fifty-six workers attending a two-year course at the Workers' University in Zagreb,[17] have analyzed the perceived and ideal (desired) control curves as seen by the respondents. The results refer to the two hierarchies within enterprises: one, including the workers as producers at one end, followed by supervisors, heads of economic units, and the director at the other; the second including the workers' council at one end, followed by the managing board and the director at the other.[18]

The authors of this study point out the large discrepancy between actual and ideal degree of control for the workers as a group. Since the workers' council is selected by the workers and is composed in large part of workers, this discrepancy seems to suggest that the workers' council does not give the workers a sufficient sense of control.[19] One partial explanation is indicated by the results of another study published in 1961, which found the workers' council oriented toward management and official views.[20] There is also evidence to the effect that management, including the management staff, the director, and frequently members of the management board, are the most active participants in meetings of the workers' council. The complexity of many of the issues under discussion and the control over relevant information in the hands of management, can give the latter a powerful advantage in having their proposals accepted by the workers' council.

The establishment of economic units and the increasing delegation of authority to them has been one attempt to reduce the discrepancy between actual and desired control. This introduction of direct democracy is one of the more significant political innovations in recent years. Županov and Tannenbaum suggest that the discrepancy between the ideal and the actuality can also be attributed in part to the rather high ideals expressed by the respondents. They point out that discrepancies are smaller in American industrial organizations studied, "not because the actual curves are more positive, but because the ideals are more negative."[21]

The high ideals held by respondents in this sample and others which have in the main supported these findings, are one of the hopeful signs in the development of self-management in Yugoslavia.

The survey undertaken by Bogdan Kavčić and released in 1968 is similar in its conclusion to a number of other studies and can thus be viewed as presenting a more or less accurate picture.[22]

In summarizing the results of several studies, Veljko Rus points out:

1. Workers tend to favor an increase in the influence of all groups other than top management.

2. Workers' desires are consistent with the theory of workers' self-management (the workers' council should have the most influence).

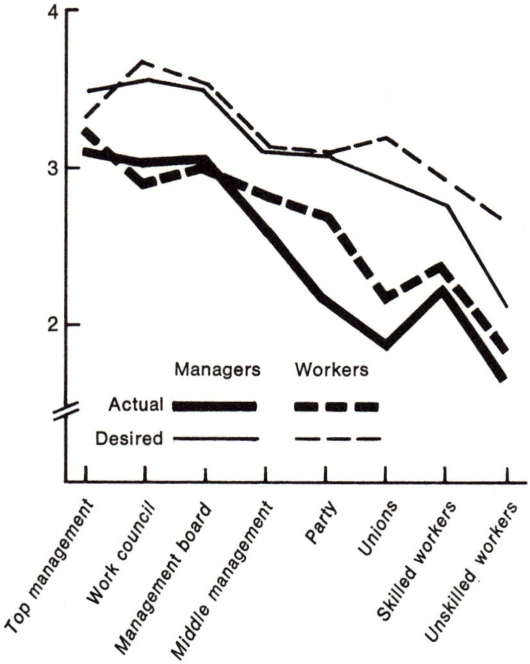

Influence as perceived and desired by managers and workers, in ninety-two industrial organizations

N = 1,489 workers and 501 managers. Amount of influence: 4 = very great; 3 = great; 2 = little; 1 = none. (This chart originally appeared in Yugoslavia in Bogdan Kavčić: "Distribucija vpliva v podjetjih industrije in rudarstva v Sloveniji," R S ZSS *Javno mnenje, stev.* 15, 1968. *Source: Industrial Relations,* Vol. IX, No. 2, Institute of Industrial Relations, University of California, Berkeley. Chart by Veljko Rus.)

3. These aspirations seem to have weakened somewhat by 1968. Latest studies show that workers' desires still place the workers' council at the top, but the desired influence of managers is now almost equal to that of the workers' council.[23]

The changing role of the trade unions, from transmitters of the directives of the central authorities to a position where they begin to act more openly on behalf of the worker, is evident in the large gap between the actual and desired influence of the trade unions as perceived by workers.[24]

NOTES

1. *Workers' Management in Yugoslavia (1950–1970),* Belgrade: Medunarodna Politika, 1970, p. 36.

2. B. Kavčić, V. Rus, E. E. Tannenbaum, *Control, Participation, and Effectiveness in Four Yugoslav Industrial Organizations* (mimeographed), Ljubljana (March 1969), p. 1.

3. This provision is, in practice, frequently violated.

4. It is not clear what effect Amendment XV has had on these provisions. In general, all decisions as to tenure and election are now to be made by the workers' council of each enterprise.

5. For a part of a working organization to be able to become a working unit, the following prerequisites are necessary:

—That there exists an integrated technological and operational process on a specified area, plus the necessary means of production;
—That tasks can be determined, within the plan of the working organization as a whole, for such a narrower framework of a working organization within the latter's plan as a whole;
—That it is practicable to observe the execution of the planned tasks for such a narrower organizational part of a working organization as well as to ascertain separately its economic results, viz., as a quantity demarcated from the working and operating results of the rest of the working organization;
—That a material base can be established for such a narrower organizational part of a working organization, to provide the foundation for the transfer of a series of self-management functions from the central indirect bodies of the working community to a narrower organizational part; and
—That it is economically justified to establish a working unit.

Vojislav Vlajić, *The Working Unit,* Belgrade: The Central Council of the Confederation Trade Unions of Yugoslavia, pp. 20–21.

6. The Confederation of Trade Unions of Yugoslavia (C.T.U.Y.) has been the most consistent advocate for the extension of decision-making authority on the part of working units.

7. There is really no adequate treatment in the English language on these important innovations. The best available source on the working unit is: *Stellung und Aufgaben der ökonomischen Einheiten in den jugoslawischen Unternehmungen,* by Gudrun Lemân, Berlin: Verlag Duncker & Humbolt, 1967.

8. The holding of a referendum is compulsory for certain important questions such as the decision to merge with another enterprise. The results of a referendum are binding on the workers' council. If an issue is defeated in a referendum, it cannot be raised again for six months.

9. The appointment of the foreman requires a two-thirds majority of all members of the working unit, as well as the approval of the management board of the enterprise. His removal takes place by the same procedure, and his term of office prior to the passing of Amendment XV was four years.

10. *Workers' Management in Yugoslavia,* Geneva: International Labor Office, p. 91.

11. Ichak Adizes, *Industrial Democracy: Yugoslav Style—The Effect of Decentralization on Organizational Behavior,* New York: The Free Press, 1971, p. 46.

12. *Ibid.,* p. 37.

13. By influence we mean actual as opposed to merely potential power. Influence derives from formal and informal positions.

14. The last large-scale appointment (by the workers' councils) of directors prior to the enactment of Amendment XV took place in 1963. At this time, 2,727 directors were renominated. Four hundred and twenty-one were not renominated and were replaced by new appointments. It is interesting to note that about two percent of directors (in enterprises) are women. Their percentage increases to over thirteen percent in Social Service Institutions (*Statistički Godišnjak Jugoslavije 1969,* Belgrade: Federal Institute for Statistics, pp. 69 and 71).

15. Adizes, *op. cit.,* p. 47.

16. According to Adizes, the Majstors are a highly cohesive group and very influential (*ibid.,* p. 47).

17. These respondents comprise a very special group, which includes a relatively high proportion of formally educated, highly skilled, and highly aspiring workers. Approximately eighty-nine percent are members of the LCY (as compared to 10.6 percent of workers in the district of Zagreb). Thirty-nine percent are first line supervisors. The respondents spend part of their time at the university while working four hours a day in Zagreb industries.

18. Josip Županov and Arnold S. Tannenbaum, "The Distribution of Control in Some Yugoslav Industrial Organizations as Perceived by Members," in Arnold Tannenbaum, *Control in Organizations,* New York: McGraw-Hill Book Co., 1958, pp. 98–99.

19. *Ibid.,* pp. 97–98.

20. David S. Ridell, "Social Self-Government: The Background of Theory and Practice in Yugoslav Socialism," in *British Journal of Sociology* (March 1968), p. 66.

21. Županov and Tannenbaum, *op. cit.,* p. 109.

22. Reprinted by Veljko Rus, "Influence Structure in Yugoslav Enterprise," *Industrial Relations,* Vol. IX, No. 2 (1970), p. 150. *Note:* B. Kavčić is director of the Center for Public Opinion Research of the Republican Council of Trade Unions of Slovenia.

23. Veljko Rus, pp. 155–57. *Note:* This trend *could* be interpreted as resulting from a more sophisticated understanding of self-management on the part of the workers and a greater degree of satisfaction with the functioning of the workers' council vis-à-vis management.

24. The relatively weak influence of trade unions on the enterprise level should be seen in its historical context. Self-management was introduced from the top, that is, by decision of the Communist party and the government, and the traditional function (prior to 1950) of the trade unions was challenged overnight. It would seem reasonable to expect that if self-management came about through the pressure and action of trade unions, their role, function, and influence would not suffer the decline evidenced in Yugoslavia.

11. Participation and Influence

JOSIP ŽUPANOV

The point of departure in this paper is the idea that there is or there should be no qualitative difference between the employees' participation in industry and citizens' participation in politics. Both notions refer to the "acts to influence the behavior of those empowered to make decisions." Or looking from the opposite angle, no "participative technique" intended to secure a "ceremonial" or "support" participation by manipulating employees' or citizens' feelings and behavior can be considered participation. According to Sidney Verba, "the definition [of participation] stresses *intention* to influence decision-makers."[1]

How to influence decision-makers (or anybody else)? There are many ways to induce others to produce an intended result. However, two of them are especially important: persuasion and coercion. "*Persuasion* involves an effort to influence by argument, reasoning, or a presentation of ideas. The person who is the object of persuasive efforts may refuse to produce without fear of reprisal. Coercion, on the other hand, involves an effort to influence through the use or presentation of force, and the person who refuses to obey a command may expect reprisal. People who can produce an intended result through the use or presenta-

Reprinted from *Employees' Participation and Social Power in Industry* (Zagreb: Institut za društvena istraživanja, 1972), pp. 33–40, paper presented at the First International Conference on Participation and Self-management, Dubrovnik, December 1972.

tion of force have power. *Power* may be defined, then, as an ability to influence through coercion."[2] In organized forms of human life the power of a person (or a group of people) is his ability to induce others to produce an intended result through the application (or possible application) of sanctions.

To these two types of influence correspond two types of participatory acts: those which carry sanctions or the threat of sanctions and those which do not carry any sanctions, though "the borderline between these two types of participation is not clear."[3] It follows from this that participation as the process of social influence involves, at least in some situations, a power relationship between those who attempt to influence the others' behavior and those who are the objects of such attempts. This raises a significant and probably crucial issue: how to influence those who are very powerful if the attempts at persuasion fail? If any attempt at influence has failed, i.e., if participation is unsuccessful, this will discourage further attempts or further participation. In other words, social power of decision-makers may constitute a barrier to an effective participation. This is not merely a theoretical possibility: this is what actually happens and can be observed or inferred from the observable behavior of actors in the process of social interaction.

The power barrier

It is a commonplace that the participation of employees is more often preached than practised. It is seldom wholeheartedly welcomed by management. Why do many management people not accept the idea of employees' participation? A very simple and not entirely incorrect answer is that they fear that participation might reduce or even challenge the managerial power within the business organization. But even if the increase in the amount of power of the employees would involve the decrease in the amount of managerial power, and this is not necessarily true,[4] the question still remains: why are management people so deeply concerned about their power within the organization?

A social psychologist might offer at least two interpretative hypotheses:

First, the hypothesis of the "authoritarian personality": that on the average, managers score higher on the scale of authoritarianism (F-scale) than the general population, and that they value power very highly as a social reward (Dubin's "power pay"). Put in more popular terms: managers are "powerseekers."

Another hypothesis relates to the perception of the managerial role by managers themselves. According to this hypothesis, managers are inclined to see their own role in terms of the master-servant relationship or in the perspective of the "boss" and "his workers." If participation is to be successful it requires a redefinition of the "traditional" managerial role;[5] however, such a concept of the managerial role is so deeply ingrained, especially in the developing countries, that it stubbornly resists any change. For that reason managers do not fully accept the idea of participation though sometimes they pay lip service to it.

If these hypotheses were true, and this is a factual question to be answered by empirical studies, then the remedies could be easily prescribed: a better selection of managers on the basis of personality testing and the clarification of the managerial role through an intensive and systematic management training. However, even in this case the sociologist would still be justified in pointing to a structural source of pressure on managers to try hard to preserve their dominant power within the organization. This source of pressure is, of course, the institutionally approved vertical pattern of the organization structure, which is essentially bureaucratic in the Weberian sense (though real organizations usually deviate, in significant respects, from the Weberian ideal type of bureaucratic organization). As is well known, the positions in the bureaucratic hierarchy are defined in terms of authority, i.e., in terms of power (according to R. Bierstedt authority is "institutionalized power") which originates on the top and is distributed in smaller and smaller amounts down the line. The duties and privileges of the position represent a compelling force on the actual behavior of managers regardless of their personality traits and ideal role concepts. Moreover, since the organizational structure is a self-selecting mechanism it may account for a disproportionate number of authoritarian personalities in managerial positions, who are naturally inclined to see their role in terms of a master and servant relationship and, by the same token, such a structure might frustrate the efforts at selection and training of managerial personnel.

The bureaucratic structure deprives the ordinary employees of sanctions in their attempts to influence managerial behavior, but it is not clear why it should prevent their efforts at persuasion. To put it differently, why could a powerful manager not sit down with his subordinates and decide jointly upon the matters of common concern? I would venture to say that the bureaucratic structure discourages even those participatory acts carrying no sanctions or threat of sanctions. We should not forget that the process of social interaction is patterned by social power. The most powerful participants initiate the interaction, they talk and the less powerful are expected to listen to them respectfully and approvingly; the former ask the questions and the latter are expected to submit the answers. Needless to say effective participation requires quite a different pattern of interaction: any member of the group (irrespective of his formal position) must be free to initiate interaction, to ask questions, to agree and disagree with any other member, in other words, effective participation implies that all participants talk on an equal footing. Such an egalitarian interaction pattern introduced into an authoritarian structure may be seen by managers as a disturbing and subversive influence.

The status differentials between the managers and the ordinary workers work in the same direction, reinforcing the patterning effects of social power.[6] A lower status person should know his "place" (his position on the status ladder) when talking to a higher status person. If he "forgets" this, his behavior will be considered "indecent" and possibly subject to retaliation.

Though this explanation sounds convincing, it fails to account for the fact that in some organizations which are bureaucratic in terms of structure, management does adopt a participative philosophy and style of leadership. This suggests that quite different philosophies and policies can be adopted and followed under basically the same structural arrangements. If so, the previous argument of the patterning influence of social power and status seems to lose much of its explanatory power. However, it should never be forgotten that managers are ultimately responsible for any decision made in the organization, and hence the ultimate power lies with them. Participation may be allowed insofar as the group is able and willing to reach a decision which the manager considers appropriate. But "if the group is so divided in opinion that there is no time to reach decisions by consensus which adequately meet these (situational) requirements, the superior has the responsibility of making a decision which does meet them." Or if the members of the group disagree with their superior and he thinks that the course of action suggested by the group will result in a costly mistake, "the superior may feel that he has no choice but to do what his own experience indicates is best. . . . If he overrules the group, the superior usually reduces the amount of work-group loyalty which he has 'in the bank.' . . . But whatever course of action taken, *he is responsible and must accept full responsibility for what occurs.*"[7] The awareness of employees that they are free to suggest or even to pass any decision which is likely to please their boss will hardly encourage their effective participation.

Here is the crux of the matter: an effective system of democratic participation in industry requires that the ultimate responsibility and authority be shifted from the executives to the employees as a group. And this is exactly what has been done under the Workers' Self-management system in Yugoslavia. Of course, this involves major changes in the very definition of the business enterprise and in the structure of the working organization. Let us briefly describe these changes.

The "labor controlled" firm

Underlying the bureaucratic work organization in industry is the "capital controlled" firm where the prerogatives to make major decisions, such as those referring to the allocation of profits and appointment of management, lie with the owners of capital (be they individual entrepreneurs and shareholders or the "Socialist State"). In contrast, in the "labor controlled" (or "labor managed") firm this decision-making power lies with the owners of labor (as a productive resource), i.e., with the workers' collectivities.

"The institutional system gives the working collective prerogatives for making decisions on employing the productive factors and on deciding on the distribution of the net revenue, if there is any, this being not guaranteed in a market economy. Losses rather than profits may result: these would have to be covered by those who decided on the allocation of productive resources, i.e., by the working collectives. It follows that the position of the working collective is similar to that of the capitalist entrepreneur. Both invest and combine resources and shoulder the risks. The collective can in fact be defined as a *collective entrepreneur.*"[8]

It follows from such a definition of the firm that each employee is not merely a hired worker, i.e., a paid contributor of some specialized services, but is in addition to this a partner in the joint endeavor. Therefore, his participation in managerial decision-making is not merely desirable but is required by his institutionally prescribed role. And the fulfillment of the role is crucially important for any type of organization.

Here at least two basic questions may be asked: (1) Is the "labor controlled" firm viable in purely economic terms, more precisely, can this type of firm match the "capital controlled" firm in business efficiency? (2) Do employees really accept their new, entrepreneurial role, as required under such a system?

The first issue drew the attention of a number of economists both in Yugoslavia and abroad. However, even the economists who approached the problem within the same conceptual framework of neoclassical analysis came out with two different answers: on the one hand, most Western economists came to the conclusion that the "labor controlled" firm (regardless of labels they use to describe it) is definitely inferior in efficiency terms as compared with the capitalist firm in the West; while, on the other hand, an outstanding American scholar and a number of Yugoslav economists maintain that such a type of firm is by no means inferior and might well be superior to the capitalist firm in terms of business efficiency.[9] There is no room here to debate the relative merits of these two contrary views, nor am I professionally competent to enter the debate. However, the second issue (the willingness of employees to take the entrepreneurial role) is clearly relevant for the present discussion.

Here I have to refer to my own research. My studies in attitudes of employees towards some crucial aspects of "collective entrepreneurship" suggest that employees, by and large, are not willing to take any responsibility beyond the limits of their own job.[10] This seems to be due, among other reasons, to the cultural background and previous social experience of workers and to the inconsistencies of this institutional pattern of the firm itself. This pattern gives the employees entrepreneurial prerogatives but no property claims on the fruits of their entrepreneurial activity beyond their personal earnings.[11]

Whether and how this model of enterprise could be made more consistent internally is still an open question.

From the vertical to the horizontal type of organization

The change in the definition of the business enterprise involved a major structural change in the organization—the shift from the vertical or hierarchical type of organization to the horizontal or democratic type of organization. Actually, the changes in the formal-institutional blueprint of the work organization made in Yugoslavia during the last two decades are in important respects in line with the ideas of the "democratic" or "participative" organization advocated by a number of contemporary management theoreticians.

The blueprint and reality

Under such a system one would expect participation to flourish both on the policy-making and work-place levels. However, the available empirical studies, especially the study made by J. Obradović (under the general direction of R. Supek), in methodological terms the best one in the field, demonstrates that the actual participation falls short of the expectation. On the basis of a three-year systematic observation and objective coding of the interactions in the meetings of the workers' councils in twenty Yugoslav firms located in four of the six Yugoslav republics, Obradović found that participation of rank-and-file employees in the most important policy-making areas was almost nil, the discussions in the meetings being preempted by the executives and staff experts. Somewhat greater employee participation was registered in the "labor relations" areas (especially in the area of human relations); however, even in those areas the amount of participation was not impressive.[12]

No less surprising are the results of empirical studies of the power structure of Yugoslav industrial organizations carried out during the 1960's by the present writer and a number of other Yugoslav sociologists.[13] They showed no difference in the distribution of "executive power" in the surveyed Yugoslav organizations as compared with the American organizations: an oligarchic pattern was found in both of them. This finding in itself should not be disturbing since "executive power in democratic organizations usually is distributed in accord with the pyramid structure of authority."[14] However, basically the same pattern was found in the area of "legislative power" where, according to Katz and Kahn, a completely different distribution should be expected: even here the top executives as a group are more powerful than the workers' council. True enough, the workers' council is perceived to have a "medium" amount of power, but further analysis revealed that the two most influential groups within the council itself are top executives and staff experts, while blue-collar workers are the least influential group. (This finding is consistent with the results of Obradović's study.) Summarizing the results of the studies in social power, one may conclude that the hierarchical organization has survived within the new institutional shell of democratic organization. In the light of such a conclusion Obradović's findings will appear less surprising: employees' participation faces again *la bête noire* of social power.

Why did the radical change in the formal-institutional blueprint of the organization yield no results in terms of the power structure of the firm? Is this failure due primarily, if not exclusively, to specific factors (historical, cultural, social) underlying the Yugoslav industrial scene? Or some more general factors arising from the very nature of the business organizations involved? Probably both kinds of factors are at work here, but the latter are certainly more relevant for the present discussion than the former. I am unable to deal at any length here with the more general factors which are responsible for preventing any significant change in the power structure of the Yugoslav business organizations along the expected lines. This would require a separate paper. Let me just point to two structural loci of managerial power which remained unchanged within the new system:

1. The key position of management in the communication process and coordination activity has not been affected by the change in the formal structure. Note that coordination of necessity restricts participation ("the free flow of information").[15]

2. Management has retained, or, more precisely, has acquired in the course of economic decentralization, the strategic position in the organization's dealings with the external demands and environmental pressures stemming from technological and market forces. Though the Yugoslav executives are not granted the entrepreneurial function by the institutional order, this being the prerogative of workers' collectives and their representative bodies, they took it since they were better equipped to carry out this function. The increasing technological development and rising market economy have already exerted strong pressure in the direction of curtailing the formal participation of employees.[16] Although the self-management ideology resists this trend, it is likely to grow stronger.

The preceding discussion should not be understood as a case against the institutional redefinition of the business firm in terms of "collective entrepreneurship" coupled with the formal structural changes along the lines of the "democratic organization." My argument was not intended to suggest that we go back to the beaten tracks of hired and bureaucratic organization—that would be a counsel of despair! I wanted to point to the limitations of organizational changes as briefly described: that even the most radical changes in the formal-institutional blueprint do not assure an effective participation of employees, for they do not necessarily redress the power imbalance between management and employees which is inherent in industrial organizations everywhere. In other words, they do not overcome the power barrier to successful participation.

There are at least two important lessons to be learned from the Yugoslav experience in employee participation: (1) that participation by itself cannot alter the existing, asymmetrical distribution of power between managers and employees; successful participation is likely to be the result rather than the cause of the change of the power structure within the organization; (2) that the present structural arrangements stressing the horizontal organization of workers and employees in general ("Workers' Collectivities") cannot be expected to produce desirable results in terms of successful participation in the absence of a strong and autonomous vertical organization of employees capable of sanctioning their "participatory acts." Strong and autonomous labor unions vigorously representing the interests and viewpoints of various sections of employees seem to be an indispensable part of structural arrangements for effective participation.

NOTES

1. Sidney Verba, "Democratic Participation," *Annals of the American Academy of Political and Social Sciences—Social Goals and Indicators for America,* Vol. II, September 1967, pp. 53, 55.

2. Rocco Carzo, Jr., and John N. Yanouzas, *Formal Organization—A Systems Approach,* Homewood, Ill., Irwin-Dorsey, 1967, p. 186.

3. Verba, op. cit., pp. 61–62.

4. A. S. Tannenbaum argues vigorously that the total amount of control (power) in the organization is a variable rather than a fixed quan-

tity (A. S. Tannenbaum, ed., *Control in Organizations,* New York, McGraw-Hill, 1968, pp. 12–15). His general argument sounds convincing although he fails to recognize that in some situations the distribution of power may be some sort of "zero-sum game."

5. "Managers may not have fully accepted the redefinition of their functions which the new industrial system requires. Many managers are still playing, to some extent, the traditional role of 'master,' holding on to prerogatives of interpersonal control—hiring, disciplining, and assigning employees to jobs—that really should not be part of their job description." (J. Županov and A. S. Tannenbaum, "The Distribution of Control in Some Yugoslav Industrial Organizations," in Tannenbaum, ed., op. cit., p. 107.)

6. "The pyramid of hierarchical organization represents a fusion of status, prestige, rewards, and power." (D. Katz and R. L. Kahn, *The Social Psychology of Organizations,* New York, Wiley, 1966, p. 211.)

7. R. Likert, *New Patterns of Management,* New York, McGraw-Hill, 1961, p. 112.

8. J. Županov, *Samoupravljanje i društvena moć,* Zagreb, Naše teme, 1969. Summary in English, p. 306.

9. Among studies falling into the first camp the following ones should be mentioned: E. D. Domar, "The Soviet Collective Farm as a Producer Cooperative," *American Economic Review,* Vol. LVI, No. 4, September 1966; B. Ward, "The Firm in Illyria: Market Syndicalism," *American Economic Review,* Vol. XLVIII, No. 4, September 1958; B. Ward, *The Socialist Economy,* New York, Random House, 1967, Chs. 8–10. The contrary views are expressed by the following writers: Jaroslav Vanek, *The General Theory of Labor-Managed Labor Economies,* Ithaca, N.Y., Cornell University Press, 1970 (a brief summary by Vanek himself appeared in *American Review,* Vol. LIX, No. 5, December 1969, under the title "Decentralization Under Workers' Management: A Theoretical Appraisal"); Jaroslav Vanek, *The Participatory Economy: An Evolutionary Hypothesis and a Development Strategy,* Ithaca, N.Y., Cornell University Press, 1971; D. Dubravčić, "Labour as Entrepreneurial Input: An Essay in the Theory of the Producer Co-operative Economy," *Economica,* August 1970; B. Horvat, "Prilog zasnivanju teorije jugoslovenskog poduzeća," *Ekonomska analiza,* 1, 1967; A. Čičin-Šain, P. Miović, A. Vahčić, "Ponašanje samoupravnog poduzeća—centralno pitanje teorije samoupravne tržišne privrede," Zagreb, Ekonomski institut, 1971 (mimeo).

10. See J. Županov, "The Producer and Risk," *Eastern European Economics,* Spring 1969, pp. 12–28. (The author has not checked the translation for accuracy.)

11. S. J. Rawin emphasizes the structural inconsistency of the model of "collective entrepreneurship": "The worker has no intrinsic rights with regard to the earnings of the enterprise except those arising from his actual contribution 'as producer.' Nor has he any claim on the permanency of employment. In the event of relinquishing his job, voluntarily or through dismissal, his relationship with the enterprise ceases entirely. In effect, notwithstanding the formal trappings of producer-associateship status, the relation here is that of wage employment. While the worker may enjoy a measure of social and economic protection, through legal statutes or through the mechanism of self-management, essentially his position is not too different from that of a factory wage earner under other systems. . . . How can the worker collective function as an entrepreneurial unit while the individual members are placed under wage-earning conditions." ("Management and Autonomy in Socialist Industry–The Yugoslav Experiences," paper submitted at the annual meeting of the American Association for the Advancement of Slavic Studies, Denver, Colorado, March 1971, mimeo.) The constitutional Amendment 21 that has been passed recently contains an important stipulation which, if put into effect, could to some extent invalidate Rawin's argument. However, his argument is still valid at the present.

12. Josip Obradović, "Struktura participacije u procesu donošenja odluka na sjednicama radničkog savjeta o ekonomskoj politici poduzeća," Zagreb, *Revija za sociologiju,* No. 1, 1972.

13. Out of a number of studies by Yugoslav sociologists only two of them available in English are mentioned here: J. Županov and A. S. Tannenbaum, "The Distribution of Control in Some Yugoslav Industrial Organizations," op. cit.; and B. Kavčić, V. Rus, and A. S. Tannenbaum, "Control Participation and Effectiveness in Four Yugoslav Industrial Organizations," *Administrative Science Quarterly,* Vol. 16, No. 1, March 1971.

14. Katz and Kahn, op. cit., p. 212.

15. This is a fundamental organizational dilemma between coordination and communication (P. M. Blau and W. R. Scott, *Formal Organizations: A Comparative Approach,* San Francisco, Chandler, 1962, pp. 242–244).

16. In 1969 the Federal Parliament passed the 15th Constitutional Amendment allowing the business organizations more freedom in setting up the bodies of management as they see fit. In many firms managers were reported having seized this opportunity to change their formal prerogatives, especially by abolishing the "Board of Management" (which was stipulated by previous laws as an executive com-

mittee of the Workers' Council) and instituting the "Business Committee" as an organ of professional executives. This move was met by a bitter opposition—on ideological grounds—by the Trade Unions and a number of political functionaries. However, since any empirical evidence is lacking, it is impossible to assess the magnitude of the change that undoubtedly took place.

12. The Self-management System in Yugoslav Enterprises

JANEZ JEROVŠEK

At the outset, it must be explained that the economic system in Yugoslavia is substantially different from those operating in other socialist countries. Our industrial organizations do not operate in the framework of a centralized system, which might be efficient in a simple and undeveloped economy (where different subsystems are not highly interrelated and interdependent) but is inefficient and rigid in a more complex economy, where the operation of each subsystem determines the efficiency of other subsystems. Our industrial organizations operate in a market system and their efficiency is measured in economic terms of profit and growth.

All organizations are autonomous and make decisions regarding planning, production targets, investment, prices, wages, and all less critical issues. The question is, who makes these decisions within the plant?

We have introduced a most radical participative model. It is not possible to identify this model with the human relations approach which intends to make the executive human-oriented rather than task-oriented. Participation, in our model, is not manipulative and workers are not considered children. Our par-

Reprinted from *Employees' Participation and Social Power in Industry* (Zagreb: Institut za društvena istraživanja, 1972), pp. 113–22, paper presented at the First International Conference on Participation and Self-management, Dubrovnik, December 1972.

ticipative model has mainly to do with a completely different structure of organization in which the legitimacy of all decisions stems from all employees. Since workers constitute the majority, workers are the major source of legitimacy. From this point of view, our model is typically democratic.

In practice, this means that the workers make all important decisions on the policy of the enterprise and set the fundamental aims that the enterprise pursues. Top managers, i.e., the general manager and the heads of departments, are not appointed, but elected. Formally, they are responsible to the workers and to all lower participants, i.e., to those who formally elected them.

As all workers cannot directly make decisions on all important issues, they elect a Workers' Council composed of about thirty or more members. The number of members depends on the size of the enterprise.

The Workers' Council meets once or twice a month and passes all important decisions on expansion of the enterprise, new investments, prices of products, wages, the incentive system, safety provisions, etc. About 70 to 80 percent of the Workers' Council membership are workers: the others are top managers, middle managers, supervisors and professionals.

Self-management was introduced in our country as an "ideological projection" and not as a pragmatic managerial idea. It was defined and treated a priori as if self-management were identical with the greatest efficiency and with the highest degree of democracy. Some suppositions, on which self-management was based, were illusions, and all of them were insufficiently tested empirically. Scientists in the field of organizational sciences became aware that a most radical participative organization was thus introduced, i.e., an organization with a completely new formal structure which was nowhere in the world formally introduced or tested. With this a need arose to find out how this system works, how democratic and efficient it really is and which structural solutions are unsuitable and wrong. It was necessary to find out how influence is distributed in the work organization, how the system of collective responsibility works, how leadership relates to self-management, how the system of financial stimulation operates, who bears the risk, how the system of sanctions operates, who exercises sanctions, what are the conflicting roles of the general manager, his sources of power, etc. It was necessary to investigate those problems empirically and to form a new theoretical model of the work organization. Work organizations were bureaucratic, or even prebureaucratic when self-management was introduced and formally institutionalized from the top downwards (i.e., by the government).

This led to incoherence and structural inconsistency. The formal system of organizations appeared to be rather complicated, with tasks and relations among numerous committees and organs being loosely defined. Since the organizations operate as rational systems, managers simplified the formal system in everyday functioning. This led to strong informal organization, that created an inconsistent social system falling short of legitimacy. Therefore the problem arose of how to lessen the gap between formal and informal organization. The main disadvantages and insufficiencies of the self-management model are the following:

1. The essence of autonomous action is that it is not controlled, that it goes beyond the framework of the formally permissible and expected. Since autonomous action in the work organization functions disruptively—or, at least, so it seems—there exists a continuing effort to channel the action into the formal structure. When the formal organization completely frustrates autonomy of action and allows only activities that can be anticipated, and are strictly and rigidly regulated, it reduces or destroys the motivational basis for participation. We institutionalized our self-management model from the top downwards with an enormous and excessive system of laws, excessive to the extent that we greatly narrowed the motivational basis for participation deriving from autonomous action.

2. The model of self-management is based on the assumption of common interests. A work organization, however, contains a social and status system with various organizational and socioeconomic groups which hold different positions in the hierarchy and have different incomes, education, responsibilities and aspirations. Interaction among these groups having different interests leads to conflict.

3. As the model is based on the assumption of uniformity of interests, tensions and conflicts are interpreted to be residual and are not recognized as integral parts of the system. The strike, as one form of conflict, threatens the social system of the working organization and is therefore seen as dysfunctional. Since sharp conflicts are not defined as elements of the system, they are not legitimate.

4. The existing model of the self-management organization comprises two different structures: a hierarchical one functioning

within the frame of the daily work process, and a nonhierarchical one functioning only sometimes. In this latter framework, the most important decisions are formally taken and aims and policy of the working organization are defined.

Josip Županov says that "each of these structures is based upon different definitions of the function of the producer and upon different organizational principles. Not one of the structures—if we take it by itself—is internally coherent, and neither of them is compatible with the other; therefore, the rights are defined unclearly and contradictorily—or they are not defined at all."[1]

The main advantages of the self-management model are the following:

1. Through self-management it is possible to increase the degree of co-operation and involvement in working toward organizational goals, particularly on higher levels in the organization.

2. The self-management model gives greater opportunity for awareness by all members of all important events and potential happenings in the organization: this is the source of greater identification with the enterprise and of greater opportunity for participation.

3. The self-management model provides opportunities for mutual influence and control which in turn reduce the negative effects of hierarchy, improve communication, stimulate motivation and generally make the organization more flexible. This means that the organization is able to adapt to those environmental elements (market, economy, technology and system of production) most threatening to its progress and development.

4. The main point here is that all employees participate directly, or through the Workers' Council, to achieve a most rational and socially desirable allocation of financial resources. This gives employees the feeling that the success or failure of the organization can be attributed mainly to members of the enterprise and not to outside groups. (Of course, merits for success are not evenly distributed, but depend on the distribution of influence and knowledge.)

5. The value system in the wider society is dominated by participative ideals which enhance the feeling in all employees that they are the legitimate source of power.

6. The discrepancy between personal and organizational needs is not overcome; it is, however, not as great as is characteristic of

1. Josip Županov, "Samoupravljanje i reforma," *Naše teme,* 1968, No. 5, p. 688.

a typical hierarchical organization. Personal needs—especially those of employees occupying lower levels in the hierarchy, are satisfied to a much greater extent. In such a participative organization, there is more opportunity for differential reward than in the classical organization.

Prior to the introduction of self-management, our economy was strictly centralized by a system of planning which limited the autonomy of work organizations. With the introduction of self-management, not only was the social system within working organizations changed, but also the entire political system, and the economic policy of the government as well. As a result of these changes, the effectiveness of work organizations, and of the whole society, increased. The gross national product increased by 12 percent per annum, thus including Yugoslavia among those countries with the most intensive and rapid economic development in the world. Today, it is difficult to establish the extent to which the abolition of the centralized system and strict planning contributed to this rapid development, or the extent to which this extraordinary development can be attributed to self-management. The centralized system imposed substantial limitations upon individual initiative: the self-management system loosened those limitations to a great extent. There is little doubt that self-management created a more flexible organization, capable of rapid adaptation to changes in the environment.

Yugoslavia was for the last two decades among those societies (states) with the most rapid economic development and in a few years had recorded the most rapid economic development in the world. In this period Yugoslavia has changed the composition of its population.[2] That is evidence that the participation system in Yugoslavia is a viable one, and it is therefore a worthwhile subject for comparative studies.

We shall limit ourselves to the presentation of some empirical data and some indicators demonstrating indirectly that self-management has created a vital social dynamic in work organizations.

Data from a recently completed study indicate the extent to which the self-management model has been realized in our work organizations, and the extent to which the model is effective.[3]

We based this study partly on the organizational theory which

2. After the war more than 70 percent of the total population was agricultural, now less than 50 percent is agricultural.

3. Stane Možina, Janez Jerovšek, *Determiante, ki vplivajo na učinkovitost vodstva v delovnih organizacijah,* Ljubljana: Institut za sociologijo in filozofijo pri univerzi v Ljubljani, 1969.

we find in the works of Rensis Likert and Arnold Tannenbaum. Rensis Likert distinguishes four systems of organization:

1. exploitive authoritative
2. benevolent authoritative
3. consultative
4. participative

Because of the lack of space, we will describe here only systems 1 and 4, as we have adapted them to Yugoslav conditions.

System 1

Within this system, the managers of the enterprise conceive of workers as market goods which can be bought. Managers perceive their own role as that of decision-making and giving orders. They lean primarily upon coercion as a means of motivation. Human feelings and higher needs are not taken into consideration. It follows that the flow of communications is in one direction—from the top downwards.

Decisions regarding aims and policy of the enterprise are made by top managers only, and often on the basis of inaccurate and inadequate information. The lower organizational levels do not participate and they do not feel responsible for carrying out these aims and policies. Responsibility is hence found only at the top. Since the managers depend primarily upon coercion, there is no real co-operation or interpersonal influence. Changes are carried out with difficulty because resistance is relatively strong. There are many conflicts and they are difficult to solve. In such a social system the dissatisfaction of lower participants is substantial.

System 4

Within this system all employees are treated as important parts of the organization. Managers are responsible for decisions, but in making those decisions they take into account the opinions and suggestions of lower participants. Workers participate primarily in determining the work processes, the area in which their fund of knowledge and experience is greatest and most useful. Communications flow vertically, in both directions, and horizontally. They are, for the most part, rapid and accurate. Employees are relatively highly motivated by the differentiated reward system, such that everyone who produces more and better work is rewarded correspondingly and those performing poorly in quantitative and qualitative terms are punished correspondingly. This system does not represent a loose organization. With mutual control and influence, a highly co-ordinated, cohesive and closely knit system is introduced. This is not a permissive system—it is a system having more formal organization in that everyone is simultaneously an object of control and exercising control over others. Responsibility is not located only at the top, but among all organizational groups. The degree of responsibility is linked to the power which the individuals and groups possess. There are fewer destructive conflicts in system 4 than in system 1, and those that exist are more likely than in system 1 to be solved integratively. Changes are more easily introduced because those concerned with the changes are not just their passive executors, but active participants in their planning. Although this system is not loose or permissive, the employees are relatively satisfied.

We have described only systems 1 and 4 because these represent extremes. Systems 2 and 3 are in between and differ only in degree. While we have labelled system 4 participative, we have defined it not only in terms of degree of participation, but also in terms of other variables—motivation, communication, interaction, responsibility, change, conflict, efficiency, and the like.

We have assumed that work organizations are managed on the basis of different social systems, and that the efficiency of those social systems is of differing degrees. We hypothesized that those working organizations approaching system 4 would be more efficient than those operating on the basis of systems 1 or 2.

For these reasons, we selected twenty work organizations, ten highly efficient and ten less efficient. We selected industrial organizations so that in each branch there would be one highly efficient and one less efficient organization.

The following criteria were used to determine the level of efficiency of each organization:

1. average personal income per employee
2. profit per employee
3. funds per employee
4. investments per employee
5. increase in number employed over last three years
6. increase in number of professionals employed in last three years

All of these criteria overlapped: average income was high in the more efficient organizations and low in the less efficient ones. In the last three years profit increased in the more efficient organizations but not in the less efficient ones. Funds increased in the more efficient organizations over the last three years, and in less efficient ones they decreased. Investments grew in the more efficient organizations and decreased in the less efficient ones. Over the last three years the number of employees and professionals increased in the more efficient organizations and decreased in their less efficient counterparts.

When selecting highly efficient and less efficient organizations we were also concerned with the social system in which they operate. We found that all the highly efficient organizations belonged to system 3. In Figure 1 we can see this difference. Calculations reveal that differences between efficient and less efficient organizations are statistically significant.

In the highly efficient organizations, superiors express trust in their subordinates, while in the less efficient enterprises, trust is absent. In the highly efficient organizations, subordinates feel relatively free to discuss their problems with their direct superiors; in the less efficient organizations, they feel less free. In the efficient organizations, superiors often seek the ideas of their subordinates in solving problems, and try to incorporate these ideas in their solutions; in the less efficient enterprises, this is done far less often. This type of influence is of primary importance since other studies[4] have shown that employees want to participate in determining their own working process—where their fund of knowledge and experience is greatest—but do not so much want to participate in decisions concerning the entire enterprise where their fund of knowledge is lowest.

In the highly efficient organizations, the total amount of influence is greater than in the less efficient organizations, meaning that in the former all levels in the hierarchy exert greater influence upon relevant events than in less efficient organizations.[5] Using Wilcox's test, the difference was found to be statistically significant.

In highly efficient organizations employees are motivated to

---

4. Veljko Rus, "Status strokovnega in vodstvenega kadra glede na komuniciranje, moč in odgovornost," *Moderna organizacija,* 1968, No. 5.

5. The association between the amount of influence and efficiency in working organizations was confirmed in several other researches. See: Arnold S. Tannenbaum, *Control in Organizations,* New York: McGraw-Hill, 1968.

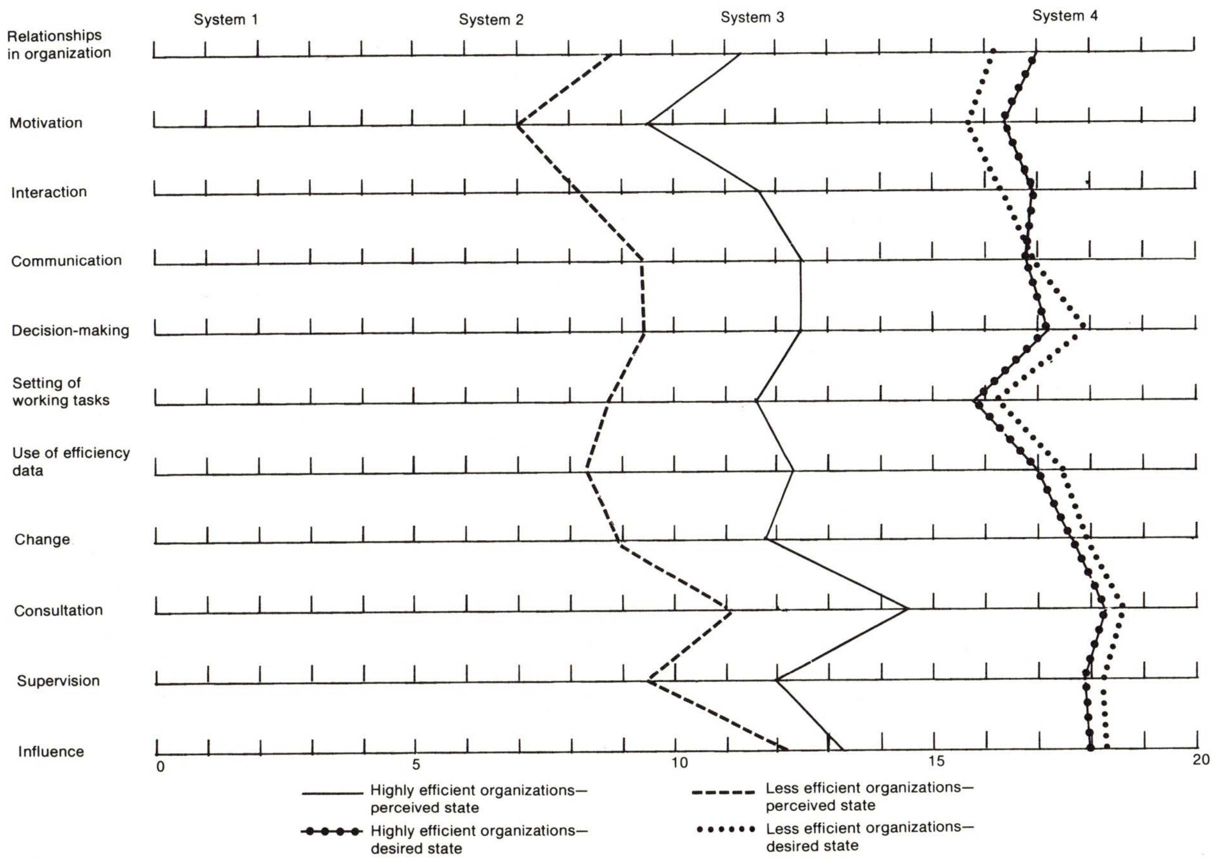

Figure 1. Organization efficiency and system of self-management

participate more than in the less efficient organizations. Nevertheless, we established that on this variable, highly efficient organizations approach system 2. This means that human potentialities are not being fully utilized even in the highly efficient organizations. Concerning the interaction variable, we established that in the highly efficient organizations extensive use is made of team work, while in the less efficient organizations little use is made of team work.

We found as well, that in the highly efficient organizations, the communications flow both upwards and downwards; in the less efficient enterprises, vertical communications flow primarily downwards. In the more efficient organizations, employees receive downward-flowing information with confidence and trust; in the less efficient organizations, such information is received mainly with distrust. In the highly efficient enterprises, the information flowing upwards is, for the most part, accurate, while in the less efficient organizations, it is carefully arranged and screened. In the highly efficient organizations, supervisors are well acquainted with the working problems of their subordinates; in the less efficient enterprises, they are correspondingly less well acquainted with such problems.

Concerning decision-making we found that in the highly efficient organizations decisions are made at the top, but with considerable delegation of authority in formulating those decisions. In the less efficient organizations, decisions are made at the top with little delegation of authority in the process. In the highly efficient organizations those making decisions on important issues possess quite enough relevant knowledge, while in the less efficient organizations they have relatively little knowledge that is relevant to the issues.

In the highly efficient organizations work tasks are defined and distributed on the basis of discussion—in the less efficient organizations, this is accomplished without benefit of discussion.

In the highly efficient organizations data on operations, expenses, income and productivity are used to a much greater extent than they are in less efficient enterprises.

Systems 3 and 4 are not characteristically loose organizations: in these two systems there is intensive supervision. Our data demonstrate that in highly efficient organizations, all organizational groups are considerably more supervised than in less efficient organizations.

In more efficient enterprises, not only are all groups more supervised but they are also more differentially supervised. From other studies[6] we know that those groups and organizations with more differentiated reward systems and structures of influence are more efficient than those groups and organizations with more egalitarian reward systems and less differentiated structures of influence. Our data also lead to the conclusion that a more differentiated system of supervision is related to higher efficiency.

Further, we found that in the highly efficient organization, a more open system of supervision is applied and in the less efficient organizations, a more closed system. In the highly efficient organizations, the employees are considerably more motivated by rewards than in the less efficient enterprises.

We found that the utilization of work time is greater in the more efficient enterprises, probably because of the greater supervision.

Although organization members are considerably more supervised in the highly efficient organizations than in the less efficient ones, they are considerably more satisfied.

The difference in degree of satisfaction is substantial. In the less efficient organizations, 84.1 percent of respondents answered that they were not particularly or not at all satisfied with the current results of the enterprise; in highly efficient organizations, only 12.5 percent of respondents were of the same opinion.

In our study, we found that all of the highly efficient organizations fell into system 3 and all of the less efficient organizations into system 2. At the same time, we asked respondents (top managers and members of the Workers' Council) in which system they would prefer to operate. In Figure 1, it can be seen that for several variables, all respondents in more and less efficient organizations preferred system 4.

A participative system, as we have defined and operationalized it, cannot be introduced from the top. Institutionalization does facilitate the introduction of a social system which appears to produce optimal results in terms of efficiency. A social system characterized by optimal utilization of human resources cannot, however, be realized through laws or institutionalization alone. This means that within a formal bureaucratic and autocratic structure, a participative social system can be introduced, but it is

---

6. Harold J. Leavit, "Unhuman Organization," *Readings in Managerial Psychology*, Chicago: University of Chicago Press, 1968.

possible that the formal self-management organization will remain in reality bureaucratic and autocratic.

Within bureaucratic organization the style of leadership can be democratic, motivating workers, raising their morale and their productivity. On the other hand, the style of leadership can be explicitly autocratic within a formal self-management organization, having a negative influence on satisfaction, working morale, attitudes toward work and productivity.

We found, in our study, that work organizations operating on the basis of a participative social system are highly efficient; those working on the basis of an autocratic social system are less efficient and operate at the lower limit of profitability.

It appears that philosophy of management differs in more and less efficient organizations. We found, for example, in interviews that the general managers of highly efficient organizations define effectiveness as the expansion of their organizations. General managers of less efficient organizations defined effectiveness as simply staying in business. For the latter, then, effectiveness is the mere existence of the enterprise, not its expansion.

The fact that highly efficient organizations have different social systems may give us the right to conclude, or at least to suppose, that this is a matter of differing philosophy and differing practice.

Managers, primarily those in less efficient organizations, often assert that their low levels of efficiency are the result of their exposure to changes introduced continuously by the government. These changes, they say, are often neither justified nor consistent, and are sometimes discriminatory. While these claims are not entirely without foundation, they are, in some respects, quite exaggerated. If they were accurate, then we would not find both highly efficient and less efficient organizations in the same industry. Economic policy can have discriminatory effects among industries, but not within one industry.

We found in our study that the social systems differ in highly efficient organizations compared to less efficient organizations. We can ask now, who determines the nature of a social system within an enterprise or who contributes most to that system resulting in optimal efficiency. It seems to us that the nature of the social system is determined by those who exert the greatest influence within the organization—the general manager and the top managers immediately below him. If this supposition is accurate then it follows that the degree of democracy in work organizations depends to a large extent on the qualifications of top managers. It follows that the education of managers and the recruitment policy of the enterprise are of primary importance.

Our research was not undertaken and the enterprises were not selected so that we could test the above hypothesis. We mention our interpretation only because our observations suggest such conclusions and because of our interest in seeing the above hypothesis tested in the future.

Although we are aware that the structure of the work organization is affected by its environment, which is different in different societies, and by the system of values and customs, which also differ among societies, the experiences of Yugoslavia in introducing the democratic structure of organization can be useful for all those who will experiment with self-management. If nothing else, the Yugoslav experience will show what should not be done and where there may be little chance to be successful.

13. Problems of Participatory Democracy

VELJKO RUS

Democratization as decentralization and democratization of decision-making

At the end of the fifties, the state of self-management already seemed so bleak that we lost our belief that workers' self-management would be realized by the broadening of the economic base. The new thesis of "bringing self-management closer to the direct producers" attempted to counter the obvious manifestations of the bureaucratization of self-management. A process began of decentralizing self-management, of forming economic units within enterprises and calling meetings of producers as direct forms of management. Compared to all previous actions, this was the most radical to date, and it seemed that it would basically change the structure of power within work organizations.

Decentralization of management was not consistently carried out, however. It got bogged down halfway, for it already provoked so many disagreements in its initial waves that it became paralyzed by them.

The conflicts that arose manifested themselves above all in the following accusations: the trade union alleged that the *technoc-*

Reprinted from *Smisao i perspektive socijalizma* (Zagreb: Praxis, 1965), pp. 207–16. Also published in Rudi Supek, ed., *Etatisme et autogestion: bilan critique de socialisme yougoslave* (Paris: Éditions Anthropos, 1973). Translated by Helen Kramer.

racy hindered the development of self-management, while enterprise directors resisted the broadening of self-management because, they claimed, it introduced anarchy into the work organization. Both accusations have some foundation, although they only symbolically express those conflicts that even today have remained unresolved.

The fact is that the overall structure of management, built on the so-called scientific organization of work, did not undergo fundamental changes with the introduction of self-management. Basing itself on the equivalence of authority and responsibility, the concentration of decision-making, and the control of information, scientific organization of work necessarily began to resist the processes of decentralization. The resistance was intensified, in particular, because decentralization tended toward collective decision-making and thus went beyond the limits of functional management in its aims. This identification of self-management with collective decisions is, of course, a necessary consequence of that fact that self-management develops from the top down, and thus institutional forms dominate over spontaneous forms of participation throughout.

Hence, it is understandable that the attempt was made to implement decentralization of self-management as decentralization of decision-making. In this way, the impression inadvertently arose that the strengthening of self-management lies in a broader transference of jurisdictions to self-management organs. But since the work organization is a highly differentiated organism in which every member has his function (and functions are simultaneously differentiated and nontransferable), it is understandable that the transference of managerial functions to local self-management organs threatened the functional unity of business operations, and that thus effective social control and effective participation of the collective in managing the entire enterprise were not insured. Our managers were correct in stating that there are limits to the decentralization of decision-making; they erred, however, in opposing self-management as a whole on the basis of a one-sided conception of self-management and in failing to warn against nonfunctional forms of participation of the work collective that spontaneously appear in modern work organizations. The trade unions were equally correct in seeking the democratization of the functions of authority, but they created nonfunctional structures when they tried to "democratize" professional functions as well.

Unchanged structure of power

In view of the many conflicts that accumulated with the introduction of self-management, it would be impossible to discuss the further development of self-management without an attempt to locate the overall background of the phenomena described above. Sociological analyses testify that, in spite of the changes made, the structures of power within work organizations remained essentially the same. Although a rather far-reaching decentralization of jurisdictions took place, we find that the central organs of the enterprise still held dominant influence. And in spite of the fact that, in formal status, the collegium (top managerial staff) was only the director's advisory body, it played a leading role in work organizations.

The conclusions cited above can very probably be generalized to the majority of work organizations. And this means that, with all the structural changes up to now, we have not achieved a fundamental democratization within work organizations. By broadening self-management jurisdictions, we have in essence developed self-management only formally, without actually changing the structure of power. Further development of self-management in the same direction would thus mean only the development of self-management formalism and, at the same time, the legalization of the irresponsibility of those who have the decisive influence on events in the work organization.

Criticism of the self-management model

The majority of "technocrats" see the cause of the past formalization of self-management to lie in the utopian model of self-management which is in essence cooperative and, as such, no longer corresponds to the modern work organization with its specialized managerial function. Our investigations of seven industrial and sixteen handicraft work organizations showed the above assertions to be justified:[1] workers in handicrafts were substantially more informed than those in industry. On the basis of these differences, we could almost agree with the thesis that, in handicraft enterprises, because of the nonspecialized function of

1. *Samoupravna problematika u industrijskim i zanatskim radnim organizacijama* (Kranj: Zavod za organizaciju rada kranj, 1963).

management and the homogeneous skill structure, collective decision-making is possible, while, in work organizations in industry and in *similar* organizations, *self-management* in the sense of collective *decision-making* is impossible. The consequence would thus be the following: we must urgently develop a type of self-management that will correspond functionally to those organizations that have already achieved a high level of division of labor.

We could conclude our reflection with this finding and leave the concern for the further development of self-management to the organizers, if there were not data which urged us to disclose other factors that hinder the development of self-management.

The conflict between institutionalized and spontaneous participation

What is involved here are phenomena common to both handicraft and industrial work organizations—phenomena not of a technological but of a sociological nature. In industry, and still more in handicrafts, we observe a marked conflict between spontaneous participation of workers and institutionalized participation. We can cite at least four factors that unambiguously confirm the above assertion.[2]

a. In all work organizations, we observe that the spontaneous participation of workers in the organization of work in the narrower organizational unit and active participation in meetings are more frequent than the institutional possibilities for collaboration. This finding appears absurd, for the institutional possibilities should, in principle, limit spontaneous participation. Nevertheless, I interpret this phenomenon differently. Spontaneous participation actually exceeds the institutional possibilities primarily because it is directed to an area other than institutionalized activity.

b. This observation is confirmed by data that hold equally for all the work organizations included in the cited study: in basic organizational units, on the average, two times more workers collaborate in the area of work organization than in discussions about determining rules for the distribution of personal incomes; likewise, two times more proposals are made on work rationalization than on problems of incomes. This fact is all the more signif-

---

2. Ibid.

icant because it relates to a period when the political organizations had limited discussion almost exclusively to the topic of personal incomes and required work organizations to draw up rules for the distribution of net incomes. It is therefore obvious that spontaneous participation developed more strongly than and in a different direction from the activity pressed by self-management institutions.

c. Our analyses showed that more than 20 percent of the proposals made by workers concerning the improvement of work and business operation in the work organization are not considered by anyone at all. We also analyzed the causes and consequences of such lack of attention and found that the workers whose proposals were ignored today comprise the most negativistic group in work collectives, and that this represents a dangerous precedent for further self-management practice. We further discovered, however, that the undemocratic behavior of the top management in neglecting proposals is not at all the main reason why the spontaneous initiative of workers comes to naught.

And thus we arrive at the "original sin" of self-management. Because of its structure and mode of operation, self-management is incapable of developing initiative "from the bottom up." In order to do this, it was conceived as developing in two directions:

1) On the one hand, self-management should implement the rule of labor over capital; in this sense, the self-management organs should take over the functions of the former owner.

2) Self-management should be the broadest model of political integration of the working people into the general politics of our society.

The institutional implementation of these two goals, of course, necessarily brought forth very generalized self-management structures that were rather ill-adapted to individual work organizations and whose function was more to carry out the general conception of society than to create an integration of work collectives that would be based on spontaneous participation and to develop original models of work and social practice. The surmounting of these deductive[3] tendencies in the organism—a process whose basic import would be to create by inductive means[4] new forms of truly socialist social practice—would allow the merging of the

3. Based on inference from principles laid down a priori by the political leadership; in French text, "deductive" is replaced by "authoritarian"—*Trans.*

4. I.e., experimentally and spontaneously at the base level—*Trans.*

spontaneous participation of workers with institutionalized participation. Spontaneous participation sometimes may not be formalized, and thus may not influence the work of self-management organs, and still less the work of top managerial bodies.

The mode of operation of self-management organs is markedly deductive. It is limited to sending the central management organs proposals to examine particular acute problems; these may not even affect the agenda of the meeting. (The rare exceptions only confirm the rule.) For the most part, meetings of producers, instead of influencing the decisions of the central organs by prior discussion, merely consider conclusions already adopted by the central organs and thus are transformed into informative meetings. In short, the entire structure of self-management in work organizations functions executively, rather than being oriented above all toward developing and broadening initiative from the bottom up. It is no wonder, therefore, that not even the existing initiative of workers is wholly realized, much less that the present functioning of self-management fails to motivate more intensive participation.

Domination of the management over the collective

The predominance of deductive tendencies within self-management, and of course within the top management as well, also implies that at present the basic conflict in our work organizations is not between the directorial and the self-managerial line, but is still between the higher and lower organizational units—or, stated very simply, between the managerial staff and the workers. If the workers cannot implement their constructive initiatives and are condemned to the status of performers,[5] then the basic balance of power within the work organization is destroyed, and a basis is created for continual intensification of conflicts.

Perhaps the above assertion will be considered a completely anachronistic idea, valid largely for the period of administrative socialism. The majority of empirical data, however, show us precisely the opposite: we still find that directorial and self-management organs of higher levels are dominant over directorial and self-management organs of lower organizational units. Likewise

5. I.e., those who carry out decisions made by others—*Trans.*

we find that disciplinary sanctions are more often imposed on workers than on staff members.[6]

Educational defeatism

If the predominance of deductive tendencies and the related domination of top management over the work collective form the basic obstacle to the affirmation of initiative in work organizations with a high as well as a low level of division of labor, then it is obviously senseless to blame technology and its "laws" for the inadequate self-management activity of work collectives.

Instead, we often cite the inadequate level of education of workers and seek a solution in long-term prospects for enlightening and educating working people. From the standpoint of our findings, this thesis is incorrect, since those initiatives that already exist are seen to be ignored; in addition, this thesis implies that self-management is a matter of the distant future, when the entire working class has become academized. Since this educational pretext has mastered our consciousness to such an extent that the workers themselves submit to it, the thesis cited must be carried to the absurd: in every historical situation, the work collective or the working class as a whole will be—with respect to its education, its work culture, and its historical experience—to a certain extent inadequate to the tasks that will be placed before it by the historical situation. According to the logic of educational defeatism, we can accordingly postpone self-management into the imaginary future, to a time when, by who knows what miracle, the working class will completely master work and social problems. The performance of work presupposes that minimal work culture which is at the same time the legitimation for managing the social process of work. Understandably, there are differences: a higher work culture allows fuller participation; nonetheless, this differential logic cannot negate the overall view we have presented.[7]

---

6. *Aktualni problemi radničkog samoupravljanja* (Belgrade: Centar za radničko samoupravljanje republičkog veća SSJ, 1960).

7. I intentionally emphasize higher work culture that is a part of education. Let me mention also that research has shown that there is practically no connection between the level of education of workers' council members and the quality of their work in various work organizations, which means that the social system plays a very important role.

There are no anarchical tendencies in work organizations

We must therefore seek the basic prospects for the further development of self-management in the elimination of those social obstacles that fundamentally limit the already existing initiative of workers. We have said that these obstacles are hidden in the deductive strivings of self-management. Are they perhaps forgivable in light of the anarchical tendencies in work collectives?

Further research in work collective X showed that the strivings for greater discipline (integrative tendencies) among a third of the collective are stronger than the strivings for greater work independence.[8] Likewise, we found that the more inadequate the practice of the managerial personnel, the greater the strivings for independence. Centrifugal tendencies, therefore, result above all from the socially and professionally unsuitable practice of the managerial staff. In spite of conflicts, the majority of the work collective favors maintaining the staff of skilled craftsmen. Other studies yield similar results. The monograph cited also showed that the social interests of the skilled craftsmen do not differ from the interests of the workers, except in those cases in which the interests concern the performance of managerial functions held by the staff of craftsmen. Furthermore we find in the worker a desire for more intensive collaboration in self-management and often a readiness to assume functions in self-management organs.[9]

Let us cite one more fact—perhaps the most important. In three enterprises in which the existing distribution of influence was studied, the same basic tendency was found: all three work collectives tended toward a polyarchic structure of power. The exception was the strivings to reduce the influence of individual central organs of the enterprise (usually only of the collegium); in addition, the demands were strong to increase the influence of the professional services, of self-management organs in economic units, and of workers. The strivings of the collective were thus

---

8. *Položaj rukovodnog kadra u uslovima samoupravljanja* (Kranj: Zavod za organizovanje rada kranj, 1964).

9. *Tendencije i praksa neposrednog upravljanja u ekonomskim jedinicama* (Belgrade: Institut društvenih nauka, 1962); *Samoupravna problematika u industrijskim i zanatskim radnim organizacijama; Integracija radnika u podužeću* (Ljubljana: Institut za sociologiju, 1963); *Analiza mišljenja o samoupravljanju* (Ljubljana, 1963).

strongly nonanarchical and coincided with the theoretically determined optimal structure of influence (A. S. Tannenbaum).

In collectives, there are no conspiratorial strivings to eliminate managers; tensions between the managerial staff and the workers are not such as to jeopardize the unity of the collective; there is still a fairly general readiness to collaborate in self-management; a tendency prevails to take into account all factors in the work organization. Fear of social anarchy therefore cannot justify the predominance of deductive tendencies in self-management.

Communication between the work organization and society

It follows that the reasons for the predominance of deductive tendencies in self-management are to be sought not in the circumstances of work organizations but rather primarily in the inertia of administrative practice. Some analyses dealing with the status of the director and relations between the work organization and the local government call our attention to the fact that directors (or managerial personnel) have very close communication with the organs of the sociopolitical communities, while the self-management organs are, so to speak, left to themselves.

The "superiority" of the director and some managerial personnel is directly manifested in their accumulation of leading membership functions in organizations outside the enterprise,[10] as well as in the fact that meetings of producers are often composed of a majority of managerial personnel. The domination of managerial personnel over self-management organs is strengthened still more by the practices of local government bodies; these usually contact the directors or the managerial personnel of the enterprise and through them try to regulate relations with the work organizations. In addition, they are often ready to bypass self-management organs in order to realize their interests,[11] and in doing so they naturally push self-management in work organizations onto a sidetrack. While the influence of managerial personnel is strength-

10. *Direktor kao društveni radnik* (Zagreb: Savezni centar za obrazovanje rukovodnih kadrova u privredi, 1959).

11. *Prikazi i studije iz društvenog upravljanja* (Ljubljana: Zavod za društveno upravljanje, 1960).

ened by their communications outside the enterprise, the self-management organs are in fact isolated and limited to the work organization. The self-management organs do not integrate into higher self-management units, nor do they communicate with the self-management organs of neighboring or similar organizations. The subordination of the self-management organs to the influence of the directorial organs is unavoidable, and the localistic tendencies that break to the surface from time to time are thus understandable. In spite of the practice of the local government bodies as described above, the producers do not oppose the diversion of funds to the commune (but they seek greater influence and control over the expenditure of these funds).[12]

The role of sociopolitical organizations

We should also, of course, have dealt with the work organizations in the context of the overall economic system (plan, market). Only by examining that system and its influence on self-management within work organizations could we obtain more precise impressions of the prospects of self-management in our society. That, however, exceeds the framework of this discussion. Nevertheless, attention should be drawn to the current role of sociopolitical organizations in work organizations precisely for this reason, for the sociopolitical organizations should be a dynamic factor in the further development of self-management in our country. From past analyses, we must conclude that the political organizations make no essential contribution to greater coherence and activity of work collectives, nor do they fundamentally influence the conduct of business policy. Their action is limited, on the whole, to attempting to influence the personnel structure of the directorial and self-management organs. They hope in this way indirectly to influence the direction of the overall activity of the work organization. This means, however, that the sociopolitical organizations do not act to make self-management processes more dynamic "at the bottom," but appear as a control filter "at the summit." Their activity is thus more strongly oriented to the organization of the directorial organs than to the activization of the self-managers.

12. *Aktivnost radnih ljudi u samoupravljanju radnom organizacijom* (Zagreb: Institut za društveno upravljanje).

Prospects

Since it is not possible to propose here what should be done for the further development of participatory democracy in our country, I shall limit myself to the following conclusion: our present social system still burdens self-management with so many hindrances that without substantial changes in structure it is difficult to imagine successful development of self-management, and consequently the more active participation of working people.

Workers' Movement, Workers' Control, and Self-management

14. Strategy for Labor

ANDRÉ GORZ

Formal recognition of the union organization and of civil liberties on the job remains an abstract demand, incapable of mobilizing the workers as long as it is not organically linked to the demand for concrete workers' powers over the conditions of work. The former demands are not ends in themselves; the organization and its civil liberties have value only insofar as they permit the pursuit of substantial workers' powers.

And these substantial powers . . . consist of union control over all aspects of the work situation, in order to:

1) subordinate and adapt the exigencies of the production process to the needs of the workers;

2) narrow the sphere of management's arbitrary powers;

3) install, finally, a true workers' counter-power, capable of challenging and of positively counterbalancing the capitalist system of decision making in the company (and by extension in the society).

These three aspects, implied in the demand for workers' control over the work situation, are in fact more concrete as themes for mobilization and action than the simple wage demand which they necessarily involve. The impenetrability of the overall production process, the workers' ignorance of the economic and technical decisions which determine the conditions of their activity, force them in practice to leave the substance of their work entirely up to managerial control. In most cases, the union now negotiates nothing but the minimum price of labor power, leaving the employer free to exploit the labor force as he sees fit and to dispense premiums and bonuses over which he often has sole control and which, by definition, are not contractually negotiable.

An increase in the basic wage either has no practical effect, or may be cancelled by a number of devices, including intensification of labor (that is, the extortion of supplementary work in the same time—a speed-up), cutting various bonuses; or the introduction of new machines which make the job more complex without granting promotions and higher wages; or demoting workers on certain jobs, a demotion which may not be accompanied by a wage cut but which entails in any case a professional devaluation for the workers concerned, a halt in the development of their capacities, and the loss of autonomy in their work.

General demands for increased wages cannot, in such a situation, improve the deteriorating condition of the worker; they cannot bring about a reduction in the rate of exploitation or of profit; they cannot even measure the impact of the proposed wage increase on the rate of exploitation and of profit. But above all, in big industry, wage demands cannot adequately cover situations as diverse as those of the laborer, the semi-skilled and skilled worker, the specialist, and the technician, whose incomes vary in each case according to sex, region, city, company, and shop.

The existing great differences in working conditions and wage levels within the same industry and for the same type of work make it impossible to mobilize the working class around general and undifferentiated demands concerning the minimum and hourly rates. . . .

This is further evidence that general and undifferentiated slogans are incapable of uniting and mobilizing a working class which itself is differentiated to an extreme; they are incapable of launching an offensive against the employers' discretionary powers over economic and technical matters, against the contradictory evolution of productivity, wages, and profits.

This is why the first task of the working class movement today is to elaborate a new strategy and new goals which will indivisibly unite wage demands, the demand for control, and the demand for self-determination by the workers of the conditions of work. The only way to unite and mobilize a differentiated working class at present is to attack the class power of the employers and of the State; and the only way to attack the class power of the employers and the State is to wrest from each employer (and from the State) a vital piece of his power of decision and control.

Concretely, the goal of this attack should not be to achieve modifications and accommodations of the workers' condition within the framework of a given management policy and a given stage in the technological development of the industry; for such a victory, besides being non-generalizable beyond the individual company, could rapidly be taken away from the workers, as rapidly as improvements in techniques and in the organization of production permit. On the contrary, the working class movement must demand permanent power to determine, by contract, all aspects of the work situation and the wage scale, so that all modifications in the productive process must be negotiated with the workers, and so that the workers can materially influence the management of the enterprise and orient it in a given direction.

For example:

—The union should be able to control the training schools to ensure that they do not train robots, mutilated individuals with limited horizons and a life burdened by ignorance, but professionally autonomous workers with virtually all-sides skills, capable of advancing in their jobs at least as fast as technological development.

—The union should be able to control the organization of work and the personnel system, to guarantee that personnel and organizational changes are made with the aim of developing the workers' faculties and professional autonomy, and not the contrary. Young workers especially should not be confined to one particularly degrading task.

—The union should thus exercise its power over the division of labor, on the company and industry level, to keep abreast of the given techniques of production and their foreseeable evolution. It should be able to impose on the employers, in each enterprise, that level and structure of employment which will result in the adoption of optimum production techniques and organization from the workers' point of view, thus guaranteeing that technological and human progress will coincide.

—The union should be able to negotiate the speed or rhythm of work, the piecework rate, the qualifications required for a job, the hours—all of which implies a continuous surveillance and negotiation of technological changes and their effects on the workers' condition, as well as the power to influence them.

—Finally, the union should demand a collective output bonus, that is to say a premium which is dependent neither on individual productivity nor on profits, but on production accomplished in a fixed number of working hours. This premium, which should be added to the basic wage (and a raise in this wage should be demanded simultaneously) constitutes a first step toward workers' control over the distribution of company revenue among labor costs, investments, and amortization—that is to say, a first step toward workers' self-management.

The purpose of this collective output premium is threefold:

1. First, the object is to take out of management's hands the annual bonuses which now are distributed as presents or as "no strike payoffs" at management's pleasure and whim. These bonuses must fall within the union's power of negotiation and should be based on objective criteria.

2. The annual premium must be linked to the true level of collective productivity, that is to say to the level of production in a fixed number of working hours. The right to negotiate this premium necessarily means that the union must have access to all information concerning the evolution of productivity in the enterprise, the real or potential evolution of profit, and, consequently, the management's policy itself.

3. On the basis of this information the union should be able to present effective opposition against any intensification of the rate of exploitation, against any enlargement in the sphere of management's power. The union will be in a position to ensure that erroneous commercial policies such as overproduction or dumping will not be carried out at the expense of the workers. It will be able to adjust its demands in such a way as to limit from the beginning whatever freedom of action the employer gains by the augmentation of productivity. In the long run the union should be able to negotiate the proportions of the company budget allocated to investment, reserves, direct and indirect wages, free time, and social expenditures, and it will thus exercise a power of control and veto over the entire management policy. Within the framework of this battle—whose general objectives are adaptable to each particular local situation and which embraces the most varied demands and specific problems in a single class perspective—there is quite naturally another fight, namely the battle for the recognition and autonomy of the labor organization in the enterprise. The latter is not the ultimate goal; it is rather the indis-

pensable means which gives the workers the power to challenge and to control management policy and to determine and to impose their own policy regarding working conditions; for it is at work that the workers experience the power of capital and their conflict with society most directly. If the transformation of society and the political power of the working class are to have a meaning, then the workers must master their oppressive condition at work.

Of course this battle will not lead to the immediate abolition of profit; it will not give *power* to the working class; it will not result in the abolition of capitalism. Victory will only lead to new battles, to the possibility of new partial victories. And at each of its stages, above all in its first phase, the battle will end with a compromise. Its path will be beset with pitfalls. The union will have to make certain agreements with management. The union will be unable to reject management's power as a whole, to challenge capitalist policy as a whole. The union will have to "dirty its hands." With each compromise, with each agreement at the end of a battle, it will endorse the employers' power with its signature. . . .

Should we reject an economic policy based on profit? Should the working class take power? Should we refuse to endorse the employers' power? Of course; that goes without saying. But the workers endorse the employers' power every day, by punching in on time, by submitting to an organization of labor over which they have no power, by collecting their wages. They thereby accept the profit system; the power of the working class remains for them a dream. Does this mean, at least, that they or the union which represents them do not dirty their hands, that they remain free to reject the whole system altogether? That may be true. But their challenge and their rejection of capitalism remain on the level of general intentions and speechmaking; the challenge is abstract, its purity is sterile. The workers lack the means to turn their rhetoric into hard facts. The power of the employer and of capital remain intact. The workers lack positive accomplishments. They end up by falling into all the traps they had hoped to avoid.

For example, in order to avoid class collaboration more effectively, the union loses interest in company- and industry-wide agreements. Collective agreements are tacitly annulled or let fall into abeyance because the union does nothing to renew them when they expire. Company level agreements are not signed at the end of strikes because the union does not want to recognize the employer's power. In order not to compromise itself, the union leadership does not present a list of demands and grievances; it organizes delaying actions which express a vague discontent and diffuse protest. Then they wait for management to make offers. No negotiation with the enemy: a verbal agreement replaces a signed contract, and the union keeps its hands clean.

What does it gain from this? A clear conscience and the feeling of independence; that is to say, in practical terms—in terms of a victory over capitalist policy—nothing. And what does the employer lose? Precisely nothing: he also keeps his independence and the power to run the company as he wishes, that is, to amortize and invest according to *his* program, to install the machines which *he* wants, to impose the rhythm and organization of labor and the personnel system which seem to *him* the most advantageous, and even to pay his manpower according to the planned budget. For we must have no illusions: the safes of the modern big businesses do not contain large wads of banknotes which the workers can hope to snatch away from their greedy bosses; these safes contain only programs. And these programs have their margin of security: they are calculated in such a manner that the foreseeable wage demands will not compromise the plan of production or the plan of amortization and investment (with their predicted variations in terms of possible economic fluctuations).

The dominant tendency in large modern industry is no longer that of maximum exploitation of its workers by means such as the individual bonus and the whip. The dominant tendency (with numerous exceptions which, however, represent the past and not the future) is to "integrate the workers." The modern employer knows that the piecework system does not "pay" any more; he knows even better that in a large enterprise where fixed capital is more important than circulating capital, regularity matters more than anything else. To obtain regularity, individual output must not be stimulated too much: each increase will be followed by a decrease. Five per cent of the workers who produce double or triple the norm are less interesting than a whole shop producing one hundred per cent of the norm permanently and on the average, and this average, moreover, represents the sum of three distinct levels of effort: a third of the workers producing at eighty per cent, a third at one hundred per cent, and a final third producing at one hundred and twenty per cent of the average output, for example.

To obtain this regularity, the employer foresees the unpredictable, especially wage demands. The tactics of the "clean handed union" thus do not bother him at all. These tactics leave the employer the power which is most important to him: the power of decision and of control; the power to determine the increases to which he will be forced to consent, in order to maintain these increases within the margins which he has fixed, and to shield these margins from all effective challenge.

Thus the union falls prey to "integration" even in the demands which it advances and the concessions which it obtains. Foreseen by management's program, these demands are integrated from the beginning into the budget and encroach very little on management's policy. Nor does the union succeed in effectively challenging a planned layoff by protest movements: the cost of protest strikes is foreseen in the company budget, and the layoffs will take place as planned after the "challenge" is over. In this way union action remains without a grip on the employer's decisions and on the details of his policy, precisely because union action rejects them totally; this rejection is itself one of the elements in management's policy. And this policy remains sovereign in practice. The employer keeps the initiative: it is he who constantly confronts the union with new situations of an economic, structural, technical, or organizational order, situations which affect the professional status, the careers, the lives of the workers, situations which force them to move in the direction intended by the employer's strategy. The union has no choice but to say "yes" or "no," and its "no" has no consequence, results in no visible progress in the succession of battles which the workers carry out. The same type of battle is always repeated, and the workers always return to the point of departure.

In this way the challenge remains abstract, does not become concrete, and does not progress. There is no meaningful link between its goals of reduction and suppression of exploitation, negotiation of all elements of wages, guarantee of employment and career, elevation of living standard according to needs, abolition of the dictatorship of profit, and its daily actions. The goals stand on one side and the actions on the other, and there is no progress from one to the other.

If, on the other hand, the union seizes control of the elements on the basis of which management policy is worked out, if it anticipates the employer's decisions, if at each step it presents its own alternative solution, and if it fights on that basis, then it will challenge capitalist policy more effectively than a hundred fiery speeches. The union will be in a position to exercise control over technical, productive, and professional developments, to push them in the optimum social, economic, and human direction. This means, for example, that instead of fighting against layoffs and reorganization plans, the union should fight *for* a plan of reorganization, reclassification, and re-employment, a plan whose every aspect is under permanent union control. Instead of fighting against new machines and the new organization of labor which these impose, it should fight over the type of machines, the process of their installation, the future organization of labor, the future job classifications, before the reorganization takes place. Instead of fighting against the intensification of exploitation, the union should fight to gain control over the program of amortization and investment to assure that the workers benefit from it.

Does the union, by acting in this way, accept the capitalist system? In a sense, it does, without a doubt; but I have already said that it also accepts the system by pretending to reject it and by enduring it. But the important thing is not to have to endure it: it must be accepted only in order to change it, to modify its bases, to counter it point by point and at each step, in order to force it to go where the workers want it to go; in short, in order to bring capitalism to a crisis and to force it to retreat to a different battlefield. And with each partial victory, with each reconversion, merger, reorganization, investment, or layoff prevented or imposed by the union, the workers' power is strengthened, the workers' level of consciousness rises; the freedom of the employers—capitalism's sphere of sovereignty—is diminished, and the essential weakness of the system is displayed: the contradiction between the logic of profit and the needs and exigencies of men.

Is this class collaboration? Unquestionably that would be the case if the union accepted the responsibilities of "cooperation" with management, if the union lost sight of its goal, which is not a little more prosperity at any price, but the emancipation of the workers and the achievement of their right to determine their own condition; it would be class collaboration if the union agreed to participate in the elaboration of policy decisions and guaranteed their execution. But precisely this participation, advocated by the *"concertistes,"*[1] must be firmly rejected. It is not a

1. "Concertistes" are advocates of closer cooperation between labor and management. (Translators' note.)

question of elaborating a neo-paternalistic company policy with management; it is a matter of opposing a union policy to that of management, of struggling for a company-, industry-, and region-wide plan, a well-elaborated and coherent plan, one which demonstrates concretely the opposition between the desirable and the possible, on the one hand, and a profit-oriented reality on the other hand.

Clearly, the battle must be concluded with a settlement, a compromise. The only ones to be shocked by this would be the left wing extremists, with whom Lenin already clashed, pointing out that there are good compromises and bad compromises. Under the circumstances, compromise would be bad if the union renounced its plan and its perspectives, in order to settle for an intermediate solution. But why should it renounce its plan? The settlement which concludes the battle simply signifies that all of the plan's objectives could not be obtained: the union has reached a compromise on the basis of the employer's adoption of a substantial part of its plan; and the union exercises its control over this plan. Thus the battle ends with a partial victory, won by force, and with a "moral" victory which, in this case, is complete. For in the course of the struggle, the workers' level of consciousness has risen; they know perfectly well that all their demands are not satisfied, and they are ready for new battles. They have experienced their power; the measures which they have imposed on management go in the direction of their ultimate demands (even though they did not obtain complete satisfaction). By compromising they do not renounce their goal; on the contrary, they move closer to it. By reaching a settlement the union does not alienate its autonomy (no more than when it accepts an eight per cent raise although it has asked for twelve per cent); it does not endorse management's plan; on the contrary, it forces management to guarantee (with union control) the execution of the essentials of the union plan.

Such is the strategy which begins to establish the power of the union to negotiate all aspects of the work situation, to diminish thereby the autonomy of the employer and, by extension, the class power of management and the State. This is not an institutional union power; it is rather a positive and antagonistic power of challenge which leaves union autonomy intact. This power, once it is achieved after necessarily long and hard struggles,[2] will

2. This particularism at present develops precisely because a perspective which tightly links local demands to class action is lacking.

establish a permanent and continuous challenge to management decisions; it will permit the union to anticipate these decisions, to influence them before they are made; it will place the workers in an offensive, not a defensive position; it will elevate their level of consciousness and competence; it will deepen their knowledge of the productive process; it will force them to specify their goals, scaled according to a strategic and programmatic vision, goals which they intend to oppose to the capitalist plan on the company, industry, and regional levels and on the level of the national economy; it will give rise to partial and local demands (which is today not the case) within the framework of an overall and coherent perspective of response ("alternative") to monopoly capitalism, a perspective which will reciprocally influence and clarify the local demands; and in this way it will stimulate a continually resurging struggle with more and more advanced goals, at a higher and higher level.

Thus, the demand for workers' power in the enterprise does not necessarily signify the development of particularism or of company "patriotism." On the contrary, this demand will have a militant and mobilizing substance, a meaning and a chance of success, insofar—but insofar only—as it is conceived as a local adaptation of an overall reponse to the model of capitalist development. This demand requires such an overall vision to be effective on the political level (on the level of the big decisions regarding national development and economic policy) , just as political action requires the support of mobilized and militant masses; it requires this vision not only in order to make progress, but also and above all in order to establish itself as a popular counterpower capable of overcoming the obstructive power of the private and public centers of decision making in a decentralized and non-bureaucratic manner.

Thus, the demand for and the exercise of workers' power, of self-determination and control, quite naturally lead to a challenge of the priorities and purposes of the capitalist model.

15. Workers' Power

SERGE MALLET

. . . This rapid glance at the workers' struggles that occurred after May 1968 permits one to draw . . . certain conclusions:

a. Wage claims in the strict sense (struggle for increasing the nominal wage) are rarely the principal objective of the struggles. Certainly, they are translated only infrequently into strike movements. Everything proceeds as if wage negotiation, since it is admitted by the system, were in some way abandoned to the trade union bureaucracy, at least where the latter is recognized by the employers. This explains, for example, the weak impact of general slogans such as the return to the sliding scale of wages and prices: it is a matter of a demand on which the workers know they cannot act directly in any case; it eludes their control.

b. In contrast, while general wage claims are abandoned to technical discussion of "social partners," there are no norms for determining these. Confronted with the increased complexity—very often artificial—of methods of remuneration, the workers seek to control the way in which they are carried out. This demand is oriented in two, sometimes contradictory directions:

—One tends toward the simplification of forms of remuneration, the guarantee of the elimination of employer arbitrariness.

Reprinted from *Pouvoir ouvrier* (Paris: Éditions Anthropos, 1971), pp. 215–21, by permission of the publisher. Translated by Helen Kramer.

The only demand totally accepted by the entire working class during this period was that of making wages monthly.

—On the other hand, there continue to exist innumerable forms of wage bonuses institutionalized some years ago, based on premiums for risk, unhealthfulness, and insecurity of work.

It is here that the nature of the demand was changed and it came to deal with the conditions of work themselves.

c. The discussion of conditions of work has certainly been integrated into collective bargaining for a long time. Nevertheless, at this level it is always converted into discussions on raising wages. Traditional trade unionism has renounced fighting for the effective modification of work conditions and has transformed their most scandalous aspects (accident risks, unhealthfulness, nervous tension) into so many more benefits of particular wage earners. The strikes that break out over these points and tend to impose the change of work conditions authoritatively—slowdowns, refusal of certain types of work, etc.—then inevitably take place outside the trade union organizations, which the workers do not trust to resolve this type of problem.

d. This generalization of wildcat strikes bearing on objectives not covered by the habitual trade union practice does not at all signify hostility of the workers toward their organizations: quite simply, they have the impression that the matter at point is something that is not within the purview of the unions.

One can explain in this way the role sometimes played in the start of these actions by political groups which, in spite of a very weak numerical base, assert a role relevant to traditional trade union activity. I refer here not to the enterprise cells of the Communist Party, the action of which generally is limited to propaganda and which are more the transmission of the trade union section of the General Confederation of Labor (CGT) than the reverse, but of various leftist groups (Maoists of the *Gauche prolétarienne,* Trotskyists of *Lutte ouvrière*) or sections and enterprise groups of the Parti Socialiste Unifie (PSU), present today—and this only since May 1968—in all the important enterprises. This role played by political groups, a role often exaggerated in the attacks made against them by the employers and the CGT, should be put in its proper place. It is the expression of the crisis of traditional trade unionism, whose institutionalized forms of action (the strike with advance notice, decided upon by consultation of all the employees) appear as inadequate as the nature of the demands ("consumerist") it puts forth.

It does not signify disaffection of the workers with trade unionism itself. The best proof of this fact—and this is true for strikes in France as well as for what are called wildcat strikes in Germany, Italy, or Sweden—is that almost everywhere, it is trade union militants who have been the instigators and slogan bearers of the strikes. Although they are not assured of the support of the industrial federations and the national centrals, and are sometimes opposed by them, the strikes voted by the trade union channel to the base; they tend, in fact, to revalue the trade union section of the enterprise in relation to the vertical and horizontal organization of the confederations.

Besides, all the struggles whose objective is control have been negotiated by the trade union channel, the trade union organization always finding itself "controlled" in the course of the negotiations by delegates sprung directly from the general assemblies of strikers.

e. If, in addition, we analyze the various aspects of the struggle for control, we find that, depending on the enterprise, it follows one of two different courses:

1. In the modern sectors of production characterized by capital intensity, the content of these struggles can express itself in a will to take over control of management itself. . . . In all cases, sectors directly or indirectly relevant to the state sector are involved, and all such struggles attack measures that favor the progressive privatization of this sector.

The governmental counteroffensive based on "progress agreements," initiated precisely in the state sector, can appear to have partly the object of counteracting this tendency by orienting it toward "consumerist" aspects through a renewal of the well-worn theme of "the workers' interest in benefits."

But the mere fact of hereafter linking the determination of wages to the management of the enterprise risks on the contrary spontaneously orienting the trade unions themselves toward demands for control of management: the determination of costs of production, then control of equipment and supply markets, control of investments and product markets, indeed, the determination of the ends of production, intervene in the elements of wage determination.

This type of contractual relations dissipates the mystifying notion of a free labor market. The objective integration of workers in the enterprise, thus institutionalized, facilitates the transition of trade unionist consciousness into the consciousness of a managing class—the will to acquire control of the enterprise by the workers and for the workers—and then into political consciousness, with this demand developing at the level of the large national sectors and against the policy put into effect by the state.

2. The struggle for workers' control in the more traditional sectors of production and services assumes a more defensive character. The struggle against speedups and for work security, the improvement of hours, and control of determination of wage norms does not express itself directly in terms of control of management, but teaches the workers not to accept as a given fact the norms of employer exploitation, which are most oppressive in precisely this sector.

In the proper sense of the term, these are still "economic struggles" that do not call into question the ends of production. How could it be otherwise, since most of the time they unfold either in particular sectors of the enterprise, which have no economic autonomy, or in subcontracting enterprises?

They are, then, nothing but struggles of resistance against capitalist exploitation. But the very terms of this resistance take the form of *nonintegrable* demands. The struggle against the productivity of labor—that is to say, here, against physical overexploitation—disequilibrates the competitive system in which the modern sector of production prospers. In refusing to transform their demands for dignity of life into integrable wage demands at the price of a mild inflation, in refusing to be paid a few centimes more an hour for risking their life and health, the workers of these enterprises are calling into question the system of unequal development of the French economy, the internal colonial pact that assures the proliferation of small and medium-sized enterprises and the superprofits of the large enterprises.

Simultaneously, these struggles manifest for the first time in a long time the revolt of the traditional working class against what Paul Lafargue denounced as "this strange madness that has seized the European working class: the moribund passion of work pushed up to the exhaustion of the vital forces of the individual." This is the most direct product of the trauma that May 1968 left in the consciousness of the worker: while the demands with a managerial orientation experienced a *qualitative* development in the modern sectors of industry in May 1968, one could find indications of this in the social conflicts since 1956—these are the elements I analyzed in 1963 in *La nouvelle classe ouvrière*. In contrast, calling into question the ends of work, surpassing the simple wage demand, is an entirely new phenomenon in the unskilled working class.

The two movements in fact join each other. Both call into question "trade unionism of antagonistic participation."

16. The Trade Union as Opposition

KEN COATES AND TONY TOPHAM

The multi-plant company has of course been with us for a long time. Since the turn of this century, when firms in cement, chemicals and cotton led the movement to form cartels and trusts, to be followed during the 'twenties and 'thirties by outbreaks of rationalisation and mergers in steel, shipbuilding and again chemicals, an increasing proportion of British workers have found themselves employed by companies with several centres of manufacture. But the spate of mergers and take-overs experienced in the past ten years has transformed the industrial landscape and created an entirely new situation.

In the decade between 1949 and 1958, £1,060 million was expended by UK companies on take-overs, a figure which represented 9.5 per cent of their funds. The comparable figure for the *single year* of 1969 was over £6,000 million, representing more than 16 per cent of their funds. During the 'sixties, 45 of the top 120 UK companies lost their independent existence through the process of merger and take-over. . . .

A factor of increasing significance is the multi-national nature of many of these companies. In the world's car industry, for example, six companies—General Motors, Ford, Chrysler, Volkswa-

Reprinted from *The New Unionism* (London: Peter Owen, 1972), pp. 86–91, 94–95, by permission of the publisher.

gen, Fiat and British Leyland—control more than 80 per cent of the total world output. In 1968 nearly three million cars from the assembly lines of these firms came from plants located outside the parent company's home country. . . .

We may take one or two examples of British-based multi-nationals in other industries. The giant General Electric–Associated Electrical Industries–English Electric Company, which quadrupled its size through mergers in two years, 1968–69, operates through 120 subsidiary companies in the UK and owns 95 overseas subsidiaries in Europe, Australia, New Zealand, Africa, Asia and the Americas. In Britain alone it employs 220,000 workers. Dunlop International, Ltd., employs 100,000 workers in 120 plants spread across 26 countries and 5 continents. Sixty per cent of its business is done outside the UK. These figures refer to Dunlop alone; since its merger with Pirelli, it has doubled its size and now ranks second only to Goodyear amongst world rubber manufacturers.

It is clear that in this kind of structure the problems of industrial democracy and workers' control take on a new dimension. The international company can play one national group of workers off against another—as, for example, when the motor companies continually threaten, during strikes in one country, to shift production to another country. The transnational giant firm has a literally world-wide choice of sites for development, between which it can pick and choose according to its assessments of relative labor costs, and according to the degree of sympathy shown it by governments, in taxation policy, grants, loans, trade-union laws and so forth. It is to a large extent beyond the legislative control of national governments, because it exists in a higher dimension, in which it can shift its resources almost at will and conceal its financial and ownership structures. It goes without saying that its centres of authority are so remote that purely plant-level trade unionism or workers' control strategies will never come to grips with them. It stands as the ultimate example of pyramided arbitrary, unaccountable private power in industry and society. And it makes the general political and social case for workers' control and social accountability even more relevant and convincing; for the interests of the giant corporation do not at all apparently or in reality coincide with the social and economic interests of the communities within which they operate. When the GEC (or Dunlop, or Ford) decides to close plant A in country B, and to expand plant C in country D, it is concerned solely with its own interests, as measured by its overall financial balances and by its need to strengthen its competitive position in relation to the other, rival monsters in its industry.

The trade-union movement has constantly adapted itself, throughout its history, to the changing technology and industrial structures with which it aims to bargain. Craft, industrial and general unions arose in Britain in turn, to meet particular stages of the Industrial Revolution, in successive attempts to create structures which would match the needs of workers. Similar evolution has taken place in other countries. In the United States, the outmoded craft unionism of the American Federation of Labor was challenged by the more radical and appropriate industrial unions of the Congress of Industrial Organizations. Whatever their names or their origins, the unions which most successfully cope with the phenomenon of the multi-plant company—which is often also a company operating not in one, but several industries—are those which spread their recruitment policies across the board. "Industrial unionism" was the chosen instrument of an older movement for workers' control in the 1910–22 era. Today the rigid schemes for "one union, one industry" are more likely to be favoured by governments and employers, who prefer a neat, vertical, orderly structure which is more easy to divide and control, in accordance with their interests. The pace of industrial change, moreover, is so rapid that a union which has all its eggs in the basket of a single industry is vulnerable to that very process of combined decline and innovation which is most easily observed in the fuel and transport industries, and which has left industrial unions like those of the miners and railwaymen stranded in industries which are being tapered away. The effects on the morale, the leadership quality and the militancy of the victims were all too evident in those cases, until recently.

Of course, workers anticipate changes in union structure and control long before the slow-moving processes of trade-union reform catch up with changes in industry. The shop stewards threw up their Combine Committees precisely in order to meet the problem of the multi-plant firm and the inadequacies of national union structures. It is within such committees that workers' control programmes which are appropriate for the large companies can be worked out. But as unions respond to the new needs, programmes and policy-making can be fed back into the large, conglomerate trade unions themselves, and, provided such unions are democratised and genuinely service their members with adequate communications, the whole process of matching the unity of the large employer with unity on the workers' side can be assisted.

But something more is needed if an adequate trade-union strategy is to emerge to confront the multi-national company. . . .

Individual trade unions in several countries, faced with the problems of the international motor companies, have not waited upon the formalities of the trade secretariats and have commenced the process of working out common policies and strategies to be applied, say, in Ford plants throughout the world. The British TGWU and AEU, for example, broke new ground in 1969 by organising a policy seminar on the car industry with the leaders of the American United Automobile Workers' Union. In order to achieve full international coverage between Western European and American workers, it will be necessary for the British and Americans to break free of the old divisions between communist and non-communist unions, since the majority of trade unionists in France and Italy, two of the key countries in these regions, are organised into unions with communist affiliations. The threat of the international company is in fact pushing both communist and non-communist unions towards each other, and away from the crippling hostilities of the past. This is a difficult process; it will be greatly assisted as and when workers press their unions to adopt genuinely international attitudes, and to develop appropriate workers' control programmes which stress the common interests and objectives of American, British, German, French and Italian workers. This process will be helped by progressive forces in both camps, and hindered by the old dogmatisms, which in England for instance are represented by the NUGMW and in France by the CGT. . . .

If we apply our four watchwords to this idea, we can begin to see the emergence of a strategy and a programme: information, representation, veto, supervision. We can illustrate the application of the strategy from a case which did not arise in Britain, but which did involve a British-based international company, Dunlop's. In February 1970 Dunlop's Canadian division announced publicly, with no prior warning or consultation with unions, that it would close its Toronto factory on 1st May, making 600 workers redundant. It argued that international competition—from Europe and Japan—made the factory unprofitable. Dunlop is, as we have shown, a very big slice indeed of "international competition." Whilst it was prepared to close the Toronto plant, it was opening a factory in the United States, was busy merging with the widespread Pirelli empire, and actually obtaining a public loan from Canadian authorities to automate another plant in Canada.

The workers in the factory, through their union branch, expressed complete scepticism, therefore, as to the company's reasons for closure. They suspected that the plant was perfectly viable, but was being closed because profits (in a fairly high wage area) did not come up to the level which Dunlop expected from other locations.

The union branch therefore mounted an all-out campaign behind a number of carefully thought out demands. They demanded (1) that the company postpone the closure of the plant, (2) that the time so obtained should be used to carry out a feasibility study, by the Ontario Government, the union and co-opted experts, which would establish the true financial and economic position of the factory, (3) that the company should consider an offer by the workers to buy the plant from it, using their severance pay (which would amount to 2 million Canadian dollars) if the feasibility study was favourable (the workers proposed in that case to run the plant as a co-operative), and (4) that the Ontario Government should pass a new law which would require companies to justify all closure decisions in future, and submit to feasibility studies where these were requested by the workers.

The workers in this case obtained massive public support for their campaign; the New Democratic Party (Canada's Labour Party) took up the matter as a major issue, challenging the refusal of the (Tory) Provincial Government to take any action. Two professors of economics lent their professional support to the workers' case. Moreover, the union reached out to mobilise international trade-union opinion in its support. Telegrams and appeals were sent to unions in Britain (the home of the Dunlop headquarters) and to the International Chemical Workers' Secretariat in Geneva. British MPs raised the question of the arbitrary nature of the closure decision in the House of Commons. Contact was made between the Canadian union and the British Dunlop shop stewards. This case is a pioneering example; its failure to prevent the closure should not be taken as a failure of a strategy which is still in infancy. . . .

Ultimately, what must emerge from the process of internationalising the trade-union movement, is a programme which is capable, through workers' control, of *anticipating* arbitrary decisions. The Canadian workers were still in the defensive position of *reacting after* the decision was announced. Workers' control should be established internationally over hiring and firing, over labor organisation at the level of each plant, but pre-eminently over investment decisions. It is these latter decisions which determine, months and years in advance of the event, which plants will close and which will expand. These decisions are not taken at plant level. The trade-union demand for the opening of the books, and for "feasibility studies" conducted in advance of decisions, is highly relevant at the international company level.

PART IV

Economics

General

1. Identifying the Participatory Economy

JAROSLAV VANEK

We must start our discussion by explaining what we understand by the participatory—or labor-managed—economy. The matter is not a simple one because any definition at this stage of history must be a judicial balancing of what we observe in the real world and what we can identify as the most desirable form of participatory economy on grounds of a priori scientific judgment. To say that the participatory economy is exactly the type of economy we find today in Yugoslavia would be as incorrect and one-sided as to say that labor management consists of a number of abstract principles unrelated to any real experience or actual performance.

Fortunately, there is another factor which will help us in seeking a definition. We do not have to identify the participatory economy down to the minutest detail, there being a very large number of characteristics which may be termed nonessential and which can be adjusted to particular situations or circumstances. For example, a number of minor characteristics of the participatory economy of Yugoslavia could certainly be omitted or replaced by others—indeed, this might be highly desirable—if a specific labor-managed economy were designed for, say, a country

Reprinted from Jaroslav Vanek: *The Participatory Economy: An Evolutionary Hypothesis and a Strategy for Development,* pp. 7–14.

of Latin America or Africa. We thus have to concentrate here only on what we may term basic characteristics of a system of economic participation; the rest can be left for adaption to specific conditions. In fact it is this adaptability that makes—or at least promises to make—the participatory economy universally appealing.

To use an analogy, we may liken the labor-managed economy —or for that matter, any economy—to a motor vehicle. If we want to become acquainted with the vehicle, we should learn principally about two things: one, what are the vehicle's main component parts, and two, what is its moving force? Accordingly, we will first introduce a set of defining characteristics of the labor-managed economy, and then explain what its principal moving force is—that is, the motivation on which economic actions within it are actually taken. Pushing the analogy a step further, we may also ask how the vehicle compares with other vehicles in respect to the main component parts. And going still another step, we may want to learn how the moving force—that is, the motor—compares with that of other vehicles. These other aspects of characterization by comparison will also concern us in this chapter.

The first of our five defining characteristics is quite obvious. The labor-managed or participatory economy is one based on, or composed of, firms controlled and managed by those working in them. This *participation in management* is by *all* and on the basis of equality, that is, on the principle of one man, one vote.[1] It is to be carried out in the most efficient manner—in the majority of cases through elected representative bodies and officers: a workers' council, an executive board, and the director of the firm.

Clearly, the exact form of labor management that is most efficient can vary from enterprise to enterprise and from one labor-managed economy to another, and as such need not concern us here. It could not be overemphasized that the participation in control and management derives uniquely and unalterably from *active* participation in the enterprise. Participation in ownership in no way and under no circumstances entails the right to control and manage; whether active participants are also owners of the assets of the firm or whether they contribute to the formation of such assets through undistributed earnings, it is not these contributions but their active participation that entitles them to control and manage.

The second general characteristic is related to and, in a sense, derives from the first. It is *income sharing.* The participants of the labor-managed firm, after they have paid for all material and other costs of operation, share in the income of the enterprise. This sharing is to be equitable, equal for labor of equal intensity and quality, and governed by a democratically agreed-on income-distribution schedule assigning to each job its relative claim on total net income. Of course, not all net income needs to be distributed to individual participants; a collectively agreed-on share can be used for reserve funds, various types of collective consumption or investment. In the last mentioned instance, however, . . . it may be preferable to recognize the contributions of savings to the firm's capital formation as individual claims of each participant, and express them in the form of fixed interest bearing financial obligations of the firm. Of course, recalling our first defining characteristic, such financial claims cannot under any circumstances carry a right to control or management of the firm.

These considerations of financing bring us to the third basic characteristic of participatory economies. The working community which has the exclusive right to control and manage the activities of the firm does not, as such, have the full ownership—in the traditional sense of the word *ownership*—of the capital assets which it uses. Perhaps the term *usufructus,* the right of enjoying the fruits of material goods, is a more appropriate one. The working community can enjoy the fruits of production in which the plant and equipment were used, but it must pay for this a contractual fee—or rental, or interest on the financial liability brought about by the purchases of such real assets. The community cannot destroy the real assets or sell them and distribute the proceeds as current income. In turn, the lenders of financial capital have no right of control whatsoever over the physical assets of the firm as long as the working community meets its debt-servicing obligations; the same holds for those who may lease physical assets to the firm, as long as the corresponding obligations of the labor-managed firm are met.

Whereas the first three defining characteristics pertain to individual firms, the remaining two bear on the relations among firms and, more generally, among all decision-making units of the participatory economy. The fourth characteristic is that the labor-managed economy must always be a *market economy.* This implies, among other things, that the economy is fully decentralized. All decision-making units, firms, households, associations and the public sector decide freely and to their best advantage on actions they take, without direct interference from the outside. Economic planning and policy may be implemented through use of indirect policy instruments, discussion, improved information, or moral suasion, but never through a direct order to a firm or a group of firms. The economic relations among the above-mentioned decision-making units are settled through the conventional operation of markets, which is perfectly free whenever there are a sufficiently large number of buyers or sellers. Only in situations of monopolistic or monopsonistic tendencies can the public authorities interfere—and then only by fixing of maximum or minimum prices, or, preferably, by rendering the market structure more competitive, either through stimulation of entry or through opening up of the market to international competition. This ought not to be interpreted to mean that values determined by free market operation are desirable in any normative sense; a given society may prefer values different from those established by free competition (e.g., it may desire to make cigarettes prohibitively expensive) but if it does, it must reach its aims through legitimate tools of policy (a high tax on cigarettes or an import duty on imports of tobacco) .

We come finally to the fifth basic characteristic. It bears on the human factor which in the participatory economy no longer is a mere factor of production but also—and perhaps primarily—the decision-making and thus creative and entrepreneurial factor. We may refer to the fifth characteristic as *freedom of employment.* It simply indicates that the individual is free to take, not to take, or to leave a particular job. At the same time, the labor-managed firms are free to hire or not to hire a particular man. However, the firms can, as a matter of their collective and democratic decision, limit in various ways their own capacity to expel a member of the community even where strictly economic considerations might call for doing so.

These considerations of freedom of employment—especially the one regarding the right to dismiss—lead us to the second part of identification of the participatory economy. What is the basic motivational force—or in the transposed sense suggested earlier, what is the motor—of the participatory firm and thus of the labor-managed economy as a whole?

In classical capitalism the moving force was the maximization of profit. In the Galbraithian new industrial state it is the self-interest of the upper management stratum of the large corporation, and in Soviet-type systems it is a combination of the fear of penalties attached to plan nonfulfillment and various types of bonuses extended to the plant manager.

In the participatory economy it is a combination of the interests of the members of the labor-managed firms as individuals on the one hand, and as a collective on the other. More specifically, and thinking first of the problem in pecuniary terms, the labor-managed firm's aim is the *maximization of income* for each of its members. Of course, this must be done in conformity with an income-distribution schedule reflecting the comparative shares belonging to each job agreed on democratically in advance; once the schedule is given, the highest income is attained for all participants at each level as soon as it is attained by any single participant.

This pecuniary objective of income maximization can be thought of as the crude form of the moving force of the labor-managed systems. It reflects an important part of the true motivation, and it lends itself to a simple formal analysis of the behavior of the labor-managed firms and of the labor-managed systems as a whole. It does not by any means contain the whole truth, however, and in many concrete situations will not even be seen as the principal objective by the participants of actual labor-managed firms.[2]

The true objective of the participatory firm is complex and multidimensional. If we insisted on reducing it to a single variable, we could not do otherwise than to say that the single variable is the degree of satisfaction of the individuals within the collective. Of course, monetary income may be an important ingredient of the satisfaction, especially in very poor environments, but it is definitely not the only one. The working collective can, for example, sacrifice some money income in exchange for additional leisure time, lesser intensity of work, better human relations—or even a kinder managing director. If this is so, all the alternatives mentioned must be considered as a part of the participatory firm's objective and thus as a component of the moving force of the labor-managed economy. In fact, the broader interpretation of the motivation base can include even objectives which normally would not be included under the heading of "self-interest," such as giving employment to others in the community, preventing unfavorable external effects of production such as air or water pollution, and many others.

NOTES

1. Alternatively, in a more sophisticated and generally superior voting scheme where the voters are allowed to assign different weights to alternative issues simultaneously to be decided on, each voter is given the same number of points. This reflects the principle of equality of importance among members engaging in the democratic process of decision-making.

2. In discussion with practical economists, enterprise directors or workers in Yugoslavia, the income-maximizing motive will often not be recognized—or will be recognized only after some reflection—and other objectives, such as maximum growth, maximum surplus value and maximum employment will be given. As an even more extreme point of view—one that certainly cannot be dismissed on a priori grounds—some will say that the objective of the participatory firm is simply what the majority of participants wants, there being no single identifiable motive.

2. Self-management, Oligarchy, and Proprietary Socialism

MARIO ZAÑARTU

When the "capitalists" were in power in our curious Chile, they opposed self-management, worker-operated enterprises. Now that the "socialists" are in power, they too oppose self-management. Could being in power have something to do with the rejection of self-management? Handing over enterprises and the economy to the workers is opposed for a number of reasons.

The *capitalist oligarchies* give reasons of efficiency and productivity: "The system of self-management so much discussed here implies that workers will have to assume the risk involved in the management of industry. But do they have the financial means to undertake that risk? Could a special type of insurance solve the problem?"[1]

The *statist oligarchies* cite the danger that particular groups may pursue their own divergent interests to the detriment of the common good: "Planning has to be the main guideline of productive resources. Some may think there are other ways. But the creation of worker-operated enterprises as an integral part of a

Reprinted from *Flecha roja,* No. 2 (September-October 1971), 27–41, by permission of the author. Translated by Michel Vale.

1. Luders, R. "Enjuiciamiento económico de la autogestión," *Foro sobre la autogestión de la empresa* (IHC-CIEUC, Santiago, 1968), p. 80.

free market would effectively mean placing wage laborers in the role of capitalists and persevering with a mode of production that is historically bankrupt."[2]

The *party oligarchies* refer to an unacceptable stratification in the revolutionary struggle: "The MAPU does not agree with the formation of worker-operated enterprises; since productivity will vary among the different enterprises, the net result would be a stratification of privileges within the working class."[3]

The *intellectual oligarchies* focus on the survival of egotistical motives: "By replacing the capitalist entrepreneur, whose power is based on capital and his property deed, with a socialist manager, whose power stems from workers' assemblies . . . the central liberal concept without which capitalism cannot survive remains in operation: that is, economic equilibrium can be achieved as long as the production of goods is based on the maximization of profit."[4]

These sources of opposition have one obvious thing in common: they are all different types of oligarchy.

Self-management means that decision-making power and managerial responsibility rest with all those who are a part of the economic structure. The opposite of self-management is "heteromanagement," management by others. These others will always be an oligarchy. Heteromanagement is therefore an oligarchic formula; thus it should not seem strange that the oligarchs defend it. Self-management is the antithesis of oligarchic power: it is the power of working people, exercised directly, without the alienating mediation of the "efficient ones," the "centralizers," the "mobilizers," or the "critical thinkers." All of these social types, which are always oligarchic, are indispensable for the execution of a historic project on a national scale. But there is a great difference between dominant oligarchies and service oligarchies. Oligarchies are acceptable only as oligarchies of public service, appointed and controlled by the people. They are not acceptable if they have the people serving them, if they are self-appointed and control and manipulate the people at their whim, which at bottom means to use the people to further their oligarchic interests.

---

2. *First Message of President Allende before the Full Congress* (Servicio de Prisiones, Santiago, 1971), p. 21.

3. Declaration of the Secretary General of MAPU, *La Prensa*, Friday, June 4, 1971.

4. Himkelammert, F., and Villela, H. "Autogestión, participación, y democracia socialista," *Mensaje*, June 1971.

1. The capitalist oligarchies

Capitalist oligarchies are blinded by their own efficiency and capability; they believe that it is impossible to organize human capacities for efficient production outside of the capitalist order. They imagine that in self-management, decisions on methods of production will be made by janitors. They believe that the workers will not be interested in the efficiency of the enterprise. They cannot conceive that a workers' collective—that is, a collective consisting of *all* the personnel of an enterprise (including managers and directors as well as janitors)—could have an interest in placing the most capable manager available in the management position. And they do not see that this manager would have an ever greater authority to use all of his abilities in obtaining the maximum economic surplus within the restrictions imposed by his new employers. They also fail to realize that control exercised by all over all is much more efficient than the mercenary control of a capitalist or state enterprise. The fundamental difference is that those who hire or fire managers, as they see fit, are the workers' collective, and that the new manager (that is, the person who is the ultimate source of decisions affecting the whole enterprise) is precisely that workers' collective, whose greatest interest is the maximization of economic output within the restrictions dictated by national planning, that is, within the requirements of the historic national mission.

2. The statist oligarchies

The statist oligarchies have always believed that the only way of bringing the decisions of groups and individuals into accord with the interests of the historic national mission is by centralizing decisions in their own hands. At the factory level, this means state management. They believe it impossible for autonomous management by individuals or groups, no matter how much they are contained within limits, to be compatible with the national mission. They think that the only alternative to a system of economic incentive, which functions poorly because it functions within a free market (by definition defective because it encourages exploitation and a system of production marked by an unjust distribution of income) is the replacement of economic incentives by direct bureaucratic control. They cannot imagine that a group of human beings, a workers' enterprise, seeking to insure its own well-being could also thereby contribute to the general welfare. They cannot imagine that, given certain conditions of control, planning, and intervention, the monetary surplus which would accrue to the advantage of the personnel could serve as a measure of the social utility of the productive unit in question.

By social utility or economic surplus, we mean the difference between the benefits or welfare contributed by the product of the production unit (material goods or services of any type) to the community as a whole and the social cost or effort that the production of that product requires from the community as a whole. Welfare is created by satisfying the needs of the community. Expended effort or social cost pertains to the use of production factors (personnel and physical capital) and resources (raw materials, intermediate products, and energy) which require present effort (man-hours and machine-hours) or past effort (training of personnel and production of capital and materials).

To maximize the economic surplus is the ultimate social goal of every productive unit, whatever or however it may produce, and however the economic system of which it is a part may be organized. The fundamental managerial decision, which is part of the managerial function, is the decision to maximize the difference we have called economic surplus. It is therefore of major social interest that, whoever fulfills that function (the capitalist oligarch in a capitalist system, the state in state capitalism, the consumer in a consumer cooperative, the workers' collective in a self-managed enterprise) be highly motivated to make the best decision.

The statist oligarchy is not capable of imagining a system in which the workers' collective would be highly motivated to make the best decisions for maximizing the economic surplus. As long as we are part of history (the coming of the "new man" is the end of history), man will make better decisions, the more he is affected by them, the more his standard of living depends on them. For this it is sufficient that some percentage of the economic surplus produced by his decision be allotted him. If he errs, he loses; if he judges correctly, he wins.

The problem is that the allotment is a monetary one, or is reducible to money. And we know very well that, in our defective market system, it is possible for a person who fulfills a managerial role to increase his monetary surplus without increasing the economic surplus (by exploiting the consumer, the worker, the provider of capital, or the provider of raw materials).

The monetary surplus (total income minus total costs) would be an exact measure of the economic surplus (overall well-being minus total effort expended) when and only when all the prices (of product, of raw materials, of wages and salaries, of interest on capital) are an exact measure of all the values (consumer satisfaction, production cost of resources, marginal productivity of personnel, and marginal productivity of capital).

Since this is not the case, instead of making the appropriate corrections in the various prices through planning, control, and intervention, the statist oligarchs are quick to take over management, to assume control of the managerial function, at the same time thereby excluding from it the personnel as a whole, who in the best of cases are left with only an infinitesimal measure of participation. The inevitable result is the state enterprise, whose motive force—bureaucratic control—does not even remotely approximate the driving force that would ensue from mobilizing the entire collective of workers toward the goal of improving their standard of living.

3. The party oligarchies

Party oligarchies, whose primary concern lies in mobilizing for the revolution and the dictatorship of the proletariat, prefer a homogeneous mass, proletarian where possible, but in any case with income close to the subsistence level. This gives them a number of advantages: simple and homogeneous slogans and actions along with heightened revolutionary potential. And for this reason they cannot look with favor upon a workers' economy and workers' enterprises. Workers' control tends to divert the working mass into endeavoring to produce a greater social utility and to give them a sense of involvement in the maintenance of a system which, moreover, means a higher standard of consumption for them. For the purposes of revolutionary mobilization, it is more convenient to have a mass of state wage laborers or workers who could not care less about economic surplus as long as their jobs are secure, and whose pay therefore has little to do with their productive effort and, in addition, is so low that it would be difficult for them to come out on the losing end in any revolutionary transformation. One of the most common arguments raised by the revolutionary mobilizers against workers' control is the claim that outrageous privileges would be created by income differences between workers in the various productive units, owing, they argue, to the different "productivity" levels of different enterprises.

The productivity that is relevant for determining the personal income of workers is called "marginal productivity," which answers the question: by how much does the volume of production change when one and only one factor changes by one unit? Marginal productivity obviously defines the contribution made by one unit of the factor in question. This indicator is very different from the "average production" per person in general, or per person in a determined category, which results from dividing the total product by the number of persons. Furthermore, this indicator has nothing to do with the contribution of the individual or efficiency of the intensity of capital employed in the productive unit in question.

It is very typical of those who do not attribute any productivity or cost whatsoever to capital (machinery, sites, installations, tools) to confuse these two indicators. It is a distortion common to naive Marxism. But today there is not a single system of economic organization that does not concern itself with the most productive allocation of capital, which after all is scarce everywhere. Some who would not venture to talk about the rate of interest or return on the productivity of capital speak instead of the rate of capital recovery, which is nothing but the inverse of the former.

Now, given workers of the same capacity, expending the same amount of effort, if there are productive units in the economy in which the productivity or contribution of these same workers varied, this would mean that the work force was poorly distributed among those enterprises, and it would be necessary to introduce corrective measures into the Chilean economy until the contribution of all balanced out. Only then would workers be contributing their utmost to the creation of economic surplus for the national commonwealth. Furthermore, the state must take care to insure that the compensation (only now do we introduce money!) of the workers is commensurate with their contribution, avoiding any exploitation on the part of enterprises and any abuse on the part of the workers (beware of professional societies!). This is valid for any type of industry: capitalist, state, consumer cooperative, or workers' self-management. As long as the national community prefers to compensate different contributions with correspondingly different pay, a source of income inequality among workers will continue to exist. However, this inequality could be subsequently diminished or abolished through taxation mechanisms.

Monetary surplus is also a source of income differences. In self-managed enterprises, this monetary surplus belongs at least in part to the workers' collective, because it is the workers who are performing the entrepreneurial function. But, once again, an incentive is needed, as we noted before. Furthermore, besides the adjustments necessary to bring the monetary surplus in alignment with the economic surplus, a whole series of measures can be taken to reduce the former, if it seems that factors independent of the effort expended by the workers cause a disproportionately large economic surplus to be produced in any one enterprise. For example, any copper enterprise could be maintained under self-management without danger of excess profits by employing any of the following expedients:

1) by determining the sale price of copper not by the London Exchange but by what the state pays the enterprise in accordance with the current unit cost; any productivity difference would fall to the workers; the difference beween the state price and the London price goes to the national commonwealth;

2) by leaving prices intact but returning close to 100 percent of the monetary gain of the enterprise to the commonwealth through taxes;

3) by charging the enterprise a fee for the rental of physical capital whether it belongs to the state or to another party, thereby reducing the monetary surplus to zero; and

4) by charging the enterprise a fee sufficient to diminish the monetary surplus to almost zero for a major portion of the raw materials (copper minerals), inasmuch as they belong to the nation.

What these measures show is that since monetary surplus represents a differential in monetary flow, it can be substantially altered not only directly, but also by altering any of the three flows mentioned (product value, resource value, capital cost) without fundamentally changing the incentive mechanisms.

There is not an economy in the world that operates efficiently without paying for this privilege the price of income inequality in order to gain greater productive effort on the part of its workers. Nor does it seem possible for that to happen on a national and permanent scale before the advent of the new man. The case is different for smaller groups (family, religious community) or for exceptional periods (national catastrophe, short war) in which solidarity, disassociated from personal or group advantages as regards the standard of living, is able temporarily to prevail.

4. The intellectual oligarchies

It would be interesting to find out who among those socialist intellectuals dedicated to denigrating self-management in Chile is not or has not at some time been a priest, seminarian, or leader of a religious movement. Their general tone has been that self-management, by basing itself on the workers' interest in maximizing economic surplus, is committing the sin of selfish interest, and, like all economic sins, this one should be attributed to capitalism, or at least to the remnants of capitalism. A common characteristic of this group of intellectuals is their deficient economic analysis and terminological confusion (for example, monetary profit is confused with economic surplus). They are ignorant of some problems (such as the entire incentive problem) and confuse others (the distortions of an unrestricted free market with the various trends that a controlled market may take in the face of an adjusted income structure; or the inevitable effects of technical progress with the defects of a bad employment policy).

In general, they are eschatologists who try to organize economies that would function only with the new man, who consider the advent of the new man already to be an accomplished fact, and who indignantly reject any compromise with the vestiges of egoism. They see in the new Chilean Marxian socialism a new opportunity for eschatological fulfillment which they did not find in their previous political options. If they are deceived by the new system, they will turn against it, vilify it as they now do the previous one, and become the great defenders of the moral and Christian values of more extremist options. And, since extremes meet, if they survive the compromises these options demand, they will come full circle by giving their support to ultra-rightist solutions.

In any case, they are the oligarchs of value judgments on political options. They cannot act simply within politics, as political beings, basing their actions on political diagnoses, analyses, and strategies. Their action proceeds from the pulpit of the world of values. From there they anathematize and bless in the name of politics. They cannot accept the fact that the political systems open to them are simply that; for them, political options must be canonized options.

Their present object of canonization in the economy is the program and practice of the Popular Unity Party. Since that program and practice reject workers' enterprises, these doctrinaire socialists must also reject self-management. They argue that self-management perpetuates the faulty structure of an unrestricted free market. But this objection is not valid in a perfect market structure or, what is the same thing, in a market structure that is planned, controlled, or corrected so that the monetary surplus (or "profit") is an exact measure of the economic surplus, as has been explained earlier.

In this case, the decision which is best for the workers' collective is also the best for the society as a whole.

But even assuming a functioning within a faulty market structure, there is a phenomenon which radically changes the social setting: the loss of power and the loss of surplus, which pass from the owners of capital to the workers, and which therefore strongly influence the redistribution of income within the community.

The intellectual oligarchs criticize incentive mechanisms which artificially link group interests to the interests of the community as a whole, but they offer no alternative except an appeal to solidarity. They do not see that the problem is precisely how to achieve solidarity. For us, solidarity is the fruit of mechanisms that are able to bring divergent interests into harmony. For them, the only way to achieve solidarity is through an eschatological convention. Part of the eschatological attitude of the intellectual oligarchs translates into a blanket rejection not only of capitalism but of many of the elements found in the economic structures out of which capitalism emerged. They tend to leave capitalism undefined, so that it is easy for them to consider it to include such elements as the market and price system, free enterprise by citizens and groups, incentives to productive effort, competition to provide the best product, etc. They reject these elements with the same fervor as they reject capitalism, without realizing that they are independent of capitalism and are found, in different forms and degrees, in every economic system. They do not realize that supporting free enterprise (after instituting all the correctives mentioned above) means heeding the indications of individuals and groups as to what they perceive their own needs to be.

They do not realize that capitalism can be defined, albeit very or individual interest, they are immortalizing it and declaring it indestructible, and thus making any alternative system unviable. They do not realize that in rejecting product competition (an example of which is the bidding system) they are proposing its opposite—monopoly.

They do not realize that capitalism can be defined, albeit very roughly, as the economic system in which decisions and surplus are appropriated by those who contribute capital.

An analysis of the arguments of the various types of oligarchs shows the inconsistency of their attacks on self-management. But we must still account for the fact that they attack it.

The explanation would seem to lie in the monopoly of power that is characteristic of all oligarchies. Self-management is the transfer of power to the people, and the oligarchies cannot but look jealously upon this transfer, which means a loss of power or, in any case, the loss of their monopoly of it.

The capitalist oligarch does not accept sharing his privilege as regards efficiency and rationality with the working population.

The statist oligarch does not believe it possible for small groups to move in consonance with the historic national mission unless the movement is under his centralized direction.

The party oligarch does not accept the possibility of grass-roots mobilization unless he himself sets its pace and goals.

The intellectual oligarch does not accept that people might be able to align their interests with those of the society as a whole by means of simple mechanisms independent of the eschatological adventure to which he holds the key.

3. Social Ownership—Collective and Individual

ALEKSANDER BAJT

As a basic legal institution and basic socioeconomic relation, ownership—and, in particular, social ownership—is the object of intensive research by scholars in the social sciences, from lawyers and economists to sociologists and psychologists. The domestic (Yugoslav) literature on ownership has grown so much that it has become almost vast. Yet in spite of this, many essential characteristics of ownership, and even some basic concepts related to it, appear to have remained unclarified. The decentralization of investment decision-making and of the corresponding resources, and changes in Yugoslav economic policy resulting from the reform, especially the changes that will be further brought about by the successful implementation of the reform, pose the question of ownership in a new light and still more urgently demand its answer.

In this contribution, I shall attempt to distinguish some basic concepts relating to ownership and employ them in analyzing the basic forms of ownership in the Yugoslav economy—the private ownership of small peasants and craftsmen and the social ownership of work collectives—in order to bring out some ideas about the regulation of property relations in Yugoslav society in the future. . . .

Reprinted from *Gledišta,* April 1968, 531–44, by permission of the publisher. Translated by Helen Kramer.

I. The legal and economic concepts of ownership

Ownership in the legal sense is an institution of the legal order, which gives real and legal persons the exclusive right to dispose of things. We call this right the right of ownership. The legal order decides who is the legal owner of a thing. It says nothing, however, about who is the owner of something in the economic sense. More precisely, while the legal owner of a thing may also be its economic owner, this need not be the case. Its economic owner can be an entirely different person. Who the owner is in the economic sense is a question of fact: it is he who acquires benefit from the thing or, to use Marx's expression, he who appropriates.

By the benefit from a thing, the benefit that the thing gives, we mean its product, i.e., the *increase* of the output of the production process caused by the increased share of that thing in it, or the reduction of the output of the production process caused by reduction of the share of that thing in it. Including a parcel of land in the production process increases its output; we call this increase in output the product of that parcel of land. An increased share of labor, for example, the inclusion of an additional worker in the production process, increases its output; we call this increase the product of that worker, or the product of his labor. Including a patented invention or process in production increases its output; we call this increase of the output of the production process the product of the patented invention. He who appropriates the product of the parcel of land is the economic owner of that parcel. He who appropriates the product of the patented invention is its economic owner. He who appropriates the product of labor is the economic owner of the corresponding manpower.

This concept of economic ownership requires two supplements. First, the product can have a nonmaterial as well as a material form. In the most general sense, it means the sum of benefits that people can expend, the sum of welfare. This means that not only things that we conventionally include in means of production but also things that we usually classify as consumer goods, especially durable goods, yield products in the cited sense. An apartment, for example, is not directly the object of consumption; the object of consumption is the benefits it offers. The apartment thus takes the role that factors of production play in the processes we usually have in mind when we use that expression. . . . Therein lies the economic reason that, in many socialist countries, apartments (and similar consumer goods) are treated practically the same as means of production, in that housing ownership also is limited in our country, although officially we include apartments in consumer goods. Second, since things participate in production not only in the short term but also in the long term, during which their legal owner and the appropriator of their products change, in defining the owner of a thing in the economic sense we must have in view the appropriation of the thing in all periods in which the thing yields products. Ownership of a thing at the last moment in the thing's existence is necessarily only partial ownership.

From the forgoing we can derive the following significant differences between the legal and the economic concepts of ownership:

1. While legal owners can be both real and legal persons, economic owners can be only real persons. Legal persons cannot appropriate in the sense of consuming, destroying benefits.

2. The object of ownership in the legal sense is a thing; the object of ownership in the economic sense is a good, which means a *useful* thing, a thing which gives benefits.

3. The legal owner of a thing can be one person, and the economic owner another. This is partly due to the fact that legal owners can be legal persons, while owners in the economic sense can be only real persons. Essential in the assertion that the legal owner of a given thing can be one person and the economic owner another, is the idea that the economic owner of a thing can be another *real* person, but not its legal owner. Several examples can illustrate this point: the legal owner of an apartment house is the one entered as the owner in the deed books; the economic owner is the one who pays rent, insofar as this rent does not exceed the amount necessary for maintaining the building. If it exceeds the maintenance costs but falls below the size of the benefits the apartment yields, then the economic owners are proportionally both the owner and the renter. The owner of a patent (of a technological process, and so on) is always its purchaser, at least legally; if he paid a price for the patent equal to the present value of all future products of the patent, then in spite of the purchase of the patent, he has remained only its legal owner. The economic owner has remained the seller of the patent. The same holds for the owner of land, of a machine, of an entire workshop or enterprise, and, in general, for the owner of every factor in the broader sense described.

II. The content of legal ownership

The institution of the legal order that we call the right of ownership understandably would have no meaning if it had no socioeconomic content. Its purpose is undoubtedly to allow the appropriation of the products yielded by the objects of the right of ownership and everything that appropriation and accumulation of products makes possible. It is surely not on account of things that are not useful that the right of ownership is legally formulated. In addition, one should be aware that the range of such things is substantially reduced if we keep in mind the fact that the thing which is useless today can yield products tomorrow; it is for this reason that we emphasized in the first part that economic ownership of a thing should be judged according to the benefits it gives during the *entire* period of its existence.

When we speak of the content of the right of ownership, we have in view precisely these economic motives of its legal formulation. In other words, we have in view the actual socioeconomic relations which the legal order shapes and legally protects in the institution of the right of ownership. In this respect we can determine the following:

1. The content of the right of ownership is different in various legal orders, especially in legal orders that belong to different socioeconomic systems. Between the Roman *jus utendi, fruendi ac abutendi* or liberal capitalist private property, on the one hand, and the medieval *jus procurandi et dispensandi,* on the other, there are substantial differences. The differences in the content of the right of ownership between legal orders that belong to the same socioeconomic systems are also substantial. From this we can conclude that every socioeconomic system and every legal order adapt the content of ownership to their social and economic goals.

2. Every legal order recognizes numerous civil rights by which it is possible to limit the right of ownership legally and economically. . . .

3. In addition to private legal institutions, public law, particularly the administrative laws of the state and of other territorial-political communities, also determines the concrete content of the right of ownership. Direct and indirect taxes, including tax on inheritances, compulsory sales [*prisilni otkup*], and fixed prices can be cited as examples.

4. In a market economy, the price structure also decides the concrete content of the right of ownership. At a given volume of

output of things, the price structure differentiates the incomes that things yield, and thus changes the economic position of their owners. Through prices and real incomes, it enables the appropriation of products by those who are not the legal owners of the corresponding factors and even prevents the legal owners of factors from appropriating their products.

The state can take advantage of this circumstance; in such a case, however, it is a matter of shaping the content of the right of ownership as cited in point 3.

The factors molding the content of private ownership that were cited in points 1–3 can be classified as belonging to the institutional structure of the economy. The fourth originates directly in the socioeconomic structure of the economy.

III. Ownership per se and ownership of labor capabilities (manpower)

Products or benefits of things do not arise by themselves alone, by the influence of only one factor or thing, but arise in production processes (in the broader sense presented above) as the fruit of the mutual influence of several factors. In every economy it is useful to distinguish those factors or sets of factors that operate to a greater or lesser extent in all production processes: land, capital, labor, entrepreneurship, and inventiveness. Only labor and capital require special explanation. Since entrepreneurship and inventiveness are cited as separate factors, it is clear that by labor we mean only labor that is repeated, that remains qualitatively the same from period to period. By capital we mean those parts of the income of preceding periods that were not spent during those periods but were saved and invested in obtaining new products or benefits. In this sense, capital exists in every economy. In a market economy, the position on the buying and selling market, degree of monopoly, or, in short, monopoly, should be added to the cited factors. It is understood that this is only a factor of income and not of the product.

In primitive processes, the contributions of individual factors to the total product are not mutually differentiated; it is not clear which parts of the total product are the consequence of individual participating factors. The reason for this lies in the lack of differentiation of the *owners* of the factors. One and the same person or collective (old Slavic family cooperative or *zadruga,* peasant farm, medieval craft shop) is the owner of all factors that act in the process. Historically, land and its product, land rent, were differentiated first. In the period of capitalism, when technology requires more and more capital which the producers or entrepreneurs themselves cannot provide out of the production process, capital and the income of its owner, interest, are differentiated with regard to ownership. Thus capital is activated as capital in the Marxian sense, as value which brings surplus value to its owner.

Although land and capital are necessary to every process and both enable the increase of output above the existing volume, and although land produces in the physical sense as well, these factors nevertheless give income to their owners only under a certain institutional structure. Without this institutional structure, whose core is private ownership of land and capital, there would be neither land rent nor interest as private income (which as a whole is categorized as monopoly income). In other words, the incomes of other factors would be proportionately greater. Participation in production with land and capital therefore means participation in production with property per se, without any contribution of the work capabilities of the owner. Hence ownership of land and capital is categorized as ownership of others' labor, and in this lies the reason that the idea of socialism is always linked with the idea of socialization of land and capital. The same holds also for market monopoly, which gives the owners of factors monopoly income that is first of all the result of entrepreneurship. The abolition of entrepreneurship, i.e., market economy in general, here corresponds to the socializaton of land and capital.

Participation in the production process with other factors represents some effort on the part of their owner, whether it is predominantly of a physical or of an intellectual nature. Both work in the narrow sense, and entrepreneurship and inventiveness therefore mean the *direct* participation of their owners in production. The relative incomes of the owners in a modern economy, of course, do not reflect the effort related to their participation in production, however we measure it. This would occur only where there was free competition among the owners with respect to the disposal of work capabilities, where each could dispose of either entrepreneurial, inventive, or work capabilities in the narrower sense, that is, of any one of these capabilities. Since this is not the case, ownership of work capabilities is a source of similar inequalities among people as arise from ownership of land and capital. This thought is contained in Marx's ideas when, in the *Critique of the Gotha Program,* he says: "As far as the distribution of means of consumption among the individual producers is concerned, the same principle prevails as in the exchange of commodity equivalents: a given amount of labor in one form is exchanged for an equal amount of labor in another form. Hence *equal right* here is still in principle *bourgeois right. . . .* This *equal* right is an unequal right for unequal labor. . . . *It is, therefore, in its content, a right of inequality, like every right.*" In other words, similar to the way in which we determined that land and capital give their owners incomes only under a certain institutional structure, so work capabilities also give their owners incomes disproportional to the actual work effort only under a certain institutional structure. Nevertheless, we emphasize that it is a matter of similarity only, which we shall see immediately in what follows.

IV. Socioeconomic functions of private ownership

I shall cite two basic socioeconomic functions of private ownership that are important for the question we are considering. From the viewpoint of socialist economy, the first is negative, the second positive.

1. Private ownership of productive factors, which makes possible the appropriation of incomes by their owners in accordance with the prices that the factors obtain in the corresponding economy, implies the exploitation of the owners of less productive factors by the owners of more productive factors. Nevertheless, there is an essential difference here between the owners of land and capital, on the one hand, and the owners of work capabilities, on the other. The point is not so much that some obtain products without any real contribution to production (in the sense of effort), while others obtain products on the basis of it. What is more significant is that the accumulation of work capabilities in one person, even when it is a matter of entrepreneurship, is clearly limited by the importance of these factors themselves, while the accumulation of land and capital is not limited in this way. Hence private ownership of land and capital allows the concentration of power over owners of other factors, which is the basis of class social orders. Accordingly, private ownership of land and

capital, insofar as they are not limited by some exogenous factors, constantly *give rise to class exploitation.* This is the reason we spoke in the preceding section only of the *similarity,* and not the identity, of relations between owners of work capabilities, on the one hand, and owners of land and capital, on the other.

2. Private ownership is an important *stimulator* of people's productive activity. This holds for ownership of work capabilities as well as for ownership of land and capital. The motive that stimulates people's productive activity can be consumption or accumulation. In the case of ownership of work capabilities, the motive is, as a rule, consumption, although the source of initial accumulations is the incomes of work capabilities. In the case of ownership of land and capital, the predominant motive is accumulation of property and social power.

Private ownership has both the cited functions in the legal and in the economic sense. The reason is understandable. The economic motive of the legal institution of ownership is, as we have seen, ownership in the economic sense, the appropriation of the products of the things that are the object of ownership.

V. The criterion of social ownership in the economic sense

According to what we have established with respect to ownership in the economic sense, it is certain that only the structure of the distribution of national product can give us the answer to the question of what social ownership is in the economic sense. Relations of distribution are the reflection of property relations, says Marx. Hence we can determine property relations only if we know the distribution relations. The question of what social ownership is in the economic sense, therefore, reduces to the question of how national product must be allocated in order for us to be able to speak of social ownership.

Part of the answer to this question is undisputed, while the rest is to some extent uncertain. There is no disagreement as to the requirement that private incomes from land and capital be abolished. This is the negative side of this part of the answer. The positive side is the requirement that the distribution of the national product be proportional to work. The uncertain part of the answer relates to the conception of work contained in the socialist principle of distribution according to work. Shall we understand work to include inventiveness and entrepreneurship? How do we measure the amount of work when we know that work does not have inherent measures, while the market judges different work according to its position on the market, or concretely depending on whether there is free competition among producers and how strong this competition is? At least for the initial period of socialism, it is possible to answer this question only as Marx did: "bourgeois" equality continues to measure the amount of work (inventiveness, entrepreneurship) ; hence, incomes correspond to the relation of the supply of the respective type of labor to the demand for it. Socialization of work capabilities, for example, in the form of income leveling, has shown itself to be inefficient everywhere it was introduced; the stimulatory function of private ownership was forgotten.

The answer we gave to the second question, understandably, means that there are different types of social ownership, and that a different type of social ownership, i.e., a different structure of distribution "according to work," than the present one corresponds to developed socialism.

The question is raised as to the importance of the legal formulation of ownership for social ownership in the economic sense. We saw that private ownership leads to the concentration of property and power. Private ownership in the legal sense thus in some way favors private ownership in the economic sense. This could lead to the conclusion that the introduction of social ownership in the legal sense in and of itself favors social ownership in the economic sense. The matter is not so simple, however.

As we know, the legal order together with the price structure formed by the economy determine the content of ownership. Today there are public instruments (progressive income tax, property tax, progressive inheritance tax, and so forth) that can bring the distribution of national product in a system of private ownership to approach the principle of distribution according to work, and hence very close to that which corresponds to social ownership. In this way, private ownership, instead of being formally abolished, is economically transformed into social ownership. The structure of relative personal incomes, which in economically developed countries changes in favor of strenuous work, also contributes to this. Prices, which form the incomes in these activities, operate in the same way, particularly in agriculture and partly also in handicrafts. From the viewpoint of its first function, private ownership can be immobilized.

On the other hand, the proclamation of ownership as social (state) does not by itself create social ownership in the economic sense. If the surplus product is appropriated by a stratum of people—for example, a state bureaucracy or state hierarchy—economic ownership nevertheless remains private and can even be class ownership, although it is proclaimed constitutionally as social. A similar situation arises when the product of land and capital is appropriated by individual collectives. In that case, it is a matter of collective private ownership (in the economic sense). It is obvious that in a legal system of social ownership, relations of distribution that correspond to social ownership can materialize only with the aid of a corresponding system of factors that form private ownership. Although legally formulated social ownership combined with the corresponding economic policy measures favors social ownership in the economic sense, nevertheless legal social ownership alone is incapable of affirming itself economically and maintaining itself independently. By itself, therefore, it is much weaker than the private right of ownership.

VI. Self-management as a criterion of social ownership

In Yugoslavia both conceptions of social ownership are affirmed. Since private ownership of land and capital make possible the concentration of property and social power—and concentration of property and social power is usually understood to include both private capitalistic and state capitalistic (but also state socialistic) concentration of property and social power—it appears that the abolition of private ownership and the introduction of social ownership, not only in the legal but also in the economic sense, is insured by the abolition of private capitalistic and state authority over work and by the introduction of self-management.

Such a conception is mistaken for several reasons. First, it interprets social power narrowly in the sense of the direct relationship capitalist–worker, or the direct relationship state organ–worker. However, it is typical of the sphere of ownership that it controls social labor, and thus distribution, *as a whole,* regardless of the concrete manifestations of this control in individual processes. The direct relationship capitalist–worker and state–worker is to a large degree the relationship *entrepreneur*–worker, or even the relationship director–worker. In spite of the undisputed private ownership of land and capital, and the control of society and of distribution on the basis of concentrated ownership, the element of power as shown by contemporary capitalism can be separated to a large extent from the relationship entrepreneur—worker. On the other hand, self-management in and of itself does not exclude that element of power from the direct relationship within the collective . . . either sociologically or psychologically, and, in particular, does not by itself alone liquidate the power of ownership in relations among collectives. Previously we determined that appropriation on the basis of ownership of land and capital can be prevented only by suitable economic policy measures. If the state authorities concern themselves only with such action, if they fail to use their power gradually to strengthen their position in distribution and close up into a sociological and economic whole, the social significance of ownership cannot be disputed. Even if they take over the entrepreneurial function—and planning doubtless means the partial takeover of this function—it cannot be negated. Otherwise, we would have to identify socialism with self-management, although, all things considered, there are socialist economies without self-management and self-management can be easily deformed into appropriation on the basis of ownership. Finally, there are different levels of self-management. If the essence of the control of ownership over work is macroeconomic control, then it is a priori very probable that it can be eliminated only by macroeconomic measures, and not by mere self-management within work collectives, that is on the lowest level. By a suitable mechanism of direct and indirect decision-making (choice), the etatist element of these measures can be eliminated and importance given to self-management on a higher level. . . .

VIII. Social ownership of work collectives

The greatest unclarity with respect to ownership is found in the area of socialist production organized by work collectives. Since this concerns the most important area of the Yugoslav economy, great damage results from such unclarity, damage that is much more extensive than appears at first sight. The main source is the incorrect allocation of social capital, means of production, and the labor force, which is the consequence of lack of comprehension of relations in production and lack of clarity of the corresponding concepts.

First, the difference between capital as we defined it at the beginning and the means of production that the collective uses in production has been completely wiped out. When we speak of means (or capital) we refer sometimes to means of production, sometimes to the amounts of money that the enterprise transforms into means of production. In the constitutional provision that establishes the means of production as social property, they are interpreted physically, in the sense of objects of labor and means for labor. This corresponds more to a natural production process than to a modern market economy, in which the function of capital is clearly separated from the entrepreneurial function, ownership of capital from ownership of means of production. There are two owners of the same means of production. The entrepreneur is the owner of the physical means of production, and the capitalist is the owner of the capital which he has loaned to the entrepreneur. The ownership function is exhausted in the undifferentiated form of capital that is offered to production, while the entrepreneurial function consists of giving that undifferentiated capital the form of concrete means of production, choosing the amount, location, technique, and product of the process.

The lack of separation of these two functions in our socioeconomic system, which is based on unified social ownership of the "means of production," on the one hand leads to the construction of the "right of use," the "right of managing," and similar rights inadequate to modern production for the market that limit the enterprise in developing its entrepreneurial capabilities, and on the other, creates a situation in which social ownership is fragmented and economically approaches private ownership because the system of income distribution virtually fails to recognize interest on capital. The analysis of property relations in a capital economy presented in the preceding section makes possible the following solution: what society gives individual work collectives to manage in our economic system is not means of production. It is *capital,* in the sense we defined it at the beginning of the discussion. That capital is therefore social property. Work collectives themselves decide on the form of concrete means of production to be given to the capital which is social property. They freely buy and sell these means, whether in the country or abroad. More precisely, that is how it ought to be insofar as we consistently maintain the ideas of a market economy.

If this is so, then it is very probable that the "management" of work collectives far surpasses management in the sense of economic activity with given means of production. Work collectives in Yugoslavia are not managers of land and factories that are the property of someone else. The fact that these are social property still does not mean that they are another's property. Their "management" approaches *ownership* disposal of the means of production. Understandably, this ownership has an essentially different content than all previously known forms of ownership. It is significant because it does not make possible the appropriation of income on the basis of ownership as such, but only of the incomes of entrepreneurship, which in essence derive from the capabilities of enterprises to transform undifferentiated social capital into such means of production and to direct it into those areas that yield satisfactory surpluses of income above costs. The economic socialization of social ownership of undifferentiated capital which is insured by interest at a uniform rate gives individual collectives a social norm for the lower limit of the profitability of the capital they use and simultaneously gives them a norm for the separation of income into the incomes of labor (including entrepreneurship) and the incomes of property as such.

Thus we have delineated the area of social ownership in the economic sense and determined the forms in which it appears in the economic activity of individual and collective producers in the Yugoslav economy. It is, on the one hand, private ownership of land and capital (naturally, also means of production), which the institutional frameworks and economic laws keep on the soil of social ownership and thus economically change into *individual* social ownership; and, on the other, private ownership of the means of production of work collectives, or their enterprises, required by the market character of the economy, which, because of economically realized social ownership of capital (similarly for land), is in essence *collective* social ownership. This justifies the title of this discussion, "Social Ownership—Collective and Individual," which is at first glance paradoxical, and which after this discussion is, I hope, founded at least as a hypothesis. . . .

Because of its stimulatory function, it would be useful actually to use private ownership as the "metaphysical and legal illusion," as Marx called it outside of real social relations, during the period of its general dying out, insofar as it can still perform this function (above all in connection with entrepreneurship), and to insure social ownership in the economic sense by a system of distribution according to work, hence, by the development of socialist social relations among people.

4. The Labor-managed Enterprise

BRANKO HORVAT

Self-management

Self-management is undoubtedly the most characteristic of Yugoslav institutions. Further developed into social self-government, it is the pivotal institution of the Yugoslav socioeconomic system. Moreover, Yugoslav social scientists are quite unanimous in believing that without self-government socialism is impossible (Fiamengo, 1965). Thus the fate of socialism depends on the feasibility and efficiency of self-government. In this section we will be concerned only with self-government as applied to business firms, which is usually denoted as self-management.

Self-management is not a Yugoslav invention. The development of this institution can be followed from the beginning of the last century (Horvat, 1969, Ch. 5). Every social revolution from the Paris Commune onward attempted to implement the idea of self-management. In the very beginning of the revolution in Yugoslavia, in 1941, workers were assuming control over factories in various places (Tanić, 1963, p. 30). With the establishment of central planning, the idea of self-management suffered a setback. However, already in 1949 it was revived; by the end of that year

Reprinted from "Yugoslav Economic Policy in the Postwar Period," *American Economic Review,* 61, No. 3, Part 2 (June 1971): 99–108, by permission of the author and the publisher.

workers' councils were created as advisory bodies in 215 major enterprises and in June 1950 the law passed that inaugurated the era of self-management.

For more than a decade the basic organizational principles of self-management remained unchanged. All workers and employees of a firm constitute the work collective [*radni kolektiv*]. The collective elects a workers' council [*radnički savet*] by secret ballot. The council has 15 to 120 members elected originally for one year and recently for a two-year period. The council is a policy-making body and meets at intervals of one to two months. The council elects a managing board [*upravni odbor*] as its executive organ; the board has 3 to 11 members, three-quarters of whom must be production workers. The director is the chief executive and is an ex officio member of the managing board.

As soon as it was established, self-management met with criticism and skepticism. Both came mostly from abroad. It was said that self-management would erode discipline and that workers would distribute all profits in wages, thus reducing the growth potential of the economy. In 1955 Ward suggested that workers had no real choice in the election of the council and that actions reportedly taken by the councils might represent rubber stamping (Ward, 1957; Horvat and Rašković, 1959). In evaluation of these criticisms one may point out that, regarding labor discipline, an International Labor Organization mission found in 1960 that "while the self-government machinery for labor relations has curtailed the former powers of the supervisory staffs, it would not appear to have impaired their authority. . . . It has undoubtedly strengthened the position of the collective vis-à-vis the management, but it does not appear to have undermined labor discipline" (1962, p. 203). As to the growth potentials, the rate of accumulation remained high with a chronic tendency toward overinvestment and with a high rate of growth. Elections are supervised by courts, and all candidates approved by the majority of the workers are included in the voting list. The safeguards against the creation of a managerial class are the workers' majority in the managing board and the provision that members of self-managing bodies may be elected only twice in succession.

The real difficulties were encountered elsewhere. The original organizational scheme proved to be too rigid, and had to be revised extensively in all its three components. It soon became evident that the director's position was not quite compatible with the new arrangement, and directorship came to be "one of the most attacked and criticized professions in the country" (Novak, 1967, p. 137). In the etatist period the director was a civil servant and a government official within the enterprise. He was in charge of all affairs in the enterprise and responsible exclusively to the superior government agency. In the self-management system the director became an executive officer of the self-management bodies, while at the same time continuing to represent the so-called public interest in the enterprise. This hybrid position has been a constant source of conflicts. At first the director was appointed by government bodies. In 1952 the power of appointment of directors was vested in the commune. In 1953 public competition for the director's office was introduced and in the selection committee the representatives of the commune retained a two-thirds majority. In 1958 workers' councils achieved parity with communal authorities on the joint committees authorized to appoint and dismiss directors of the enterprises. The present state of affairs is that the director is appointed by the workers' council from candidates approved by the selection committee on the basis of public competition. He is subject to reelection every four years, but may also be dismissed by the workers' council. Since the appointment of the director does not depend exclusively on the will of the collective—as is the case with all other executives—he has been considered a representative of "alien" interests in the firm. There have been constant attempts to reduce his power, which have made his position ambivalent and reduced his operational efficiency. On the other hand, as G. Lemân remarks, the director is expected to play the triple role of a local politician, a manager and an executive (1969, p. 28). In the context of what has just been said, the managing board was supposed to exercise control over the work of the director and the administration. Involved in problems of technical management and composed of nonprofessionals, the managing board often proved to be either a nuisance or ineffective. For professional management the director had to rely on the college of executive heads [*kolegij*], which was his advisory body and subordinated to him. Thus two fundamentally different organizational setups were mechanically fused into one system. The director's office provided a link between them, i.e., between the self-management organs and the traditional administrative hierarchy.

Finally, in any somewhat larger firm one single workers' council was not sufficient if there was to be real self-management. In 1956 workers' councils on the plant and lower levels were created apart from the central workers' council. Even this was not sufficient, because hierarchical relations between workers' councils at various levels were not compatible with the spirit of self-management. "The self-management relation in its pure form is polyarchic and not democratic," explains D. Gorupić, "the democratic relationship represents a domination of the majority over the minority. . . . The polyarchic character of the self-management relationship is revealed in equal rights of members of a certain community" (1969, p. 16).

In 1959 an interesting new development began with the creation of so-called economic units [*ekonomske jedinice*]. The enterprises were subdivided into smaller units with a score or several scores of workers. Since a year earlier the enterprises had become more or less autonomous in the internal division of income, it was thought that a strong incentive could be built into the system if economic units recorded their costs, took care of the quality of output use and maintenance of machinery, and themselves distributed their incomes according to certain efficiency criteria. In an interesting study Lemân, a German student of Yugoslav self-management, argues that economic units resulted from endeavoring to eliminate dividing lines between three fields of activities: policy making, managing and executive work (1967, pp. 38–39). Soon, economic units began to practice collective decision making on all sorts of matters. It became advisable to enlarge economic units so as to comprise individual stages of the technological process or separate services. Economic units were transformed into work units [*radne jedinice*]. The hierarchical self-management relations within the enterprise called for a revision. Important self-management rights (distribution of income, employment and dismissals, assignment to jobs) were transferred to work units. Direct decision making at meetings of all members of the work unit became the fundamental form of management. In this way the work unit provided a link between the primary group and social organization. It was both a well defined techno-economic unit, meeting the requirements of efficient formal coordination, and the basic cell of workers' self-government (Županov, 1962).

Work units, several workers' councils and managing boards, many commissions and committees—all this made the formal organization of a labor-managed enterprise rather complicated and inefficient. In order to make such a formal system work, it had to be simplified in practice and this was done in various informal ways. That in turn meant further limitations on competent professional management and a further reduction of efficiency. Workers' management is passing through an efficiency crisis caused by the need for a radical transformation of inherited organizational structures. After all, workers' management meant a fundamentally new principle in running enterprises and it would have been surprising if that did not require painful adaptations and deep changes in social relations. I must add, however, that the conclusions in this paragraph, though based on widely held beliefs, cannot be substantiated in a more rigorous way because no adequate empirical research has been undertaken so far.

Although the crisis has not yet been overcome, matters have begun to be gradually sorted out. A constitutional amendment, passed in 1969, made it possible for enterprises to drop managing boards and to experiment with various organizational schemes. Trade unions, authorities and workers have come to realize that certain developments were based on erroneous beliefs concerning various management functions in a labor-managed enterprise. Perhaps the clearest analysis of the mistakes made came from a sociologist, J. Županov (1967a). Županov distinguishes self-management [*samoupravljanje*], management [*upravljanje*] and executive work [*rukovodjenje*]. The last mentioned is a partial activity intended to carry out a decision made within a policy framework. The integration of all decisions into a consistent framework is the task of management. But management means only technical coordination, while coordination of various interests, making basic policy decisions, is a task of self-management. Self-management means social integration, the formulation of common goals, which is a precondition for efficient operational work of the management. The confusion between management and self-management generated tendencies to transfer more and more of formal coordination to bodies whose task was social integration. As a consequence, satisfactory social integration was not achieved, while nonprofessional management meant lower efficiency (Bilandžić, 1969). S. Bolčić has reminded me that this inherently complex problem was complicated even further by a rather naive ideology contained in legislation and political propaganda and advocating direct participation in administrative work as indispensable to safe-guarding the interests of the workers.

How are the problems encountered to be solved?

Gorupić (1967) and the Institute of Economic Science (Institut economskih nauka, 1968) saw the solution in a fusion of professional competence and self-management. The enterprise may be considered an association of work units. The professional managers of the work units should no longer be appointed, as in the traditional setup, but be elected by their associates. In this way they would represent the interests of their primary groups, while at the same time being also professionally competent. Managers so elected would make up a managing board which would be both an executive organ of the workers' council and a professional management body. Decisions would be made collectively. Since most of the decisions affecting the daily lives of workers would be made and implemented within economic units and by themselves, executive work would become more and more purely organizational and lose its order-giving character (Novak, 1967, p. 118). Businessmen proved susceptible to this approach (Miletić, 1969). As one might have expected in a country like Yugoslavia, as soon as these ideas had been clearly formulated the practical experimentation began, and the Constitution was promptly amended.

Before closing this section let me note another interesting phenomenon: the development of the so-called autonomous law. Enterprises appear as law-creating bodies. Their self-management organs pass charters and rules governing the organization of work, the composition and responsibility of self-management and other organs, the distribution of income and the conduct of business. The autonomous law-creating power emanates directly from the Constitution; the rules and regulations are legally binding on all persons to whom they are addressed within an enterprise and disputes are settled by the enterprise organs, except in some specific cases. In this way "a continual narrowing of the area of state law and corresponding broadening of the area of so-called autonomous law characterize the entire process of regulation of social relations in Yugoslavia" (Kovačević, 1969, p. 1).

Enterprise

. . . A new enterprise may be founded by an already existing enterprise, by a government agency or by a group of citizens. The founder appoints the director and finances the construction. Once completed, the enterprise is handed over to the work collective, which elects management bodies. As long as all obligations are met, neither the founder nor the government has any say about the operations of the enterprise. Enterprises are also free to merge or to break in parts. If a work unit wants to leave the mother enterprise, and the central workers' council opposes that, a mixed arbitration board composed of representatives of the enterprise and of the communal authorities is set up. In all these cases it is, of course, implied that mutual financial obligations will be settled.

Since the capital of an enterprise is socially owned, the fundamental obligation of the enterprise is to keep capital intact. If it fails to do so for more than a year, if it runs losses or fails to pay out wages higher than the legal minimum for more than a year, the enterprise is declared bankrupt or the founder undertakes to improve its business record. In the latter case self-management is suspended and replaced by compulsory management [*prinudna uprava*], a form of receivership administered by officials chosen by the commune (Miljević, 1965). Bankruptcies are rather rare because the commune is obliged to find new employment for workers and so prefers to help the enterprise as long as possible.

If integration processes are to proceed efficiently, the organizational forms must be extremely flexible. Thus since 1967 it became legally possible for two or more enterprises to invest in another enterprise and then share in profits. Similar arrangements were adopted in joint ventures with foreign capital (Friedmann and Mates, 1968; Sukijasović and Vujačić, 1968). In an open economy, like the Yugoslav one, foreign capital is welcome provided it does not limit workers' self-management. Therefore direct investment is impossible, but joint ventures are encouraged. The basic motivation for a Yugoslav firm to enter into close business cooperation with a foreign partner is to be found in the desire to secure access to the know-how and the sales organization of the foreign firm. In this way the Yugoslav firm tries to achieve international standards in technological efficiency and to expand its market. . . .

This brings us to the problem of entrepreneurship in a labor-managed firm. If an entrepreneur is a risk-taking and innovating agent—as Knight and Schumpeter would say and most economists would agree—then the work collective qualifies for that role (Horvat, 1964, Ch. 6). In fact the work collective is generally treated as an entrepreneur. However, doubts have been voiced as well. Županov argues that the practice of fixing wages in advance means that they are not a residual in the income distribution—as is profit in a capitalist firm—and that this sets up a barrier to entrepreneurial behavior. He quotes results of empirical research according to which in work units only managers and professionals are prepared to bear risks, while other categories of workers and employees mostly are not. S. Bolčić has drawn my attention to the fact that workers behaved rationally if they were prepared to bear risks only to the extent that they were able to control business operations. That is why managers were both prepared and expected by others to bear risks to a much larger extent. Such an explanation was spelled out explicitly by workers in a case quoted by Lemân (1969, p. 40). In another piece of research undertaken in Zagreb in 1968 it was found that all groups were more prepared to share in losses if output was diminished than if income was reduced while output remained the same or even expanded (Županov, 1967b.) On the other hand, it is an empirical fact that wages vary pretty widely depending on the business results. Wachtel quotes data on the issues discussed at workers' council meetings: two-thirds of the agenda items are concerned with general management issues (labor productivity, sales, investment, cooperation with other enterprises, work of management) and only one-third with direct worker issues (personal income, vocational training, fringe benefits) (1969, p. 58). Variable wages derived from profits amount to 8–14 percent of standard wages on the average (Wachtel, 1969, p. 100).

The ownership controversy

In Marxist sociology ownership relations are the basic determinants of social relations and thus of the socioeconomic system. The class that owns—i.e., has an economic control over—the means of production, rules the society. For a long time, and in most instances even today, it has been maintained that private property generates capitalism and state property, socialism. In fact the percentage of the national capital owned by the state has been taken as the most reliable measure of the degree of socialism achieved. It follows that a socialist economic policy must be oriented toward an overall economic control by the state and must be hostile towards private initiative.

As already noted, the above described view was generally accepted in Yugoslavia until 1950, and since then it has been thoroughly revised. It is now pointed out that there are at least three reasons why the dogma of the identities between private ownership and capitalism, and state ownership and socialism, is false: the artisans of medieval towns were private owners but not capitalists; in ancient Oriental kingdoms state ownership was frequent and yet that had nothing to do with socialism; in fascist countries the state extensively controlled social and economic life while these countries were obviously capitalist (Horvat, 1969, Ch. 4). Yugoslav scientists are now quite unanimous in believing that state ownership may be a useful device to initiate socialist reconstruction, but is otherwise as alien to socialism as is private ownership. The present position is well summed up by J. Djordjević: "state ownership of means of production creates a monopoly of economic and political power and . . . makes possible the unification of economic and political power under the control of a social group personifying the state." Thus "the essence of classical [class] ownership is not changed. . . . As the holder of the title to property, it [the state] disposes of the producers' labor and its results, on the basis of which surplus labor is appropriated by groups which have their own interests in keeping their commanding functions and thus retaining power and their social status and prestige" (1966, pp. 81, 79).

If state ownership fails to promote socialism, what is a feasible alternative? The Yugoslav answer is: social ownership. But the answer to the next question—What precisely is social ownership?—is not so easy and simple. The legal experts agree that social ownership implies self-government, that it is a new social category, that if it is a legal concept, it does not imply an unlimited right over things characteristic of the classical concept of property, and that it includes property elements of both public and private law (Toroman, 1965, p. 5). In practically everything else there is disagreement. A. Gams and a number of other writers maintain that social property also implies rights of property since property implies appropriation, enterprises are juridical persons and the basic ingredient of the juridical person is property (Gams, 1965, p. 61). Article 8 of the Constitution says that the disposal of means of production in social ownership and other rights over things will be determined by the law. S. Pejovich talks about the right of use, which is somewhat wider than *usus fructus* because it makes possible the sale of capital goods, but is narrower than ownership because the right of disposal is not absolute (1966, p. 29). A diametrically opposite view is expressed by Djordjević and most other writers who maintain that social property represents a negation of property rights (Djordjević, 1966, pp. 84, 90). Djordjević quotes Part II of the Basic Principles of the Constitution to support his view: "Since no one has the right of ownership of the social means of production, no one—neither the sociopolitical community nor the work organization nor an individual working man—may appropriate on any property-legal ground the product of social labor, or manage and dispose of the social means of production and labor, nor can they arbitrarily determine the conditions of distribution."

Legal writers differ further according to whether they stress the public law or private law component of social property. Further disagreements relate to the subjects of law (state, society as a real community of people, several subjects, no subjects). Next come disagreements on whether social property is a legal, economic or sociological concept or is nondefinable in these terms because it relates to quasi-property. And if it is a legal concept, it may be so in various ways. By applying the calculus of combinations we can easily determine the number of possible theories. It seems that available possibilities have been efficiently exploited since M. Toroman (1965) was able to describe thirteen different theories.

The legalistic controversy was somewhat less interesting than the one among economists and sociologists that followed. Bajt drew attention to the fact that the legal owner and economic owner may be two different persons. The former holds legal title, the latter derives the actual benefit from the use of a thing (Bajt, 1968). In this sense social ownership implies the nonexistence of exploitation which in turn implies the distribution of income according to work performed. If a person or a group of persons are earning nonlabor income, they are exploiting others, and insofar as this happens social property is transformed into private property. Thus self-management per se is not a sufficient condition for the existence of social property.

The institution of property already undergoes gradual disintegration under capitalism. Shareholders are legal owners but management exerts real economic control. That is why I prefer to replace the traditional concept of property by a more fundamental concept of economic control (Horvat, 1969, Ch. 15). The latter always means "control over labor and its products," which is Marx's definition of capital as a social relation (Marx, 1953, p. 167). In this respect legal titles are irrelevant. If artisans or peasants possess no monopoly power—which in an orderly market system is likely to be the case—then they represent no alien elements in a socialist society. And there can be little doubt that they practice self-management. Horvat and Bajt came to the conclusion that individual initiative is not only compatible with but is an integral part of a socialist system. In fact the process of production can be organized individually or collectively and that is why Bajt talks about two forms of social ownership: individual and collective.

Agreement about the matters mentioned so far is quite universal by now. Differences in views appear when intermediate cases are considered. Yugoslav law makes it possible for artisans and innkeepers to employ 3–5 workers. V. Rašković (1967, pp. 106–107) and many others consider this to be a form of exploitation, a remnant of the old society, something alien to the system but which has to be tolerated at the present level of development. In support of this view Rašković argues that the employer would not hire workers if this were not profitable for him. It may, however, be argued in reply that a worker, by choosing an individual employer instead of a firm, reveals that he finds such employment more profitable for himself. Such a line of reasoning leads clearly to an impasse. To resolve the question whether workers may be hired by individual employers, and if so how many of them, a sociological argument has been advanced as a criterion. As long as an individual employer works himself in the same way as his employees and has not become an entrepreneur merely organizing the work of others, employees may be considered as (often younger) associates in the work process, direct personal relations of a primary group are preserved and the alienation phenomena of wage labor relations are not present.

Discussion of the scope and role of individual work was invited by political bodies and very soon decisions were made following more or less the ideas expounded above. Individually organized production became a constituent part of a socialist economy.

REFERENCES

A. Bajt, "Društvena svojina-kolektivna i individualna," *Gledišta,* 1968, vol. XIX, 531–44.

D. Bilandžić, "Odnosi izmedju samoupravljanja i rukovodjenja u poduzeću," in *Savremeno rukovodjenje i samoupravljanje,* Belgrade, 1969, pp. 67–96.

J. Djordjević, "A Contribution to the Theory of Social Property," *Socialist Thought and Practice,* 1966, 24, 73–110.

A. Fiamengo, "Samoupravljanje i socijalizam," in Janičijević, ed., *Društveno samoupravljanje u Jugoslaviji,* Belgrade, 1965, pp. 11–38.

W. Friedmann and L. Mates, eds., *Joint Business Ventures of Yugoslav Enterprises and Foreign Firms,* Belgrade, 1968.

A. Gams, "Društvena svojina i društveno usmeravanje," in *Usmeravanje drustvenog razvoja u socijalizmu,* Belgrade, 1965, pp. 50–67.

D. Gorupić, "Tendencije u razvoju radničkog samouprevljanja u Jugoslaviji," *Ekonomist,* 1967, vol. XX, 593–638.

D. Gorupić, "Razvoj samoupravnih društvenih odnosa i samoupravno odlučivanje u privredi," *Ekonomski pregled,* 1969, vol. XX, 1–26.

B. Horvat, *Towards a Theory of Planned Economy,* Belgrade, 1964. (Serbo-Croatian, ed., 1961.)

B. Horvat, "Prilog zasnivanju teorije jugoslavenskog poduzeća," *Ekonomska analiza,* 1967, vol. I, 7–28.

B. Horvat, *Ogled o jugoslavenskom društvu,* Zagreb, 1969. (Eng. ed.. *An Essay on Yugoslav Society,* New York, 1969.)

B. Horvat and V. Rašković, "Workers' Management in Yugoslavia: A Comment," *Journal of Political Economy,* 1959, vol. LXVII, 194–98. B. Ward, "Reply," 199–200.

Institut Ekonomskih Nauka, *Sumarna analiza privrednih kretanja i prijedlozi za ekonomsku politiku,* Belgrade, 1968.

International Labor Office, *Workers' Management in Yugoslavia,* Geneva, 1962.

M. Kovačević, "Enterprise Rules and Regulations," *Yugoslav Survey,* 1969, 1, 1–8.

G. Lemân, *Stellung und aufgaben der ökonomischen Unternehmungen,* Berlin, 1967.

G. Lemân, *Ungelöste Fragen in jugoslawischen System der Arbeitselbstverwaltung,* Cologne, 1969.

K. Marx, *Rani radovi,* Zagreb, 1953.

M. Miletić, "Da li je upravni odbor prevazidjen," *Direktor,* 1969, 9, 56–60.

D. Miljević, *Privredni sistem Jugoslavije,* Belgrade, 1965.

M. Novak, "O prelaznom periodu," *Ekonomski pregled,* 1952, vol. III, 203–13.

M. Novak, *Organizacija poduzeća u socijalizmu,* Zagreb, 1967.

S. Pejovich, *The Market-Planned Economy of Yugoslavia,* Minneapolis, 1966.

V. Rašković, "Osnovni idejni i politički problemi ličnog rada u sistemu društvenog samoupravljanja," in *Privatni rad: Za ili protiv,* Belgrade, 1967.

M. Sukijasovič and D. Vujačić, *Industrial Cooperation and Joint Investment Ventures Between Yugoslav and Foreign Firms,* Belgrade, 1968.

Z. Tanić, ed., *Radničko samoupravljanje; razvoj i problemi,* Belgrade, 1963.

M. Toroman, "Oblici društvene svojine," paper presented at the Symposium on Social Ownership, Serbian Academy of Science and Art, Belgrade, September 20–22, 1965.

H. M. Wachtel, *Workers' Management and Wage Differentials in Yugoslavia,* unpublished doctoral dissertation, University of Michigan, 1969.

B. Ward, "Workers' Management in Yugoslavia," *Journal of Political Economy,* 1957, vol. LXV, 373–86.

J. Županov, "Radni kolektiv i ekonomska jedinica u svijetu organizacione teorije," *Ekonomski pregled,* 1962, vol. XIII, 143–69.

J. Županov, *O problemima upravljanja i rukovodjenja u radnoj organizaciji,* Zagreb, 1967. (a)

J. Županov, "Proizvodjač i riziko—Neki socijalno-psihološki aspekti kolektivnog poduzetništva," *Ekonomist,* 1967, vol. XX, 389–408. (b)

5. Balancing Environmental Requirements and Personal Needs Through an Organizational Structure

ICHAK ADIZES

A trend of contemporary management theory is to expound the advantages of increased participation by subordinates in organizational decision-making processes. This trend suggests altering organizational structure for decision-making from the vertical type of structure toward the horizontal type of structure.

It has been theorized that increased participation and responsibility in decision-making on the part of the general workers tend to yield organizational loyalty, confidence, trust, favorable attitudes toward superiors, low absenteeism, high productivity, etc. Increased participation diminishes behavior which is detrimental to the organization or to its members, behavior classified as dysfunctional. In addition, it has been claimed that "democracy . . . is the only system which can successfully cope with the changing demands of contemporary civilization."[1]

A question, therefore, arises as to whether there is a limit, a point of diminishing returns, to the amount of authority in the decision-making process which can be placed upon the shoulders of the general membership, i.e., a limit to the character and magnitude of democracy in industrial organizations. In more general

Reprinted from *Industrial Democracy: Yugoslav Style* (New York: The Free Press, 1971), pp. 232–38, 243–50, 254–56, by permission of Macmillan, Inc.

1. W. Bennis, *Changing Organizations* (New York: McGraw-Hill), p. 17.

terms, what is a desirable organizational structure? In order to answer this question, an analysis must be made of the external (environmental) and internal (personal needs) constraints which an organizational structure has to satisfy.

The holistic and behavioristic approaches to organizational design differ primarily in the amount of importance they give to external and internal constraints. The holistic approach views organizations as a goal-fulfilling system, and, through departmentalization and specialization, designs the structure for efficient realization of given goals. Membership's personal needs are considered mainly as a means to be manipulated toward the achievement of the goal which is influenced by environmental forces.

The behavioristic approach focuses on behavior primarily within the organization. Through job enlargement and participative structures, the realization of membership needs is sought. External environmental pressures are considered, but, for the most part, only in terms of how they affect the behavior of the participants.

In answering the above question on the desirable organizational structure, the researcher intends to consider an optimal structure as a goal in itself. For this purpose, a third approach is taken: an organization is viewed as a social boundary mechanism which encompasses resources and operates within an environment. In order to answer the question of what kind of structure is necessary for this mechanism to work, both the environment within which an organization operates and the personal needs of the participants who are bound by the organization must be analyzed. An organizational structure is viewed, then, as a mechanism which buffers and balances between external and internal pressures, a structure which optimizes between the conflicting requirements rather than a structure which maximizes any one of them separately.

This chapter analyzes the manner in which both the environment *and* the psychological needs of the participants in the Yugoslav companies observed affected organizational behavior and change in the organizational structure. In addition, a comparison is made of these changes in relationship to those taking place in American companies. From this comparison of environments and structures, some insights are derived, which should answer the question of how much democracy is feasible in an industrial organization.

Organizational structures

The vertical model at work

The vertical structure and its related organizational structures are found throughout the American industrial organization scene. The general structure is usually a pyramidal formation, with authority, power, and financial rewards increasing as the pyramid is ascended. Legislative and executive directives are formulated at higher levels in the pyramidal structure, and are received and carried out at its lower levels. Thus, major decisions, including those concerned with tenure, hiring, firing, modernization, or relocation of the firm, as well as the power to veto such decisions, are made within certain constraints in the higher levels of the organization.

The horizontal model at work

In terms of structure, the assumption upon which the Yugoslav organizational theory is built is that all the members of the organization have equal voice and authority in the determination of plans, rewards, and operations of the company.

Since the total membership has all the legislative authority, while executives have only the authority derived from their professional expertise or specifically assigned to them to implement these decisions; and since the general membership makes decisions on selection, tenure, and dismissal; and since the power of the veto is rendered to the general membership through the referendums, the Yugoslav self-management system qualifies as the horizontal edge of the spectrum of organizational structures. . . .

Environmental forces and organizational adaptation

The Yugoslav environment

Yugoslavia changed from a centrally planned to a highly regulated economic environment which lately has become more competitive. On the political level, the country seemed to move toward more pluralism than was true in its former structure of a tightly knit political elite ruling through a police force.

This change had two main effects: (1) it increased the uncertainty within which a company had to operate, and (2) it altered the goal structure of a company: constraint goals were relaxed and deterministic goals were emphasized.[2] Uncertainty increased since the various alternatives for action in a competitive market increased. Goals became more deterministic since the socio-political decentralization allegedly relaxed the processes required for decision-making and allowed organizations to determine their own courses of action. As constraint goals were relaxed and profit maximization became the criterion of a company's survival, deterministic goals were emphasized to a greater degree.

Organizational adaptation in Yugoslavia

In hierarchical (vertical) organizations, the higher one ascends in the hierarchy, the greater the reward to the individual in terms of status, power, and financial remuneration. However, it is also true that the higher the level reached on the pyramid, the greater is the magnitude of uncertainty a decision-maker has to absorb. Thus, the hierarchical organization has the equilibrating quality of offering greater inducements in terms of rewards for greater contributions, i.e., larger rewards or stronger punishment for making decisions which have greater commitment and repercussions for the organization.

The self-management system does not have this quality. The differences in rewards do not necessarily represent differences in responsibility. Executives are not allocated significantly higher economic or social rewards. The economic rewards are limited because of egalitarian principles. Status allocation is limited because even though there are pressures to elevate the status of technocrats as mentioned before, the syndicalist stream of thought considers such a trend as a contra-revolutionary phenomenon. Those who formally are required to undertake responsibility, the members of the Workers' Council, are not paid for their membership in the Council, and their rotation does not facilitate the process of decision-making.

---

2. Deterministic goals are goals the company was set to achieve—"do" goals. Constraint goals are those the company decided not to violate—"do not do" goals.

As long as the process of decision-making was not directly related to results, there was no need for responsibility to be contained effectively within the organization. Rather, the government at large undertook responsibility and handed down regulations. In a competitive situation, when someone had to account for results and take the lead in making certain decisions, group responsibility seemed to be inadequate since it was difficult to find out who was responsible for decisions.

An organization seeks to replace those of its parts which are not functioning well; however, group responsibility also can constrain such actions. Furthermore, group decisions are vulnerable to emotional factors, and thus are not always predictable, while organizations operating in a competitive environment need a level of predictability, or rationality, in their behavior in order for decisions to have a logical sequence. When an individual feels responsible for his decisions, they are more predictable since the values that affect them are relatively stable. In a leaderless group the decisions change their course as the power structure composing the group changes, and under these circumstances it is more difficult to predict the group's decisions. Predictability of decisions could be achieved in this group decision-making situation if there were a leader who felt responsible for decisions made. But in that case we would be back to our initial query: Why would anyone take responsibility in this situation without commensurate authority and adequate rewards? Moreover, in a competitive market, timing of decisions is crucial, whereas the ponderous development of consensus was time-consuming.

The comparative difficulty of identifying those individuals responsible for decisions, unpredictability of group decisions, lack of a mechanism for allocating higher rewards for greater risk absorption, and time pressure to make faster decisions are some of the instances where the pure, democratic (horizontal) structure and the competitive environment seemed to conflict. Because of this conflict, pressure was exerted on self-management to become less participative and more hierarchical, although this does not imply development into a pure vertical structure. . . .

Organizational structures and the fulfillment of individual needs

The above discussion analyzed environmental pressures and organizational structures; this, however, is only half the answer. A pure hierarchical structure designed because of environmental forces may be found to be disadvantageous because it may have an adverse effect on the behavior of its participants. It was stated above that a vertical structure will be more welcome in an environment where short-run economic results are desired and the process of achieving them is ignored. What effect such a structure has on its participants is important, since it was claimed at the outset of this chapter that an organization should meet not only environmental constraints but internal personal needs as well.

The following is a brief analysis of the effect extreme vertical organizations (with workers on production line) have on the fulfillment of individual needs. The researcher discusses his experience with the horizontal structure.

The vertical structure and individual needs

The hierarchical organization with its unity of command, span of control, and emphasis on specialization generates incongruity with personal needs for growth, self-realization, involvement, etc. The point is that people possess complex needs; they desire that sense of "mastery" or "competence" in dealing with the working environment. When the organization thwarts the fulfillment of these needs, the worker often responds with dysfunctional behavior. Along this line of thought, Argyris stated, "the more the rigidity, specialization, tight control, and directive leadership the worker experiences, the more he will tend to create antagonistic adaptive activities."[3] The incongruity between the vertical structure and individual needs is a well-known theory. . . .

It is interesting to note that the horizontal structure imposes a set of constraints on individuals within the organization which are incongruous with a different set of personal needs. The following section presents this phenomenon by means of an analysis of the organizational constraints imposed on executives by the horizontal structure; of those executive needs which are being constrained and unfulfilled; and of those symptoms of dysfunctional behavior observed by the researcher, which can point to the above-mentioned incongruity.

3. C. Argyris, *Integrating the Individual and the Organization* (New York: Wiley, 1964), p. 59.

The horizontal structure and individual needs

1. The constraints of the structure[4]

a) In group decision-making by workers, risk-taking is not necessarily related to skill.

b) Long-range planning may be constrained because of the rotation of the decision-makers.

c) Executives are in a passive role—a staff position—but are expected to be responsible for the outcome of the decision they formally did not make.

d) Executives are not *formally* making tactical, strategic decisions. Such decisions are left to the governing bodies. Executives have to deal with routine operations.

e) Generally, there is no place for individual responsibility (unless specifically defined as a personal responsibility)—only group responsibility. What an executive is really responsible for is ambiguous.

f) Harder work on the part of the executive does not necessarily mean that the results achieved will be attributed to him, since the major part of his work is in convincing the group to accept a decision. Once the group is convinced, the decision may be considered their achievement rather than his.

g) Role ambiguity and group decision-making reinforce the difficulties of predicting behavior, since they postpone feedback and make this feedback somewhat ambiguous.

Are these constraints congruent with individual needs fulfillment?

2. Executive needs

This analysis concentrates only on the executives. The researcher, however, realizes that in dictatorial vertical organizations, management that is one level below the President is as alienated as the workers. And in an anarchistic horizontal organization, workers are as alienated as executives. This analysis, however, concentrates on executives' behavior which can be attributed to constraints imposed *specifically* by the horizontal organizational structure.

---

4. It should be re-emphasized that we are dealing with a pure horizontal structure where self-management is being fully observed.

One assumption made here is that entrepreneurial needs are similar enough to executive needs to make the forthcoming conclusions valid. An additional and crucial assumption is that, for the purposes of the analysis, it is unimportant that the horizontal system was forced on the executives. The researcher claims that because of the incongruity between organizational structure and executive psychological needs, a pure horizontal structure will always be somewhat forced and never fully accepted voluntarily. (Except if a "New Man" is created, which is a matter of "religious" belief.)

According to McClelland, the executive has a need for "moderate risk-taking as a function of skill."[5] This implies a need to make important, not routine, decisions in the organization. At the same time, McClelland notes the executive need for individual responsibility. The executive gains great satisfaction from initiating successful action, as well as from creating and selecting the plan of action. Another executive need is related to the fact that executives "appear to work harder only when . . . personal efforts will make a difference in the outcome."[6] McClelland also states that the executive performs better when given a concrete feedback on how well he is doing. He states, too, that executives have a need to make long-range plans.

Thus, while the entrepreneurial executive seeks individual responsibility and risk-taking, desires to make strategic, long-range decisions where his personal effort will make a difference in the outcome, and seeks rapid feedback on how well he is doing, he is being constrained by the self-management structure. Furthermore, even though he is forced into a staff position, he is still expected to create results and to be responsible for them. While a good staff person should have the ability to keep away from the center of attention, the good line executive in Yugoslavia has to manifest leadership traits in time of need which may put him in a focal, influential position. This position can be interpreted as power rather than mere influence, and power is condemned as an abuse of one's position.

The Yugoslav executive thus was required by the post-reform conditions and organizational structure to be unnoticed, yet able to lead. He was expected to be responsible voluntarily, yet he was not given any large differential in rewards as an inducement. A

---

5. D. McClelland, *The Achieving Society* (New York: Free Press, 1961), p. 207.

6. Ibid., p. 230.

decision made by the Workers' Council did not necessarily represent the risk he was willing to absorb. He would lead the way to strategic decisions, but he was restrained legally and socially from forcing the decisions or making them himself. His personal efforts would make a difference in the outcome but only after the decision had filtered through numerous group decision-making processes until it was impossible to identify the executive with the outcome. He did not receive rapid feedback on how well he was doing, since what he was supposed to be doing or what results might be attributed to him was not clear.

Incongruity between personal needs and organizational demands leads to dysfunctional behavior which is analyzed in the following section.

Dysfunctional behavior

Dysfunctional behavior in vertical organizations has been researched extensively.[7] Some of this research will be repeated here, since the dysfunctional behavior displayed by the executives in horizontal structures is similar although not identical.

Behavioral responses: vertical structures

According to Argyris, dysfunctional behavior may take many forms. An initial form is caused by a sense of conflict. It can be resolved if the worker is "to leave the conflict situation," which he may do either physically or mentally. Physically, he may transfer or quit, or otherwise remove himself from the situation. Mentally, in order to leave the situation, the individual "may decrease the psychological importance of one set of factors (the organization or the individual).[8] This mode of adaptation enables the individual to decide that he is capable of working only in the present job situation, or he may decide that the job means very little to him. According to Argyris, the result of conflict, in terms of dysfunctional behavior, is "apathy, lack of interest, decreased

---

7. Argyris, *Personality and Organization* (New York: Harper & Row, 1957), Chap. IV, summarizes major findings.

8. Ibid., p. 78.

involvment, and lessened loyalty toward the set of factors rejected."[9]

The conflict between organizational demands and workers' personal needs may also yield frustration for the worker. Of the many responses to frustrations, one of the most common is aggression which manifests itself variously as absenteeism, turnover, quota restrictions, rate setting, goldbricking, slowdown, stealing, cheating (on production records), causing waste, and making errors which reduce the quality of the work. Also, singularly or in combination, the individual may react by:

1) regressing, i.e., becoming less mature and less efficient;

2) giving up and leaving the situation;

3) becoming aggressive and attacking what is frustrating him; developing a tendency to blame others;

4) remaining frustrated by doing nothing. This choice leads to still more tensions.

Behavioral responses: horizontal structures

Unfortunately, there are no extensive research findings on the dysfunctional behavior that pure horizontal organizational constraints impose on executives. In the following statements, the researcher has utilized only his own observations.

One pattern of behavioral response is characterized by the individual's leaving the conflict situation either physically or mentally. In terms of a physical withdrawal, it is a known fact that many organizations in Yugoslavia find it difficult to locate candidates for executive positions. As a consequence, some companies have been forced to operate without a top executive. Along the lines of adaptation by physical withdrawal was absenteeism. Participation in Workers' Council meetings was considered a necessary evil by many executives; consequently, they tried to avoid them. There was also a desire to quit, which was manifested by wishful waiting for retirement age. Those who do not physically leave the conflict situation display apathy toward the self-management system, and they abhor even discussing it. In such cases, the executives have decreased their personal involvement to a minimum.

Leaving the situation mentally if not physically was another

9. Ibid.

observed phenomenon. Daydreaming was common behavior, though leaving the situation mentally was done in other ways as well. For instance, in one company, the Director made loud phone calls during all sessions of the Governing Board, thereby obstructing the work of the Board; he also wrote letters, and seldom participated in the discussion. In another company the Director came to the meetings to suggest topics for discussion, but then would leave once his presence had been noted.

The Finance Director of one company provides an illustration of dysfunctional behavior resulting from the prevention of personal executive action. He was always late to work and tried to avoid meetings. When he was finally forced to attend a meeting, he would make a sincere attempt to explain his suggestions. When his highly sophisticated financial arguments were not accepted because apparently they were not understood, his response to the frustration was to turn inward, or to converse with other executives and then to lose interest in the discussion.

Responses to frustration created by the system also appeared as what Berleson and Steiner classify as "displaced aggression,"[10] typified by the individual's hitting the table, clapping his hands in anger, and generally being fidgety. This type of aggression was displayed also when executives repeated the same idea, same sentence, or same word several times at a meeting. And further, the frustration seemed to cause the individual to regress, to revert to less mature modes of coping with his frustration.

This conflict between executives' needs and the horizontal organization also caused some executives to act as if they had lost their self-confidence. Thus, when a worker questioned them on their suggestions, they would react by saying, "I really don't know; I have only suggested; just tell me what you want and I will carry it through." In addition, the tendency to blame others in times of business difficulty is not an unknown phenomenon in Yugoslav organizational behavior. For instance, in one company, production quality fell for almost fifteen months, but discussions at the meetings still concentrated on blaming each other for the situation, rather than identifying and attacking the source of the problem.

The outcome of executive dysfunctional behavior was the creation of informal groups—"kitchen cabinets"—where decisions

---

10. B. Berelson and G. Steiner, *Human Behavior* (New York: Harcourt, Brace & World, 1964), p. 267.

were made on which the Workers' Council was then asked to vote. As the workers would "get back at the system" by slowdowns in production in the hierarchical organizations, the frustrated Yugoslav executives seemed to get back at the system by not making the decisions which were within their authority, or by slowing down communications, not answering letters, confusing data, etc. The red tape that evolved from this behavior was a major crisis with which the Yugoslav system had to cope.

Thus, at both ends of the continuum—the *pure* vertical or horizontal structures—certain organizational demands placed upon member individuals conflict with their needs. The result, on both ends of the continuum, is dysfunctional behavior. . . .

Conclusions

Taking into account the environment, we note that both horizontal and vertical structures in their pure form are inappropriate, since they are not designed for effective absorption of uncertainty and, thus, are based on the erroneous assumption of a closed system.

From the researcher's study of internal organizational behavior, it appears that the continuum of organizational structures, ranging from the vertical to the horizontal structure, has a circular and inverse effect upon organizational behavior. That is, the effect is circular in that dysfunctional behavior, which plagues the vertical structure, decreases in magnitude with increased worker participation in the decision-making process, but then reappears to plague the horizontal structure. The effect is inverse in that the dysfunctional behavior found in the vertical organization is displayed by the workers, while similar, though not identical, dysfunctional behavior in the horizontal organization is displayed by the executives.

It is suggested that the dysfunctional behavior on either end of the spectrum stems from the fact that organizational demands which are rigid, constrictive, and beyond the control of the recipients tend to elicit dysfunctional behavior on the part of the recipients themselves. The vertically structured organization imposes rigidity and constrictiveness on the worker and the horizontally structured organization imposes both factors on the executive.

Thus, while an organizational structure may be designed functionally to meet environmental constraints, this structure may be rigid and dysfunctional to some of its participants. And conversely if the structure is changed to fully meet individual needs, it may be inadequate to meet environmental requirements. The suggested approach to organizational design is one that enables sufficient flexibility in duty assignment, authority distribution, and allocated rewards, i.e., organizational structure, to meet both the changes in the environment and the psychological needs of its participants. The organization should allocate authority for uncertainty absorption and proportionate to this assignment, allocate rewards. Therefore, the "three-legged stool," where all legs must be equal in size, turns out to be a "four-legged stool": authority, duty, responsibility, *and* reward. All four components have to be well balanced in order to achieve an effectively operating organization.

6. Economic Units in Yugoslav Enterprises

GUDRUN LEMÂN

The term "economic unit"

It is representative of all Yugoslav authors that they define the economic unit by the following characteristics:[1]

1) an exactly defined task which is part of the overall task of an enterprise's collective,
2) a certain degree of independence regarding the organization and administration of the process of work,
3) exactly ascertainable costs of fulfilling the task,
4) the quantitative measurability of the relation between input and output or of the result of work.

The differences in defining the economic unit result from emphasizing different components.

Franc especially underlines the measurability of input:[2]

> The economic unit is a part of the production process or of the administration which operates in a certain, delimited framework and for which the following can be determined: a task for a year or a certain period, the standards for material input, the input of labor and of general costs as well as the necessary capital assets and working capital. The director or-

Translated from *Stellung und Aufgaben der ökonomischen Einheiten in den jugoslawischen Unternehmungen* (Berlin: Duncker & Humblot, 1967), pp. 19–20, 41–48, 51–59. Reprinted by permission of the author.

> ganizes the work in view of the tasks to be fulfilled, he instructs the working team, and renders account for the result reached by the economic unit by its work.

Bandin[3] gives the following definition oriented towards economy:

> Economic units are organizational parts of an enterprise and the economic interests of their members are closely connected. The aim of the profit and loss accounting of the individual economic units is defined by the efforts towards a close connection between the economy [*ekonomija*] of production and the amount of personal income.

This definition shows that the economic units permit a comparison with similar phenomena in other economic systems, such as with those American profit centers which serve as a control of the profitableness of capital invested and of capital employed. The Czech firm Bat'a followed an aim similar to that of the economic units regarding its profit and loss accounting in the individual departments.

Of new and purely Yugoslav origin is the sociological definition of economic units with a political accent:

> . . . they are not only the scientific basis for management and administration on the level of the enterprise, nor do they lead only to stimulating work, but they are the fundamental cells in which a gradual process is going on, viz., of changing the worker from being merely an operator into an organizer and executive with his own creative activity.[4]

For Yugoslav Communists the direct connection of production workers with management as it functions in an economic unit means the realization of the principles of direct democracy. . . .

The economic unit as a social group

> The economic units are based on the new revolutionary principle of the social organization of work, on the principle of integrating managing and practical work.[5]

The sociological aspect of the economic units, as it appears in the effort to humanize work, shows quite a few parallels to the efforts of many countries of the West to reform social relations in the modern working world. The sociological view of economic units began with Karl Marx, but was soon amplified by the investigations and results of the American and French literature on industrial sociology.[6]

In 1960, the first Yugoslav sociological study about economic units was published in Zagreb.[7] About the same time, representative surveys in industry began to a greater extent. They produced the empirical material for further investigations.

The tasks of economic units in view of industrial sociology

Intensifying workers' self-management

The introduction of the economic units, with their own self-management organs, defends against the undesired process whereby—especially in large enterprises—workers' self-management freezes into mere formalism. As the organs of workers' self-management mainly consist of non-specialists, the workers cannot be expected to make decisions based on an economic understanding in such a complex institution as an enterprise. In the smaller economic units which can be surveyed easier and with the results of which the workers' income is so closely connected, the worker can very well take part in decision making.

Overcoming the alienation processes

One of the special sociological problems of industrial sociology is the alienation process. Whereas in Marx's time people believed that these disadvantageous features could be eliminated by socializing the means of production, within the last decades experience has shown that the problems of alienation processes continue to exist even in the nationalized or—in the sense of the Yugoslav system—socialized enterprises.[8]

The origin of the alienation processes lies in the increasing separation of brainwork and physical work and in the subordination of man to material processes, i.e., in the dehumanization of work. The extent of these alienation processes is connected with the size of the enterprise. Therefore, from the social aspect as well as in regard to the economy of production, it belongs to the task of the enterprise to counteract the obstructing factors resulting from the alienation processes and, if possible, to eliminate them.[9]

The difficulties arising from the relation between man and work cannot be overcome by merely constituting economic units. The economic units are rather a starting point from which the social relations within an enterprise can be investigated and influenced.

As a rule, the worker in modern industrial society is not the owner of the means of production and this is generally felt as discrimination. But profit shares and decentralization within an enterprise have proved an effective means against the negative influences of the alienation of property.

The consequences of the alienation of work resulting from the mechanization of production are as disadvantageous as the alienation of property. In a big enterprise with a high level of technology the worker to an increasing extent has only partial functions. The result is—whether desired or not—a specialization of the operating process, and at the same time the loss of the inner connection to one's own work. It happens very often that the worker does not even know the finished product in the manufacture of which he takes part.

The process of spatial alienation results from the separation of the place of work and the place of living and from the impersonal working area designed for the purpose of the machines only. Thus, when factory shops for special working processes are planned, the needs of the worker are mostly neglected, i.e., the need for freedom of movement at one's working place, for an overview of the work process, for attractively painted rooms and the need for communication.

The alienation of man results from anonymous cooperation at work and from the separation of brainwork and physical work, often resulting in a supercilious attitude of socially superior persons empowered to give instructions toward persons who merely follow these instructions.

In solving these social problems in Yugoslavia, one could depend on the experiences in the former factories of Bat'a in Borovo, where pioneer work had been done not only in steering the firm by means of internal transfer prices [*pretiale lenkung*], but also in the reformation of social relations.[10] In the same way as in the Bat'a factories before the First World War, the efforts regarding the economic units today aim at leading the worker away from the attitude of a wage earner toward a more entrepreneurial attitude.

In the economic units the principle is abandoned of carrying out orders which were planned in every detail by a central institution. The individual departments get a task which is part of the whole enterprise's program and which has to be carried out according to the instructions governing for the whole enterprise. Thus, the director—and in the desired case the collective—of the economic unit has to fulfill a variety of tasks, whereby every employee is invited to contribute to brainwork and to influencing working conditions.[11]

One way to overcome the alienation processes is the cooperation of all members of the economic unit in the organization of work, the layout of space, the composition of small working teams, etc. Transferring the decision-making process about the performance of work to the economic units is furthermore a rather optimal solution because of the direct practical connection.

The personality of the director of an economic unit is most important for the good functioning of the social processes. Therefore, special attention has to be paid to the selection of persons for these positions and to their special training.[12]

But exactly in this field there are quite a few unsolved problems in the Yugoslav enterprises. The director of an economic unit stands on the lowest rank of the industrial hierarchy. He is nominated by higher organs, though in agreement with the working collective, and is responsible for the economic unit subordinate to him. This subordination of the collective under the orders of the director, however, contradicts the Yugoslav aim of direct democracy, i.e., the possibility for all workers to participate in the management of the enterprise.[13]

The work collective is expected to adopt managerial rules to counteract this tendency toward an extreme strengthening of the director's position.[14]

In spite of all this, it is up to the director whether the employees are induced to active cooperation or whether the advantages of decentralization are employed only by the director himself, with the majority of the workers consequently lacking the possibility of overcoming the alienation of work. One way to prevent this is to discuss all important problems during the meetings of the economic units.

A further problem is that the worker not only has to be ready to take over responsibilities, but has to be able to do so. Therefore, in the Yugoslav enterprises great importance is attached to improved in-service training and to instruction in thinking in macro economic terms. In this connection, it has a positive effect on the intellectual horizon and the general knowledge of the worker when he acts in the self-management organs where new tasks and new impulses are produced.[15]

In participating in the administration work of the self-managing organs of the economic units, the worker comes out of the monotony of specialized work and is faced with tasks which require brainwork and produce a feeling of common responsibility. The consequence of cooperation in the self-management organs is that the other economic units and the entire enterprise—on which ultimately the success of the individual unit also depends—are taken into consideration, and thus the connection to the marketed product is guaranteed.

Increasing production by direct relationship to the group's success

Generally, in a system of stimulative income distribution the emphasis lies on the individual worker. When a system of wage incentives for the economic units was worked out, the experiences of the industrial sociologists—above all of the Americans Mayo, Dickson, and Roethlisberger—served as a basis; for them the main interest lies on the actions of the group.[16] Already in the twenties of this century, Mayo, with his Hawthorne interview program, came to the conclusion that the relation between the working groups and the management is one of the principal problems of a large industrial concern.

From the beginning, the economic units are organized in such a way that it is possible to ascertain the economic success of their own work, and a certain part of the additional profit gained by the work of the economic unit raises the planned wages of the workers. Thus, the influence of group cooperation on the success of an economic unit makes it possible to pressure individual workers in a way that would not be tolerated if it was done by the management. The group consciousness within the economic unit will be strengthened by the transference of certain decisions about personnel and discipline, such as employment and dismissal of workers, disciplinary punishment, co-termination in the election of the director, etc.

In a similar sense also Štaudaher and Štaudaher write about practical experiences with the distribution of income according to economic units:

> The efforts for improved quality are greater. The relation to one's own work improves. There are growing tendencies to a better utilization of labor. The attitude towards 'work shirkers' becomes more critical. A sound self-criticism towards one's own technical qualification is the consequence.[17]

The utilization of industrial sociology in constituting an economic unit

Already since the experiments of Elton Mayo it has been known that other factors, in addition to material ones, influence the worker's effectiveness. Only much later, however, were these experiences accepted in the ideas of industrial management and used in practice. And socialist Yugoslavia utilized these methods of industrial sociology still later than the capitalist world.

The importance of human relations in the work area

In different sociological studies[18] it was pointed out that the social phenomena accompanying industrial work, such as growing self-confidence and the feeling of belonging to a certain workshop, play a much greater part in the effectiveness of the worker than pecuniary incentives.

The consideration of human relations in the work area is one of the most important factors of social influence; the national economic system of which an enterprise is a part is irrelevant. Experience has shown that the workers of nationalized firms as well as of private enterprises have the same attitude regarding human relations. Alienation processes and signs of monotony develop because of the general passiveness of the workers, which is a consequence of the present form of industrial organization confining the brainwork in a factory to a certain percentage of the employees and excluding the majority.[19] This was taken into account by the German entrepreneur Spindler[20] when he carried out his experiments.

The introduction of workers' self-management in Yugoslav enterprises did not basically change the industrial organization.

> . . . Alongside the new, democratic and self-management structure in the enterprise, the old hierarchic structure still exists, based on the division of labor into mental and physical work or, in other words, into directing and performing work.[21]

In many Yugoslav enterprises the creation of an effective connection between the guidance of production and workers' self-management is still an unsolved problem. Some of the most progressive Yugoslav enterprises which provided an example for the organization of economic units based their personnel combinations of working groups on sociological and psychological investigations. In these firms the main task of the industrial sociologist is human relations. Already today, this task is considered to be more important than the development of stimulative wage systems.

> Not until the new organization produces a real connection between the worker and his work does work cease to be alienated. Understanding this problem makes us comprehend many other things, first of all the fact that the productivity trend during the last years has not taken such a course as normally could have been expected.[22]
>
> Therefore, for workers' self-management as a total and indivisible system the following question is essential: How can a connection be created between the production process and self-management in the form of a social process? This problem became especially urgent with the introduction of stimulative pay which involved many internal problems in connection with wages. Do there exist already approaches toward a new organization still to be developed? It seems that they do exist: they are the economic units.[23]

Redirecting interests by co-determination

One of the main goals of the decentralized enterprise management is the drawing of, if possible, all the workers into brainwork, which is not limited to participation in the income distribution within the economic units. By the organization of an economic unit the workers should have the possibility of influencing processes that are important for them, as, e.g., the distribution of work according to qualification and ability of the individual, cooperation in the organization within a department, participation in the profit reached by joint efforts, and abolition of strict subordination under superior persons.

If in the framework of effective co-determination in the industrial processes, the worker regards himself as an entrepreneur, on whose prudence and attentiveness success also depends, a redirection of interests will be the consequence, i.e., a turn from interest in short-run advantages—to get as high wages as soon as possible—to interest in a long-term stable economic position in the market. Dahrendorf[24] among others realized this dichotomy of interests in an enterprise when workers cooperate in management. This is a socially very important process not bound to a certain economic system.[25]

Training for economic thinking and joint responsibility

The training for economic thinking is closely connected with the system of departmental profit and loss accounting and the related distribution of income. The basis of personal income is the complex efficiency [*kompleksan učinak*] of every worker, i.e., not only the quantitatively measurable result of his work, but also the qualitative components of his performance, his technical qualification, personal initiative and creative cooperation, responsibility of the individual, and the work result of the group as well as of the whole enterprise. The worker no longer has fixed, more or less guaranteed wages to which a varying sum is added, but, in principle, the total wages depend on the final result of work.[26] This means that the economic success of the enterprise in the market—i.e., the profitableness—also influences the workers' wages.

Self-management and joint responsibility in the framework of an economic unit encourage the worker to a better education. As the results of cooperation have a direct effect on personal income, it widens the mental horizon of the individual for economic processes.[27]. . .

The economic unit as an industrial category

With the transition from administrative control to workers' self-management and with the acceptance of the principles of supply and demand, production planning was transferred from the technical to the commercial departments because production now has a marketing function and is no longer confined merely to the function of distribution.[28]

With the decentralization of economic decision-making, the enterprises will show some features of the free market system. The basic principles which determine the functions of the national economy are only of secondary importance for the efficiency of decentralized enterprise control.[29]

Enterprise control under the condition of decentralized economic decision-making

. . . The causes for the general introduction of decentralized enterprise management in Yugoslavia are to be found on two levels, though one must not forget that the development of workers' self-management had mainly political motives.[30] Under the appeal of Marx's doctrine of the withering away of the state, the initiators of the new Yugoslav economic system are striving to make economic organizations as independent as possible, i.e., mainly decentralizing the planning system by strengthening workers' self-management. On the other hand, such a strengthening of self-management requires additional rights for the enterprises. The subdivision of an enterprise into smaller and surveyable units (economic units) is the consequence of these endeavors, which the Marxian economists justify by direct democracy. Thus, the decentralization of the national economy and of political power is extended by the decentralization of industrial organization. In an economic unit the worker can in principle be a producer as well as—in his capacity as a member of self-management—a manager. Here, the purely economic considerations begin, centering about the attempt to increase the good management of the enterprises by utilizing the possibilities of industrial organization. . . .

A condition for decentralized enterprise control is the delegation of managerial and initiatory authority connected with the transfer of responsibility to the corresponding personnel of the independent parts of the firm.[31] From the standpoint of the national economy, a restriction of decentralized economic decisions must be seen in the fact that a series of very important decisions is reserved to the state.[32]

The advantages and disadvantages of decentralization have been sufficiently discussed already in the literature so that they need not be explained here in detail.[33] Attention shall be directed, however, to some facts which are especially relevant for Yugoslav enterprises. Thus, in the less developed parts of the country with a high percentage of illiterates it will be difficult to bring workers unaccustomed to industrial work to adopt economically rational conduct, above all if they lack material interest going beyond the satisfaction of their subsistence minimum.[34] In cases in which the educational status of the working class does not permit expectation of voluntary behavior in its short-term self-interest, central controls are more effective. A frequent disadvantage of decentralization is the clumsiness and slowness of decision-making processes in matters which do not show a direct and effective advantage in the short run for the deciding persons.[35] This often appearing lack of initiative leads to disadvantages, especially with decisions which are important and urgent for the whole enterprise. These weak points of decentralization become nearly insignificant at the same time as the professional qualification of the deciding persons improves and as the decision-making process is prepared and organized more effectively.

The advantages of this form of organization must not be underestimated. They lie in the strengthening of personal initiative and responsibility, the shortening of lines of authority as the decisions are made on the lowest possible level, the immediacy of decision-making and the training for businesslike thinking and transactions.

NOTES

1. Stevan Kukoleća and Živko Kostić, *Organizacija kolektiva* (Zagreb, 1961), p. 284.

2. Franc, Pavlašepić, and Antonić, *Organizacija poduzeca po ekonomskim jedinicama* (Zagreb, 1960).

3. Tomislav Bandin, "Uticaj obračuna po ekonomskim jedinicama na ekonomiju proizvodnje," *Ekonomika preduzeča,* 12, 1964, p. 893.

4. Josip Županov and Ilija Marjanović, *Ekonomske jedinice kao socijalne grupe* (Zagreb, 1960), p. 21.

5. Ibid., p. 3.

6. Above all, Mayo, Roethlisberger, Drucker, Friedmann.

7. Županov and Marjanović, *Ekonomske jedinice.*

8. Hyacinthe Dubreuil, "Bildung autonomer Gruppen—eine Form der Betriebsorganisation," *Soziale Beziehungen in der Industrie,* 3, 2/1952, p. 8; Rudi Supek, "Humanizacija rada i radničko samoupravljanje," *Naša stvarnost,* 1, 7–8/1957, pp. 99–114.

9. See also Götz Briefs, "Betriebssoziologie," in *Handbuch der Soziologie* (Stuttgart: Alfred Vierkandt, 1959), pp. 45, 50.

10. Udo Gerd Schweder, "Innerbetriebliche Dezentralisation, Dargestellt am Beispiel Batas," *Der österreichische Betriebswirt,* 2, 1952, pp. 41–61; Bat'a, *Menschen und Wurk,* complete edition, A. Cekota (Zlin, 1935).

11. The process of developing intentions within the economic units is directed by factory regulations for the concrete details of which the legislator gives only the frame.

12. See Josip Županov, "Ekonomske jedinice—nova struktura vlasti u poduzeću," *Ekonomske jedinice u praksi* (Zagreb, 1961), pp. 2, 3.

13. See also I. Štaudaher and V. Štaudaher, *Knjigovodstvo proizvodnje po ekonomskim jedinicama* (Zagreb, 1961), p. 9.

14. Vojin Hadžistević, *Odnosi,* pp. 24 ff. [*sic*].

15. *Problemi organizacije ekonomskih jedinica i unutrašnje raspodele u proizvodnim preduzećima* (Belgrade: Jugoslovenski zavod za produktivnost rada, 1964), pp. 89 ff.

16. See Elton Mayo, *The Social Problems of an Industrial Civilisation* (Cambridge: Harvard University Press, 1945); F. J. Roethlisberger and W. J. Dickson, *Management and the Workers* (Cambridge: Harvard University Press, 1949).

17. Štaudaher and Štaudaher, *Knjigovodstvo proizvodnje,* p. 9.

18. E.g., Mayo, *Social Problems,* p. 119; Dubreuil, *Autonome Gruppen,* p. 6; Renate Mayntz has a different opinion (*Die soziale Organisation des Industriebetriebes* [Stuttgart, 1958], pp. 58, 86).

19. Durbeuil, *Autonome Gruppen,* pp. 13 ff.

20. Gert P. Spindler, *Neue Antworten im sozialen Raum* (Düsseldorf-Vienna, 1964); same author, *Mitunternehmertum* (Lüneburg, 1951).

21. Županov and Marjanović, *Ekonomske jedinice,* p. 15.

22. In certain years (1954, 1958) Yugoslav industry showed no increase of productivity at all; in 1955 to 1956 the productivity increased about 3 percent.

23. Županov and Marjanović, *Ekonomske jedinice,* p. 18.

24. Ralf Dahrendorf, "Industrie- und Betriebssoziologie," *Sammlung Göschen,* Vol. 103 (Berlin, 1956), p. 78.

25. See also Spindler, *Neue Antworten,* p. 268; Alfred Horné, *Der beklagte Sieg* (Villingen, 1957).

26. This procedure corresponds approximately to Nicklisch's thesis of the wages as a part of profit paid in advance. See Heinrich Nick-

lisch, *Die Betriebswirtschaft, 7, Auflage* (Stuttgart, 1932), pp. 267 ff., 560 ff.

27. See also, Dubreuil, *Autonome Gruppen.*

28. Kosta Vasiljević, "Obračun po ekonomskim jedinicama i rezerve obrtnih sredstava," *Ekonomika preduzeća,* 9, 1961, p. 473.

29. See Eugen Schmalenbach, *Pretiale Wirtschaftslenkung,* Vol. II, *Pretiale Lenkung des Betriebes* (Bremen-Horn, 1947), p. 9.

30. Ašer Deleon, "Worker's Management," in *Collective Economy in Yugoslavia* (Geneva, 1959), p. 151.

31. See also Kurt Junckerstorff, *Internationaler Grundrisse der wissenschaftlichen Unternehmungsführung* (Berlin, 1964), pp. 193 ff.

32. E.g., import restrictions, influence on price adjustments, control of the investment policy.

33. E.g., Eugen Schmalenbach, "Industrielle Kleinbetriebe und pretiale Betriebslenkung," *Die industrielle Organisation,* 17, 1948, pp. 197 ff.; Kurt Bender, *Pretiale Betriebslenkung* (Essen, 1951), pp. 100 ff.; Albert Meier, *Organisation der Unternehmungsführung, 2, Auflage* (Stuttgart, 1965), pp. 64–67; Theodor Beste, "Verwaltungsaufblau und betriebliches Rechnungswesen," in *Festschrift für Eugen Schmalenbach* (Leipzig, 1933), pp. 110–117.

34. See also Dragašević, "Postupnost u sprovođenju organizacije," *Ekononomika predazeća,* 7, 1964, p. 668.

35. See Roko Braut, Alfred Jaeger, and Mija Novak, *Priručnik o organizaciji poduzeća* (Zagreb, 1962), p. 87.

7. Industrial Efficiency under Managerial versus Cooperative Decision-making

A Comparative Study of Manufacturing Enterprises in Israel

SEYMOUR MELMAN

Managerial versus cooperative decision-making

Apart from relatively primitive societies, the managerial mode of organization is clearly the dominant one, worldwide, in private as well as publicly owned enterprise. The managerial mode of decision-making may be identified by three primary features. First, there tends to be an occupational separation between decision-making and producing. Especially in firms beyond the workshop size, those who mainly do decision-making have distinctive occupational roles from those who primarly do production work. This differentiation is reinforced and formalized by unionization, for then the "bargaining unit" differentiates those who do the production work from those who do decision-making. A second feature of management is the hierarchical organization of decision-making. At the peak of successive layers of fewer and more powerful decision-makers, there is the final decision-maker, the person whose decision cannot be vetoed by anyone else. A third feature of managerial organization is the built-in criterion of enlarging the scope and intensity of decision-making as the priority objective for the enterprise. In this perspective, money making in

Reprinted from *Review of Radical Political Economics,* 2, No. 1 (Spring 1970): 9–34, by permission of Transaction, Inc.

the form of profit is a necessary but not a primary objective in its own right.

What sort of alternative is conceivable—as against the managerial mode of decision-making so defined? First, decision-making could be done by those who also do production work. This is feasible especially as decision process is differentiated between particularized decisions concerning details of work, and condition-setting decisions which define major goals, criteria for design, or limits (like product class) within which an enterprise is to operate. Thus, decisions about the choice of class of products, or decisions about major capital expansions are made infrequently. All persons in an enterprise have a stake in such choices and can conceivably participate in making them. Once defined, such condition-setting decisions become the boundaries within which detailed operating decisions can be made by administrators and technicians. In a non-hierarchical organization, work assignments, including the administrative and technical posts, can be subject to final decision, including removal and replacement, by the general body of persons engaged in an enterprise. Finally, it is conceivable to operate industrial facilities according to primary criteria like providing useful work and regulating volume of output to serve specified social priorities—instead of profit maximization or extension of managerial control.

These analytically abstracted contrasts in types of decision process define key elements of a cooperative as against the conventional managerial mode of production organization.

A comparative study in Israel

Such variation in mode of decision process is found within Israel where, in addition to a considerable population of industrial firms under managerial control, there is also a population of 170 industrial enterprises that are operated under a cooperative decision process. The latter group of enterprises are located in the cooperative communities called Kibbutzim. There are 230 such communites in Israel,[1] of which 170 operate industrial enterprises with 20 to 250 persons working in each unit. These cooperative enterprises use modern machine technology and techniques and are engaged in a broad array of manufacturing industries: metalworking, chemicals, various types of machinery production, tools, home appliances, woodworking, food processing, instruments, electrical goods, plastics, and others.[2]

In view of the wider theoretical interest in the problem of alternatives for decision-making on production, I decided to inquire into the comparative industrial efficiency of enterprises operating under managerial as against cooperative control. How efficient can an industrial enterprise be under cooperative control? In terms of accepted criteria of labor and capital productivity, and profitability, can there be an efficient alternative to managerial control over industry? . . .

It is well appreciated that there is some degree of variation among nations in "styles" of industrial administration. However, average national industrial efficiency, as in productivity of labor and capital, is determined decisively by relative costs of labor and machinery to industry, which, in turn, regulate the cost-minimizing intensity of mechanization. It is significant that Israeli industry is permeated with personnel trained in the United States and Western Europe, and the Israeli schools of business and technology emulate the same models, as do industrial associations and others who have continuing access to the literature of modern industrial management. From this standpoint, therefore, Israeli industry shares in the knowledge and practices of western industrialism.

The criteria for the selection of enterprises for this study were that each should represent a technically modern industrial operation, including substantial capital investment, and producing standard products for sale in an open market. Of course, it was essential that the enterprise administrators in each case should make available the required data for analysis. In the case of the Kibbutz enterprises a special criterion was applied: Kibbutz enterprises that involved more than about 10 percent of hired employees were not to be included in the sample. During the last years, numbers of Kibbutzim, endeavoring to enlarge their industrial output, sought to employ persons on a temporary basis. This arrangement sometimes continued. Since this introduced an employment relationship in what was formerly a cooperatively operated enterprise, industrial units that had this characteristic were excluded from the sample.

Procedure

About 25 industrial enterprises were contacted, and it was possible to develop a paired sample of 12 enterprises, 6 of them under managerial control and 6 under cooperative control.

TABLE 1. Capital Investment of Each Matched Enterprise
(In thousands of Israeli pounds)

Industry	Managerial decision-making	Cooperative decision-making
Tools	942	647
Instruments	753	8,393
Die casting	20,953	461
Plastics	330	2,656
Machine shop	335	1,077
Canning	6,746	4,148
Median	847	1,866
Average	5,010	2,897
Ranking (no. sets where each type enterprise leads)	3	3

These enterprises were matched with respect to industry and product. It seemed important to include in each group enterprises that produced similar products, hence using similar raw materials, similar manufacturing technologies and processes, and selling their products in similar markets.

The list of industries represented by these two groups of enterprises, and the capital investment in each enterprise are shown in Table 1. . . .

In each of the sampled firms it was possible to obtain parallel sets of data from the financial and production records.[3] These data were all for the same year, between 1963 and 1967. The actual year is not disclosed in order to shield the identity of the enterprises.

There are special features of accounting data for the cooperatively administered enterprises. The cost of labor in the managerially controlled enterprise is measured by wages paid. In the cooperatively administered enterprise no wages or salaries are paid, there being no internal money exchange within the framework of the cooperative community. (Money is used in the economic relations of the cooperative community to the rest of society and for recording inputs and outputs in the component enterprises of the cooperative community.) The cost of labor, as part of the cost of production in the Kibbutz enterprise, was measured by using an accounting category which the Kibbutzim calculate regularly and carefully: the "cost of a day of labor." This means the average cost of maintaining a person in the cooperative community per day of labor worked. This statistic reflects the sum of all expenditures for consumer goods and services during a year divided by the total number of man-days worked in the various production sections of the cooperative village economy. The resulting figure is the best available estimate of the cost of using labor by a Kibbutz enterprise and was accordingly used for accounting purposes in these calculations. (The Kibbutz "cost of a day of labor" has tended to equal or exceed industrial wages in managerial enterprises.) . . .

Industrial efficiency is measured here in terms of: productivity of labor, productivity of capital, profit generated per production worker, and the cost of administration. Labor and capital productivity reflect on the efficiency with which key industrial inputs are utilized. The general competence of enterprise administration in optimizing outputs in relation to inputs is reflected in the profit that is generated per production worker. Lastly, the manpower used for administration measures the outlays made for the productionally necessary function of decision-making: Who can do it at lesser cost?

Results

The comparative productivity of labor in managerial and cooperative enterprises was measured by contrasting output (net sales) to inputs (production worker manhours). These data (Table 2) were calculated for the sampled enterprises on an equal weighting basis. This procedure is significant for the purpose of the investigation. If the total sales in each set of enterprises were divided by total production worker manhours, the result would assign substantial weight to the enterprises in each group that were larger than the others. The present objective, however, is to contrast types of enterprises. Therefore, the enterprise is necessarily the unit of observation, and the productivity of labor and other measures of efficiency were calculated separately for each enterprise, then grouped with median and average values shown for the managerial and cooperative groups.

The results appearing in Table 2 show that the cooperative decision-making enterprises had median sales per production worker manhour of I£13.61, 26 percent higher than the I£10.76

TABLE 2. Productivity of Labor
(Sales per production manhour)

Industry	Managerial decision-making	Cooperative decision-making
Tools	I£ 7.88	I£ 6.31
Instruments	13.64	12.67
Die casting	15.48	14.71
Plastics	5.40	14.26
Machine shop	5.66	13.26
Canning	14.08	13.97
Median	I£10.76	I£13.61
Average	10.36	12.53
Ranking (no. sets where each type enterprise leads)	1	2
	3—almost equal	

for the managerially controlled enterprises. It is important that the sales statistics do not simply reflect undifferentiated money-valued sales. They represent quantities of similar products sold in similar markets, and therefore at similar prices, for each set of enterprises.

A second measure of productivity was that of productivity of capital (Table 3). This was measured in two forms, output (profit) as percent of input (capital invested), and output (sales) as percent of input (fixed assets). For the cooperative enterprises median profit was 12.9 percent of capital invested as against 7.7 percent for the managerially controlled enterprises. Sales (median) were 3.6 times fixed assets for the cooperative enterprises and 2.7 for the managerially controlled enterprises. These measures of capital productivity reflect the overall effectiveness of the use of fixed assets for generating output for sale. In this respect the cooperative enterprises outperformed the managerially controlled firms—by 67 percent greater profit/investment, and by 33 percent greater sales/fixed assets.

In order to gain another view of the overall effectiveness of the administration of these enterprises, I measured net profit per production worker (Table 4). In these terms, the cooperative enterprises showed a median profit per production worker of I£1,912, 115 percent greater than the I£899 for the enterprises under managerial control.

TABLE 3. Productivity of Capital

Industry		Managerial decision-making	Cooperative decision-making
Tools	a)	0.659	0.021
	b)	2.9	3.7
Instruments	a)	0.300	0.0195
	b)	2.5	4.7
Die casting	a)	0.038	1.125
	b)	1.1	3.6
Plastics	a)	0.024	0.095
	b)	3.4	4.3
Machine shop	a)	0.117	0.200
	b)	2.5	2.6
Canning	a)	0.026	0.164
	b)	2.96	2.6
Median	a)	0.077	0.129
	b)	2.7	3.6
Average	a)	0.194	0.271
	b)	2.6	3.6
Ranking (no. sets where each type enterprise leads)		2	7
		3—almost equal	

(a) Profit as percent of capital invested
(b) Sales as percent of fixed assets

TABLE 4. Efficiency of Management
(Net profit per production worker)

Industry	Managerial decision-making	Cooperative decision-making
Tools	I£ 3,190	I£ 118
Instruments	2,880	556
Die casting	1,335	4,350
Plastics	74	2,771
Machine shop	463	2,287
Canning	461	1,537
Median	I£ 899	I£ 1,912
Average	1,401	1,937
Ranking (no. sets where each type enterprise leads)	2	4

A further contrast for these two sets of enterprises is given in Table 5, showing the comparative cost of administration. This is measured in terms of the number of administrative employees required per hundred production workers. In the cooperative enterprises, the median value was 17.3; the same relationship for the managerially controlled enterprises was 19.9.

In sum: the cooperative enterprises showed higher productivity of labor (26 percent), higher productivity of capital (67 and 33 percent), larger net profit per production worker (115 percent) and lower administrative cost (13 percent).

The relative performance of the two types of enterprises may also be viewed by ranking the position of each of the firms in the study with respect to each criterion. In Table 6, there is an entry M (managerial) in the "Tools" industry row under the "Labor productivity" column. This means that for the labor productivity criterion in the Tools industry, the managerial enterprise was the better performer. Again, under "Labor productivity" for the "Instruments" industry, the managerial and cooperative firms were almost equal, with the managerial unit being somewhat better than the cooperative, hence the designation in the Table as M-C. Similarly for the rest of the Table.

Discounting the 8 almost-equal performances (M-C or C-M), in 15 enterprise-criteria cases the cooperative units were better

TABLE 5. Cost of Enterprise Administration
(Administrative staff per 100 production workers)

INDUSTRY	MANAGERIAL DECISION-MAKING	COOPERATIVE DECISION-MAKING
Tools	12.1	19.2
Instruments	24.0	15.4
Die casting	21.5	21.1
Plastics	26.5	24.1
Machine shop	11.1	13.3
Canning	18.3	14.2
Median	19.9	17.3
Average	18.9	17.8
Ranking (no. sets where each type enterprise has lower value)	2	2
	2—almost equal	

TABLE 6. Summary Ranking of Managerial (M) versus Cooperative (C) Enterprises by Criteria of Efficiency

INDUSTRY	LABOR PRODUCTIVITY	CAPITAL PRODUCTIVITY	PROFIT PER PRODUCTION WORKER	COST OF ADMINISTRATION
Tools	M	M C-M	M	M
Instruments	M-C	M C	M	C
Die casting	M-C	C C	C	C-M
Plastics	C	C C	C	C-M
Machine shop	C	C C-M	C	M
Canning	M-C	C M-C	C	C

Note: The M, C designations in this table may be used as rank values in the sign test of significance of difference, single-tailed. Were the Cooperative enterprises, as a group, significantly more efficient than the Managerial enterprise, with 15 of the former and 7 of the latter emerging first in the various measures of industrial efficiency? Chance factors alone would produce the Cooperative lead at probability .067. This gives confidence in the inference that the sampled Cooperative enterprises, as a group, were significantly more efficient than the others. See S. Siegel, *Nonparametric Statistics for the Behavioral Sciences,* McGraw-Hill, New York, 1956, pp. 68 ff.

performers, compared with 7 where the managerial units led. By industry type, only in the Tools case was there a clear first for the managerial type in more than two criteria. In ranking under efficiency criteria, the cooperative units led in capital productivity and profit per production man-hour, were ahead in labor productivity and broke even in cost of administration.

Analysis of results

The data assembled here bear upon three widespread assumptions: first, that there is no workable alternative to the managerial form of control for operating modern industry; second, that even if there were an alternative, the managerial mode of organization is inherently most efficient; and finally, that technology itself sets the requirement for managerialism. Whatever constraints may be assigned to the data of this paper, it is evident that they do not support these familiar themes. Evidently, there is a cooperative mode of organization that is a workable alternative to managerialism for industrial operations, and the use of machine technology does not itself exclude the use of cooperative decision-making.

However, some reservation is in order for interpreting the data of this study for the second proposition. It is not warranted, given the characteristics of the data, to infer any general statement as to the degree or predictability of relative efficiency of cooperative versus managerial decision-making in industrial operations. Thus, while the enterprises examined here tend to show greater efficiency for the cooperative units, as a group, the limitations on the data (number of units, single time and single locale of observations) point to the following as the relevant inference: cooperatively administered industrial enterprises can be as efficient, or more efficient, than managerially controlled units. This, albeit qualified, inference suggests that the cooperative organization of industry can be a workable option for some societies. What characteristics of cooperative organization account for its apparent effectiveness in industry?

The main differentiating features of cooperative organization of production include the following: (1) Authority for major decisions is vested in all the participants; there is no occupationally codified separation between those who decide and those who do the work. (2) The mode of internal decision-making is based upon mutuality and is essentially democratic, as against the hierarchical organization of managerial control. (3) In the cooperative organization there is formal, institutionalized equality and anti-inequality in decison-making and in consumption through the pervasive system of sharing final authority in decision-making and in consumption. This contrasts with the managerial pattern of differential, competitive individual gain (i.e., one man's gain, to be a competitive gain, must include another's relative loss). (4) Finally, the cooperative enterprise is oriented toward enlarging its output and affording participation in useful work for members of the cooperative community, rather than profit maximization or expansion of managerial control.

The above-mentioned characteristics of the cooperative organization have not been ordinarily linked to industrial efficiency. Indeed, some of these features are often presumed to lead to industrial inefficiency. It seems appropriate at this point to examine each of the above features of the cooperative system in light of their possible consequences for industrial efficiency.

Participation and democracy in control. In the cooperative industrial enterprise, final authority over basic decisions—products, capital investment, number of workers—is vested in the general body of workers in the enterprise and in the cooperative community as a whole. Responsibility for organizing implementation of basic decisions is the task of democratically elected enterprise administrators who are required to report regularly to the general body and to justify their decisions and proposals.

As a consequence of cooperative control, the workers in these enterprises tend to have interest and concern about technical conditions of work which is rare in the managerially controlled enterprise. Thus, instead of the suggestion box and individual money rewards for particular technical suggestions, the cooperative industrial enterprise operates with a fairly sustained free flow of communication among all members of the enterprise, both in production and administration.

The cooperative enterprises deal with mechanization and automation of production in ways that contrast with the managerial firm. Thus, the elimination of a manual work task by mechanization benefits all concerned in the Kibbutz-managed enterprise since the gains are shared by all. Also, the Kibbutz industrial enterprises usually operate under conditions of labor shortages relative to goals for enlarging production. As a result there is little problem of having useful work available for people whose tasks have been mechanized. Furthermore, each person knows that the members of the cooperative care for each other. There is little likelihood here of producing a situation where a particular work skill, no longer required, could cause a person to be discarded, no longer needed or wanted. Such an event contradicts the essential conditions of mutuality and cooperation in the Kibbutz.

Equality in "income." In the cooperative enterprise, the principle of equality in major decision-making is paralleled by a code of consumption equality—more exactly, consumption without money exchange and on the basis of need, community capability, and in accordance with mores of anti-inequality and material non-ostentation. There are no problems of wage systems administration since there are no wages. The cooperative enterprise has no trade union relations problems or costs in the absence of an employment relationship. Production work-load problems are usually resolved by the working group in terms of mutual understanding of what is an acceptable day's work, taking into account the capabilities of production equipment and the requirements of the enterprise.

Instead of individual financial incentives, the people in the cooperatively controlled enterprise receive an acceptable level of living, the right and duty to participate in mutual decision-making, mutual care and esteem—especially for carrying group decision responsibilities. For example, the Kibbutz enterprise gets the benefit of wide-ranging cooperation among its members owing to the use of extra-work-shift hours on behalf of the enterprise. Frequently, when some of the administrators or workers of an enterprise eat dinner together in the community dining room and discuss the problems of the work place, this is not an "overtime" task that requires special payment as would be the case in a managerially controlled enterprise where work is done by employees. Though discussions on enterprise problems in the dining hall of the cooperative can be lengthy, it is unthinkable to "charge" for this, for there is no theory, category, or procedure by which such a "charge" could be made.

It is commonly assumed that the presence of individual money incentives combined with opportunity for rising in a managerial hierarchy comprises a very powerful incentive system for efficiency in industry. In the Kibbutz there is no differential income reward for varied work. Therefore election to a post of administrative responsibility confers status only. Also, it is ordinarily assumed that the managerial decision process, because of the attraction of individual gain, uniquely produces a major incentive to minimize costs in production and to maximize net return to the enterprise. The administrator of the cooperative enterprise does strive for efficiency, and meeting enterprise goals of profit, output, and employment, for that is the requirement for his status. However, in contrast with the managerial system, success in Kibbutz industry administration does not necessarily bring accretions of decision-power. For rotation of administrative personnel is a general policy in cooperative enterprises. This produces a sophisticated administrative cadre because people with these talents are moved among administrative tasks within and among enterprises. The unwritten code of the cooperative community often requires that administrators do manual production work as one of their rotating responsibilities.

Among the administrators and technicians in the cooperative

enterprise, there is considerable pressure to have good personal relations with the other men in the work place. This is owing to the fact that only by mutual agreement are major decisions made and effectively implemented.

None of this is to say that in the Kibbutz community all men are equal. Work tasks differ. Differences of ability make for inequality of responsibility, and those who bear it receive the esteem and attention of their fellows while having to devote typically more than average hours to their work. In the cooperative community one's standing, the degree to which others take you seriously, means a lot. The use of a vehicle often goes with some administrative jobs and that gives a fringe-benefit of mobility as a result of simply doing the work. But the vehicle goes with the job, not with the man. Identification of the individual with the wider community, and cooperation to achieve its goals, are the main operative incentives of the cooperative enterprise—in contrast with the individual competitive incentive pattern of managerially controlled production.[4] The apparent workability of the cooperative form of organization in production suggests the importance of greater understanding of the worth of non-monetary and other than direct-work-efficiency factors in influencing productiveness in industry.

Useful work and increased output as goals. . . . The combined effect of the main features of cooperative organization, summarized above, is to induce automatically a pervasive pattern of detailed cooperation in the performance of work. Such cooperation is the crucial element for stable, hence optimal, operation of a given production system. This is a key factor, in my judgment, for explaining the efficient performance of cooperatively controlled industrial enterprise.

Optimum input-output performance in modern industrial facilities is expected, on both theoretical and empirical grounds, when the unit functions as a stable system.[5] A stable system is one whose output varies within predictable and acceptable limits. When operations are, in this sense, "under control," there is an optimum production result from the combined inputs of machines, men, and services that constitute the principal inputs of an industrial facility.

The sort of cooperative pattern of workaday functioning that is found in the Kibbutz enterprise is rarely found, or even approximated, in the managerially controlled enterprise. This is owing to the conditions of competitive individual incentives and competitive bargaining between managers and employees within the managerially operated enterprise. Beyond a certain level of intensity these competitive incentive factors produce conditions which work against stable operation of the production system. Stated differently: competitive managerial rule over production often interferes with the optimization requirements of modern production technology.

This is not to say that stability in production is not obtainable under managerial control. However, the price is usually costly managerial control over production workers (one foreman to ten workers), or the creation of conditions which induce cooperation among production workers, and between production workers and management. The latter can significantly alter the competitive incentive factors that differentiate the managerial from the cooperative mode of decision-making.[6] Having considered the efficiency effects of features that are unique to cooperative decision-making, we now turn to other factors that may bear on the findings of differences in efficiency between the two types of organizations.

Size, environment and ideology. In manufacturing industry it is widely appreciated that large enterprises operate with significant advantages over small enterprises. Larger firms have superior access to capital and technical talent, and usually operate with higher rates of profit. Also, investigations of administrative costs[7] show that larger enterprises, on the average, have lower administrative to production ratios than smaller enterprises.

The managerially controlled enterprises of this study were all located within or near large urban centers. Therefore, the managers of these enterprises had access to a large and diverse labor pool. By contrast, the cooperatively run enterprises of a particular cooperative community were, in each instance, located on the premises of a particular cooperative community and could draw their labor supply only from the members of that community or from neighboring ones. The cooperative village populations vary in size within a range of 300 to 2000. This is, at maximum, a significantly smaller labor pool than the one that is open to the management of the managerially run enterprises. . . .

In the present study, advantages of size for the paired enterprises are substantially balanced out since in three industries the managerial enterprises are larger (tools, die casting, and canning) and in three the cooperatively controlled units have larger investments (instruments, plastics, and machine shop). Therefore, the average differences in enterprise efficiency that have appeared here must be explained primarily in terms of factors that are specific to, and associated with, the contrasting types of decision-making among the paired enterprises. These associated factors include conditions of environment (integration of the enterprise in a wide community) , ideology, and motivation.

There are definite relations between the mode of functioning of an organization and the social structure of its wider society. The Kibbutz enterprise is sharply differentiated from the managerial unit by its total integration into the surrounding Kibbutz community. Thus the individual does not differentiate sharply between his role in the Kibbutz enterprise and his role in the community. He is not, as in a managerial enterprise, an "employee" —while being a "citizen" of a wider community. The conventional firm is a work organization, formally unconnected with the family, home, consumption activities, and the provision of various community services. In the Kibbutz, all these functions are integrated and the individual sees them as related parts of one community. As a result members identify with and have a strong commitment to the whole community of which the enterprise is a part. This is a central characteristic of Kibbutz organization, apart from variation in individual behaviors owing to all manner of reasons.

The operation of the cooperative enterprise is strongly influenced by the integration of the enterprise within the cooperative community where it is one among several "branches" of the economy. Integrated operation produces certain economies for component enterprises. For example, when manpower is needed in the industrial enterprise for a short period of time, say to make up for persons away for military training, then, depending on community priorities, manpower from other branches of the community can be temporarily assigned to the industrial enterprise.

When a Kibbutz factory needs the use of special equipment like a tractor for moving heavy machinery, then this equipment and its driver are borrowed from their normal work to do the special task. Thereby, there are no problems of renting heavy equipment, billing, paying for transportation time of the equipment to and from the industrial location, etc. Similarly, when Kibbutz vehicles go to town the drivers are able to do chores that are helpful to the industrial plant, like picking up or delivering materials or machine parts. Also, the cooperative community often includes manpower for particular tasks needed by industrial administration. For example, if a letter has to be written in a foreign language which someone in the community knows, he is easily asked to do this job and would normally do the task of letter translation and writing during an off hour. A similar task in the managerial enterprise usually requires hiring a secretarial service.

However, integration and commitment of the individual to the enterprise is by no means unique to the cooperative enterprise. The professional behavior and life style of modern corporate executives includes extensive involvement of the individual with his occupational role: work is carried home at night, to the golf course and to the dinner table. As in the Kibbutz enterprise, it is unthinkable to "charge" for this "overtime" (not counting the expense account). This sort of integration of occupation with other facets of life is ordinarily appreciated as contributing to the effectiveness of the managerially controlled enterprise.

It may appear from the above that the managerial and cooperative organizations are more alike than different with respect to commitment of members to the enterprise. The similarity, however, lies particularly in the commitment and integration of individuals who are decision-makers. In the managerial enterprise this means the management. But in cooperative organization this includes the total work group. To the extent that involvement of the individual in responsibility for the enterprise and its purpose affect morale and work efficiency, then the cooperative organizations have an inherent advantage in this respect.

Even allowing for the built-in strengths of cooperative organization, it would be erroneous to infer its competence from the structure of decision-power alone. An important contribution to its competence is the support that comes from the explicit ideology and moral values of the community: mutual care, responsibility, and cooperation. This is different from the ideal value system that permeates the managerial organization, with its affirmation of individualism and competitiveness—values that contradict the operational efficiency requirements of modern productive systems. The conditions of involvement of the individual in the Kibbutz enterprise, and accompanying ideological factors, are important in motivating the individual.

The people working in the Kibbutz enterprise are motivated to feel needed and wanted within the context of the total community. Such feelings, among people who share in a common task, are powerful motivating forces for individuals to give their best in the performance of shared responsibility. The entire social system of the cooperative reflects voluntary participation, voluntary cooperation, and mutual control: these are democratic communities that operate internally without coercion (no courts, no police, no jails), and without money. The Kibbutz approximates—within community capabilities and priorities—the principle "from each according to his ability, to each according to his needs."

NOTES

1. Total Kibbutz population: 1949, 63,500; 1964, 80,900. *Annual Statistical Abstract of Israel,* Central Bureau of Statistics, Government of Israel, Jerusalem, 1949, 1965.

2. S. Melman, "The Rise of Administrative Overhead in the Manufacturing Industries of the United States 1899–1947," *Oxford Economic Papers, 1951; Dynamic Factors in Industrial Productivity,* John Wiley, New York, Basil Blackwell, Oxford, 1956; *Decision-Making and Productivity,* John Wiley, New York, Basil Blackwell, Oxford, 1958.

3. For each of the sampled enterprises I secured the following data from their balance sheets and profit and loss statements: capital invested, value of fixed assets, sales, and profits. These data categories are the ordinary sorts of financial records that are kept by industrial firms. In each instance, the financial statements were private, unpublished data. The following employment data were also obtained: administrative personnel, production manhours per year. The accountants or bookkeepers made the data available, being directed to do so by the responsible administrators of each enterprise. In each instance I checked for consistency of definition of the data categories, and in several enterprises I found it necessary to reclassify the data in order to assure consistency. The data, arrayed for all the enterprises, were altered by an unstated factor—thereby shielding the identities of the cooperating firms while retaining proportional relationships.

4. Among the relatively few organizational studies that are relevant for a comparison of managerial versus cooperative decision-making, two are noteworthy: Stephen C. Jones and Victor H. Vroom, "Division of Labor and Performance Under Cooperative and Competitive Conditions," *Journal of Abnormal and Social Psychology,* 68 (March 1964), pp. 313–320; Bernard M. Bass, "Business Gaming for Organizational Research," *Management Science,* 10 (April 1964), pp. 545–556, especially fn. 3.

5. S. Littauer, "Technological Stability," *Transactions of the New York Academy of Science,* December 1950; S. Littauer, "Stability of Production Rates as a Determinant of Industrial Productivity Levels," *Proceedings of the Business and Economic Statistics Section* (Washington, D.C.: American Statistical Association, 1955), pp. 241–248; S. Melman, *Decision-Making and Productivity,* pp. 165–166.

6. This is one consequence of bilateralism in production decision-making. See diagnosis of bilateralism in L. B. Cohen, "Workers and Decision-Making on Production," in L. Tripp (ed.), *Proceedings of the Eighth Annual Meeting, Industrial Relations Research Association,* 1956, pp. 298–312; also see data on impact of bilateralism on management in S. Melman, *Decision-Making and Productivity.*

7. S. Melman, "Administration and Production Cost in Relation to Size of Firms, Applied Statistics," *Journal of Royal Statistical Society,* 1954.

8. Economic Efficiency and Workers' Self-management

MITJA KAMUŠIĆ

In the development of the model of self-managed enterprises a dilemma has been constantly present: whether to give preference to the social-political principle of direct participation of the workers in the management by any means, or to the economic and organizational efficiency of management. The Yugoslav Basic Law on Enterprises tries to solve this dilemma by requesting at the same time:

a) the greatest decentralization of management possible;

b) as direct a participation of the working people in management as possible;

c) the most efficient organization possible; and

d) assurance of the best conditions for the operation and business activities of the enterprise.

Two compromises are embodied in this postulate of the Law, namely:

a) a compromise between the democratic principle of immediate participation in management and the imperative of efficient organization and management, where capable and appropriately stimulated professionals are called upon to decide on matters of business and work;

Reprinted from M. J. Broekmeyer, ed., *Yugoslav Workers' Self-management* (Dordrecht, Holland: D. Reidel, 1970), pp. 86–87, 108–13, by permission of the publisher.

b) a compromise between the principle of democratic decentralization of management, according to which workers in all parts of the enterprise should decide on all matters directly, and the idea of the enterprise as a working and business unity aiming at the greatest economic efficiency possible.

These conciliatory solutions are a result of a particular disposition in the parallelogram of political forces in Yugoslavia. One of its components is represented by the political ideology requiring maximal and immediate realization of an organization of work and apportionment where the working people will be on an even footing with each other, and where they will be able to make the best of their personal ability, i.e., the ideology requiring in radical form the ideal humanistic concepts of the society transferring at the same time ideal human relations from a communist society of a remote future into the present time. A second component represents a more realistic observation of the operation of economic laws and tried practice of scientific organization of work which, however, tends to keep alive and even to aggravate the material and social inequality of people and which compels them to adopt such forms of their work as expressed by the term of "alienated work" invented by the philosophers. . . .

In the model of self-managed enterprises where the interests of the working community occupy the first place, and in which parts of the enterprises—organizations of united labor—apportion their income independently, the workers are interested first of all in investments that can ensure an immediate increase of their earnings, stable employment, better working conditions and similar benefits. They are less interested in investing in other parts of the enterprise, in long-term investments, in those that would require reduction of manpower or the re-qualification of the employed. They are interested least in investments—though they might be the most rentable—in other enterprises or even in enterprises situated elsewhere in the country. In decisions concerning the investments we can often notice a compromise between the immediate needs of the working community and the considerations of the business managers who, also for the sake of their reputation, seek the most rentable placement of the investments; in these endeavors they are usually supported by public opinion and by political and administrative organs. As a consequence of this compromise, enterprises invest partly to satisfy the short-term needs of the working community and partly on the basis of the estimations of long-term and optimally rentable placements. If an enterprise decides to invest so as to meet the immediate interests of the working community its members feel to a greater extent the economic consequences than when investments are decided upon solely after economic consideration, especially if these are placed in other parts of the enterprise, in other enterprises, or even in other places. It is possible, of course, that the enterprise lays down in its internal provisions that the results of investments, positive or negative, be apportioned among all members of the working community without regard to the place of investments. Some enterprises have recourse also to another possibility, namely, that independent parts of the enterprise lend and borrow their means mutually under the same conditions as these are available to other lenders. Such internal arrangements meet immediate local needs, but they do not meet social and short-term personal needs of the workers. Therefore even with such arrangements compromises are necessary. . . .

Means formed by the deposits of private citizens are particularly interesting. These means have been constantly increasing as compared to other sources. Some regard this phenomenon as a tendency toward the privatization of accumulation. It is obvious, at least, that producers prefer saving their money individually to the accumulation of their enterprises; this could be explained by the fact that deposits are their property, while the means saved by their enterprises are not—not even collective. If the workers A and B are in the same department and are both equally efficient, they will get equal personal incomes, though A might have worked in the same enterprise for ten years and contributed considerable sums to the funds of the enterprise and thus to its present prosperity, while B has worked in the enterprise a short time and his contribution to the funds was insignificant. A transfer of individual contribution (i.e., savings) is equally impossible when a worker leaves the enterprise. The problem appears in a particularly sharp light when a worker is dismissed because of technological changes that were made possible by his contributions to the funds of the enterprise. On individual deposits, on the other hand, he gets 6–8 percent interest. . . .

The pluralistic model of self-managed enterprises and the pluralistic system of self-managing relationships such as they at present exist in Yugoslavia do not ensure the greatest economic efficiency of particular enterprises or of the entire economy automatically, but they do not oppose it. They can be realized in various aspects of the organization in enterprises and in various aspects of the policy of the state, of which some heighten and ensure the economic efficiency of individual enterprises and the whole economy, while some of them hamper it or even prevent it altogether. As to the wide range of the possibilities it offers, the pluralistic model of self-managed enterprises and the pluralistic system of self-managing relations generally do not differ essentially from the capitalist model of enterprises and from the modern type of mixed capitalist economic system.

Economic efficiency of particular forms of organization of self-managed enterprises as well as the economic efficiency of the state economic policy depend on an appropriate evaluation of the agents influencing it, and on able and enterprising business managers. If these conditions are sometimes absent in our practice, we cannot ascribe this imperfection to the system as such.

If we compare impartially our system of self-managing relationships both in enterprises and in the society at large to the model of capitalist enterprises and the system of capitalist economy of the mixed types as to their economic efficiency we should admit that the latter fulfills its functions at least in the economically most advanced countries and for a long period, better than the first. But in saying this we must take into account the psychological and moral-political advantages of self-management. It would be rather superfluous to contrast economic efficiency as the exclusive attribute of the capitalist model of management with psychological and moral-political satisfaction as the exclusive advantage of our model of management. We are not obliged to do this because, according to my opinion, it is possible to improve our system and ascertain its economic efficiency to the same extent as is now characteristic for the modern and most advanced capitalist system, preserving at the same time all the psychological and moral advantages lacking in the capitalist system.

9. Does Self-management Approach the Optimum Order?

Comments on Professor Kamušić's Paper

JAN TINBERGEN

The subject dealt with by Kamušić is the *"efficiency"* of the system. Since efficiency means the ratio of result to effort, the widest sense given to that phrase is the degree to which the aspirations of the people as a whole are met. This degree will be highest in what I have called elsewhere the *optimum order*. I have defended the thesis that the optimum order is of a *mixed* character, somewhere between extreme freedom of the old type (implying complete private ownership of the means of production) and extreme regulation (of the primitive socialist type of the early days of the Soviet Union). One can expect the Yugoslav system to be close to the optimum. There are two ways of ascertaining this, to be called the *empirical* way and the *deductive* way. I will discuss what evidence of both types there is to evaluate the Yugoslav system. The empirical evidence shown by the author is of a crude character only and could hardly have been different. At most it seems to show that Yugoslavia does relatively well. A rate of growth of per capita real income of about 6 percent together with a considerable degree of democracy in the everyday environment of the mass of the producers is not easily found elsewhere. . . .

The *theoretical* method to judge the distance between any

Reprinted from M. J. Broekmeyer, ed., *Yugoslav Workers' Self-management* (Dordrecht, Holland: D. Reidel, 1970), pp. 119–21, 123–24, 126–27, by permission of the publisher.

given order and the optimal order is to apply welfare economics and to formulate the conditions the optimum has to satisfy and then compare these with the given order. Such an analysis will be undertaken in the remainder of this paper.

A general remark may precede this attempt. It is highly improbable that the proponents of a "laissez-faire theory" of self-management are right. It can be convincingly shown that in the optimum order some tasks must be performed in a centralized way and cannot therefore be left to the lowest levels, even if on these levels workers would have the decision power, which is by itself a desirable thing. . . .

It is of some relevance to ask the question what *influence on productivity* is exerted by various *forms of self-management.* Professor Kamušić's paper contains a reference to the observed fact that in Western co-operatives an increase in the degree of direct participation of their members in the management tends to lower business efficiency (quotation of H. Decroches). My tendency is to say that for very low levels of participation an increase in participation will raise productivity, but after a certain level Decroches's finding will probably apply. From there on we will have to *compromise* between two incompatible aims: more participation or more production (and consumption) . . . .

As a general rule there is an *optimal level* of decision making characterized by a *minimum of "external effects."* By external effects influences outside the jurisdiction or authority of the decision maker are meant. If there are such external effects, and sometimes there exist important ones, decision making on a relatively low level may neglect these effects and the decisions may not be the best ones for the community as a whole. In such cases there is a strong reason for making the decision on some higher level. As a counteracting force there is a smaller degree of participation of individuals, since only some representatives of them may be involved. These principles must be considered as the basic principles to be used in the search for the optimal degree of decentralization in society. If no external effects exist, and this may be the case for many activities, the principles imply that a low level of decision making and hence a high degree of participation is optimal. For industries with small equipment and whose products can be sold in small units, external effects will be absent or small as a rule and here the Yugoslav system is optimal. It may be different for activities using large indivisible units—as a technical datum—or whose products for organizational reasons cannot be sold in small units or cannot be sold to the real beneficiaries of the product. Examples of products which cannot be "sold" in small units are the so-called *collective goods* such as security, radio and television and some other types of information, which can only either be available or not available, but not made available only to those who wish to have it. Examples of products which, for organizational reasons, cannot be sold to the actual beneficiaries are the services of a road system, with the exception of turnpikes where individuals can pay a toll. . . .

Another well-known optimum condition is that in the same region the same type of labor must have a uniform wage. This is one example only of *uniform pricing* which is characteristic for the optimum and which comes along, i.e., if prices are determined by markets. To be sure there are other institutions which can lead to the same result, but only with uniform wages can we be sure that the correct use is made of the available manpower. There may be regional differences, if for reasons of cultural preferences workers in poor regions want to stay there instead of moving to the regions where higher wages are being paid. . . .

It is in the light of the preceding remarks that we want to comment on Professor Kamušić's paper where he discusses the question whether decisions on the correct income scale can be taken in a democratic way, that is, in the context, decisions by the workers' council or by parliament. The outcome of our welfare economic exercise is that some aspects of the optimal income distribution depend on scientific propositions and in a general way *science cannot be developed by public opinion polls or majority decisions.* Imagine that Marx instead of developing his own ideas had formulated what the majority of his contemporaries thought to be true! There are limitations therefore to what should be left to deliberate democratic procedures. The decision, e.g., to pay different wages to persons doing the same work in more profitable and less profitable enterprises, while natural when decided upon by the various workers' councils, is definitely incorrect from a welfare-economic, that is, scientific, point of view. The decisions taken in many parliaments to reduce inequalities by an income tax is also suboptimal. It would have been better if wages were determined for all enterprises in a region simultaneously and uniformly and it would be better if parliaments had chosen to impose higher wealth and lower income taxes; preferably even a tax on personal capabilities. But the *degree of inequality desired* is a matter of preference of the community; it is part of choosing the preference function of society. This can be a decision by parliament. Hence also the tax *rates* may correctly be decided upon by democratic procedures. . . .

Let us try to sum up the conclusions we have reached with regard to the optimal income distribution and the means to be applied in order to let it materialize. I think I have shown that wage systems cannot be detached from the tax system and that the desired distribution can at best be attained by applying both types of instruments: an "incomes policy" cannot only be a wage policy. I have also shown that, in order to be optimal, both wage and tax policy have to fulfil certain conditions. Wages paid for the same sort of labor must be uniform and the taxes to be paid by a person of given quality and education must be independent of the job he chooses. But then, unfortunately, we have found that the best tax system should be based on a principle for which the objective assessment is not yet possible; in order to maintain the full stimulus for each person to choose the job by which he serves society best, we should tax only his productive capacity. This capacity consists of two elements at least, his personal wealth and his personal capabilities, and while the former can be ascertained and hence taxed, the latter can only be assessed in a very imperfect way. I think we should make efforts to improve that assessment. It would help us to organize society in such a way that a maximum of stimulus goes together with a minimum of inequality. There remains some scope for democratic decision making about the rates of taxation, but at a higher level than that of the single enterprise. There also results the need for educating citizens so as to let them understand the societal mechanism in order that voluntarily they agree that some decisions should be taken at higher levels than the enterprise level.

10. On the Theory of the Labor-managed Firm

BRANKO HORVAT

Published and unpublished literature deals with three types of labor-managed firms: the (Yugoslav) firm under workers' management, the (Soviet) agricultural cooperative, and the (Israeli) kibbutz. Each of the three types has some special characteristics.[1] I will, however, confine my observations to the first type, which at present is the only type that is dominant in at least one economy (in Yugoslavia).

1. The Illyrian firm

The description of the behavior of economic agents is based on the assumption that they maximize a particular target

This article is based on papers presented to two international conferences held at Florida State University in 1970 and at the Istituto di Studi e Documentazione sull Est Europeo, Trieste, 1972. The first paper was published under the title "On the Theory of the Labor-Managed Firm" (*The Florida State University Slavic Papers,* 4, 1970, 7–11); the second, under the title "Critical Notes on the Theory of the Labour-Managed Firm and Some Macroeconomic Implications" (*Ekonomska analiza,* 4, 1972).

1. But it is also possible to develop a general theoretical approach. For instance, a kibbutz may be considered as a special case of a workers' council firm which (a) distributes income among the members equally and (b) engages in neither buying nor selling the land, nor in admitting or dismissing members in response to market stimuli. What both firms have in common is (a) social ownership and (b) self-management.

function. What target function does a labor-managed firm maximize? In his pioneering article [9; see also pp. 241–60 of the present volume], Ward decided that such a firm maximizes (or ought to maximize) income per worker. He was not sure that workers really behave in this way, however, and he called his construct the Illyrian firm. E. Domar [1] and, in particular, J. Vanek [7, 8] accepted the same answer and developed the theoretical implications.

In the simplest case of one product and one variable factor, the production function is given by

$$q = f(x), \tag{1}$$

where q is product and x is the number of workers employed. If k is some sort of fixed cost to be covered (depreciation charge, interest, capital tax, or just a lump-sum tax), income per worker appears to be

$$y = \frac{pq - k}{x}. \tag{2}$$

It must be maximized assuming the price of the product p to remain invariant. The first-order equilibrium condition readily follows:

$$pq' = \frac{pq - k}{x} = y \tag{3}$$

The value of marginal product is equal to income per worker (and not to the wage rate, as in a capitalist firm). Rewrite (3) to get

$$q - xq' = \frac{k}{p}, \tag{4}$$

$$\frac{d}{dx}(q - xq') = -xq'' > 0. \tag{5}$$

Now assume that k and p are variable and differentiate (4) once with respect to k and then with respect to p:

$$\frac{\partial}{\partial x}(q - xq')\frac{\partial x}{\partial k} = \frac{1}{p} \qquad \therefore \frac{\partial x}{\partial k} > 0 \tag{6}$$

$$\frac{\partial}{\partial x}(q - xq')\frac{\partial x}{\partial p} = \frac{-k}{p^2} \qquad \therefore \frac{\partial x}{\partial p} < 0 \tag{7}$$

It follows that an increase in taxes increases employment and an

Effects on Output and Employment

TYPE OF CHANGE	NEOCLASSICAL FIRM	ILLYRIAN FIRM	U-MAXIMIZING FIRM*	YUGOSLAV FIRM
Increase in wage rate	–	0	0	0
Increase in lump sum tax	0	+	0, +	0 (?)
Increase in product price	+	–	0, –	+

*See Part 2, below.

increase in the product price reduces employment. Changes in employment change output in the same direction, as is obvious from the production function (1). It remains to compare how a labor-managed firm and a capitalist firm (in its neoclassical version) react to changes in wages, lump-sum tax, and product price (see table).

If the neoclassical capitalist firm reacts in an economically efficient way, as the conventional theory of the firm seems to have proven, then the Illyrian labor-managed firm operates inefficiently, since it reacts in an exactly opposite way. Besides, the equalization of the value of the marginal product with income per worker and not with the wage rate implies smaller employment (because $y > w$). What is particularly disturbing is a negatively sloping supply curve, which renders the economy unstable.

As Domar [1] and Horvat [3] have shown, a more realistic production function with two or more variable factors and joint products modifies the relations of a labor-managed firm appreciably. Yet even so, the firm is sinning against an efficient allocation of resources. Such sins cannot be forgiven in pure economic theory. And so the verdict was passed: a labor-managed firm is less efficient than a capitalist firm.

This is now a universally accepted opinion among Western economists; there is therefore no need to quote published and unpublished statements to illustrate the point. Yet the proponents of this view somehow failed to ask what would seem an obvious question: does a firm run by a workers' council really behave in the assumed way? The cautiousness of Ward has been forgotten. Ward's hypothetical Illyrian results have been generally interpreted as the Yugoslav reality. Thus, the verdict now reads: the Yugoslav firm, run by the workers' council, is inherently less efficient than its capitalist counterpart.

2. The utility-maximizing Illyrian firm

S. Parrinello [6] accepts the basic behavioral assumptions outlined above, but he tries to make the approach more general by introducing two risks: dismissal and employment risks. The workers dislike dismissing their fellow workers and, even more, being dismissed themselves, and they are not eager to employ new workers because they may change the preference map of the collective in an undesirable way. Parrinello constructs two simple utility functions by modifying the income per worker, as a target, by the effects of the two risks quoted:

$$\begin{aligned} U &= ye^{mr}, & -1 \leqslant r \leqslant 0, \\ U &= ye^{-nr}, & r \geqslant 0, \end{aligned} \qquad r = \frac{x - x_0}{x_0} \tag{8}$$

where r is the relative change in employment, m is the coefficient of dismissal risk, and n is the coefficient of employment risk, $m, n > 0$.

If utility is maximized, the equilibrium conditions are now as follows:

$$\begin{aligned} pq' &= y - \frac{m}{x_0}(pq - k), & 0 \leqslant x < x_0 \\ pq' &= y + \frac{n}{x_0}(pq - k), & x > x_0 \end{aligned} \tag{9}$$

In the case in which the two risks are absent, $m = n = 0$, (9) is of course identical with (3). When the risks are present, fewer workers will be dismissed than otherwise, $(pq' < y)$; and in the alternative case of new employment, fewer workers will be employed than otherwise, $(pq' > y)$. This result is not surprising, of course, since the model assumes that the workers are reluctant to change employment in either direction.

The introduction of the two risks has rendered the behavior of the firm indeterminate, though biased in the Illyrian direction, as shown in the third column of the above table.

3. Alternative approaches and elaborations

The conclusion as to the relative inefficiency of a socialist firm did not go unchallenged. If with Joel Dirlam we define capitalism as a system in which capital employs labor, and socialism as a system in which labor employs capital, then in socialism the period of analysis can be defined in terms of labor. Thus, the short run will be defined as a period in which the membership of the firm remains constant. It follows that in the short run a working collective, by hiring other factors of production up to the point where their values of marginal products are equalized with their prices, maximizes both total income and per-worker income. Similarly, a capitalist in the short run, defined by invariance of the capital invested, maximizes both total profits and the rate of profit. The possible remark that Marshall defined the short run in capitalism in terms of physical characteristics of the production process cannot be taken too seriously. As every businessman knows, a certain amount of investment (i.e., changes in fixed capital) is going on all the time; on the other hand, a group of workers cannot easily be either hired or (even less so) dismissed in a modern economy in order to satisfy marginalist equations.

D. Dubravčić [2] pointed out that, regardless of how one defines the period, one must treat the twin firms symmetrically. If a labor-managed firm maximizes income per worker, a capitalist firm must maximize profit per unit of capital. In this case, a socialist firm will economize on labor (and develop capital-intensive techniques), while a capitalist firm will economize on capital (and use labor-intensive techniques). This approach implies—but Dubravčić failed to spell this out—that the supply of capital is inelastic to changes in the interest rate and that the capitalist uses largely his own capital in financing investment. I leave to the reader to judge whether the assumptions are realistic or not.

Perhaps the most interesting is the third challenge by J. Vanek [7, 8]. Vanek assumes Ward's target function but goes on to explore implications in a general equilibrium setting. He ends up by refuting some of the criticisms and by describing a dozen or so advantages that an Illyrian firm enjoys in comparison with its capitalist rival. Out of this list I have chosen those that do not require lengthy explanation.

1. Under perfect competition (same technology, free entry) the Illyrian firm will attain Pareto optimum because factor returns are equated to factor marginal products.

2. Workers will not dismiss their colleagues just because a small change in product price has occurred. Thus, in the short run the supply elasticity is zero and this eliminates the possibility of instability. (This reasoning corresponds to observed facts.)

3. There will be stronger demand for and higher returns to capital. As a consequence, accumulation and growth will proceed

at higher rates. (This has been observed in reality, but the causes may be different from those implied by Vanek.)

4. Because of the inherently democratic organizational structure of the firm, monopolistic tendencies will be weaker. (Observed.)

5. Because of point 2, wages and prices will be flexible downwards. (Wages have in fact proved to be much more flexible downwards than in Western market economies.)

6. Because of point 2, fluctuations in effective demand and employment will be small. (Observed.)

7. There will be little national cause for secular inflation because of lack of systematic upward price changes. (Not observed.)

8. Collective decision-making increases the welfare of the workers as compared with authoritarian rule in a capitalist firm.

Vanek concludes: "In brief, the labor-managed system appears to me to be superior by far, judged on strictly economic criteria, to any other economic system in existence."

Vanek's conclusion and his paper were promptly attacked on the grounds that all this might be fine in theory, but surely one must take a close look at what happens in practice before passing judgment. Vanek's results somehow appealed to pure theorists in the West less than did Ward's.

Vanek was not familiar with empirical research and did not have firsthand experience with a workers' councils economy. Thus he could not meet criticism on that count. Parenthetical remarks about observed facts are mine. It is of interest to note how many of Vanek's theoretical predictions proved to be correct. However, it is important to realize that hardly any of Vanek's points depend on the assumption that the firm maximizes per-worker income. This assumption may be changed without changing his picture of a socialist economy.

4. Evaluation of the Illyrian theory

Any meaningful theory has to pass two fundamental tests: verifiability of assumptions and predictability. A theory may pass both tests and still not be a correct one. However, if it fails to pass one or both, then it is surely not the correct one. The latter determination is much simpler and more conclusive, so I shall consider it first.

The Illyrian theory predicts that an increase in price will reduce output, or at least leave it unchanged. *Nothing of the kind has been observed in the Yugoslav economy.* Increases in prices, as *signals of unsatisfied demand,* have been followed rather quickly by efforts to increase supply. It suffices to read newspapers to realize that.

The theory also predicts that a reduction of k will reduce supply. It is not possible to verify or reject this prediction without a special empirical inquiry. Yet when in the 1960s the 6 percent capital tax was abolished, I did not observe a depressing effect on output—and no one, to my knowledge, reported anything close to it.

Finally, the theory predicts that the labor-managed economy will be a labor-saving economy. But the Yugoslav experience shows, on the contrary, chronic overemployment in the firms. The government is constantly lamenting the "extensiveness" of production.

It is still possible to save the Illyrian theory by introducing special factors accounting for observed effects, while retaining the basic assumption as to the per-worker maximization. However, it is much simpler to replace the theory by another which corresponds more directly to the facts. Besides, there is a universally accepted rule in scientific research which says that of two theories with equal predictive capacities, the simpler is preferable.

As far as the basic behavioral assumption is concerned, my own experience has led me to postulate the following target function (3):

$$\pi = pq - [(d + \Delta d)\, x + k] \tag{10}$$

At the beginning of a new business year, the workers' council sets the level of personal income the firm will aspire to achieve. The aspired income consists of the last year's or some standard personal income (d) and a change, normally an addition, to be achieved in the current year (Δd). The aspired income is a function of (a) expected sales, (b) incomes in other firms, (c) incomes in the last and earlier years, (d) labor productivity, (e) costs of living, and (f) taxation policy, and perhaps of some other factors.

Once the aspired income has been decided upon, it becomes an obligatory target for the management. This means that for all practical purposes ($d + \Delta d$) performs the allocational role of the wage rate, without, however, being a wage rate. What the worker will actually get as his share in the firm's income may be different from the aspired income, $d' \gtreqless (d + \Delta d)$, and depends on the business results of the firm. In fact, the actual Δd may turn out to be negative if the firm suffers losses. Thus, instead of reducing employment, the firm will simply reduce d, which is also observed behavior.

Mathematically, (10) is identical to the standard neoclassical target function, and so the equilibrium conditions will be the same. Thus, at least qualitatively, the theory predicts the observed behavior.

In which way does the Yugoslav firm differ institutionally from the Illyrian firm? This is best seen when we consider savings decisions. There are three pure cases. Savings decisions can be made (1) by the state, (2) by the work collective (the firm) and (3) by individuals. The Illyrian firm fits into (1) and (3). If saving is done by the state, total net income of the firm is distributed among workers and they may be concerned only with maximizing their wages. Assuming that the state's savings approximate capitalist profits, in this case per-worker income of an Illyrian firm will equal the wage of its capitalist twin, $y = w$. If saving is done by individuals, total income of the firm is again distributed among workers, but they now buy securities with the part of their income they wish to save. In this case, $y > w$ and employment is accordingly reduced.

In its pure forms, case 1 corresponds to an etatist setup, and case 3 to a blend of private ownership and collective management. The Yugoslav firm, with its capital socially owned and the working collective performing the role of entrepreneur, is behaviorally alien to both classes 1 and 3. It belongs to class 2. In order to survive in a competitive environment, the collective-entrepreneur has to save part of the firm's income and follow a vigorous investment policy. Given the uncertainties of real life, the expansion of the firm is the basic guarantee that the incomes of its members will be rising. Thus it is natural to focus on the maximization of the absolute value of the residual, and not on the residual relative to the changing number of workers. If the residual happens to be exceptionally great (small), a less (more) than proportional amount will be distributed in wages because: (a) it is considered that wages should not differ too much from firm to firm (which is a derivative of the socialist principle of distribution according to work), and (b) it is wise to accumulate reserves in order to speed up expansion of the firm. In short, the Yugoslav or workers' council firm uses aspired wages as an accounting device for cost calculation and resources allocation. It apparently maximizes the residual and then divides the residual into the part that will be accumulated and the part that will be distributed in additional wages (in cash or otherwise). How the distribution of the residual is determined is an interesting question for both the theory and the empirical research concerned with the Yugoslav type of labor-managed firm.

5. Maximizing income versus maximizing profit

Groups of Yugoslav economists have been engaged in long and bitter debates over whether a socialist firm maximizes income or profit. What can be said about this matter?

Suppose we deal with an Illyrian firm whose income per worker

$$y = \frac{pq - k}{x}$$

is represented as a sum of two components, the standard wage, w^s, and the profit per worker, $\frac{\pi}{x}$,

$$y = w^s + \frac{\pi}{x}. \tag{11}$$

Since w^s is fixed, maximizing y implies maximizing $\frac{\pi}{x}$. In other words, maximizing income per worker and maximizing profit per worker come to the same thing. The behavioral and allocational consequences are identical.

Suppose we deal with the Yugoslav firm, and the production function depends on two variable factors, labor (x) and raw materials (z). Suppose the target is to maximize the surplus, which we may call conditionally the profit.[2]

2. Conditionally, because part of it will be used to adjust wages upwards or downwards.

$$\pi = pq(x, z) - [(d + \Delta d)\, x + p_z z + k]$$
$$\frac{\partial \pi}{\partial x} = pq_x - (d + \Delta d) = 0,\; pq_x = d + \Delta d \qquad (12)$$
$$\frac{\partial \pi}{\partial z} = pq_z - p_z = 0,\; pq_z = p_z$$

The result is familiar: in equilibrium the value of the marginal product is equal to the price of the factor.

If the aim is to maximize total net income,

$$D = pq(x, z) - (p_z z + k)$$
$$\frac{\partial D}{\partial x} = pq_x = 0 \qquad (13)$$
$$\frac{\partial D}{\partial z} = pq_z - p_z = 0,\; pq_z = p_z$$

the condition for the nonlabor factor is the same. But the labor equation is different and states that employment ought to be increased until the marginal productivity of the last worker falls to zero. Since overemployment is an empirical fact, it may be thought that $pq_x = 0$ describes the reality well. Yet I prefer to consider (12) as a more accurate description of normal behavior and would explain overemployment (which implies $pq_x < d + \Delta d$) as a deviation due to strong pressures generated by the large latent unemployment.

6. Some macroeconomic implications

An extensive empirical inquiry into business cycles in Yugoslavia revealed that the labor-managed firm behaves differently from the capitalist firm in a number of important respects [4].

1. Since capital is socially owned, risk and uncertainty are greatly reduced. As a consequence, the work collective—performing the role of entrepreneur—shows a much higher propensity to invest and to increase employment, aiming at a fast expansion of output, than is the case in the capitalist environment. Hence, a high rate of investment often not matched by adequate finance and overemployment are to be expected.

2. Since the firm is collectively managed, there is a great reluctance to dismiss fellow workers. In general the firm prefers to reduce wages rather than dismiss workers. But before wages are reduced, the firm will exhaust all its internal reserves and credit possibilities. If the workers are not dismissed, they must produce. And if there is no market, they will produce for inventories. On both counts, in a recession aggregate demand will be higher than in a comparable capitalist environment. In the acceleration phase of the cycle, firms will decumulate inventories, which is again opposite to the behavior of capitalist firms. Consequently, a labor-managed economy is inherently more stable.

3. Because of points 1 and 2, the firm will tend to produce even when it cannot sell immediately and/or continue to sell its products even when the buyers cannot pay immediately. Thus one should expect large involuntary inventories and trade credits, particularly in the recession phase. This may generate cycles of severe illiquidity which render monetary policy completely ineffective.

4. In the acceleration phase, unit costs will tend to decrease, and, in the recession phase, they will tend to increase. Thus we should expect stable prices when the rate of growth is high (except in booms, when demand-pull inflation becomes operative) and rising prices when the market is slack.

5. Without regulatory activities of the policy-making authorities, wage rates for the same type of work will tend to differ more than in a capitalist economy. Intraindustry differences are beneficial, because they imply adjustment to local conditions making it possible for the firm to survive. However, interindustry differences are highly undesirable because they reflect the violation of the basic distributional principle—distribution according to labor. Since this principle is deeply engrained in a labor-managed economy, any violation generates counteracting forces. Since productivity increases at very different rates in different industries, the lagging industries will not be able to absorb wage increases and will have to increase prices. Thus, in an unregulated or inefficiently regulated labor-managed economy, there will be strong inflationary pressures of the cost-push type. On the other hand, because of the absence of the fundamental employer-employee conflict, it is much easier to control a cost-push inflation in a labor-managed environment than in a capitalist environment.

6. For obvious reasons, self-management creates an aversion to

large units. The openness of self-management makes collusive trade practices difficult or impossible. Thus, in a labor-managed economy, one should expect strong pressures toward decentralization and against cartelization and monopolization.

REFERENCES

1. E. D. Domar. "The Soviet Collective Farm." *American Economic Review,* 1966, 734–57.

2. D. Dubravčić. "Prilog zasnivanju teorije jugoslavenskog poduzeća: mogućnosti uopćavanja modela." *Economska analiza,* 1968, 120–27.

3. B. Horvat. "A Contribution to the Theory of the Yugoslav Firm." *Ekonomska analiza,* 1967, 7–28.

4. B. Horvat. *Business Cycles in Yugoslavia.* White Plains, N.Y.: International Arts and Sciences Press, 1971.

5. B. Horvat. "Analysis of the Economic Situation and Proposal for a Program of Action." *Praxis,* 3–4, 1971, 533–62. (This paper was published in Serbo-Croatian in *Pregled,* 1970, 462–98.)

6. S. Parrinello. "Un contributo alla teoria dell'impresa Yugoslava." *Est-Ovest,* 3, 1971, 43–66.

7. J. Vanek. "Decentralization Under Workers' Management: A Theoretical Appraisal," paper presented at the December 1969 AEA annual meeting.

8. J. Vanek. *The General Theory of Labor-Managed Market Economies.* Ithaca, N.Y.: Cornell University Press, 1970.

9. B. Ward. "The Firm in Illyria: Market Syndicalism." *American Economic Review,* 1958, 566–89.

10. B. Ward. "Beleške o Iliriji: Model jugoslovenskog planiranja." *Univerzitet danas,* 1966, 21–31.

11. B. Ward. *The Socialist Economy.* New York: Random House, 1967.

11. The Illyrian Firm[1]

BENJAMIN WARD

The Yugoslavs have gone further than any other communist country in developing market exchange relations. Their approach, based on workers' management as an important aspect of enterprise decision making, is only one among many possible ways of organizing socialist market decision processes. It will be given primary attention here, partly because there is some experience with the system which can be used to suggest casually empirical analytic assumptions, and partly because the workers' council approach has considerable appeal elsewhere both in and beyond the communist bloc. That is, this form has a past and some prospect for a much greater future.

However, following the procedure used in the rest of this study, we will be dealing with Illyria, a place which bears some resemblance to Yugoslavia, but in which affairs are much simpler and behavior much more uniform. The present chapter deals with microeconomic aspects of resource allocation which are derived from a model of the enterprise. . . .

The key features of productive organization in the Illyrian economy are two. First there is the operation of individual material self-interest as the dominant human motivation. This assumption is basic to the laissez-faire models of capitalism, but operates differently in the Illyrian environment because the workers are at the same time managers. They are interested in profits as well as wages.

The second key feature is the resort to markets as the means of allocating resources. There is no state plan of production and allocation which sets targets for each firm, at the same time providing the firm with its needed inputs. Instead the firm must purchase what it needs from other firms on the relevant markets at the going prices, and endeavor to sell its own output in a similar manner. The incentives of the worker-managers thus play a key role in the allocative process. They are the Illyrian equivalent of the soviet incentive criteria and the capitalist's profit incentive.

The state plays a special role in relation to the Illyrian productive apparatus because it owns the means of production. This may be interpreted as meaning that the state has acquired a right to a functional share in the income of the enterprise, by virtue of granting the enterprise the right to use the state's property. This interpretation need not be made, however. It may simply be assumed that the state in Illyria, as elsewhere, has a taxing power which it may use in the public interest. In addition it serves the usual watchdog functions of the capitalist state, refereeing disputes arising out of the market system and controlling fraudulent activities.

We shall begin with the problem of current allocation. That is, we assume that the state has already provided the means of production to each firm, and that the firm has no incentive at the moment to expand its capacity. What sort of current allocation decisions will our Illyrian firm make under these conditions?

The competitive firm

The Illyrian firm is paid for its product by purchasers, just as is its capitalist counterpart. It must pay for its purchases of inputs from other firms in a similar manner also. But other aspects of costs differ a bit from the capitalist situation.

In the first place there is the state, the owner of the means of production. For the moment we will assume that the state takes its putative functional share of the firm's income in the form of an interest charge on capital. Let us assume that a rational depreciation system permits state and firm to reach a valuation to be placed on the total capital in the form of plant and equipment which is in the hands of the firm. The tax then amounts to a percentage of this value—the state fixes the percentage—or a fixed amount to be paid over by the firm. Under certain assumptions the charge could be equal to the scarcity price or rent of capital. This will be the only tax paid by the firm.[2]

Secondly, there are the worker-managers. Activated by their own material self-interest, the workers will be interested in profits as well as wages. Their obligation to the state ceases with the payment of the fixed interest charge. Their obligation to other producers ceases when they have paid for goods obtained from them. Since there is no investment the remainder of the firm's revenue belongs to the workers. It is thus difficult to make a distinction between wages and profits, since the workers are residual recipients of the firm's income.

A distinction will however be made between wages and profits since it is useful for comparative purposes. The initial assumption is that the state fixes the contractual wage, which is to be treated on the firm's books as its labor cost.[3] The remainder, when all costs have been deducted, is profits. These are to be distributed to the workers in proportion to the accounting value of their work. The firm may operate at a loss, in which case wages paid out will be less than the contractual wage.

The mechanism of decision making is a simple one. The workers at a general election choose from among their members a council, which serves a function analogous to that of the board of directors of a corporation. It appoints a manager to operate the firm, gives him general instructions as to how to act, and checks periodically on his performance. On the job, all workers are under the manager's orders. They may not disobey these orders unless they violate the general instructions. Grievances are handled by the council as part of its responsibility both for maintaining the worker's security against arbitrary action by the manager and for maintaining the worker's income by judicious action in the market place. Workers are free to leave the job at any time. They may also be laid off. Hiring and firing is the ultimate responsibility of the workers' council, though it may decide to act merely as a board of appeal against the manager's decisions.

Finally, we assume that the firm is operating in purely competitive markets both for inputs and outputs. That is, our firm sells or buys too small a share of total output of any product for variations in its own level of activity to have a significant effect on price.

The one-output–one-variable-input case

A simple case which brings out the principal features of the model is that in which there is a single variable input and a single product. The variable input to the firm is labor, which is homogeneous—only one skill type of worker employed—and whose accounting cost per worker, w, is fixed by the state. Variations in output can be achieved only by varying the *number* of workers employed since hours of work also are fixed by the state.[4]

Thus we have a production function which describes the technical conditions under which the firm may transform labor, x, into the salable product y:

$$y = f(x) \tag{1}$$

Over the feasible range of output, the marginal product of labor will be assumed to be positive but declining as output increases.

The manager makes the decisions as to how much to produce. What is his criterion? The workers' council is interested in maximizing the incomes of the workers. Indeed, each member of the workers' council is interested in maximizing his own income. But in this case there is no conflict of interest among the workers, since each receives the same wage and the same share in profits.[5] The workers' council instructs the manager to produce up to the point at which the average income (wage plus profits share over the time period in question) per worker is a maximum. The manager, being himself a worker, is only too happy to oblige.

The manager's job now is to calculate the desired output and then to produce it. As a basis for his calculation he knows the firm's production function, the prices p and w—given by the market and the state respectively—and the criterion prescribed by the workers' council. He might proceed by considering

$$U = py/x, \tag{2}$$

the average receipts per worker, and

$$K = w + R/x, \tag{3}$$

the average costs per worker. The difference between U and K is average profits per worker, so maximizing this difference will satisfy the workers' council's criterion.[6]

Equilibrium for the Illyrian competitive firm is described graphically in Figure 1, where the values of U and K are plotted against x, the number of workers. The solution is not altered by making

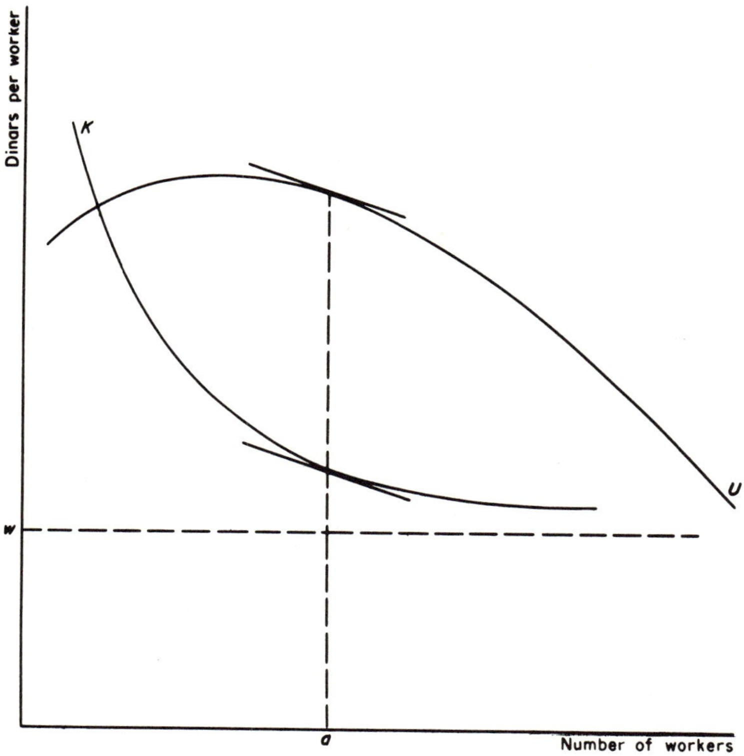

Figure 1

x rather than y the formal choice variable. U has its maximum value at the point at which marginal and average product are equal, and declines as the number of workers is either increased or decreased from this value. The k-function is a rectangular hyperbola asymptotic to $x = 0$, $K = w$. Profits per worker reach a maximum when the difference between U and K is greatest, which is the value of x for which the slopes of U and K are equal. According to Figure 1 the equilibrium value of x is a.

Our equilibrium condition is that the slopes of U and K be equal, or alternatively that marginal per-worker revenue equals marginal cost per worker.[7] This is the Illyrian equivalent of the capitalist condition that price will equal marginal cost under rational management, or of the market socialist rule that managers act so as to set marginal cost equal to price. The Illyrian condition states that wages per worker (or, what amounts to the same thing, profits per worker) are maximized if the competitive firm chooses the output at which marginal per-worker revenue equals marginal cost per worker. This condition has more in common with the capitalist "rule" than with the Lange-Lerner rule. For the Illyrian rule represents the *result* of behavior of a specified kind (wage-maximizing behavior), as does the neoclassical rule (profit-maximizing behavior). In the market socialist economy of the Lange-Lerner type, however, the managers are directed by the state to act in a certain way, the rule not being connected explicitly with the motivations of the managers.

What is the meaning of this equilibrium? How does it compare with the equilibrium position of the traditional firm? We may consider first the effects of changes in the parameters on the Illyrian firm's behavior, and then contrast the equilibrium positions of Illyrian and capitalist firms under similar technological and market conditions.

Referring to Figure 2, suppose that the firm is in equilibrium producing, under revenue and cost conditions represented by U_1 and K_1, an output corresponding to the level of employment a. The state now raises the interest rate, so that R is increased. This shifts the cost curve up to K_2. But at the output corresponding to a, curve K_2 is steeper than is U_1.[8] That is to say, at employment

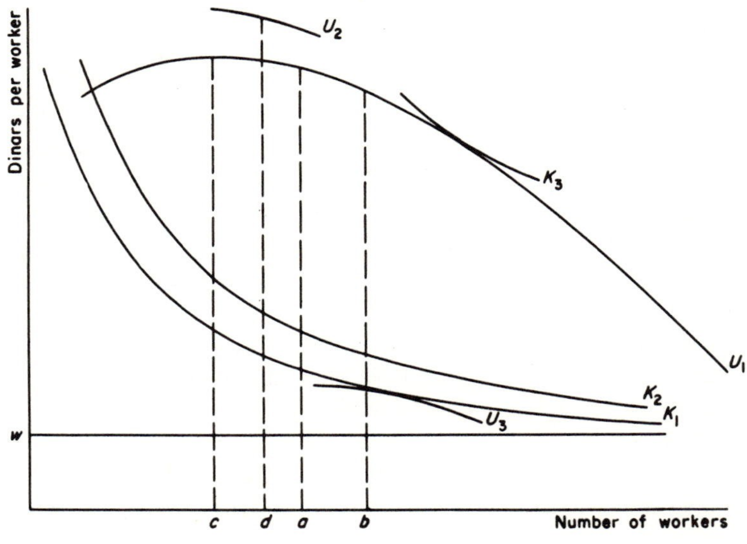

Figure 2

level a the rate of decrease of average cost per worker is greater than the rate of decrease of average revenue per worker. Consequently it will be to the workers' advantage to raise output until average cost and average revenue per worker are decreasing at the same rate. In Figure 2 this is represented by employment level b where the slopes of U_1 and K_2 are equal. This result can be generalized into the theorem: *A change in the fixed costs of the competitive Illyrian firm leads to a change in output in the same direction.*

Further increases in R would lead to further increases in output. If K_3 were the relevant cost curve, the firm would be earning zero profits. Even if R were increased beyond this point, output would continue to increase, as the worker-managers strove to minimize losses. Under these circumstances the workers would be receiving less than the calculated wage w. So long as no better alternatives were available elsewhere, the workers would continue to work in the given firm despite this fact, under our assumption.[9] Decreases in R of course have the opposite effect. At $R = 0$, the cost function becomes $K_4 = w$, and output would be at the level corresponding to the maximum value of U_1. A negative interest rate would convert K into a hyperbola asymptotic to the same lines as before, but located below w on Figure 2. Employment would be less than c and the competitive Illyrian firm would be in equilibrium with average costs falling.[10]

Price changes may be considered in a similar way. Suppose that an increase in demand for the industry's product leads to an increase in the market price p of our firm, which is currently in equilibrium at employment level a of Figure 2. This will shift U_1 upward to position U_2. But at the current employment level, U_2 will be steeper than K_1.[11] That is, at a the rate of decrease of average revenue per worker is greater than the rate of decrease of average cost per worker. Output and employment will contract until these rates are again equal, as at employment level d. Our theorem is: *A change in price to the competitive Illyrian firm leads to a change in output in the opposite direction.*

The lower limit to a price-induced output contraction is, roughly speaking, at employment level c where average and marginal product are equal. If falling price were to shift the revenue curve down to U_3 a zero-profits position would be reached. The remarks above regarding operations at a loss would apply equally if falling price rather than rising fixed costs were the cause of the losses.[12]

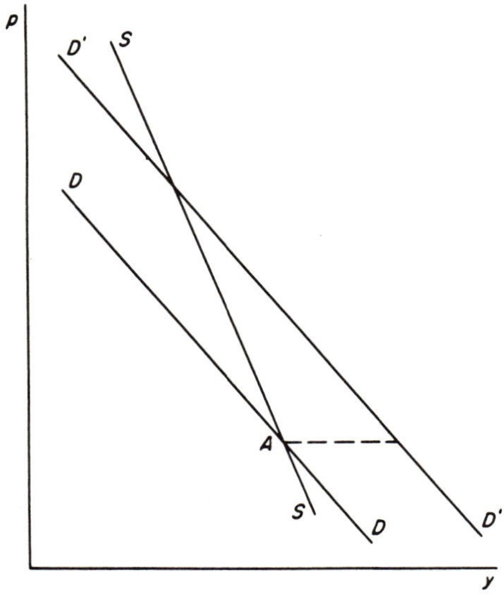

Figure 3

Under the usually hypothesized market and technological conditions, the Illyrian competitive firm possesses a negatively sloped supply curve. This does not mean however that Illyrian competitive markets are inherently unstable. For example, Figure 3 depicts the industry supply and demand curves in such a market. If demand were to shift from *DD* to *D′D′*, point *A* would no longer be an equilibrium position. If this is a "price-adjusting" market in the usual sense, the adjustment mechanism is such that the direction of price movement over time has the same sign as the amount of excess demand. In the diagram, excess demand is now positive so price increases, and eventually equilibrium is restored.

On the other hand, if the demand curve has a steeper slope than the supply curve, the adjusting mechanism described above will lead away from equilibrium and the market will be unstable. To be assured of stability this possibility must be avoided, which means that some further constraint must be imposed on the structure of the firm specified above.[13] The problem of instability is most likely to arise when product demand is relatively inelastic, or when marginal product is relatively large and declining slowly as output increases.

If the state changes the calculated wage w, there is no change in any of the variables relevant to the firm. The K function (see Figure 1) shifts vertically up or down as a result. The income of the workers is unchanged, though more income is in the form of profits (if w is reduced) and less in the form of wages.

The Illyrian equilibrium can now be contrasted with its capitalist counterpart. Consider two firms, one in Illyria, the other in the capitalist country. They have identical production functions and are operating in purely competitive markets. In addition, market prices are equal in both cases, as are fixed costs, and the Illyrian calculated wage w^I equals the going capitalist wage w^c. In Figure 4, the U and K functions describe the revenue and cost positions of the Illyrian firm under alternative levels of employment. The rates of change are also drawn in. At the intersection of the latter, the Illyrian firm is in equilibrium, producing the output corresponding to exployment x^i.

In describing the equilibrium of the capitalist firm, it will first be noted that U also expresses the value of the average product of the capitalist firm under our assumptions, since $U = py/x$. The capitalist value-of-the-marginal-product function bears the

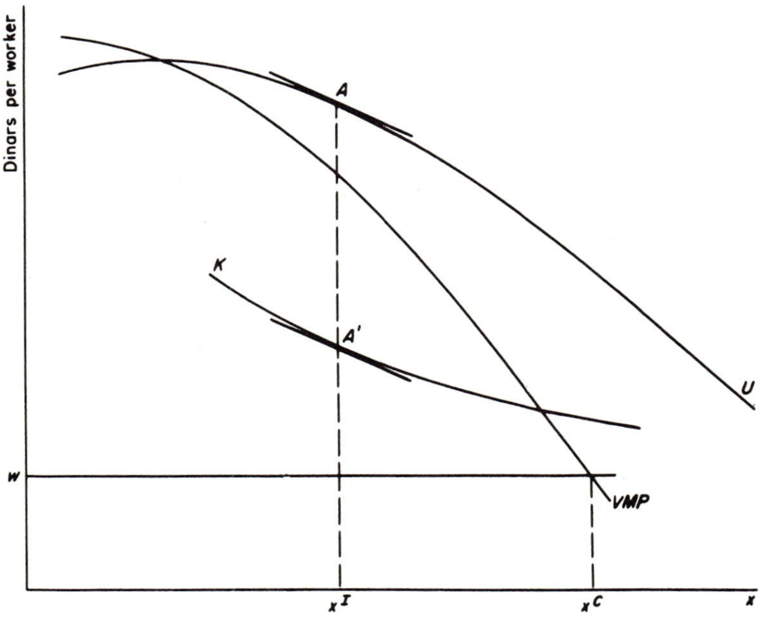

Figure 4

usual relation to U, and the capitalist output is found at the point x^c where VMP equals the wage, since output y^c is a single-valued function of labor input.[14]

In the diagram the capitalist output exceeds that of the Illyrian firm. But this need not be the case. For example, by increasing w^c it would be possible to reduce the equilibrium output level of this firm to the Illyrian level or even below. Under our assumptions, a necessary and sufficient condition that the outputs of the two firms be equal is that the equilibrium marginal products be equal. The capitalist value of the marginal product is equal to w^c. In Illyria the value of the marginal product is equal to the "full" wage, i.e., the calculated wage plus the profits share to each worker.[15] Therefore the Illyrian full wage equals the capitalist wage, and equality of outputs implies zero profits.[16]

Thus the Illyrian firm is capable of producing, in the short run, at a level equal to or even greater than that of its capitalist counterpart. And the state can affect output decisions of the firm via its ability to alter the parameter R. If it is willing to use the fixed tax for capital use as an instrument of policy in attaining desired levels of output, and consequently is willing to make discriminatory charges on this basis, it may create an environment in which it is in the material interests of the worker-managers to produce at the competitive capitalist output, or at some other preferred rate. Alternatively, if the industry were in long-run equilibrium in both countries and demand, labor force, etc., conditions were identical, both firms would produce the same output.

Finally, the case of constant average product y/x may be noted. In capitalism this means one of three things: (1) if $VMP < w$ the firm produces at capacity; (2) if $VMP > w$ the firm produces nothing; and (3) if $VMP = w$ output is indeterminate. In the Illyrian case this means that U is a horizontal line. The maximum positive, or minimum negative, difference between U and K consequently is at infinity whatever the position of U on the diagram. The Illyrian firm always produces at capacity when average product is constant, regardless of the level of w.

The case of two variable inputs

In Illyria a single class of inputs, labor, is singled out for special treatment. The distinctive features of Illyrian behavior stem entirely from this fact. By extending our previous model to include the use by the firm of a variable nonlabor input, the special position of labor in the firm can be brought out more clearly. The production function will now have the two arguments,

$$y = f(x, z). \tag{6}$$

If the usual assumptions of positive marginal products and diminishing returns to the factors are made, the equilibrium condition for labor use will correspond to that in the previous section, i.e., the value of the marginal product of labor will be equal to the full wage. For the nonlabor input however, the value of the marginal product will be equal to the price v of the input.[17] The workers react to changes in nonlabor inputs in the same manner as do capitalists: they will increase their use of the factor as long as it contributes more to revenue than to cost. On the other hand, they seem to use a different criterion in evaluating labor use. An additional laborer must contribute more to revenue per worker than to cost per worker in order for him to be employed. In fact, *only* the latter criterion is being employed in the model. It simply happens that the capitalist and Illyrian criteria lead to the same behavior with regard to nonlabor inputs. Whenever one of these factors contributes more to revenue than to cost it also contributes more to revenue per worker than to cost per worker. As a result the equilibrium conditions are the same. However, the two criteria do not lead to the same behavior when it comes to labor use. Because each laborer gets a share of the profits, it does not follow that an additional worker who contributes more to revenue than to cost will necessarily also contribute more to revenue per worker than to cost per worker. As a result, the equilibrium conditions for labor use are not the same in the two regimes.

An analysis of the effects of changes in the parameters R and p leads to less clear results in the two-input case than it did in the previous section. In the case of a change in fixed costs, the analysis may be illustrated by means of the factor-allocation diagrams of Figure 5. The curves in 5A are drawn on the assumption of a fixed input of factor z, and those in Figure 5B on the assumption of a fixed level of employment. From an initial position of equilibrium in which x_1 of x and z_1 of z are being used, fixed cost is increased. This shifts K_1 upward to K_2, increasing labor input from x_1 to x_2, and consequently tending to increase output. However, there is now an additional effect which must be taken into account: namely the effect of the increase in labor use on the marginal product of the nonlabor input. If the latter is unaffected or increases, shifting VMP_1 upward to VMP_2, the increase in output is either unaffected or magnified. However, if VMP is reduced by the increased labor use, the amount of z used decreases, and the output effect of the increase in fixed cost is indeterminate by means of qualitative analysis alone. The latter, however, is a rather unlikely eventuality, since in the short run more labor will generally not decrease the usefulness of the other variable factors, and conversely. Consequently a change in fixed cost in the multifactor case will also tend to lead to a change in output in the same direction.

A more serious indeterminacy appears in the analysis of price changes. Without a good deal more information, it is not possible

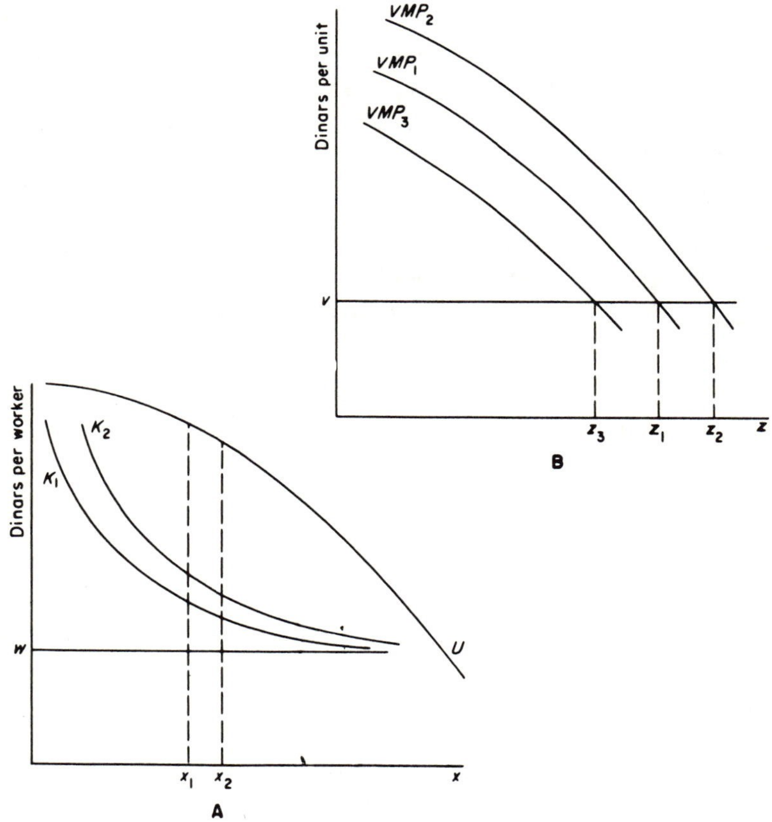

Figure 5

to state the effect on output of a change in price. The possibility of a positively inclined supply curve emerges clearly however, and some presumption that the danger of instability, resulting from a negatively inclined and relatively elastic supply curve, has diminished. Whether or not a negatively sloped supply curve will result in the multifactor case depends on the importance of labor in the bill of inputs.[18]

Similarly, changes in the parameter v, the supply price of the nonlabor input z, have indeterminate effects on output. This is also true in the case of analysis of the capitalist firm with the same amount of information, though information sufficient to remove the indeterminacy in one case may not be sufficient in the other.

The statements made earlier comparing competitive capitalism with competition in Illyria generally apply in the somewhat more complicated two-variable-input case. We will consider here the problem of comparative factor allocation. As before, our two firms have identical production functions and are operating under identical market conditions so that:

$$p^I = p^c$$
$$w^I = w^c$$
$$v^I = v^c$$
$$R^I = R^c$$

the superscripts, as before, standing for "Illyria" and "Capitalism" respectively.

The situation is described in Figure 6 in which isoquants Q_i which are identical for both firms are drawn. Let us assume first that the capitalist firm is producing output Q_1. BB is the factor-cost line based on the values of w and v, so that the capitalist firm is in equilibrium at a factor mix represented by point N. Let us assume further that the capitalist firm is earning a profit at this level of operation. At the same output the Illyrian firm would be earning a profit too. But it would not be in equilibrium at point N. This is because BB is not the relevant factor-cost line for the Illyrian firm. In Illyria the value of the marginal product of labor is equated to the *full* wage, which includes the profit share. Consequently BA, representing a larger wage "cost," is the relevant factor-cost line for the Illyrian allocation decision. The Illyrian firm is in equilibrium then at point M, producing less output and using less labor than its capitalist counterpart.

Suppose now that market price falls to the zero-profits point. Capitalist output and factor mix contract along Y^c, say to point L.

Illyrian output and factor mix contract along Y^I, but also to point *L*, since the zero-profits full wage is equal to *w*. If price should fall further, so that both firms are incurring losses, the full wage will then be less than *w*. For example, under conditions which would lead the capitalist firm to produce at *H*, the Illyrian firm would produce more than the capitalist firm and would use more labor, so as to spread the losses around among as many of the worker-managers as possible.

The Y^I line, like Y^c, is positively sloped in the diagram, indicating that supply responds positively to an increase in price. It is perfectly possible for Y^I to have a negative slope under suitable cost and technological conditions, but it will still intersect Y^c at the zero-profits point.[19]

The slopes of the two supply curves can also be compared. When labor is the only input, the supply curves have opposite signs, but in the multiple-input case this need not be true. Both may have positive slopes. In note 2 of the Appendix to this chap-

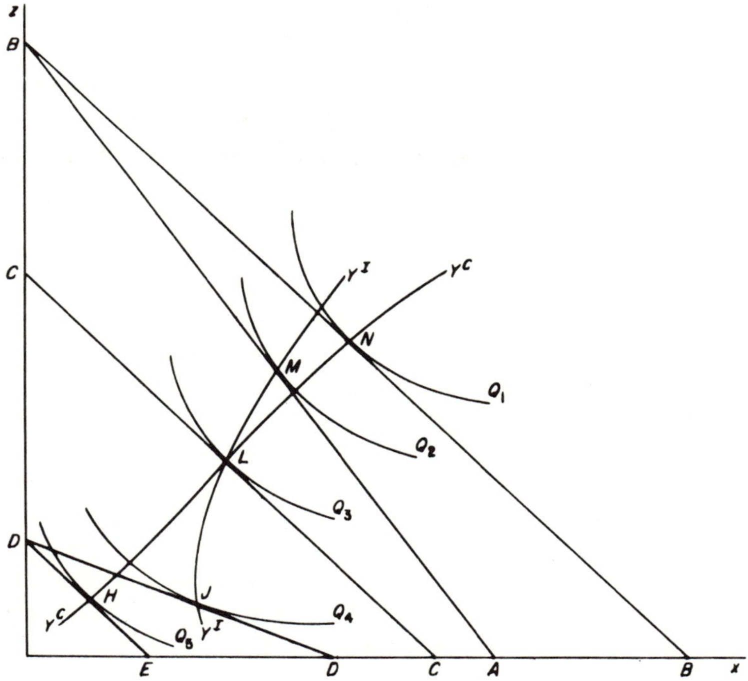

Figure 6

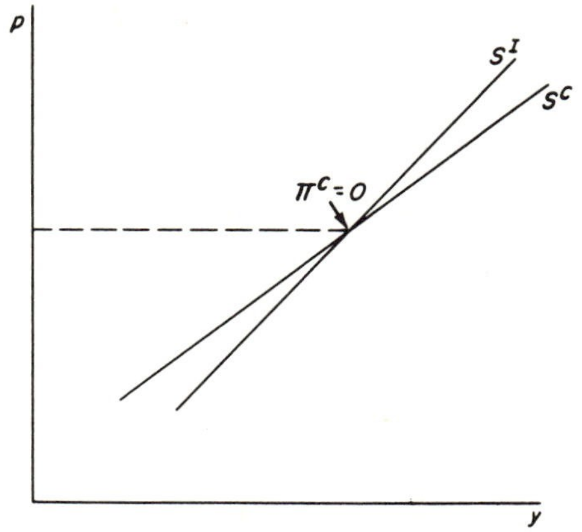

Figure 7

ter [not reprinted here] it is shown that under assumptions sufficiently strong to ensure that the capitalist supply curve is positively sloped, the Illyrian supply curve will be either negatively sloped or steeper than its capitalist counterpart, for each level of output. One situation is shown in Figure 7, where the two supply curves intersect at the capitalist zero-profits point.

As a final aspect of the multiple-input case, we may consider a firm which is highly automated so that labor does not enter significantly into the short-run production function as a variable input. In this case, factor use and output are determined by the usual equilibrium conditions of capitalism. That is, with a fixed labor force, any addition to profits is also an addition to profits per worker. Such a firm would behave in exactly the same way as its capitalist counterpart, equating marginal cost to price and the marginal value products to the fixed input prices.

Market imperfections: monopoly

A comparison of output levels under competitive and monopolized market conditions in Illyria can be made using Figure 8. Labor again is the only variable input, and technology and demand conditions are assumed identical for the two situations. The output generated by employing *b* workers is the equilibrium output for each of the identical competitive firms. Is this output level optimal from the point of view of the monopolist? The cost

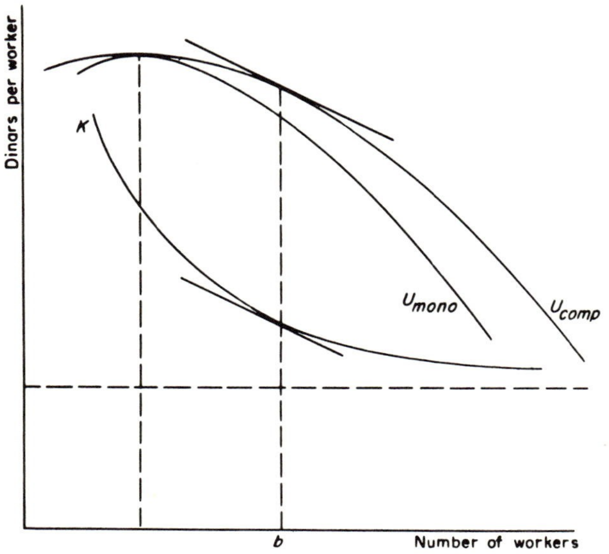

Figure 8

function, *K,* will not change in the monopoly case. However, *U,* the average-revenue-per-worker schedule, will be different—reflecting the monopolist's ability to anticipate the price effects of altering his output rate. The effect of lowering price on intra-marginal units is to make *U* steeper at the output rate determined by using *b* workers in each firm. Thus, to equate the slopes of *K* and *U,* the monopolist will move back toward a lower rate of output in each plant. This is true so long as the competitive equilibrium occurs at a point of decreasing average product and the demand curve is downward sloping.[20] A similar conclusion holds for the multiple input case. An Illyrian monopolist will tend to produce less than his competitive counterpart.

The Illyrian monopolist's behavior in response to changes in the capital charge, in fixed costs generally, or in price is similar in direction to that of Illyrian competition. If the demand curve is negatively sloped and not concave to the origin, a parallel rightward shift in demand will lead to a decrease in output if average product is declining. And for the same kind of demand and declining average product, an increase in the capital levy will lead to an increase in output.[21]

By an argument similar to those in the previous sections another comparative statement can be made: *Given the possibility of operating at a profit, the Illyrian monopolist will produce less and charge a higher price than his capitalist counterpart.*[22]

NOTES

1. A slightly revised version of "The Firm in Illyria: Market Syndicalism," *American Economic Review,* 48 (1958), 566–89.

2. The state also owns the land, but for the moment we shall assume that land is a free good.

3. Alternative assumptions will be treated in the next two chapters.

4. Alternatively, hours of work are fixed by the workers' council by majority vote, in which case the work-leisure choice could be made differently in different firms.

5. Conflicts might arise in case the criterion specified by the workers' council would lead to layoffs. But as long as these amounted to less than half the work force (and less than half of the members of the workers' council) a majority decision would still follow the criterion.

6. Since wage cost per worker is fixed by the state, maximizing profits per worker is equivalent to maximizing the sum of wage per worker and profits per worker. We are also deliberately idealizing the decision process by which the manager determines his appropriate level of output.

7. Marginal per-worker revenue, it will be noticed, is not the same thing as marginal revenue per worker. The former measures the change in average revenue per worker brought about by a small change in output, while the latter measures the average marginal revenue per worker. In symbols, marginal per-worker revenue is:

$$\frac{d(py/x)}{dy} = p \cdot \frac{x - yx'}{x^2}$$

(here and elsewhere in this chapter primes denote derivatives) while marginal revenue per worker is:

$$\frac{d(py)/dy}{x} = \frac{p}{x}\,.$$

8. Since $K = w + (R/x)$, $dK/dx = -R/x^2$. Therefore, if $R_2 > R_1$, $|dK_2/dx| > |dK_1/dx|$ at $x = a$.

9. In the Yugoslavia of the mid-fifties wages up to 80 percent of the

calculated wage were guaranteed by the government. If this were true of Illyria, then at outputs beyond that which yielded $0.8w$ to the workers the maximization criterion would cease to apply. Continued operation at such a level would eventually lead to bankruptcy.

10. As in capitalism, this would only be true over the range in which marginal product was declining. Beyond that range the second-order condition for equilibrium would not be satisfied, so that if a solution existed it would not be a maximum. It may also be noted that over this range of values the supply curve would be positively sloped.

11. $dU/dx = (p/x)[y' - (y/x)]$. Hence if $p_2 > p_1$, then $|dU_2/dx| > |dU_1/dx|$ at $x = a$.

12. The workers' criterion, $S = w + \pi/R$, where π is profits. Then maximizing this subject to the constraint of equation (1), the effects of changes in p and R can perhaps be seen more clearly by considering the resulting equilibrium condition:

$$\frac{dS}{dx} = \frac{p(xy' - y) + R}{x^2} = 0 \tag{4}$$

or

$$\frac{y}{x} - y' = \frac{R}{px} \tag{5}$$

Thus the right-hand term of (5) measures the difference between average and marginal product in equilibrium, which will be positive (decreasing average product) if R is positive. But the difference between average and marginal product is a monotonic increasing function of output, beyond the point of maximum average product (at which point the difference is nil). So, from equation (5), if R is increased, the difference between average and marginal product, and hence equilibrium output, will be increased. On the other hand, an increase in p means a decrease in the difference between average and marginal product, and hence a decrease in equilibrium output.

13. See the Appendix to this chapter [not reprinted here].

14. We are assuming that the capitalist firm too can vary only the number of workers employed and not the hours of work.

15. From footnote 12, $S = (py - R)/x = py'$ in equilibrium.

16. We assumed at the start that $w^I = w^C$. Since the value of w^I really does not make any difference, a more significant statement would be: equality of outputs implies equal wages.

17. See the Appendix to this chapter for derivations in the two-variable-input case.

18. Cf. equation (2) in the Appendix to this chapter.

19. Figure 6 may also be used to contrast other comparative static changes. For example, an increase in w will increase the slope of BB without affecting that of BA. This will tend to move the capitalist equilibrium position at N closer to the Illyrian at M. An increase in R, on the other hand, will tend to make BA less steep without affecting the slope of BB. This will tend to move the Illyrian equilibrium position at M closer to the capitalist at N. When the equilibria coincide, in either case profits will be zero.

20. It also assumes that the monopolistic firm faces no problems of obtaining a consensus among workers in different plants. This point is discussed in Chapter Ten.

21. The assumptions are as above, except that p is now a variable. Assume

$$p = g(y, \alpha)$$

where $\partial p/\partial y < 0$ and α, a shift parameter, is defined so that $\partial p/\partial \alpha > 0$, and further that $\partial p/\partial y$ remains invariant under the shift. Solving for the first-order condition for a maximum:

$$y'(p + p'y) = (py - R)/x, \text{ where } p' = \frac{\partial p}{\partial y}.$$

This equilibrium condition may be differentiated with respect to R and α respectively, and solved:

$$\frac{\partial y}{\partial R} = - \frac{x}{2p'x + p''xy - x''(py - R)}$$

and

$$\frac{\partial y}{\partial \alpha} = - \frac{(\partial p/\partial \alpha)(x'y - x) - xy\dfrac{\partial^2 p}{\partial y \partial \alpha}}{2p'x + p''xy - x''(py - R)}.$$

Knowledge of signs tells us that, as long as the demand curve is linear or convex to the origin, a change in R leads to a change in y in the same direction. With a similar demand curve, an upward shift in demand of the hypothesized kind will lead to a decrease in output if the firm is operating beyond the point of maximum average product, but an increase in output if average product is still increasing.

22. Evsey Domar in a recent paper, "The Soviet Collective Farm as a Producer Cooperative," *American Economic Review,* Vol. 56, September, 1966, 734–57, has developed the comparative static analysis discussed in this appendix using a generalized production function. This

gives a much more detailed picture of enterprise reactions under the assumed conditions, but does not change the general picture given by the results. Contrary to his assertion, no result of mine is reversed by his analysis, as the reader may see by comparing note 2 in the Appendix below (and especially equation 20) with his appendix note 3 (pp. 753–56) and especially paragraph (c) (i) (p. 755). For a discussion of his altered assumption about the supply of labor see Chapter Ten below.

12. The Firm, Monetary Policy, and Property Rights in a Planned Economy

SVETOZAR PEJOVICH

The thrust of proposed reforms in most East European countries, as well as the steps toward economic decentralization in Yugoslavia, suggest an important inference: something has occurred to the Socialist belief that administrative planning is superior to the market-oriented allocation of resources. Moreover, some prominent East European economists, such as Liberman and Šik, have recently suggested that their respective governments have failed to devise an effective incentive and control system to induce public administrators to direct production efficiently.

The implementation of proposals to substitute economic for administrative criteria in the conduct of economic life would present decentralized socialist states with a set of new problems. To deal with some of these problems, their governments would have to rely on fiscal and monetary policies. Yet knowledge of the role that fiscal and monetary policies might be expected to play in decentralized socialist states remains rudimentary.

The purpose of this paper is to contribute toward an understanding of the nature and limitations of monetary policy in a decentralized socialist state which seeks to attain the market-ori-

Reprinted from *Western Economic Journal,* September 1969, 193–200, by permission of the author and the publisher.

ented allocation of resources and, at the same time, retain public ownership over the means of production. While the model is intended to be a contribution to the pure theory of property rights, it has some correspondences—which will be pointed out—to the economic situation in Yugoslavia.

I

Let us assume that the firm in a socialist state operates within the following institutional framework:[1] (1) The right to manage the firm is in the hands of its employees. This right includes output and employment decisions, wage determination, production planning and disposition of the total revenue. (2) The firm's profit is equal to total revenue minus the cost of all inputs excluding labor costs but including turnover tax, interest on capital and other legal obligations. The firm's profit represents the employees' income. They can choose either to allocate the entire profit to the Wage Fund, or to leave part of it with the firm. (3) The employees have only the *right of use* of the means of production held by the firm. This right allows the collective to produce, buy, or sell capital goods. The firm must maintain the book value of its assets via depreciation or other means (e.g., the firm must reinvest the proceeds from sale of capital goods). If the firm sells assets to another firm for less than their book value the difference must be deducted from the firm's profit and earmarked for investment.[2] The firm must also pay interest to the state on the value of its capital. In addition to asserting the state's ownership rights, the purpose of this obligation is to provide funds for investment projects, as well as to induce the profit-oriented firm to use capital goods sparingly and efficiently. The firm selling capital goods can transfer only the right of use to the buying firm.[3] (4) Product prices are administratively determined, i.e., they are exogenous to the firm. (5) The bank loan rate and interest paid on savings accounts are also determined by the state.

Given the assumed institutional setting,[4] two possible behavioral goals of the firm are suggested: *wage maximization* and *wealth maximization per worker*. We assume the wealth maximization hypothesis henceforth.[5]

II

Employees have two major alternatives available for investing their nonconsumed income in nonhuman wealth.

Investment in nonowned assets. Workers may choose to accept a reduction in their current take-home pay and leave some of the profit with the firm for investment in physical assets. Their property rights to new assets acquired by the firm would be limited[6] to benefits from the increased future profits, and only for as long as they remain employed by the enterprise. The behavioral implication of this quasi-ownership is a shortened time horizon for the employees (which is assumed to depend on the average length of employment expected by the employees) and a high time preference relative to what it would be if the workers were granted the right of ownership in capital goods acquired by the firm during the period of their employment.

Investment in owned assets. Savings accounts are owned by depositors. Thus, employees would find it advantageous to allocate the entire profit of the firm into the Wage Fund and let each person save for himself, *unless* there exist investment opportunities in nonowned assets at least as attractive to the workers as the rate of interest paid on individual savings deposits.

The understanding of the investment behavior of the firm, as well as the formulation of monetary and fiscal policies, requires a common denominator for comparing these two investment alternatives. Since employees cannot withdraw their nonconsumed income once it is invested in nonowned assets, they might envision the two wealth-increasing alternatives as an annuity for a fixed number of years with no return of capital versus a savings account.[7] The rates of return that would make investment in nonowned capital goods as attractive to the employees as savings deposits at 5 percent are 23 percent, 19 percent, 13 percent and 9 percent for time horizons of 5, 6, 10 and 15 years. This relationship is shown in Figure 1. The *rr* curve shows the rate of return from nonowned assets that would make an average member of the collective indifferent between investment in nonowned and owned assets at a stipulated rate of interest (i) on savings for alternative time horizons of the collective. Since curves similar to *rr* can be established for any rate of interest (i), the *rr* curve makes it possible to compare all investment alternatives available to the employees.[8]

III

If the workers choose to allocate none of their earnings to the Investment Fund, the amount they would save at each possible rate of interest paid on savings accounts can be summarized in a hypothetical saving schedule for the collective. The S_1S_1 curve in

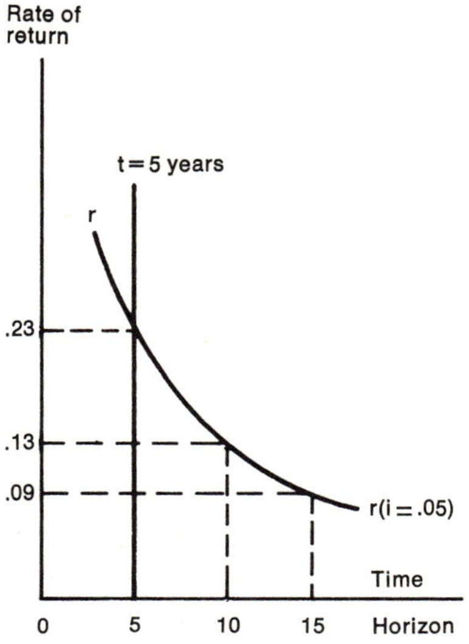

Figure 1

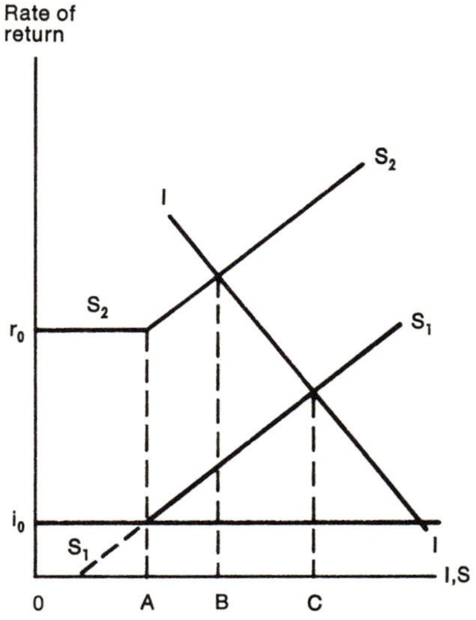

Figure 2

Figure 2 represents the savings that will be forthcoming at various interest rates. Following the usual textbook formulation, it shows the amount of income the collective is willing to divert from current consumption to accumulation of owned assets for the various rates of growth of wealth.

Given the average length of employment expected by the employees of the firm (t_0) and the analysis in Section II pertaining to Figure 1, the S_2S_2 schedule can be easily calculated. It shows the amount of income the collective is willing to divert from current consumption for investment in nonowned assets. More specifically, the S_2S_2 curve is the S_1S_1 curve *adjusted* for the behavioral effects of a change in property rights from owned to nonowned assets. The rate of return (r) on nonowned assets has to be greater than the corresponding rate of return (i) on owned assets to elicit any given volume of savings from the collective.[9]

The portion of the S_1S_1 curve lying above the rate of return (i_0) paid on owned (savings) assets would not come into effective play. It follows that employees would have no incentive to divert their nonconsumed income to investment in nonowned assets unless the yield promised by such investment is at least equal to the rate of return (r_0) in Figure 2—where (r_0) is the rate of return on nonowned assets that is equivalent to the official rate of return (i_0) on owned assets.

The investment demand schedule *II* shows the expected increase in wealth per marginal unit of investment in capital goods; that is, the return that employees can expect from diverting current consumption to investment in nonowned assets. While the concept is analogous to the conventional marginal efficiency of investment function, the schedule has some unique features of its own. It reflects the opportunities the *given firm* possesses for the use of additional capital.

It is now possible to discern the effects of various property rights structures on the *voluntary* allocation of the collective's income between present and future consumption. If the employees' property rights in capital goods are similar to the property right known as *usus* (the right to use a thing belonging to someone else, but not to rent it, or sell it, or change its quality, or appropriate profits arising from its use), then they would have no incentive to leave any of their earnings with the firm. Under *usus*, the amount of income diverted to saving (*OA* in Figure 2) would be determined by the government-controlled rate of interest paid on savings accounts and the workers' propensity to save. If employees are granted the property right to income from capital goods *(the right of use)*, the amount of income diverted to saving would be *OB* for the time horizon in Figure 2. For a shorter time horizon the S_2S_2 schedule would be higher and the rate of income diverted to saving lower, and vice versa. Thus, the factors determining the average length of employment expected by employees of the firm are important in a decentralized socialist state. Finally, if workers are granted full ownership of capital goods acquired by the firm during the period of their employment, the S_1S_1 schedule would be the only relevant one, and the volume of saving would be *OC*. The first case has correspondences to the situation in a centralized socialist state such as the U.S.S.R., the second to a decentralized socialist state such as Yugoslavia, and the third to a private-property capitalist society.

These results are in a broad agreement with Demsetz's analysis of the differences between the state, communal, and private property rights [1]. They also suggest two general conclusions: (1) The *voluntary* allocation of resources between present and future consumption in a centralized socialist state tends to favor current consumption relative to what it would be in a decentralized socialist state, and in the latter it tends to favor current consumption relative to what it would be in a private-property capitalist society. It follows that a change in the structure of property rights affects the choices individuals make with respect to present and future consumption, other things remaining the same. (2) Investment projects with a relatively long gestation period would tend to be discriminated against in a decentralized socialist state. These projects have to be financed either by banks or by the central treasury.

IV

A growth-oriented socialist state, as most of them are, might not be happy with the firm's allocation of its profits between the Wage and Investment Funds. If the government is reluctant to fall back on a system of administrative controls, the importance of monetary and fiscal policy becomes obvious. Leaving aside fiscal policies,[10] the monetary authority (National Bank) could attempt to raise the rate of market-oriented investment by the existing firms,[11] either by reducing the rate of interest paid on savings accounts or via bank credit. The sources of the bank credit are assumed to be savings deposits, interest on capital goods held by business firms, and new money.

A reduction in the rate of interest in Figure 2 would leave the S_2S_2 curve above point A unchanged. Consequently, the firm's rate of net investment would remain at OB. A fall in the rate of interest would have some effect on the firm's *investment in capital goods* only if its investment demand schedule happened to cut the S_2S_2 curve somewhere along its horizontal stretch. This case is shown in Figure 3.

The amount of income diverted to saving is OA. Out of this amount the employees invest ON in nonowned assets and NA in owned assets (individual savings accounts). A fall in the rate of interest paid on savings accounts to i_2 would reduce the amount of saving to OA_1. Moreover, a reduction in the rate of interest from 5 percent to 3 percent would reduce the required rate of return from investment in nonowned assets with a five-year time horizon from 23 percent to 21 percent (r_2 in Figure 3). The result would be an increase in the firm's investment in capital goods *(NN_1)*, but a *decrease* in the employees' income diverted to investment in owned assets by the amount $A_1A + NN_1$.

The National Bank can also influence the rate of market-oriented investment via bank credit. We assume that the price of a

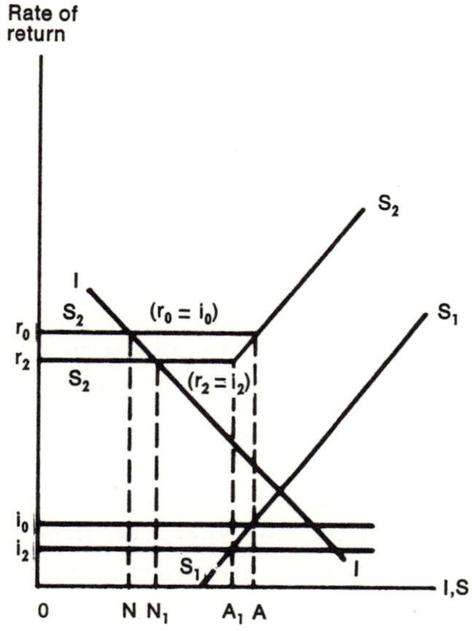

Figure 3

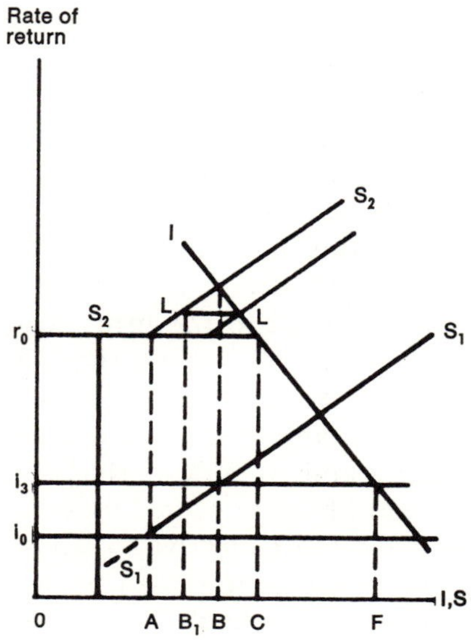

Figure 4

bank loan is administratively set at i_3 in Figure 4. The conclusions of the analysis would not be different if the National Bank were instructed to auction the supply of bank credit.[12] Suppose the firm receives a loan of *LL* dollars. The employees' saving schedule S_2S_2 would shift to the right by the amount of credit at every point on the horizontal scale in Figure 4. The resulting schedule cuts the firm's investment schedule at a lower point showing that one effect of bank credit on the firm's investment is a higher rate of purchase of nonowned assets and a lower rate of return, other things remaining the same.

The implication is that the National Bank in a decentralized socialist state can increase the rate of market-oriented investment in capital goods via bank credit. Unfortunately, this is not entirely true. The bank credit also results in a decrease in the amount of employees' income (BB_1 in Figure 4) allocated to the Investment Fund. Figure 4 shows that each additional dollar borrowed from the bank would *increase* the firm's investment *by less* than $1 because the employees would reduce the share of their income allocated to investment in nonowned assets. If the rate of return falls below r_0 the collective would allocate the firm's entire profit to the Wage Fund. The amount of income diverted to saving would fall to *OA* in Figure 4, and the employees would invest in owned assets only.

Given the bank loan rate i_3 the firm's demand for credit is *OF*. Whether the firm can borrow that amount or not depends on the total supply of bank funds and the investment schedules of other enterprises.[13] In either case, however, the analysis suggests that the amount of income which the collective allocates to the Investment Fund decreases with an increase in the amount of bank credit granted to the firm. Suppose the firm receives bank credit in excess of *OC* but less than *OF*. The firm would behave as if its demand for investment funds were insatiable, while at the same time the employees would allocate the firm's entire profit to the Wage Fund. It follows that an important effect of an attempt to increase the rate of market-oriented investment via bank credit is to make the collective's disposition of its income (i.e., the firm's profit) even more biased in favor of current consumption than it was before the bank credit was made available to the firm. Monetary authorities may find the pursuance of this policy rather difficult, and yet necessary in order to increase the rate of market-oriented investment.[14]

V

The analysis presented here shows that our understanding of the role and limitations of monetary policy in a socialist state cannot be separated from the analysis of property rights structures. Moreover, it appears that a growth-oriented socialist state seeking to increase the scope of the market mechanism in its economy would be faced by what it is bound to consider as an undesirable allocation of resources between current and future consumption, this distortion being caused by the fact that capital goods cannot be privately owned. The effectiveness of monetary policy in achieving a "preferred" rate of investment via the market mechanism seems to be open to serious doubt.

The paper also indicates that a major problem of economic decentralization in socialist countries is not their willingness to substitute economic for administrative criteria but their *ability* to solve the problem of maintaining a high rate of investment via the market mechanism in an environment in which physical assets cannot be privately owned. More generally, the success of currently debated economic reforms in Eastern Europe will depend on how successful those states are in developing a set of institutions that yield a rate of investment at least equal to the one which, *ceteris paribus,* would prevail in a capitalist society, and at the same time retain public ownership over the means of production. This problem may turn out to be a difficult one indeed.

NOTES

1. The Yugoslav economic system is used as the prototype for the assumed institutional framework. The implication is not that the rest of Eastern Europe is going to follow the Yugoslav example. The model used here incorporates some of the ideas present in the currently debated reforms in Eastern Europe and forecasts their possible future. Moreover, Yugoslavia is the only East European country that has actually decentralized its economy without falling back on the institution of private rights over the means of production.

2. To deal with the problem of inflation the Yugoslav government has periodically revalued the stock of capital held by business firms.

3. For an analysis of the *right of use* and its implications see [5]. As of 1965 the Yugoslav firm pays 4 percent of the value of its stock to the state.

4. The postulated institutional setting reflects the conditions in Yugoslavia after the 1965 reform. The collective of the Yugoslav firm, through its elected body, the Workers' Council, makes all major decisions such as the level of employment, the rates of investment and output, hiring and firing of workers, etc. The Workers' Council also has power sufficient to ask the removal of the firm's director which, in turn, suggests that he can afford to be neither a director nor a paternalistic supervisor; he has to sell his ideas to the collective. The most important change instituted by the 1965 reform was to transfer the power to distribute the firm's profit between the Wage and Internal Funds to the collective.

5. See [2].

6. This is the difference between the right *of ownership* and *the right of use*.

7. The employee's annuity from investing one dollar in owned assets is $y = i(1 + i)^n/[(1 + i)^n - 1]$, where i is the rate of interest paid on savings accounts. One dollar invested in nonowned assets must yield at least the same annual return. It follows that the rate of return from

investment in nonowned assets is $r = i(1 + i)^n/[(1 + i)^n - 1]$, where n stands for the time horizon of the collective.

8. Another investment alternative open to the collective of a Yugoslav firm is to lend funds to other firms. This opportunity can be ignored for at least two reasons. First, the rate at which funds can be lent to other firms is currently set at 10 percent. Assuming the wealth maximizing behavior of the collective, this would require a relatively long time horizon (about 14 years) to make this alternative preferable to private savings at 5 percent. Second, earnings from lending funds to other firms *must* be allocated to the firm's Investment Fund.

9. The assumption is that owned and nonowned assets are alike with respect to risk level and liquidity. As W. Nutter has pointed out to the author, the assumption could be relaxed and the indifference analysis used to incorporate some elements other than expected monetary returns into the calculated difference between the S_1S_1 and S_2S_2 curves. This point is well taken, because individuals are likely to prefer diversifying portfolios of savings (owned assets) and income from capital goods (nonowned assets). For the purpose of this paper, however, the assumption that owned and nonowned assets may show differences in effective returns, but are alike in other essential respects, is a useful simplification which does not affect our conclusions.

10. For the role of fiscal policy in a decentralized socialist state see [3] and [6].

11. The term *market-oriented investment,* admittedly a strong term, is used to signify the difference between self-financed investments and bank loans on the one hand, and administratively allocated investment funds on the other. The latter represents a direct administrative intervention by the government and lies outside the purpose of this paper. Incidentally, the sources of total investment in Yugoslavia in 1967 were: self-financed investments (including depreciation) 37.5 percent, bank loans 44.9 percent, and administrative funds 17.6 percent [7, p. 257].

12. The policy of auctioning bank credit was abandoned by the Yugoslav government some years ago. See [4].

13. Obviously the state can raise funds via taxes and extend bank credit. This possibility is ignored in the paper for two reasons: (1) it would imply a change in tax rates that would take us into the realm of fiscal policy and (2) a change in tax rates would result in a shift in both the saving and investment schedules.

14. The Yugoslav press has repeatedly and unfairly criticized the

firms for distributing their profits as wages while borrowing extensively from the banks. Yet, the property rights structure imposed by the Yugoslav government induces the collectives to behave as they do.

REFERENCES

1. H. Demsetz, "Toward a Theory of Property Rights," *American Economic Review,* May 1967, 57, 247–59.

2. E. Furubotn and S. Pejovich, "The Firm, Its Behavior and Property Rights Structures in a Planned Economy," presented at the annual meeting of the Southern Economic Association, November 1968.

3. E. Furubotn and S. Pejovich, "Tax Policy and Investment Decisions of the Yugoslav Firm," presented at the annual meeting of the Southwestern Association for Advancement of Slavic Studies, April 1969.

4. E. Neuberger, "The Yugoslav Investment Action," *Quarterly Journal of Economics,* February 1959, 73, 88–115.

5. S. Pejovich, "Liberman's Reforms and Property Rights in the U.S.S.R.," *Journal of Law and Economics,* April 1969, 12, 155–62.

6. S. Pejovich, "Taxes and the Pattern of Economic Growth," *National Tax Journal,* March 1964, 17, 96–100.

7. *Statistički Godišnjak Jugoslavije, 1968,* Belgrade, 1968.

13. Plan and Market in Yugoslavia

DEBORAH MILENKOVITCH

Planning and the market for economic development

The Marxist attitude over the years had been plan *versus* market. The Yugoslavs had slowly freed themselves of the dichotomy of this approach and accepted the principle of plan *and* market. Given the desire to combine plan and market, the Yugoslavs had to ascertain what combination of aggregative and selective controls was most suitable for economic development. Organizational possibilities ranged from complete centralization of all decisions and a continual flow of administrative orders, on the one hand, to a market economy with purely aggregative controls, on the other. In addition, the Yugoslavs required a strategy for economic development. Nor was development the sole objective. Yugoslavs have a distinct preference for worker-managed enterprises. They therefore had to establish whether the methods suitable for attaining economic development were compatible with the commitment to independent worker-managed enterprises.

No model had existed for the Yugoslav economic system. The discussion in the West in the thirties and forties over the economic possibilities of socialism did not deal with the problems

From *Plan and Market in Yugoslav Economic Thought* (New Haven, Yale University Press), pp. 127–28, 145–53, 158–62.

specific to economic development in a backward economy and was not considered highly relevant for the Yugoslav economic problems. Most economists agreed with Samardzija, who stated that "the discussion about the socialist economy among Western European economists, which took place after 1920, did not have, and still does not have, any direct influence on economic practice nor on the leading theoretical conceptions of economists in socialist countries."[1] . . .

The rate of investment and its allocation are the heart of development policy. Yugoslav practice in allocating investment funds represented the belief that the initial stages of socialist development require planning. The Yugoslavs did not analyze criteria for investment allocation at a high level of economic sophistication but they touched on most of the real problems involved. Despite deficiencies in their logic, they adopted a method of allocation that was potentially consistent with their objectives of rapid economic growth and with the principle of competition among enterprises within sectors. This arrangement permitted political determination of the overall structure and was viable as long as the political leaders could agree on the allocation of investment by sector and by region. When they could not, this arrangement began to break down.[2]

Implementation of the plan

Yugoslavs had dual objectives, an organizational pattern, on the one hand, and a vision of socialist rational development and equality, on the other. The dual nature of the objectives created ambiguities about ends and means. It was not always clear whether the organizational pattern was an end in itself or a means for attaining the socialist objectives. To the extent that the workers' management was an end, this posed limits on the instruments that could be used to attain other social goals. This dilemma, given some attention during the discussion of the economic reforms, assumed greater significance later, when sharp differences in the concepts of socialism began to emerge.

Independent worker-managed enterprises

The preference for independent, worker-managed enterprises is based on a number of considerations. Some authors, regardless of their attitudes about the relative merits of planned versus market methods of allocation, accepted the independent enterprises under worker management as desirable in and of themselves. The economic experiment is closely tied to a political philosophy concerning the withering away of the state and alienation. Decentralization of decision making in work and political affairs means the elimination of bureaucracy and provides greater economic and political democracy. These aspects of the system continued to play an important role in the arguments of political leaders. The concept of worker-producers directing their own affairs is equally important to the new Marxist humanists. These philosophers show an acute concern for alienation of the individual in contemporary society and some see in workers' management a means to end that alienation.[3]

Additional economic and noneconomic reasons were offered in support of worker-managed enterprises. Horvat argued that workers' control over production is inevitable since it is more efficient than the historically antecedent form of state capitalist bureaucracy.[4] State capitalism (which may be regarded either as the last stage of capitalism or the first stage of socialism) had developed because it was more rational than private capitalist organization. It operates on the bureaucratic principles of hierarchy, subordination, and obedience.

Workers' control over production is inevitable, according to Horvat, for three reasons. First, the bureaucratic method of state capitalism, which involves long lines of control and information, is dysfunctional. Decentralized economic organization offers greater efficiency of information and a better incentive mechanism than bureaucratic command. Further, the basic allocation principle of decentralized market socialism is full cost pricing which, Horvat argues at some length, is an adequate basis for the vast majority of economic decisions.[5]

Second, not only is decentralized organization more efficient. The decentralized units should be managed by workers because workers are more efficient when they participate in management. He supports this view by empirical studies in various countries. He also recognizes entrepreneurship as a critical factor of production necessary to assure efficiency in a world of risk, uncertainty, and dynamic change. Decentralized market socialism without an entrepreneurial agent is impossible and only workers can assume that function. The third part of his argument is historical: worker participation in decision processes has increased in the twentieth century. Thus he concludes that "a federation of self-governing associations—political, economic, and any other . . . is a possible and more efficient alternative to bureaucratic social organization."[6]

As Ward points out, Horvat's argument about the inevitability of this trend is not entirely convincing.[7] He has not demonstrated rigorously the process that brings state capitalism tumbling down nor has he shown that workers' management is necessarily superior. It is relatively easy to make a case that central planning is inefficient at certain stages of development, and rationality may force a reorganization of the central bureaucracy. It is not clear, however, that this reorganization must inevitably move toward workers' management. There is at least the possibility that, with further advance in mathematical, communication, and computer techniques, decentralization will be reversed. Finally, it is not clear that worker-managed enterprises are more efficient. There are two sources of increased efficiency, a better psychological milieu for operation and the fact that workers' incomes depend on the profits of the enterprise. (Horvat emphasizes both types of efficiency but does not commit himself irrevocably to the particular institutional forms.) It may be possible to have participation in the planning process[8] and to have incomes depend on financial results without making workers entrepreneurs and residual income recipients. Indeed, one problem the Yugoslavs face is the possible inefficiency of worker-managed enterprises that behave like producers' cooperatives. If such difficulties are important, it would pay to consider alternative arrangements. . . .

Permissible economic instruments

The instruments available to attain the plan may be classified, first, as to whether they are used generally or selectively and, second, as to whether they operate primarily on price variables or primarily on quantitative variables, or affect decisions directly. The Yugoslavs would have preferred to rely on general, price-affecting variables (fiscal and monetary policy, primarily) to attain objectives. These means were entirely compatible with the preferences for independent enterprises in a market environment.

> The new model of social planning in Yugoslavia must take into account, at the very least, the institutional setting of the

> new association of direct producers . . . and the market mechanism as a special economic form of independent relations between working collectives and consumers within the framework of socially planned norms.[9]

But the Yugoslavs also valued other social objectives. In cases in which production units are independent and managed by workers and when they respond to market forces, it may not be possible to attain desired targets with respect to output, investment, and wage payments by using general fiscal and monetary policies. The question then is, to what extent does the preferred institutional pattern restrict the range of policies acceptable for attaining the plan? Yugoslavs recognized the dilemma.

> The debate has been directed to the more practical problems of how the plan is to fit into the system of enterprise self-management and the self-government of administrative-territorial units. . . . It is particularly emphasized that we have to distinguish planning as such from state intervention in the economy.[10]

Obviously, the preferred institutions ruled out direct government production. The form of an independent enterprise was to be maintained. But there was considerable debate about the use of price-affecting tools selectively by sector (selective credit allocation, price controls, export subsidies, differential sales taxes, tax exemptions), even though these tools were actually employed in the economy. Finally, the most crucial question was whether the instruments could be applied selectively to individual enterprises, and whether direct intervention in enterprise decisions could be tolerated.

All conceded that state intervention in the market was occasionally necessary. Lavrač saw such intervention as the exception rather than the rule.[11] If the social plan established the rate and structure of investment, there would usually be no need for further intervention. In the short run the effects of the market are beneficial. If prices rise above normal, this stimulates production and constricts consumption. "Short range decisions about production, that is, decisions about production within the framework of existing capacities could in principle be left to the commodity producers themselves."[12] This does not mean that society should never intervene in the market process; indeed, when there are acute shortages, intervention may be warranted. But state action should not operate primarily to restrict price movements but to influence the supply of, or demand for, the commodity.[13]

Jelić argued that the more rapid the rate of change in the structure of the economy, the greater the need for intervention in the market. Temporary bottlenecks influence exchange relations and prices become deformed. In such circumstances the market does not provide a stimulus for individual decisions that are rational from the point of view of society as a whole. Therefore, the lower the level of economic development and the more rapid the rate of change envisioned, the greater must be the level and degree of regulation in the economy.[14] Horvat argued similarly about the greater need for regulation at early stages of development.[15]

By and large, Yugoslavs maintained in principle that the right to intervene did not extend to the affairs of the firm. Rakić appears to be an exception. He took a strong view on the obligatory character of the plan.[16] He held that the reason for using economic instruments is merely one of convenience, to reduce the need for direct intervention in the affairs of the firm. The use of general economic instruments, however, "does not exclude the possibility . . . for society to intervene through concrete decisions, irrespective of the specific forms of commodity production and even against their logic. . . . Therefore the market modes of business operation are not inviolable in Yugoslav economic practice."[17]

In general, however, the preference for independent production units and market methods of allocating factors and products restricts the range of methods available for controlling and directing the economy. . . .

The political, as well as the economic, rationale of the Yugoslav firm precludes direct intervention and requires working through indirect measures. Using a large number of nonfinancial instruments and intervening directly reduces the incentive of the enterprise to maximize its profits. Financial indicators must therefore guide the isolated production units in making the proper responses.[18] Indirect financial pressures are exerted by economic instruments: price policy, wage policy, and tax and credit policy. . . .

Plan and market in a more mature economy

The Eighth Congress of the League of Communists of Yugoslavia, held in December 1964, emphasized that with the attaining of a per capita income of approximately $500, Yugoslavia had entered the ranks of the moderately developed countries. It was recognized that a more mature economy required a different organization.[19] For an economy engaged in the process of rapid, discontinuous development, the various reasons for circumventing the market had been persuasive. As the period of radical transformation of the Yugoslav economy drew to a close, the Yugoslavs had to reconsider what combination of plan and market was suitable for an economy engaged in smooth and continuous growth. Yugoslavs were not of one mind about what changes in policy were required. The nature of the changes required depended on the assessment of the current situation and of the nature of changes to come, and on the basic initial view about plan and market.

On the one side were those who regarded the market mechanism, appropriately modified, as basically efficient. The chief need for planning arises from discontinuities in the initial, developmental stage. In their view, the plan constituted a corrective to the market to be used only when market decisions failed to produce results conforming with the general objectives of society. In general, with higher levels of development, there were fewer cases requiring intervention in the market. On the other side were those who regard the plan as the basically efficient mechanism. In their view a market exists because of the inability of planners to collect and process all information at present levels of technique. In the future more planning could be expected because of the technological requirement for fewer, larger, and more integrated production units, thus reducing the amount of market exchange among autonomous producers. However, even strong advocates of planning recognized the market as useful to convey the preferences of consumers to producers.

As for the more distant future in which communism (characterized by the principle "from each according to his ability, to each according to his needs") would be attained, and as for the method of economic organization therein, little was heard.

Plan to correct the market

The philosophy underlying this view is that of the market tradition modified by welfare economics. These authors (including Horvat, Jelić, Bajt, Bićanić, Pjanić, and Maksimović) considered consumer satisfaction to be the ultimate objective of economic activity and believed the market mechanism to be most suitable for attaining that objective. A rather liberal position on the role of the market was also taken in the White Book.[20] The papers advocated expanding the scope of the market, arguing that the task of socialism is to arrange institutions and policies so as to increase the role of decentralized decisions and to permit consumers' preferences to determine what should be produced. Accordingly, the plan should continue to determine certain long range investment decisions, as well as to specify collective consumption and some aspects of personal consumption. Admitting that decisions about investment could not be left entirely to the market, the authors also argued that, as the differences between the initial system and higher degrees of development diminished, market criteria expressing consumers' preferences could ultimately govern even the allocation of most investments. With few exceptions, decisions about current production could be left to the exclusive domain of the market and of individual firms. For these purposes a more or less competitive market structure is necessary. These arguments were in part directed at the theoretical issues of the optimal functioning of the system. The White Book also had a specific political viewpoint and significance as well, representing the view of the more developed regions.

These proposals met with some resistance on the general plane. Maksimović objected on several grounds, in particular questioning the feasibility of a competitive market structure.[21] He doubted that Yugoslavia could sustain a market structure with sufficient numbers of producing firms. While not disagreeing fundamentally with the White Book proposals, Lavrač emphasized that adequate decisions cannot always be made exclusively on the basis of market criteria and from an individualist vantage point even when the economy has passed the initial stages of discontinuous development. The market cannot allocate investment funds, Lavrač argued, for the reasons noted previously: duplication of facilities, optimum size, and so forth. Therefore the plan would be a permanent feature of socialism, used to achieve results different from those which would have been obtained from the market alone.[22] But the plan is not meant to serve as a substitute for the operation of the market. "The demarcation line between the role of the plan and that of the market mechanism is in principle clear. In commodity production the plan makes sense and is effective only insofar as the objectives laid down in it differ from the effects of the free play of the law of value, and provided the course of spontaneous movement is really changed by it."[23] The plan should not attain major status in making day to day economic decisions. Decisions about production within the framework of existing capacities should be left to the enterprises themselves.[24]

NOTES

1. Miloš Samardzija, "Problem cena u socijalističkoj privredi," *Naša stvarnost* 14, no. 12 (Dec. 1960), 488.

2. In addition, as Bajt has pointed out, the Yugoslavs have been concerned with the problem of distribution in the socialist economy at the expense of giving adequate attention to the problem of stabilization and other macroeconomic problems. Aleksandar Bajt, "Decentralized Decision-making Structure in the Yugoslav Economy," *Economics of Planning* 7, no. I (1967), 73–85.

3. Daniel Bell has suggested that there are two paths leading from Marx's concept of alienation, namely exploitation and dehumanization. Most Marxists concentrated on the first concept and sought to remedy it by the elimination of the capitalist ownership of property. The second path was less elaborated and followed a different tradition, often visualizing the solution in some form of workers' councils. The Yugoslavs rejoin the two strands of the problem. Their organizational pattern is designed to eliminate the dehumanized aspect as well as the exploitation of the worker. Daniel Bell, *The End of Ideology* (New York: Collier, 1961), chap. 15.

4. Horvat, *Towards a Theory of Planned Economy* (Belgrade: Yugoslav Institute for Economic Research, 1964), chap. 3.

5. Ibid., pp. 23–32, for his rejection of the general applicability of marginal cost pricing and for the acceptability, in most cases, of full cost pricing.

6. Ibid., p. 97.

7. Benjamin Ward, "Marxism-Horvatism: A Yugoslav Theory of Socialism," *American Economic Review* 57, no. 3 (June 1967), 521.

8. Adolph Sturmthal, *Workers' Councils* (Cambridge: Harvard University Press, 1964).

9. France Cerne, "Planning and the Market in Yugoslav Economic

Theory" (Berkeley: University of California, Center for Slavic and East European Studies, July 1962), mimeo p. 27.

10. Ibid., p. 20.

11. Ivan Lavrač, "Plan i trziste," *Ekonomist* 16, no. 1, (1963), 208.

12. Ibid., p. 208.

13. Ibid.

14. Borivoje Jelić, *Sistem planiranja u jugoslovenskoj privredi* (Belgrade: Ekonomska biblioteka, 1962), chap. 8.

15. Horvat, *Towards a Theory of Planned Economy,* p. 119.

16. Vojislav Rakić, "Fundamental Characteristics of the Yugoslav Economic System," in Radmila Stojanović, ed., *Yugoslav Economists on Problems of a Socialist Economy* (New York: International Arts and Sciences Press, 1964), pp. 123–40.

17. Ibid., p. 131.

18. Miloš Samardzija, *Naša stvarnost* 14, no. 12 (Dec. 1960), 503.

19. Mijalko Todorović pointed out that the economic policy which had been followed previously had been necessary because of the low level of economic development. "The practice hitherto followed by socialist revolutions of beginning socio-economic socialist development with a high degree of centralism, is not the only and inevitable road for all. It is very likely that countries with developed productive forces . . . will, from the very beginning, organize socialist construction, consequently, also the planned management of the economy, *on the basis of definite specific forms of self-government.*" "Some Observations on Planning," *Socialist Thought and Practice,* no. 17 (Jan.–Mar. 1965), 13–14.

20. *Ekonomski pregled* 14, no. 8 (1963), 145–567.

21. Ivan Maksimović, "Trziste i plan u nasem ekonomskom sistemu," *Ekonomist* 16, no. 1 (1963), 161–68.

22. Lavrač, *Ekonomist* 16, no. 1 (1963), 207–08.

23. Ivan Lavrač, "Competition and Incentive in the Yugoslav Economic System," in Radmila Stojanović, ed., *Yugoslav Economists on Problems of a Socialist Economy,* p. 148.

24. Lavrač, *Ekonomist* 16, no. 1 (1963), 208.

14. The Trial and Error Procedure in a Socialist Economy

OSKAR LANGE AND FRED M. TAYLOR

In order to discuss the method of allocating resources in a socialist economy we have to state what kind of socialist society we have in mind. The fact of public ownership of the means of production does not in itself determine the system of distributing consumers' goods and allocating people to various occupations, nor the principles guiding the production of commodities. Let us now assume that freedom of choice in consumption and freedom of choice of occupation are maintained and that the preferences of consumers, as expressed by their demand prices, are the guiding criteria in production and in the allocation of resources. Later we shall pass to the study of a more centralized socialist system.[1]

In the socialist system as described we have a genuine market (in the institutional sense of the word) for consumers' goods and for the services of labor. But there is no market for capital goods and productive resources outside of labor.[2] The prices of capital goods and productive resources outside of labor are thus prices in the generalized sense, i.e., mere indices of alternatives available, fixed for accounting purposes. Let us see how economic equilib-

Lange, Oskar, and Fred M. Taylor. *On the Economic Theory of Socialism,* edited by Benjamin E. Lippincott, pp. 72–89. University of Minnesota Press, Minneapolis.

rium is determined in such a system. Just as in a competitive individualist regime, the determination of equilibrium consists of two parts. (a) On the basis of *given* indices of alternatives (which are market prices in the case of consumers' goods and the services of labor and accounting prices in all other cases) both the individuals participating in the economic system as consumers and as owners of the services of labor and the managers of production and of the ultimate resources outside of labor (i.e., of capital and natural resources) make decisions according to certain principles. These managers are assumed to be public officials. (b) The prices (whether market or accounting) are determined by the condition that the quantity of each commodity demanded is equal to the quantity supplied. The conditions determining the decisions under (a) form the *subjective,* while that under (b) is the *objective,* equilibrium condition. Finally, we have also a condition (c), expressing the social organization of the economic system. As the productive resources outside of labor are public property, the incomes of the consumers are divorced from the ownership of those resources and the form of condition (c) (social organization) is determined by the *principle of income formation adopted.*

The possibility of determining condition (c) in different ways gives to a socialist society considerable freedom in matters of distribution of income. But the necessity of maintaining freedom in the choice of occupation limits the arbitrary use of this freedom, for there must be some connection between the income of a consumer and the services of labor performed by him. It seems, therefore, convenient to regard the income of consumers as composed of two parts: one part being the receipts for the labor services performed and the other part being a social dividend constituting the individual's share in the income derived from the capital and the natural resources owned by the society. We assume that the distribution of the social dividend is based on certain principles, reserving the content of those principles for later discussion. Thus condition (c) is determinate and determines the incomes of the consumers in terms of prices of the services of labor and social dividend, which, in turn, may be regarded by the total yield of capital and of the natural resources and by the principles adopted in distributing this yield.[3]

A. Let us consider the subjective equilibrium condition in a socialist economy:

1. Freedom of choice in consumption being assumed,[4] this part

of the subjective equilibrium condition of a competitive market applies also to the market for consumers' goods in a socialist economy. The incomes of the consumers and the prices of consumers' goods being given, the demand for consumers' goods is determined.

2. The decisions of the managers of production are no longer guided by the aim of maximizing profit. Instead, certain rules are imposed on them by the Central Planning Board which aim at satisfying consumers' preferences in the best way possible. These rules determine the combination of factors of production and the scale of output.

One rule must impose the choice of the combination of factors which minimizes the average cost of production. This rule leads to the factors being combined in such proportion that the marginal productivity of that amount of each factor which is worth a unit of money is the same for all factors. This rule is addressed to whoever makes decisions involving the problem of the optimum combination of factors, i.e., to managers responsible for running existing plants and to those engaged in building new plants. A second rule determines the scale of output by stating that output has to be fixed so that marginal cost is equal to the price of the product. This rule is addressed to two kinds of persons. First of all, it is addressed to the managers of plants and thus determines the scale of output of each plant and, together with the first rule, its demand for factors of production. The first rule, to whomever addressed, and the second rule when addressed to the managers of plants perform the same function that in a competitive system is carried out by the private producer's aiming to maximize his profit, when the prices of factors and of the product are independent of the amount of each factor used by him and of his scale of output.

The total output of an industry has yet to be determined. This is done by addressing the second rule also to the managers of a whole industry (e.g., to the directors of the National Coal Trust) as a principle to guide them in deciding whether an industry ought to be expanded (by building new plants or enlarging old ones) or contracted (by not replacing plants which are wearing out). Thus each industry has to produce exactly as much of a commodity as can be sold or "accounted for" to other industries at a price which equals the marginal cost incurred *by the industry* in producing this amount. The marginal cost incurred by an industry is the cost to that industry (not to a particular plant) of doing whatever is necessary to produce an additional unit of output, the optimum combination of factors being used. This may include the cost of building new plants or enlarging old ones.[5]

Addressed to the managers of an industry, the second rule performs the function which under free competition is carried out by the free entry of firms into an industry or their exodus from it: i.e., it determines the output of an industry.[6] The second rule, however, has to be carried out irrespective of whether average cost is covered or not, even if it should involve plants or whole industries in losses.

Both rules can be put in the form of the simple request to use always the method of production (i.e., combination of factors) which minimizes average cost and to produce as much of each service or commodity as will equalize marginal cost and the price of the product, this request being addressed to whoever is responsible for the particular decision to be taken. Thus the output of each plant and industry and the total demand for factors of production by each industry are determined. To enable the managers of production to follow these rules the prices of the factors and of the products must, of course, be given. In the case of consumers' goods and services of labor they are determined on a market; in all other cases they are fixed by the Central Planning Board. Those prices being given, the supply of products and the demand for factors are determined.

The reasons for adopting the two rules mentioned are obvious. Since prices are indices of terms on which alternatives are offered, that method of production which will minimize average cost will also minimize the alternatives sacrificed. Thus the rule means simply that each commodity must be produced with a minimum sacrifice of alternatives. The second rule is a necessary consequence of following consumers' preferences. It means that the marginal significance of each preference which is satisfied has to be equal to the marginal significance of the alternative preferences the satisfaction of which is sacrificed. If the second rule was not observed certain lower preferences would be satisfied while preferences higher up on the scale would be left unsatisfied.

3. Freedom of choice of occupation being assumed, laborers offer their services to the industry or occupation paying the highest wages. For the publicly owned capital and natural resources a price has to be fixed by the Central Planning Board with the provision that these resources can be directed only to industries which are able to "pay," or rather to "account for," this price.

This is a consequence of following the consumers' preferences. The prices of the services of the ultimate productive resources being given, their distribution between the different industries is also determined.

B. The subjective equilibrium condition can be carried out only when prices are *given*. This is also true of the decisions of the managers of production and of the productive resources in public ownership. Only when prices are given can the combination of factors which minimizes average cost, the output which equalizes marginal cost and the price of the product, and the best allocation of the ultimate productive resources be determined. But if there is no market (in the institutional sense of the word) for capital goods or for the ultimate productive resources outside of labor, can their prices be determined objectively? Must not the prices fixed by the Central Planning Board necessarily be quite arbitrary? If so, their arbitrary character would deprive them of any economic significance as indices of the terms on which alternatives are offered. This is, indeed, the opinion of Professor Mises.[7] And the view is shared by Mr. Cole, who says: "A planless economy, in which each entrepreneur takes his decisions apart from the rest, obviously confronts each entrepreneur with a broadly given structure of costs, represented by the current level of wages, rent, and interest. . . . In a planned socialist economy there can be no objective structure of costs. Costs can be imputed to any desired extent. . . . But these imputed costs are not objective, but *fiat* costs determined by the public policy of the State."[8] This view, however, is easily refuted by recalling the very elements of price theory.

Why is there an objective price structure in a competitive economy? Because, as a result of the parametric function of prices, there is generally only *one* set of prices which satisfies the objective equilibrium condition, i.e., equalizes demand and supply of each commodity. The same objective price structure can be obtained in a socialist economy if the *parametric function of prices* is retained. On a competitive market the parametric function of prices results from the number of competing individuals being too large to enable any one to influence prices by his own action. In a socialist economy, production and ownership of the productive resources outside of labor being centralized, the managers certainly can and do influence prices by their decisions. Therefore, the parametric function of prices must be imposed on them by the Central Planning Board as an *accounting rule*. All accounting has to be done *as if* prices were independent of the decisions taken. For purposes of accounting, prices must be treated as constant, as they are treated by entrepreneurs on a competitive market.

The technique of attaining this end is very simple: the Central Planning Board has to fix prices and see to it that all managers of plants, industries, and resources do their accounting on the basis of the prices fixed by the Central Planning Board, and not tolerate any use of other accounting. Once the parametric function of prices is adopted as an accounting rule, the price structure is established by the objective equilibrium condition. For each set of prices and consumers' incomes a definite amount of each commodity is supplied and demanded. Condition (c) determines the incomes of the consumers by the prices of the services of ultimate productive resources and the principles adopted for the distribution of the social dividend. With those principles given, prices alone are the variables determining the demand and supply of commodities.

The condition that the quantity demanded and supplied has to be equal for each commodity serves to select the equilibrium prices which alone assure the compatibility of all decisions taken. *Any price different from the equilibrium price would show at the end of the accounting period a surplus or a shortage of the commodity in question.* Thus the accounting prices in a socialist economy, far from being arbitrary, have quite the same objective character as the market prices in a regime of competition. Any mistake made by the Central Planning Board in fixing prices would announce itself in a very objective way—by a physical shortage or surplus of the quantity of the commodity or resources in question—and would have to be corrected in order to keep production running smoothly. As there is generally only one set of prices which satisfies the objective equilibrium condition, both the prices of products and costs[9] are uniquely determined.[10]

Our study of the determination of equilibrium prices in a socialist economy has shown that the process of price determination is quite analogous to that in a competitive market. The Central Planning Board performs the functions of the market. It establishes the rules for combining factors of production and choosing the scale of output of a plant, for determining the output of an industry, for the allocation of resources, and for the parametric use of prices in accounting. Finally, it fixes the prices so as to balance the quantity supplied and demanded of each commodity. It follows that a substitution of planning for the functions of the market is quite possible and workable.

Two problems deserve some special attention. The first relates to the determination of the best distribution of the social dividend. Freedom of choice of occupation assumed, the distribution of the social dividend may affect the amount of services of labor offered to different industries. If certain occupations received a larger social dividend than others, labor would be diverted into the occupations receiving a larger dividend. Therefore, the distribution of the social dividend must be such as not to interfere with the optimum distribution of labor services between the different industries and occupations. The optimum distribution is that which makes the differences of the value of the marginal product of the services of labor in different industries and occupations equal to the differences in the marginal disutility[11] of working in those industries or occupations.[12] This distribution of the services of labor arises automatically whenever wages are the only source of income. *Therefore, the social dividend must be distributed so as to have no influence whatever on the choice of occupation.* The social dividend paid to an individual must be entirely independent of his choice of occupation. For instance, it can be divided equally per head of population, or distributed according to age or size of family or any other principle which does not affect the choice of occupation.

The other problem is the determination of the rate of interest. We have to distinguish between a short-period and a long-period solution of the problem. For the former the amount of capital is regarded as constant, and the rate of interest is simply determined by the condition that the demand for capital is equal to the amount available. When the rate of interest is set too low the socialized banking system would be unable to meet the demand of industries for capital; when the interest rate is set too high there would be a surplus of capital available for investment. However, in the long period the amount of capital can be increased by accumulation. If the accumulation of capital is performed "corporately" before distributing the social dividend to the individuals, the rate of accumulation can be determined by the Central Planning Board *arbitrarily*. The Central Planning Board will probably aim at accumulating enough to make the marginal *net* productivity of capital zero,[13] this aim being never attained because of technical progress (new labor-saving devices), increase of population, the discovery of new natural resources, and, possibly, because of the shift of demand toward commodities produced by more capital-intensive methods.[14] But the rate, i.e., the *speed,* at which accumulation progresses is arbitrary.

The arbitrariness of the rate of capital accumulation "corporately" performed means simply that the decision regarding the rate of accumulation reflects how the Central Planning Board, and not the consumers, evaluate the optimum time-shape of the income stream. One may argue, of course, that this involves a diminution of consumers' welfare. This difficulty could be overcome only by leaving all accumulation to the saving of individuals.[15] But this is scarcely compatible with the organization of a socialist society.[16] Discussion of this point is postponed to a later part of this essay [not reprinted here].

Having treated the theoretical determination of economic equilibrium in a socialist society, let us see how equilibrium can be determined by a method of *trial and error* similar to that in a competitive market. This method of trial and error is based on the *parametric function of prices.* Let the Central Planning Board start with a given set of prices chosen *at random.* All decisions of the managers of production and of the productive resources in public ownership and also all decisions of individuals as consumers and as suppliers of labor are made on the basis of these prices. As a result of these decisions the quantity demanded and supplied of each commodity is determined. If the quantity demanded of a commodity is not equal to the quantity supplied, the price of that commodity has to be changed. It has to be raised if demand exceeds supply and lowered if the reverse is the case. Thus the Central Planning Board fixes a new set of prices which serves as a basis for new decisions, and which results in a new set of quantities demanded and supplied. Through this process of trial and error equilibrium prices are finally determined. Actually the process of trial and error would, of course, proceed on the basis of the prices *historically given.* Relatively small adjustments of those prices would constantly be made, and there would be no necessity of building up an entirely new price system.

This process of trial and error has been excellently described by the late Professor Fred M. Taylor. He assumes that the administrators of the socialist economy would assign provisional values to the factors of production (as well as to all other commodities). He continues:

> If, in regulating productive processes, the authorities were actually using for any particular factor a valuation which was too high or too low, that fact would soon disclose itself in unmistakable ways. Thus, supposing that, in the case of a particular factor, the valuation . . . was too high, that fact would inevitably lead the authorities to be unduly economical in the use of that factor; and this conduct, in turn, would make the amount of that factor which was available for the current production period larger than the amount which was consumed during that period. In other words, too high a valuation of any factor would cause the stock of that factor to show a surplus at the end of the productive period.[17]

Similarly, too low a valuation would cause a deficit in the stock of the factor. "Surplus or deficit—one or the other of these would result from every wrong valuation of a factor."[18] By a set of successive trials the right accounting prices of the factors are found. . . .

As we have seen, there is not the slightest reason why a trial and error procedure, similar to that in a competitive market, could not work in a socialist economy to determine the accounting prices of capital goods and of the productive resources in public ownership. Indeed, it seems that this trial and error procedure would, or at least could, work *much better* in a socialist economy than it does in a competitive market. For the Central Planning Board has a much wider knowledge of what is going on in the whole economic system than any private entrepreneur can ever have, and, consequently, may be able to reach the right equilibrium prices by a *much shorter* series of successive trials than a competitive market actually does.

NOTES

1. In pre-war literature the terms *socialism* and *collectivism* were used to designate a socialist system as described above and the word *communism* was used to denote more centralized systems. The classical definition of socialism (and of collectivism) was that of a system which socializes production alone, while communism was defined as socializing both production and consumption. At the present time these words have become political terms with special connotations.

2. To simplify the problem we assume that all means of production are public property. Needless to say, in any actual socialist commu-

nity there must be a large number of means of production privately owned (e.g., by farmers, artisans and small-scale entrepreneurs). But this does not introduce any new theoretical problem.

3. In formulating condition (c) capital accumulation has to be taken into account. Capital accumulation may be done either "corporately" by deducting a certain part of the national income before the social dividend is distributed, or it may be left to the savings of individuals, or both methods may be combined. But "corporate" accumulation must certainly be the dominant form of capital formation in a socialist economy.

4. Of course there may be also a sector of socialized consumption the cost of which is met by taxation. Such a sector exists also in capitalist society and comprises the provision not only of collective wants, in Cassel's sense, but also of other wants whose social importance is too great to be left to the free choice of individuals (for instance, free hospital service and free education). But this problem does not represent any theoretical difficulty and we may disregard it.

5. Since in practice such marginal cost is not a continuous function of output we have to compare the cost of each additional *indivisible input* with the receipts expected from the additional output thus secured. For instance, in a railway system as long as there are unused carriages the cost of putting them into use has to be compared with the additional receipts which may be obtained by doing so. When all the carriages available are used up to capacity, the cost of building and running additional carriages (and locomotives) has to be compared with the additional receipts expected to arise from such action. Finally, the question of building new tracks is decided upon the same principle. Cf. A. P. Lerner, "Statics and Dynamics in Socialist Economics," *Economic Journal,* 47:263–67 (June, 1937).

6. The result, however, of following this rule coincides with the result obtained under free competition only in the case of constant returns to the industry (i.e., a homogeneous production function of the first degree). In this case marginal cost incurred by the industry equals average cost. In all other cases the results diverge, for under free competition the output of an industry is such that average cost equals the price of the product, while according to our rule it is marginal cost (incurred by the industry) that ought to be equal to the price. This difference results in profits being made by the industries whose marginal cost exceeds average cost, whereas the industries in which the opposite is the case incur losses. These profits and losses correspond to the taxes and bounties proposed by Professor Pigou in order to bring about under free competition the equality of private and social marginal net product. See A. C. Pigou, *The Economics of Welfare* (3rd ed., London, 1929), pp. 223–27.

7. Ludwig von Mises, "Economic Calculation in the Socialist Commonwealth," reprinted in *Collectivist Economic Planning* (F. A. von Hayek, ed., Routledge, London, 1935), p. 112.

8. G. D. H. Cole, *Economic Planning* (New York, 1935), pp. 183–84.

9. Hayek maintains that it would be impossible to determine the value of durable instruments of production because, in consequence of changes, "the value of most of the more durable instruments of production has little or no connection with the costs which have been incurred in their production" (*Collectivist Economic Planning*, p. 227). It is quite true that the value of such durable instruments is essentially a capitalized quasi-rent and therefore can be determined only after the price which will be obtained for the product is known. . . . But there is no reason why the price of the product should be any less determinate in a socialist economy than on a competitive market. The managers of the industrial plant in question have simply to take the price fixed by the Central Planning Board as the basis of their calculation. The Central Planning Board would fix this price so as to satisfy the objective equilibrium condition, just as a competitive market does.

10. However, in certain cases there may be a multiple solution. . . .

11. It is only the *relative* disutility of different occupations that counts. The absolute disutility may be zero or even negative. By putting leisure, safety, agreeableness of work, etc., into the preference scales, all labor costs may be expressed as opportunity costs. If such a device is adopted each industry or occupation may be regarded as producing a joint product: the commodity or service in question *and* leisure, safety, agreeableness of work, etc. The services of labor have to be allocated so that the value of marginal *joint* product is the same in all industries and occupations.

12. If the total amount of labor performed is not limited by legislation or custom regulating the hours of work, etc., the value of the marginal product of the services of labor in each occupation has to be *equal* to the marginal disutility. If any limitational factors are used, it is the marginal *net* product of the services of labor (obtained by deducting from the marginal product the marginal expenditure for the limitational factors) which has to satisfy the condition in the text.

13. Cf. Knut Wicksell, "Professor Cassel's System of Economics," reprinted in his *Lectures on Political Economy* (L. Robbins, ed., 2 vols., London, 1934), Vol. I, p. 241.

14. These changes, however, if very frequent, may act also in the opposite direction and diminish the marginal *net* productivity of capital

because of the risk of obsolescence due to them. This is pointed out by A. P. Lerner in "A Note on Socialist Economics," *Review of Economic Studies,* October, 1936, p. 72.

15. This method has been advocated by Barone in "The Ministry of Production in the Collectivist State," *Collectivist Economic Planning,* pp. 278–79.

16. Of course, the consumers remain free to save as much as they want out of the income which is actually paid out to them, and the socialized banks could pay interest on savings. As a matter of fact, in order to prevent hoarding they would have to do so. But *this* rate of interest would not have any necessary connection with the marginal *net* productivity of capital. It would be quite arbitrary.

17. "The Guidance of Production in a Socialist State," *American Economic Review,* Vol. XIX (March, 1929). . . .

18. *Ibid.*

15. The Pricing of Factors of Production

BRANKO HORVAT

The moving force in the economic process is Man. In this sense, Labor is the only factor of production. But variations in productivity of labor cannot be determined or analyzed in any simple way; labor productivity is a function of a complex set of conditions. These conditions, according to their economic characteristics, may be classified in four broad categories which, using partly the traditional terminology, we shall call Monopoly, Capital, Labor and Entrepreneurship. As the economic process can be conveniently analyzed in terms of these four categories, we shall call them Factors of Production. The prices of Factors of Production we shall call, using again the traditional terminology, Rent, Interest, Wages and Profit.

Monopoly replaces what has traditionally been called Land. The reason for the change in terminology is rather obvious: we need a perfectly general rent earning factor and Land does not exhaust this species. Monopoly will mean a nonreproducible factor (condition) of production like a unique advantage in production, ownership of mineral deposits or ownership of land. As to land, it is often said that unlike capital (which is a product of labor) land has productivity of its own. But this is not so. If we

Reprinted from *Towards a Theory of Planned Economy* (Belgrade: Yugoslav Institute of Economic Research, 1964; distributed in the U.S. by International Arts and Sciences Press, White Plains, N.Y.), pp. 37–38, 50, 67–68, 73, 114–30.

compare two economies alike in every respect except in the endowments of natural resources, the economy with more fertile soil and richer mineral deposits will generate a large social product (measured, say, in terms of consumption goods). This is obvious, but the distinction is irrelevant for our purpose. The economy with more natural resources is quite likely to generate less rent. Or take another example. Imagine a closed economy whose agriculturalists have just applied a costless innovation, say rotation of crops. As a result the "productivity" of land will rise while rent is likely to fall (because demand for food is very inelastic and so a fall in prices will reduce output in value terms).

The last observation helps also to explain the difference in meaning of the concept Factors of Production in my usage and in the more traditional usage. This difference in approach will turn out to have far-reaching consequences. Here we are not concerned with factors productive in any absolute sense. When we speak of Factors of Production, we only assume that they somehow influence the volume of production—the productivity of social labor—and that there are four analytically meaningful types of these influences. Apart from this fundamental meaning, in a number of instances the term "factors of production" will be used to mean resources, or units of resources, in other words it will be used in the traditional sense. Terminologically it would be more correct to distinguish these uses by two terms. However, it is usually quite obvious from the context which meaning should be attributed to the term and so we may stick to our rule of minimizing terminological changes.

Finally, there is a strong tendency in modern economic analysis to treat Factors of Production as in every respect symmetrical. Insofar as this aim is achieved, the distinctions between the four classes disappear and we consider only the marginal productivity of a unit of an amorphous productive factor, whatever it is. In some circumstances this approach may have its advantages; in addition, pure marginal productivity theory undoubtedly represents an appealing logical system and is a historically significant achievement in the development of economic analysis. However, insofar as we are interested in economics, the usefulness of the generalized approach is relatively modest; for whenever we try to think in terms of potential economic policy, this approach is bound to become misleading. Factors of production are not symmetrical, the four classes enumerated differ widely in their functioning in the economic process, and in what follows our main business will consist in an examination of these differences within the framework of planned economy. . . .

Rent

Rent is that part of the price of factors of production which represents surplus over their minimum supply price. From this definition the general rule of distribution in the planned economy follows straightforwardly: Rent, bearing no influence on the supply of factors of production, should not accrue to suppliers of factors but to the general fund of the economy administered by the Planning Authority. One part of this fund consists of rent proper while the other part consists of interest charges. . . .

Interest

Three different rates of interest may be distinguished conceptually and numerically. The first two govern the organization of production, the third one is a device for redistributing consumption. The investment determination rate of interest reflects the aggregate marginal productivity of social capital. It assumes zero value when the economy is pushed on to the path of maximum growth. The allocation rate of interest ensures the most productive application of new capital. It is always positive because the economy is growing. The optimally organized production leads to a maximum possible output of consumer goods; to make the best use of the goods produced their time distribution to the consumers should be optimal. Wages, i.e., the appropriation of purchasing power, represent the main device of distribution. But for the individual consumer the time pattern of the appropriation of purchasing power does not correspond to the best possible pattern of consumption. Necessary adjustments are achieved through saving and overspending regulated by the consumption rate of interest, which may be negative, zero or positive. Each one of the three interest rates is a device for achieving a local optimum. Together, they make up a mechanism for achieving an optimum optimorum. . . .

The categories of Monopoly and Capital may be attributed a technical sense, which means that they are equally applicable in any exchange economy. But it would be absolutely inadmissible to treat the human factor in the same way because it depends on social relations in production and these relations typically change. . . .

Kolektiv-entrepreneur and profit

It is safe to say that entrepreneurship, and the corresponding category of profit, represent the weakest link in formal economic theory. Classical economists knew only three productive agents, of which one, Labor, was basic. Neoclassical economists formalized the analysis and introduced Entrepreneurship (or Enterprise, or Management) as a fourth agent. But this innovation has always remained controversial. The controversy has centered around the notion of entrepreneurship as a factor of production analogous to land or labor, i.e., as something marketable in physical units which could be used for building up a clearly defined production function. As the concept of the factor of production as used in the present study is not based on the notion of tangible resources, that part of the problem disappears. . . .

. . . If Schumpeter's innovating entrepreneur who creates profit is a somewhat artificial construct in a capitalist society, why should we not make better use of this undoubtedly appealing concept in the theory of a socialist economy? In other words, we may attempt to make use of the following scheme: capital is socially owned and thus accessible to every entrepreneur after paying the price for its use (interest) ; entrepreneurs innovate and thus create profits; if the results of innovation are applicable elsewhere, they will be made accessible to other entrepreneurs and after a while profits will be absorbed by consumers and so disappear; this continual "creative destruction" fosters economic development (though it does not exhaust it as in the Schumpeterian scheme) . . . .

In the economy consisting of self-government entities, managerial functions are not exercised by the particular class of individuals but by the collectivity of the members of the economic organizations whom we shall call working kolektivs. Social valuations and risk-bearing (also an aspect of valuation) are manifest functions of the kolektiv. Supervision is a two-way process in which every member of the kolektiv takes part. The remaining function, co-ordination, is purely technical and as such performed by technical experts, themselves members of the kolektiv. We thus reach the first important conclusion: The kolektiv qualifies for the exercise of the entrepreneurial function.

Co-ordinating activity is not a purely technical activity by itself, in other words, it is not independent from social relations. If supervision is a one-way process, i.e., if it is bureaucratic supervision, efficiency of co-ordination diminishes. And changes in efficiency are clearly of paramount importance for economic theory. We may therefore pause to examine the problem a little more closely.

Efficiency of co-ordination boils down to the problem of centralization versus decentralization. Bureaucratic authority requires very strict centralization. And this means—as von Hayek, arguing his case for the use of the market mechanism, was quick to point out—that the existing and potential resources are wasted due to the sheer technical necessity of condensing knowledge of facts. For, there is a kind of knowledge "which by its nature cannot enter into statistics and therefore cannot be conveyed to any central authority in statistical form. The statistics which such a central authority would have to use would have to be arrived at precisely by abstracting from minor differences between things, by lumping together, as resources of one kind, items which differ as regards location, quality and other particulars, in a way which may be very significant for the specific decision." Von Hayek suggests that in order to secure the best use of resources known to any of the members of society, the price mechanism must be allowed to operate. Undoubtedly the market provides a much more efficient communication mechanism than an administrative hierarchy. But this is only one aspect of the problem; the other two are: co-ordination of market choices—for they are made in space and time—and communication below the level of the firm. And in order to be solved efficiently the co-ordination problem must be solved in its totality.

Insofar as other things are kept equal, independence in decision-making increases efficiency. Then it does not mean splitting and breaking up an organization with the resulting uneconomic and anarchic atomization. It means, on the contrary, maximum economy, because direct initiative and direct responsibility are transferred to direct performers of tasks, workers and junior executives on the level of the firm, kolektivs on the level of the national economy. Bureaucratic control and management cannot successfully react to changes and problems emerging in immediate work; slow as well as inadequate and generalized reacting causes great economic losses. Inside the firm hierarchical relations exert a depressing effect on individual performers, stifle initiative, undermine the will to work, cause resistance, in short, lower labor efficiency. For these reasons initiative and responsibility must be transferred to those in immediate contact with the tasks to be performed. Various social systems have satisfied this requirement in various degrees. And the system of workers' self-government is in this respect surely superior to any other existing alternative. Compared with private capitalism state-capitalist organization proved to be significantly more efficient, as measured by the rate of growth of production, because it could make use of planning on the national scale. Compared with state-capitalism socialist organization will be more efficient because by removing class antagonism it is able to make better use of the existing knowledge, as well as of the intellectual and emotional energy of the members of the community.

Though autonomous to a great extent, the kolektiv clearly cannot be completely autonomous. In matters of valuations which affect significantly the interests of some other kolektivs there must be a superior representative body to make decisions. This is a very serious and little explored problem, but we cannot discuss it here. In matters with which we are primarily concerned the upwards dependence of kolektivs will be largely technical in nature. It would be ideal to separate "regulative" functions from "operative" functions and leave the former to the representative bodies while the latter should be displayed by the working kolektivs and their associations. In this way supreme co-ordination, including the Social Plan together with the financial instruments necessary to ensure its execution, would be vested in Parliament. It should be stressed, however, that a certain amount of co-ordination will have to be done by the specialized state apparatus on the spot, in which case regulative functions shade into operative ones. This interference of the state apparatus may be very pronounced in the early days of the new system. But as the process of normalization and institutionalization develops it can be gradually relaxed and reduced to routine activities. Banks play a special role in overall co-ordination in that they combine customary business criteria with the intentions of the Social Plan. Finally, the Planning Authority supplies enterprises with relevant data which provide elements for their economic policies. The enterprises report their own important decisions which enables the Planning Authority to prepare a new set of data for the use of all concerned. The Social Plan, the banks and the availability of information represent an efficient co-ordinating mechanism which enables smooth functioning of the economy without centralized management. The upshot of all this is that risks and uncertainties are minimized and the entrepreneurial function presents itself in a completely new light.

In the realization of economic plans the main task of the Planning Authority is to preserve normal market conditions. Insofar as price fluctuations can be avoided, windfall gains and undeserved losses will be avoided as well (in this, of course, foreign trade poses a thorny problem). And insofar as stability is achieved, profits and losses of enterprises will depend on productive contributions of kolektivs.

The next question relates to income distribution. There is no necessity for the total amount of gross profit achieved by a particular kolektiv to be appropriated by it as well. The share of profit to be distributed among the members of the kolektiv is a function of the incentives it provides. In general we wish to maximize the "supply of entrepreneurship," and we achieve this by institutionalizing a certain scale of distribution which is universally agreed to be "fair." Thus gross profits break into two parts: net profits which as a reward to members of the kolektiv are used to induce the supply of the productive factor "entrepreneurship," and the remainder, if any, which by its nature represents rent and as such is taxed away. Speaking of profit as a price for entrepreneurial services we shall therefore imply net profit, or that part of profit which is left to the free disposal of the kolektiv.

Negative profit, or loss, requires similar treatment. Within a certain range it will be regarded as the market penalty for failure to supply the average amount of "entrepreneurship." In this sense—and regarding absolute loss only as a special case of a perfectly general opportunity loss—the entrepreneurial function of a kolektiv involves risk-bearing as one of its essential component parts, which is reminiscent of Knight's case. However, the reduction of wages below a certain level will be considered as socially intolerable. Then the state—or the commune more properly—will have to intervene and subsidize for super-losses similarly as it taxed away super-profits. It may also happen that a particular venture is not profitable without the kolektiv being subjectively responsible for the failure and will therefore require either a permanent subsidy or even liquidation. In this sense, risk is borne by the owner of capital, i.e., by the community—and as such reflects the Schumpeterian case in which risk bearing is excluded from the entrepreneurial function.

We reach our second and final conclusion. The kolektiv-entrepreneur is engaged in a continuous process of technological, organizational and commercial improvements, being thus essentially an innovator. The supply of innovations is geared to material rewards and penalties. Appealing to the material interests of the people, this institution provides a strong motivation—though, of course, this is not the only motivation operating in the same direction—for a constant increase in efficiency which results in greater production which, in turn, increases the well-being of the community at large. Analytically it establishes a separate factor of production whose price is profit.

Wages and optimum distribution of income

In the economic process, producers appear not only as kolektivs but also as members of kolektivs, i.e., as individuals. The productive services of individuals are remunerated by Wages. Profit and Wages are two aspects of pricing of productive services of labor. In passing let us note once more an interesting parallelism. It is possible to classify all factors of production into two categories of which the first describes the technical and the second the human side of the economic process. We have found that in the first category Interest is only a special kind of Rent; we now add that, similarly, Profit is a special kind of Wages.

In the restrictive analytical sense the wage-rate is the price of labor. As such it may be supposed to vary in accordance with the relations of supply and demand. In this respect, two separate problems stand out clearly. The first one relates to the allocation of available labor. Mobility of labor being for well-known reasons very imperfect, the desired allocation cannot be achieved simply by manipulation of wage-rates. However, in order to simplify the analysis, and also because pecuniary incentives are perhaps still predominant, it may be taken as a first approximation that the proper allocation is effected by wage-rates. Then, if the supply of a certain type of labor is inadequate, the wage-rate will be increased so as to allocate available labor to those industries where it will be socially most productive. If demand is inadequate, the wage-rate will be lowered so as to restrict supply. This is the gist of the traditional wage theory which then may or may not be recast in marginalist terms. . . .

The second problem relates to the distribution of income. In this respect we must ask the question whether there is any reason why gross wages used to allocate labor should be equal to net wages appropriated by workers.

The traditional marginal productivity theory answers the question positively. In order to distribute the available labor force among various industries, the wage-rate must be equal to marginal product of labor and equal to the marginal worker's valuation of alternative employments. If free choice of occupation is accepted, the second condition is automatically fulfilled. The first condition must be satisfied if maximum output is to be produced. As workers' valuations are assumed to depend on net wages, it appears that net and gross wages must be equal, and no place is left for taxation. If a tax is necessary, it must not be levied as a proportional income tax, let alone a progressive tax, but as a lump-sum tax so as not to interfere with marginalist equations. Exceptionally, individuals with special native abilities (artists, for instance) may be taxed in the usual way, because they will not change their "industry" and so the "rent of ability" can be extracted from them.

Lump-sum taxes were imposed by Turkish Sultans on the Christian peasantry when the Turks conquered the feudal Balkan states in the Middle Ages. Progressive income taxes are used by modern administrators. Should these historical facts lead us to conclude that the Grand Viziers were more efficient economists than the present-day Chancellors of the Exchequer? And is socialist society condemned to have an eternally unequal distribution of income lest it be labeled irrational? To ask these questions is to give an answer: the marginal productivity theory is a very unsatisfactory theory and if we wish to explain the events of the actual world, we must try to think of something better.

It would seem to be a fair description of reality if we postulate that inducement to work does not depend on the absolute wage —a Yugoslav worker is paid three times less than a British worker —but on the relative wage. Relative wages, in turn, depend on social norms. These norms are to a certain extent independent of the distribution of natural abilities, and therefore the marginal product and marginal wage may differ without affecting the rationality of allocation. Also, these norms change in a regular and empirically observable pattern, which we shall attempt to establish. Finally, we shall probably not distort the fact too much if we assume that workers choose industries according to gross wages and, independent of this choice, accept taxes as a social institution, thus being satisfied with net wages. . . .

Suppose that the Planning Authority is free to choose any wage system it likes and that it decides to design the system of wage differentials so that it will be generally accepted as "fair" and as such will induce people to work with their maximum (long-run) energy. What is fair depends not only on the vague idea of productivity but also on the characteristcs of jobs (dirty, strenuous, dangerous, more skilled and more responsible jobs involve generally greater "disutility" and thus call for higher remunerations). Is the fair-wages policy the right policy to be pursued? The answer to this question depends on what we can say about a theoretical difficulty inherent in the procedure. Namely, it may be assumed that after maximum production has been achieved by a proper system of wage differentials, it will still be possible to redistribute income between, say, *B* and *A* so that a certain amount of income of *B* is transferred to *A* while the resulting loss in product, due to "dissatisfaction" of *B*, is less than the gain in income of *A*. In other words, total product is less than maximum, but total consumption, in utility terms, is greater than before because the loss of *B* is more than compensated by the gain of *A*.

The assumption of a possible discrepancy between production and consumption implies a possibility of a conflict of valuations. For, we assume that *A* and *B* have agreed on what are "fair" wages and hence the possibility that another distribution of income will increase total welfare means a conflicting valuation. If two conflicting valuations of equal "rank" are considered, logical deductions cannot provide a solution. However, in our case the "agreement" valuation is more general and includes the "distribution" valuation as a special case, because the "agreement" is reached after a consideration of all possible consequences. Hence, the conflicting "distribution" valuation must be ruled out as inconsistent with rational behavior.

If *A* and *B* have fully agreed on what is the appropriate distribution of income, then we know that they will work with maximum efficiency and that no discrepancy between best distribution and maximum output can arise. The argument can be reversed and then we get the following useful result. Assuming that it is possible to induce both individuals to supply maximum work, we may find the desirable distribution of income even without asking the individuals explicitly. We need only manipulate wage differentials so as to induce each individual to produce maximum output. But our assumptions are still too restrictive; we must consider a community of many individuals and then we need an additional device to make the problem tractable. Passing from the two-person to a multiperson community we shall assume that *A* and *B* reflect public opinion with regard to the respective classes of labor. The concept of public opinion raises many questions which, however, we need not discuss here. It will suffice to assume that (1) public opinion exists and (2) that in a homogeneous society the existence of public opinion implies that a great majority of people concerned are prepared to agree on a particular matter. The first assumption is hardly controversial, while the second is based on empirical observations—supplemented by experiments (Sherif, Asch, Crutchfield and others)—that individual valuations are molded by and tend to conform to collective valuations. Now, if wage differentials satisfy public opinion, individuals will supply maximum work. There will be some exceptions, but just because they are exceptions they can be disregarded. Accepting collective valuations and supplying maximum work does not imply full agreement. Individuals may have their doubts and private reservations, but these are valuations of the "second" rank because they do not affect general agreement on the remuneration of work. If and when they do affect it public opinion changes and a new "agreement" replaces the old one. Maximum output is thus indicative of the fact that the community accepts the respective income distribution and so we cannot argue that it ought to accept a different one. One modification is needed, however. Public opinion is not an automatic result of individual valuations as such but always of the individual valuations as they arise in a definite institutional system. To solve the problem completely we must design an appropriate institutional system as well. In this respect the economists can advise that the system be designed so as to be conducive to maximum economic equality. There are two reasons for recommending this course. First, historically greater equality was conducive to greater economic efficiency. And secondly, the empirically observable drive towards equality indicates that greater equality means an increase in the welfare of the community. Thus the most egalitarian distribution of income consistent with maximum output appears to be the condition for the optimum distribution of income. . . .

It remains to sum up the results of the analysis. We have found that two different criteria guide the formation of wage-rates. The first criterion is based on a "fair" wage structure. The evaluation of fair wage differentials changes is a result of an interplay of technical and social factors. The former—the scarcity of superior grades of labor due to biological limitations or due to material poverty of the society—render some grades of labor more productive than others. To more productive labor society attaches higher value because in the world with a still very low standard of living, material improvements are highly valued. With the increase of general economic welfare productivity differences decrease for technical reasons (universal education, medical attendance available to everybody, proper diet, shelter, etc.) and insofar as they remain social valuations of more productive labor are likely to grow less important because of the "diminishing marginal utility" of successive improvements in living standard. In a society not socially polarized it is in principle possible to find what these social valuations are and to express them in an agreement on "fair" wages. Net wage-rates include not only "efficiency" differentials, but also positive differentials for dirty, strenuous, dangerous, more responsible, etc., work and, conversely, negative differentials for agreeable and leisurely work, i.e., they include "cost" differentials as well. From the point of view of income distribution these wage differentials do not represent inequalities because they cancel out with the costs incurred. Wages as just described are "net" wages and, as such, relevant for the problem of income distribution.

The second criterion relates to the formation of "gross" wage-rates. They serve, as all other prices do, for proper allocation of the productive factor labor. Ideally the gross wage is equal to the marginal product of the respective kind of labor. In practice, however, the possibility of applying marginal product calculus is rather questionable and so even great "distortions" of gross wages are not likely to affect appreciably the desirable allocation of labor.

The difference between gross wages and net wages represents rent which is taxed away by the Planning Authority. One may say that net wage-rates represent the supply price of labor, while gross wage-rates are its demand price.

The wages of individual workers plus the profits of kolektivs determined as total demand and supply prices for labor services ensure that available labor resources are maximally utilized. Thus total output will be maximized. For the same reason the income distribution is universally accepted as "fair" and, because of the social institutions, is the most egalitarian attainable. In this sense it represents the optimum distribution of income.

In a general case the optimum distribution is historically determined and so always relative; it is conditioned by the mode of production and changes with it. The analysis shows that today both private and state capitalism are inherently incapable of achieving optimum distribution of income, because by changing the institutions it is possible to improve the distribution of income without reducing output. Thus it is a priori impossible to solve the problem of optimum distribution by assuming capitalist institutions. The analysis also shows that production too is likely to be more efficient in socialism than in the other two systems. Thus, the socialist mode of production—workers' councils, planning and the rest—has both properties which we have found to be associated with the historical succession of social systems: it produces greater material wealth and greater equality simultaneously. In the last analysis the problem of the optimum distribution of income reduces to the problem of the most efficient economic system. The ultimate cause of this historical identity ought to be sought in the fact that economic efficiency depends on human motivation in production and so production relations which are socially most acceptable at a given stage of development of productive forces produce also the most efficient economic machine.

16. An Institutional Model of a Self-managed Socialist Economy*

BRANKO HORVAT

1. Defining self-management socialism

Strictly speaking, "self-management (or associative) socialism" is a redundancy, for without self-management there is no socialism. Nevertheless, the term "self-management" (or "associative") is necessary for precision and to avoid misunderstanding. "Socialism," like all frequently used words with marked emotional content, is used to mean so many different things that it has become completely indefinite as a scientific concept.

In its original meaning—which I also accept as the meaning with the most sense—socialism is a socioeconomic system based on equality. In fact, capitalism was also founded on equality—in relation to feudalism, whose basis is inherited status—and that is what makes capitalism so vital.

However, the equality of liberal capitalism is defined formally and negatively: it is a matter of freedom from state or some other compulsion; and it is freedom of action *within the framework* of

Reprinted from *Samoupravni socijalistički ekonomski sistem* (Zagreb: Informator, 1971). Translation reprinted from *Eastern European Economics,* 10, No. 4 (Summer 1972): 369–92.

*The model presented here is not a description of the Yugoslav institutional structure, although based upon it, but rather should be conceived as a proposal for its reform.

a market system that is accepted as natural, and hence the consequences of that freedom of action are not questioned. Equality in socialism is defined essentially and positively: the system is regulated by social action so that real equality is guaranteed to all members of society. It is worth noting that equality does not mean sameness; people are not the same, and therefore their positions in society are not the same. This is one of the defects of socialism that can be mitigated to some extent (especially in the noneconomic sphere), but cannot be eliminated. This defect is objectively conditioned, and this must be kept in mind if one does not wish to fall into frivolous utopianism.

Man has three basic roles in social life: he appears as a producer, as a consumer, and as a citizen. Consequently, equality should also be defined in terms of these three roles. *Equality in production* means guaranteeing to all who wish to work the possibility of using the means of production under the same conditions. This implies: (a) social ownership of the means of production; (b) the right to work; (c) the right to manage production (performing the entrepreneurial function, which involves making decisions about the quantity and assortment of production, purchases and sales, prices, investments, and distribution of income). Individual labor and individual initiative represent a special case of equality in production (defined positively). In that sense individual labor is equal to both socialist and collective labor.[1] Social ownership should be interpreted as an economic, and not a legal, category. Legal private ownership (of land, a handicraft shop, etc.) that does not provide its owner with distinct income above and beyond the income of labor represents economically socialized ownership. And, conversely, constitutionally legal social ownership can permit a high degree of privatization if the collective using it exploits its monopolistic position and extracts monopoly incomes that are not the result of work. Consequently, social ownership in the economic sense can be defined only according to the manner of distribution and appropriation, and not according to the formal legal title of ownership.

Equality as a consumer amounts to distribution according to work (which refers to distribution according to the results of work, and not according to some physical expenditure of labor power). It is obvious that producer and consumer equality are two sides of the same self-management coin, and that without producer equality there is no consumer equality. The latter also requires that the conditions of economic activity be equalized by social regulation. Unequal conditions of economic activity exclude distribution according to work. Polemics often occur over what equalized conditions of economic activity ought to mean. It follows from the above that equality of conditions of economic activity is measured by the degree to which the postulate of distribution according to work is satisfied. Distribution according to work implies two requirements: (a) income differentials must result from the autonomous decisions of work collectives, which evaluate the differences among various categories of work; and (b) an individual worker should obtain the same reward for the same work regardless of the branch of market or nonmarket production in which he is employed (but the reward can vary substantially from enterprise to enterprise depending on business efficiency).[2]

Equality as a citizen implies political democracy. A high degree of political democracy is impossible without equality of producers and consumers. In capitalist society, both political democracy and market equality are defined formally. In reality, however, the citizen is to a large extent an object of manipulation by hierarchically organized bureaucratic structures. Such structures can be eliminated—or at least more effectively controlled—in a situation in which there is equality in production and distribution. This explains the order in which I presented roles in social life. However, it would be a mistake to forget that there are also strong feedbacks. The absence of effective political democracy can prevent, or at least hinder, the development of socialist relations in the sphere of production and distribution. The latter represents the contemporary Yugoslav situation.[3]

To the extent that equality of producer, consumer, and citizen is achieved, we can speak of socialist society. To the extent that there are defects in the three spheres, the given socialism is also defective. If the defects are great, then—in the sense of the well-known principle of the transition of quantity into quality—there can be no talk of socialism. In that respect it is irrelevant whether, from the formal legal standpoint, private ownership is expropriated or not. This three dimensionality of socialism makes measurement of the extent of socialism somewhat more complicated and does not permit the construction of any sort of simple index (for example, the percentage of nationalization) as a reliable instrument of measurement. In principle, however, it is not impossible to arrive at a quantitative measure of socialism (for example, by using discrimination analysis).

The three dimensions of equality are not, of course, a goal in themselves. They represent operationally defined spheres of man's positive freedom in contemporary conditions of production. Socialism is both desirable and historically necessary, for it represents an essential broadening of individual freedom. That is why self-management autonomy is the essential definition of socialism.

In this paper I shall be concerned with only the first two—economic—dimensions of socialism. I shall examine the simplest institutional model which makes it possible to satisfy the postulates of producer and consumer equality.

2. Types of linkages in coordinating the economy

Every economic system—precisely because it is a system—achieves a certain coordination of the activities of economic decision-makers. This coordination can be accomplished by various types of linkages. In fact, economic systems can also be classified according to the dominant type of link by which the coordination of economic activity is achieved.

1) Historically, the first form of economic coordination was the *laissez-faire market*. The free market served as the means for integrating the earlier fragmented feudal economy into a unified national economy. In principle the state is outside the economy and its role is to protect property and permit unlimited private initiative. Since one can sell only what someone wishes to buy, everyone who wants to make a profit must orient his activity so that he satisfies social needs as well as possible. It is from such reasoning that Adam Smith drew his theory of the *invisible hand*: motivated exclusively by their personal interests, private producers nevertheless produce in the social interest, for they produce precisely those commodities that are necessary, at the lowest costs of production.

2) The "invisible hand" did not prove to be especially efficient. Periodic crises of overproduction and unemployment alternated for an entire century and a half. Growth was relatively slow (about 2 percent annually, compared to the world average today of 5 percent and 10 percent in the most rapidly growing contemporary economies). In addition, monetarily effective demand is not identical with social demand—in fact, it can greatly

differ from social needs. Consequently, the socialist critics of the capitalist market oriented themselves toward the *visible hand* as the instrument of coordination. State initiative replaced private initiative, and *central planning* replaced the market.

3) The great economic crisis at the beginning of the 1930s brought the capitalist type of economic coordination to the verge of complete collapse. Central planning and expropriation of private property were obviously not acceptable alternatives in the capitalist countries. Besides, central planning had severe defects when conceived and implemented as administrative planning. An escape was found by introducing the state only partially into the economy, as an organ of *economic policy*.

4) The development of economic statistics, economic analysis, and the technology of gathering and distributing information enabled economic decision-makers to obtain incomparably more relevant information than hitherto. The more the market represented an information system, the more this technological progress represented a perfecting of the market. This improvement had two aspects: (a) up-to-date and comprehensive economic statistics offer economic decision-makers complete information about the economic situation without delay (whereas the old market gave partial information belatedly) ; and (b) modern forecasting methods permit the reduction of uncertainty about future events, and thereby the earlier *ex-post* decisions are elevated into *ex-ante* decisions. Both mean that economic decision-makers obtain a rather complete collection of the parameters important in making correct decisions, i.e., those that will lead to the production of precisely those commodities which can be sold. We can call such improvement of the operation of the market by *organized informing* of economic decision-makers the improvement of the "invisible hand."

5) Finally, the "visible hand" can also be improved. *Agreement, consultation,* and *arbitration* constitute a nonmarket means of coordination which, however, is different from administrative orders of the state.

These five types of economic coordination—laissez-faire, administrative planning, economic policy, production of information, nonmarket-nonadministrative coordination—developed historically in the order just cited. But historical sequence does not mean either hierarchical order or evolution in the biological sense. Individual types are complementary and it is a question of attaining the organizational optimum. Different socioeconomic systems show different degrees of efficiency of economic organization.

Liberal capitalism was based on the free market, which means that laissez-faire was the dominant principle of macroeconomic coordination. Administrative planning is the basis for etatism, in which the state bureaucracy replaces individual entrepreneurs as organizers of production. The Keynesian revolution in the theory of economic policy made possible the submission of market instability to the efficient control of the state as an organ of economic policy. Together with the creation of state (public) corporations and the ever-greater use of *ex-post* and *ex-ante* information systems, this led to the so-called *mixed economies* (or "welfare state") characteristic of the contemporary highly developed capitalist countries. Finally, a *socialist economy* should be characterized by optimal use of all five types of linkages in order to maximize the welfare of the members of the social community.

3. The federation

An economic system consists of a certain number of subsystems that are in constant interaction. For the purposes of this work we shall distinguish four basic subsystems with precisely defined functions. These are: (a) the federation, (b) the republic, (c) the community, and (d) the enterprise (work organization). However, I will consider only three of the subsystems because I do not know the fourth, the community, adequately.

The federation's task is to integrate the work of the subsystems and thus to ensure the aggregate functioning of the entire system. In the economic sense, this task reduces to permanently solving the following three components: (a) equalizing conditions of economic activity; (b) achieving short-run equilibrium; and (c) achieving long-run equilibrium. Task (a) means creation of the preconditions for distribution according to work, (b) means eliminating cyclical fluctuations, and (c) means attaining the maximum rate of economic growth.

All three tasks require making uniform decisions for the entire economic territory of the country. Consequently, in this context the "federation" represents a synonym for making uniform, or centralized, or general social decisions. But the uniformity of decision does not predetermine the way in which they are made, which depends on the political system and organizational solutions. That way can be autocratic, oligarchic, or democratic and participative. In particular, the federation, as I define it, is *not* identical with the federal government, nor are centralized decisions with official arbitrariness (which is in large measure characteristic of Yugoslav practice, because of which sharp reactions occurred). What is more, it is desirable, whenever possible, to exclude the state from federal economic regulation, or at least to limit it as much as possible. It can be established as a general organizational principle (a) that in making decisions the relevant interests must be directly represented; and (b) that the decision-maker must bear full moral-political responsibility for carrying out decisions.

In considering an institutional model of the federation, we can again conform to the historical order of the appearance of coordinating links. We proceed from the complete autonomy of the enterprise in the free market and a state that stands outside the economy and concerns itself exclusively with public administration. Since the market is inherently unstable, regulation is necessary, which is the concern primarily (but not exclusively) of the state. Hence the state establishes a certain number of its organs that specialize in various aspects of economic policy. These organs are connected by administrative political links and are obliged to execute the directives of the political center. How that center ought to look (the government, legislature, presidency, etc.), and how it should make decisions, is a matter for political science and lies outside the framework of this discussion. It is sufficient to state that such a center exists, so that we may move on to the analysis of the regulation that should be accomplished.

The social plan represents the basic social agreement in the area of the economy. Once the plan is accepted, it becomes an *obligation* for governmental bodies. The plan is not an obligation for enterprises, which should retain full independence and freedom in determining their actions.

The theses just presented once appeared—and to many appear also today—contradictory. Hence a dilemma was—and is—talked about: plan or market. But that is a false dilemma. The market is only one—and until now the most efficient—of the planning mechanisms, and the plan is the precondition for the proper functioning of the market. Contemporary economic theory, quantitative analysis, and information technology make it possible for planning forecasts to be essentially more efficient than *ex-post* market solutions and for planning goals to be reached by nonadministrative methods, along with the full autonomy of enterprises. In this context, the state political center emerges as the source of regulatory impulses which reflect the constant, previously anticipated rules of the market. On that basis economic decision-makers obtain reliable parameters for their decisions and, seeking to maximize their incomes, carry out the intentions of the plan by their own initiative. In that way the plan and its adequate fulfillment represent the necessary condition for the autonomy of enterprises. Since only federal (i.e., central, or general social, or nationally uniform) regulation can achieve this, this is a necessary condition of self-management. In a situation in which the plans or economic policy or both are inexpertly formulated, in which the rules of economic activity are constantly changed, in which the obligations of the state are not performed, the economy is extremely unstable and uncertainty in decision-making is extreme —all of which are characteristic of the contemporary Yugoslav economy; the business success of enterprises depends more on chance, the force of circumstances, speculative activities, or arbitrary decisions by the state than on productive contribution. When one's position does not depend on one's own work, then only the form of self-management remains. In essence it disappears, and this arouses massive frustrations and the false sense that "self-management is responsible for the disorder in the economy."

The federal government establishes economic ministries to carry out economic policy measures. In a market economy, one segment of the market—the money market—has special significance, and a separate institution, the *National Bank,* which has a certain degree of independence from the ministries, is founded for its control. The National Bank regulates the functioning of the system of commercial banks, which enter directly into the market, by means of the instruments available to it.[4] The lawfulness of the activity of enterprises and institutions is controlled most simply by the control of money flows. This function is performed by the *Social Accounting Service,* which alone among the federal institutions we have considered establishes direct administrative contact with economic decision-making units. This contact occurs because of the character of the SAS as inspector; hence this administrative contact does not represent command, but rather verification. Simultaneously, the SAS is an exceptionally important source of information about monetary flows.

The market would still not function well with the cited bodies.

The economy is constantly subjected to certain shocks that create disturbances which individual enterprises and their associations are not able to eliminate. Consequently, general social—i.e., federal—intervention is again necessary, the most suitable form of which is interventional funds.[5] The *Office for Agricultural Raw Materials* smoothes out fluctuation in the supply of agricultural products by means of its reserves. In addition, the Office conducts a program of protective and guaranteed minimum prices for agricultural products, by which stable and equalized conditions of economic activity are created for farmers (who currently represent about half the Yugoslav labor force) in spite of the extreme instability of production (which in Yugoslavia fluctuates in the interval of ± 20 percent). The *Office for Industrial Raw Materials* has a similar task, except that in this case it must eliminate disturbances that arise because of fluctuations of prices and supply conditions on the world market. Both offices function as compensatory funds. Once the regulations of these funds are determined and several principles adopted, all the rest is for the most part routine work. Both offices have functioned well until now, and hence there have been no objections to their work—if delays in making decisions, for which political bodies and not the offices bear responsibility, are excepted.

The work of the third interventionary fund, the *Fund for Exports,* is much more delicate. Here the possibilities of favoritism, discrimination, and arbitrariness are much greater, and it is therefore necessary to work out the organization of this fund's management very carefully. However, the necessity of the fund's existence is undisputed. Yugoslavia already exports a fifth of its production, and that percentage must be further increased. Expansion of exports represents the main constraint on the acceleration of the economy's growth. The world market is under the control of mammoth multinational corporations,[6] international cartels, and state and intergovernmental organizations. Under such conditions, Yugoslav exporters can emerge as equal partners only if they are supported by the concentrated economic power of the entire Yugoslav economy and the political power of their government.

In order for the system described to function well, one more institution is needed to eliminate the possibility of abuses by monopolies—whether state bodies or individual enterprises—which inevitably occur in the market. This institution is the *Arbitration Board for Incomes and Prices,* which upon the demand of interested parties will decide on proper incomes and prices. The Arbitration Board functions like the Constitutional Court and is composed of representatives of the economy, trade unions, institutions of higher learning, and the government, who are appointed by the Parliament for a limited period and whose decisions are definitive and binding on all, including the government. The Arbitration Board is the guarantee that government bodies will in fact act to equalize the conditions of economic activity. If the government adopts measures which discriminate against some industry, that industry will turn to the Arbitration Board, which will make an estimate of the damages. If policies applied in the market put an industry in an unfavorable position, and the government does not undertake the necessary corrective measures, the Arbitration Board will determine the facts and designate a deadline for resolving the problem. The Arbitration Board is also a suitable body for determining the level of compensation. If the government has to carry out some important but unpopular measures, it can seek the prior judgment of the Arbitration Board, and with its consent can overcome the resistance of privileged groups much more effectively than at present. The Arbitration Board will determine the level of protective and guaranteed minimum prices in agriculture, representative income differentials according to qualifications, etc. In short, arbitration will make it possible to avoid political pressures, unprincipled compromises, and irresponsible decisions, which occur when the solution of the cited problems is left exclusively to government bodies. The Arbitration Board will rely in its work on an expert body such as the present Price Bureau.

From all that we know about the contemporary market economy in general, and the Yugoslav one in particular, the battery of institutions just described would allow for the irreproachable stabilization of the market. But economic growth would be slow. To accelerate economic growth it is necessary to carry out *ex-ante* harmonizing of economic decisions, to use science to the maximum in developing modern technology and in managing the economy (and society), and to ensure the necessary proportions in productive capacities, both regionally and according to individual industries. The latter is technically the easiest to do, but it has been the most politically abused and today evokes resistance to the point of complete prevention of its use. We begin, therefore, with the problem of harmonizing the structure of investments.

A large part of investment has an activization period of under two years. If, therefore, some plants are not built on time and the economy is growing slowly, the insufficiency of supply will be covered without great difficulty by increased imports. However, for construction of a large hydroelectric power plant or steel mill, or for the opening of a sizable mine, five to seven years, or even more, are necessary. In addition, for such projects and for the transportation network, large investment funds are needed. If the funds are not assured on time, if construction is not begun on time, and if the economy is growing rapidly, there will appear such disproportions in the material balance of the country that the balance of payments will be unable to bear them and the unavoidable result will be powerful inflationary pressure along with a slowdown of growth. Still other very negative consequences will follow. On the one hand, the lack of large concentrations of capital will lead to the construction of atomized, unprofitable plants. On the other hand, attempts to achieve sufficiently large concentrations of capital will lead to the formation of production and financial monopolies outside of social control. All these phenomena are well known in Yugoslav experience.

A solution should be sought in the formation of an *Interventionary Investment Fund,* whose tasks would be: (a) to participate in financing those projects that require an exceptionally large concentration of capital and/or long period of construction; and (b) to intervene in eliminating disproportions in capacity—at the moment the best illustration of such a case is the two million tons deficit in production of cement that was once permanently on the list of exports—whenever for any reason the market does not sufficiently succeed in balancing supply and demand. Investments also have their regional aspect. Economic growth can always be accelerated if pockets of insufficiently employed human and natural resources are eliminated, or in other words if the development of the underdeveloped regions is accelerated. This aim is served by the Fund for the Insufficiently Developed Regions, which, however, should not be a mere redistributor of funds collected by taxation but should function like the corresponding international institutions for economic development. It is hardly necessary to mention that this fund has a purely social function besides its economic one; economic equality is impossible in conditions of excessive differences in the degree of economic development, and therefore these differences should be reduced as fast as possible.

The *Federal Bureau for Economic Planning* is responsible for *ex-ante* coordination of economic decisions. Its function is primarily informational. The federal government has two factories of information: the *Federal Bureau of Statistics,* which produces information about the past, and the *Planning Bureau,* which produces information about the future.

It is unnecessary to emphasize separately the role of science in a modern economy. The central government—as well as all other bodies—should directly rely in its work on the work of scientific institutes. A *Council of Economic Advisers,* composed of outstanding economists, could play an exceptionally important role in introducing science into the formation of economic policy. A *Bureau for Programming Scientific Research,* together with a corresponding fund, would ensure an orientation toward those types of research which from the standpoint of the country are most fruitful.

The list of federal institutions is thus exhausted. The economy, on its side, also creates some institutions which fill the gap between the market and the federal political center. These are first of all *cooperative chains,* which represent market subsystems and which lead to a more lasting structuring of the market. Then there are *business associations* with the usual integrative functions. The tasks of *chambers of commerce* are to harmonize the interests of industries and to influence current economic policy as a representative of the economy in consultations with the government. Finally, "industries" in my scheme represent a particular type of business association, whose task is the integration of certain functions along with the preservation of the individuality of enterprises. It is obvious, that is, that a modern economy does not tolerate atomization and demands integration. It is also obvious that integration by means of administrative merger means the creation of large concentrations of economic power, the creation of monopolies and the liquidation of self-management. Therefore, I see a solution in enterprises preserving their business independence and integrating only those two functions for which direct coordination is essential: (a) basic research and development work, which is the precondition for constant modernization of technology in all the areas of the given industry; and (b) forecasting supply and demand and effective entry into the domestic and foreign market. With regard to (a), the development bureaus of industries are directly linked to the Bureau for Programming Scientific Research; with regard to (b), the planning and analysis bureaus of the industries are linked to the Federal Planning Bureau.[7] These links are informational and consultative, enabling all parties to be fully informed and to continually harmonize the majority of decisions or uncover areas of disagreement. With respect to the latter, the chambers of commerce and executive state bodies undertake the task of finding a satisfactory solution. In that way the system of permanent planning is completed.

4. The republic

Once we have defined socialism in the sense of self-management, that definition implies maximum decentralization from the organizational point of view. Maximum decentralization means that, in principle, decision-making is carried out on a lower level and that only those decisions are reserved to a higher level which otherwise would lead to damage to the interests of some individuals or groups by other individuals or groups. Honoring that principle, entire areas of decision-making should be brought down below the level of the federation. This demands territorial decentralization, which again should be carried out not only in harmony with types of decisions but also by taking into account historical development, cultural heritage, and tradition. In a multinational state, it is natural for such territorial decentralization to be implemented by forming national republics.[8]

A republic is also a state, and therefore the republican political center has a structure similar to the federal one. With respect to specific state affairs, there is a division of labor between the republic and the federation, in the sense that the federation is primarily responsible for foreign relations (foreign affairs and national defense) while the republic is responsible for domestic affairs (justice and public order).

Since the majority of federal institutions in the sphere of the economy are engaged in equalizing the conditions of economic activity and stabilizing the market—which can be achieved for the country as a whole, assuming a unified market, only by centralized decision-making—the republic is freed of these activities, with the result that its institutional structure in the sphere of the economy is much simpler. In the area of economic development, the basic task of the republic is to achieve even development over its territory. An *Interventionary Investment Fund* serves this purpose. The republic can also hasten the development of the economy in its territory to a certain extent by attracting investors from other areas and from abroad by tax exemptions and favorable treatment (by solving communal problems, training labor, participating in loans, etc.).

In the area of market stabilization, the republic can intervene by creating a *Mutual Reserve Fund,* which is used to cover losses and reorganize unprofitable enterprises. It would be necessary, however, not to stop at redistribution of funds, but to form alongside the funds personnel exchanges, or special bureaus for business organization, which would function by offering the struggling enterprise complete financial, technical, and personnel aid, including replacement of the entire management.

While the function of the republic in the sphere of the economy is, in the nature of things, relatively modest, it is basic in the sphere of nonproductive services. Consequently, only councils which have the role of informative-coordinating bodies remain for the federal level. Republican bodies formulate and carry out policy in the fields of education, culture, health, etc. The task of the federation, aside from coordination, is only to ensure financially (by supplementary funds from the federal budget) and legislatively certain minimum health and educational standards for the population of the underdeveloped regions.

In an effort to separate the state from the sector of nonproductive services in some way—to avoid the patronage of political forums, which in our conditions have always been a very negative influence—*interest communities* were formed. The Parliament by a political decision allocates funds to individual types of services. Interest communities receive these funds and pay them out, on behalf of consumers, for the services provided by schools, hospitals, museums, etc. This solution, although it has many drawbacks with respect to concrete organization, appears to be correct in principle. The following effects are achieved: (a) separation of the state from the final users of funds prevents the dictatorship of the administrative-political apparatus in this delicate sphere; (b) work collectives in the sector of nonproductive services in principle are placed in the same position as work collectives in the productive sector; (c) replacement of budgetary financing by contractual agreement develops consciousness of the economic aspects of the educational, health, and similar processes and can lead to more efficient use of the available funds; (d) in contrast to the productive sector, where distribution according to work prevails, in consumption of nonproductive services distribution according to needs prevails on the whole. In a socialist society, a young person should be educated and a sick person cured regardless of their property standing. This communist principle of distribution and market stimuli to efficiency in the production of services can be harmonized by the system of interest communities, or quasi-market system.

There are also direct links between the productive and nonproductive sectors. At present these links are still very weak and sporadic, consisting of direct purchase of services provided by the nonproductive sector, the founding by enterprises of nonproductive service organizations, participation by the productive sector in the interest communities, and occasional patronage. However, it can be expected that these links will be extended in time, and to the extent that this happens the independence of work collectives providing nonproductive services will be strengthened.

Universities, education, culture, and health are of fundamental importance for the life of a people and are of equally fundamental importance for the building of socialism. Technology is the same in all social systems. Equal or differentiated opportunity for education and health protection distinguishes the nonclass from the class society. For this reason, while it is the task of the federation to maintain the good performance of the overall system, the daily task of the republic is to instill socialist content into the system. This conclusion would be still firmer if we had also included the political component in the analysis.

5. The enterprise

In a more complete treatment it would be worthwhile to analyze the work organization in general. For the purposes of this study, however, I shall limit myself to consideration of the dominant type of work organization, the enterprise, and in relation to the enterprise I shall limit myself to a basic institutional analysis, since I have written more about this elsewhere.[9]

Like the federation and the republic, the enterprise in a self-management society also represents not only an organizational but a political (sub)system, although *sui generis*. This political component is so essential that failure to comprehend it leads to complete confusion in the institutional foundation of the self-managed enterprise. In fact, the most complete self-management —direct democracy—is possible just in the enterprise.

The basic problem in constructing the organization of the self-managed enterprise is maximizing democracy in making decisions while also maximizing efficiency in carrying them out. In poor organizational solutions, these two goals turn out to be mutually contradictory, which is quite a frequent occurrence in Yugoslav practice. Adequate organizational solutions not only harmonize these two goals but make them complementary—just as effective planning is the precondition of the self-managed autonomy of enterprises in the socioeconomic macrosystem.

It is important to determine as precisely as possible what is understood by maximizing democracy and efficiency. At first glance it might appear that maximizing democracy ought to mean that the opinion of each member of the collective has a weight in making relevant decisions that is determined exclusively by the objective value of that opinion, and that is therefore independent of the personality that has presented it. It is obvious that in this case maximal democracy and maximal efficiency would coincide. But reality rarely permits redundancies of abstract reasoning, and that holds in this case as well. In practice, that is, these two questions are immediately posed: (a) who will judge the objective value of some position; and (b) what is the objective value of value judgments? The answer to these two questions should be sought in the determination of the extent of democracy by the *way* in which decisions are made, and not by the *quality* of the decisions. Then democracy and efficiency are not only not identical, but it is obvious that there exists the possibility of conflict.

Maximal democracy is attained in a collective of one member. With the rise in the number of co-decision-makers, the democracy of decision-making is reduced, for each individual opinion is limited by the opinions of all the others. In addition, there is always the possibility—often realized—of manipulating opinions, of forming coalitions and cliques—in short, of deforming the "true" opinion of the group. The majority's decision is not necessarily the best decision, for even in ideal conditions it can represent the outvoting of someone's legitimate minority interest. Accordingly, the first principle in the organization of a self-managed enterprise will be the *creation of sufficiently small and sufficiently homogeneous work groups,* which allow direct participation of all the members in making decisions and where decisions are sufficiently transparent. Homogeneity reduces the possibility of forming a majority on the basis of minority interests, and participation and transparency reduce the possibility of manipulation and the imposition of opinions. This is, after all, the explanation for the formation of work (economic) units in our enterprises. A system of decision-making with the cited characteristics is called polyarchy, in contrast to democracy where decision-making is by a majority regardless of the implications.

Maximal efficiency means (a) the making of correct decisions and (b) their efficient implementation. From that follow the next two organizational principles: (2) *the bodies or individuals who make decisions bear responsibility for them,* which is ensured by suitable sanctions; and (3) *execution of decisions is a matter of expertise and not democracy.* The separation of responsibility from decision-making—which is characteristic of our entire present social organization—necessarily leads to irresponsibility, to inefficiency, and as a consequence, to the negation of self-management. Execution of decisions requires the possession of special knowledge and specialization in the social division of labor, and therefore can be entrusted only to those who fulfill these conditions. Thus, principle (3) implies the next organizational principle: (4) *separation of the value, interest sphere from the sphere of expertise; of political authority from professional authority; and of decisions about policy from the field of administration.* In the first sphere each has only one vote; in the second, weights depend on the particular expertise which is sought for the given work. The judgment about what spread of personal incomes is desirable depends upon subjective value judgments; the judgment about the suitability of some machine for production of a good depends on expert knowledge. For the former, political polyarchy is relevant; for the latter, expert hierarchy. In practice, difficulties appear in that it is not always possible to separate the political from the professional sphere—in fact, these two spheres often partially coincide; and the possession of special knowledge can be misused for the destruction of polyarchy (and the establishment of oligarchy) . A practical solution to this problem lies in (5) *institutionalizing control* over enterprise management. But this control cannot be arrived at—as individual political forums continually advise workers—by including workers in business operations and expert decisions. This naively conceived control in fact means: (a) a reduction of efficiency, because it delays operational decisions and because correct operational decisions require that full working time be devoted to them, and not only sporadic meetings of an hour or two; (b) the illusion and deception that control is exercised, when it is in fact lacking because of inadequate expertise or insufficient information (full information requires full working time) ; and (c) the irresponsibility of people in the operational apparatus, who easily obtain concealment for their dubious actions from self-management bodies entangled in operations.[10]

We shall now apply the above five principles to the organization of the self-managed enterprise. Just as Yugoslavia represents a federation of work units, so also the enterprise represents a federation of work units. The analogy goes further, and the member-firms of a large merged enterprise correspond to republics. All decisions that concern the direct daily life and labor of workers—and that do not impinge on the interests of other workers—are made in the work unit with the direct participation of all interested parties. In order to be able to develop effective self-management autonomy, the work unit must coincide with an economic unit. In other countries there have already been developed accounting-organizational systems which make possible relatively great autonomy of economic units with the objective of improving the efficiency of the entire enterprise.[11]

Work units join together in the enterprise, work groups in the *collective,* and the collective makes some exceptionally important decisions of interest to all members by means of a referendum. The chairmen of work units enter into the *workers' council.* The other elected members of the workers' council become the chairmen of various committees or of the Supervisory Board. In that way *every member of the workers' council is personally responsible for a sector of work.* He periodically presents a report on his work, just as the entire workers' council periodically presents an accounting to the collective. The workers' council makes decisions on the basis of proposals of *committees.* The *Executive Board* is also one of the committees of the workers' council, the committee responsible for operations. The workers' council, on the basis of the director's nominations, appoints the Executive Board, consisting of specialists for individual aspects of business operations. The heads of economic units enter into the Executive Board. In that way, work units are represented in the workers' council by a political line, and in the Executive Board by an expert-organizational line. A procedure can be envisioned whereby the managers of a work unit are elected on the basis of an agreement between the director and that work unit.

A collective rather than individual management is probably more suitable for the self-managed enterprise. In order for that management to be able to function efficiently, its members must be mutually compatible. Hence the need to treat the director as the mandator for the composition of the Executive Board. The Executive Board periodically submits reports on business activity to the workers' council. At the end of the year it submits an exhaustive report on business in the course of the year to the workers' council and the collective. If that report is not accepted, this means a vote of no confidence, and the Executive Board automatically resigns, the workers' council elects a new director, and the latter proposes a new Executive Board. If everything is all right, the Executive Board proposes a program of work for the forthcoming year (or years). Once that program—with possible modifications—is accepted, this means *that the Executive Board has a free hand to carry it out and the workers' council is obliged to provide full support in its implementation.* The workers' council can replace the director—and thus the entire Executive Board—but it cannot interfere in the operational implementation of a program once adopted (except, of course, with the consent of the Executive Board), for the Executive Board bears full responsibility for operations, and therefore must have full freedom of action.

Since the Executive Board can abuse its authorization, or since doubts (justified or unjustified) can appear concerning the correctness of individual decisions, institutional control is necessary. This function cannot be performed by the workers' council, for its members do not have all the necessary current information or the necessary knowledge. Hence the workers' council forms its *Supervisory Board,* which checks business operations quarterly and reacts to all complaints or warnings in that sphere. At the end of the year the Supervisory Board engages a specialized consulting firm to audit the entire business, and on the basis of the audit findings submits its report to the workers' council. *Without this report the annual report of the Executive Board cannot be accepted.*

The work units and various committees enable every worker to participate directly in management if he wishes. In addition, the committees make possible a certain combination of expertise and democracy. Committee chairmen are rotated periodically, for they must be members of the workers' council. However, there is no reason whatever for not reelecting committee members who carry out their work well. Thus it will happen that people with relatively modest formal qualifications, who have spent several years in the committee for income distribution or the committee for development, and so forth, will acquire valuable experience that will enable them to propose mature and effective measures to the workers' council.

The interaction of the workers' council and the Executive Board transforms political directives into professional, and value judgements into expert, administration. Directives begin in the work units and end in the work units. In that way the open hierarchical pyramid of a capitalist or statist enterprise is replaced by the closed organizational structure of a self-managed enterprise. The closed form of the organizational structure together with the mechanism for transformation of political decisions into professional ones is precisely the *differentia specifica* of a self-managed organization.

NOTES

1. The reader will find a more complete analysis in my book *An Essay on Yugoslav Society* (White Plains, N.Y.: International Arts and Sciences Press, 1969), Chap. 15.

2. For a more complete analysis, see my books: *Towards a Theory of Planned Economy* (White Plains, N.Y.: International Arts and Sciences Press, 1964), Chap. 6; *Ekonomska nauka i narodna privreda* (Zagreb: Naprijed, 1968), Chap. 8.

3. See *An Essay on Yugoslav Society,* Chaps. 19 and 20.

4. See my study, "Yugoslav Economic Policy in the Postwar Period: Problems, Ideas, Institutional Developments," *American Economic Review,* Supplement (June 1971), pp. 136–37.

5. For an analysis of interventional funds as well as of various policies which the federation can employ, see B. Horvat et al., *Ekonomske funkcije federacije* (Belgrade: Institute of Economic Studies, 1971).

6. The largest of them, General Motors, has a larger annual turnover than the gross national products of every country of the world except the twelve largest.

7. It would probably be most consistent to form industry economic-technical bureaus, which would perform the two cited functions. The precondition for good performance of these functions is financial independence.

8. In this work a general institutional model of a socialist economy is examined, along with suitable illustrations from Yugoslav practice. In a specifically Yugoslav model, besides republics, autonomous provinces should also be considered.

9. "Yugoslav Economic Policy," Part III.

10. As an illustration I cite a drastic, but not atypical, case relating to an economic court, which is precisely the institution responsible for protecting norms of business behavior. *Ekonomska politika,* in No. 949 of May 24, 1971, states: "The District Economic Court in Niš paid 16,500 dinars to an enterprise, paying a bill for painting that was not done. The Economic Court later recovered its money by charging an intermediary enterprise for old paper that it did not deliver. Attorneys for the accused former chairman of the District Economic Court in Niš said that in the given situation the Court resorted to a way of coping used by other enterprises and institutions to obtain funds—and the District Court in Niš freed the former chairman of the Economic Court of this complaint, for the actions with the imaginary painting and the imaginary paper were approved by the Workers' Council."

11. Gudrun Lemân gave a comparative analysis of the solutions of Yugoslav enterprises and German accounting theory in *Stellung und Aufgaben der ökonomischen Einheiten in den jugoslawischen Unternehmungen* (Berlin, 1967).

Notes on the Editors

BRANKO HORVAT was born in Yugoslavia in 1928. As a youth he participated in the Partisan Liberation War. He received D.Sc. and Ph.D. degrees from the University of Zagreb and the University of Manchester. He is a member of the League of Communists of Yugoslavia. Professor Horvat was founder of the Institute of Economic Sciences in Belgrade and of the journal *Economic Analysis.* His numerous publications include *Towards a Theory of Planned Economy.*

MIHAILO MARKOVIĆ was born in Yugoslavia in 1923. He served as an officer in the Yugoslav Partisan Army. He received Ph.D. degrees from the University of Belgrade and the University of London and currently is Professor of Philosophy and Director of the Institute of Philosophy, University of Belgrade. Dr. Marković is the author of numerous philosophical studies, including *From Affluence to Praxis: Philosophy and Social Criticism.*

RUDI SUPEK was born in Yugoslavia in 1913. He participated in the Resistance Movement in France in 1941–1945. He is Professor of Sociology at the University of Zagreb. Dr. Supek is co-editor of the journal *Praxis* and author of many books, including *Power and Socialism.*